The P

of
Ohm Totem

A NOVEL

by

Brandon Ellis

First Edition, February 2013

Copyright © 2013 All Rights Reserved

ISBN: 978-1484177792

Editor: Julie Clayton
Senior Editor: DB Gregg

www.brandon-ellis.com

Dedication:

To the child inside each and every one of us.

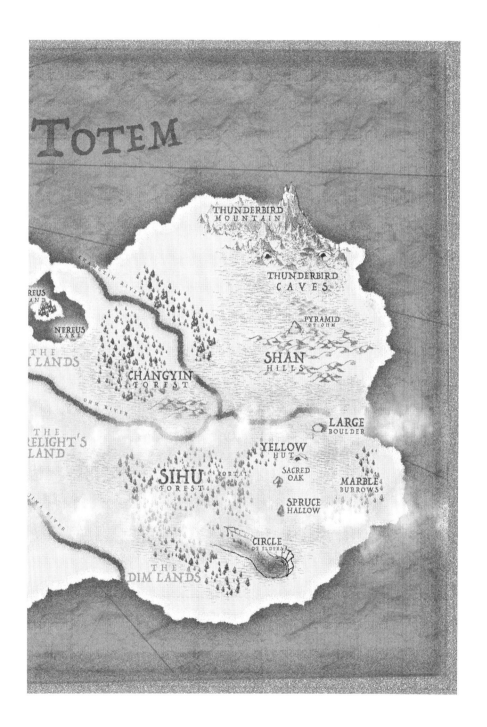

TOTEM

THUNDERBIRD
MOUNTAIN

THUNDERBIRD
CAVES

SHANTIN RIVER

REUS
LAND

NEREUS
LAKE

PYRAMID
OF OHM

THE
LANDS

CHANGYIN
FOREST

SHAN
HILLS

OHM RIVER

LARGE
BOULDER

THE
RELIGHT'S
LAND

YELLOW
HUT

SACRED
OAK

SIHU
FOREST

PORTAL

MARBLE
BURROWS

JIMA RIVER

SPRUCE
HALLOW

CIRCLE
OF ELDERS

THE
DIM LANDS

Prologue

It was nightfall. A snow leopard looked to the north, feeling a group of dim eyes burning deeply into her snowy pelt. She knew they'd killed before and she knew they wanted to kill again.

The wind howled against her body, making the snow leopard's fur cling to her skin. Leaning into the heavy gusts as she walked, she dug her claws deeply into the earth to remain upright. Her eyes were mere slits, protecting them from the flying dirt and ash swirling violently in the air. The once lush, sacred land was now burnt to a black cinder. Smoke rose from the ground, spinning wildly in the harsh wind. The old dwellings, formed from earth and fallen branches, were mostly gone, turned to embers smoldering in charcoal.

She stopped near a river's edge, facing a mountain range to the west. Like black silhouettes, the mountains stood amidst dark gray clouds. She turned her head to the north, sensing the group of eyes hidden behind a shadow of trees. They were still watching her.

She took a deep breath as a flicker of light flashed above, casting black shapes from clouds, trees, boulders, and smoke across the land. She sat on her haunches, folding her long tail over her paws, staring patiently ahead. More than just instinct had led her here.

She looked at the night sky as the gray clouds parted—one half flowed north, the other half south—revealing a star-filled canopy.

Suddenly, she winced. A comet streaked through the sky, painting a crystal-blue gash across the stars above the mountains. Her eyes intently followed as the comet slowly vanished into the western horizon. Then she nodded to the sky, as if communicating with it in some mystical way.

Dropping her gaze, the snow leopard eyed the ground. A rolled up scroll, which wasn't there a moment before, lay in front of her. She paused, then placed a paw on one end of the scroll, then nudged the opposite end with her nose, rolling it out to reveal gold paper thickly outlined in black.

She stared into it. Suddenly, a word formed, then more, until the scroll was filled with words. It read:

> *Two children from a forgotten land, ancestors of the Island of Ohm Totem, one being of the Night Walkers and the other of the Sacred Heart, will purify the energies, bring back the old ways, and unite the PureLights. They will put an end to the coming Shiver.*
>
> *~ Windstorm Prophecy*

Removing her paw from the scroll and nosing one end toward the other, she rolled it up and gently grasped it in her mouth. She stood on all fours and sniffed the air. Danger was near.

Another blast of wind unbalanced her. Closing her eyes until the wind slowed to a slight breeze, she turned and slowly walked to the east until she stopped at a large dwelling mound half-burnt to the ground. It gave off heat, but little smoke. She sniffed. It was empty of life. She glanced once more at the ruined land and felt the heavy pain of sorrow sink deep within her. Everything around her was dead—her friends, her family...everything.

Lifting her head, she stared to the north once more, narrowing her eyes as she studied a thick fog hovering over a sparse stand of trees in the distance. Still clutching the scroll, she gave a loud moan and watched the fog for several more moments, waiting for a reply.

Nothing.

Turning to leave, she noticed something on the ground. It was something important—fresh tracks. She sniffed intently—panther scent. Her head jerked up and her eyes widened. He's alive and he was here only moments ago. Why didn't she sense him?

10

Just then, she heard several yelps and turned to face seven white wolves cautiously walking toward her. With bristled fur and ears pulled back, they advanced with low growls. It was a display to induce fear, but wasted on the snow leopard.

Backing up slowly and moving her head left to right, she studied each wolf as the group began to surround her. The closer they came, the tighter she held the scroll. Suddenly she stopped, surprising and confusing the pack. Their usual slaughters involved a chase.

Then a flash of light silently appeared from above. The pack looked up as the light changed from white to crystal blue, coloring the land and then slowly fading away. Something about this omen told the pack that tonight's prey was different, something they'd never encountered before.

The pack leader glared at the snow leopard as he let out a loud, throaty growl, saliva dripping from both sides of his mouth. He had a scar on the side of his face. He had been in many fights.

The wind picked up from the north just as the leader crouched and leaped at the leopard with bared teeth.

She easily side-stepped the attack and the leader landed directly on the spot she'd just occupied. His jaws were still swiping in vain at empty air as another wolf sprang. She spun out of the way, swatting his backside and sending him further than he'd planned. His outstretched paws dug into the earth as he landed; stopping him from slamming into a burnt tree.

The snow leopard sat down, calmly looked back at the leader and exhaled as she placed the scroll on the ground. She licked her paw, wiped her forehead, and picked up the scroll. She gave a slow blink of the eyes and started to purr, seemingly content with the situation.

The leader pulsed with adrenaline as he jumped at her again; thrusting his feet out, hoping to knock her over at the shoulders. She crouched, twisted toward him and deftly moved under his body as she flipped onto her back and briskly planted her feet on his stomach and pushed firmly in the direction he had jumped.

The wolf, surprised, landed much further away than

intended and lost his balance, somersaulting head over heels and yelping with pain. When he stopped tumbling, he shook his head, flinging dirt and ash from his fur, and then sprang to his feet. He gave a high-pitched growl, signaling the pack to form a line in front of the snow leopard. Growling in unison, they obeyed. The leader barked an order and one by one they attacked.

And one by one they missed.

Finished, the snow leopard shook her body like a wet dog and sat back down on her haunches.

The leader signaled for the pack to regroup. They formed another line, standing to the east of her, blocking a throng of trees that formed the outskirts of an enormous forest.

She stared longingly beyond the pack to the forest's edge. They knew it was her only escape.

She looked up to the night sky as a thin set of clouds whisked by, uncovering a full moon. Her brow crinkled in worry. She must find the panther. The wolves, crouched low, were ready to attack. This time it was the whole pack all at once.

The snow leopard had had enough. Closing her eyes, she took a deep breath. Instantly, the growls stopped and seven thuds echoed through the air. She opened her eyes and the wolves lay on their sides, breathing deeply and looking comfortable enough to be sleeping in their own dens.

She bowed her head to them, and with a flick of her tail sped off toward the wall of trees.

Once there, she paused just before entering the forest, blinking softly and purring in gratitude for the precious scroll held within her jaws. Then she leaped, vanishing into the shadows of the thick forest.

Chapter 1

Zoey sat on a large, thick branch in a majestic maple tree looking out over the forest below. She could almost touch the beautiful orange and pink hues painting the sky by a disappearing sun. Many twelve-year-olds, and adults for that matter, would be frightened to be up so high, but Zoey couldn't imagine any place more peaceful and safe. Just as the sun dipped below a horizon of distant forest, the crickets hiding amongst the rocks and shrubs below began an ancient twilight chorus.

She heard another sound, but realized it was her tummy. Time to go home to join her family at the dinner table. It was Friday night supper, something she didn't want to miss.

Tucking thick auburn hair behind her ears, she took a final deep breath of sweet forest air. She slowly began her descent, checking carefully for the best footholds so she wouldn't slip, and hummed her favorite tune. Suddenly she stopped, glimpsing movement from below.

"Zoey?" said an unfamiliar and gentle voice.

Where did that voice come from?

Zoey pushed away a leaf-covered branch obstructing her view, and was very surprised to see a handsome gray wolf staring up at her.

Zoey knew right away that it was male, and felt strangely at ease in this wolf's presence.

She pried her gaze away from the wolf for a moment to look around for the source of the voice. She saw grass spread in huge clumps throughout a meadow surrounded by the forest. A massive, twisting tree standing alone, but magnificent nonetheless, stood at the far end of the meadow. It had a hazy golden aura around it. Or was that just the sunlight somehow reflecting off of it? She couldn't tell.

Then she had a strange feeling that she'd been in this maple tree overlooking the forest many times before, but couldn't actually remember when, and she couldn't quite recall how she had arrived here in the first place.

The voice!

Her thoughts spun back to the voice she had heard moments before.

Who had called her name? Zoey eyed the gray wolf, searching into its deep blue eyes, as if the answer might somehow be held within them. Her brow furrowed as she noticed something else rather odd. What was that peculiar teardrop-looking object embedded in the fur between his eye brows? She squinted at the object, trying to figure out what she was looking at while the wolf remained motionless. The object looked like a glowing violet crystal of some sort. Then she noticed a crystal of the same color set in his chest. The rock crystals were beautiful, she thought, but who would put such things on an animal?

After a few more moments of staring, Zoey sighed with resignation. She had the feeling that the wolf was quite content just to sit there looking up at her and she wasn't sure how to respond. She wanted to leave, but also knew that she might disturb the calm, and then who knows what might happen? She wished the wolf would walk away, finding another tree or another person to stare at.

"Please leave. I want to get down," Zoey said out loud, knowing full well that a wolf, or any other wild creature in the forest, would never understand what she was saying. She wondered if she'd have to stay in the tree for hours. *I hope not.* Her stomach grumbled again and she rubbed her tummy.

The gray wolf's sparkling blue eyes mesmerized her. She felt a tingling sensation in her body that she'd never felt before. The wolf slowly stood up on all four legs and bowed his head to her. Then his mouth moved, and to her utter amazement, he spoke.

"Yes, I can do that," he replied.

Zoey's eyes widened and she shivered with fear. There was no way she was getting down. Not now, not ever—or at least, not until that talking wolf left the forest completely.

"Please, I mean you no harm," the wolf calmly said. "I only

ask for your help." He peered intently into Zoey's eyes and her fears dissolved. The wolf seemed to radiate a sense of calm. "We desperately need your help," he quietly pleaded.

Before Zoey could recover from her shock, a large, dark green reptile emerged from the grasses and slinked quietly toward the wolf. The wolf took no notice; not even twitching a whisker. He was entirely focused on Zoey.

The reptile halted and looked up at Zoey. She could see now that it looked like one of those Komodo dragons she had once seen on the Nature Channel, except that this dragon had burning red eyes full of rage that seemed directed at her! Zoey quivered, feeling a chill run through her body from head to toe as the repulsive reptile glared at her. The dragon inched closer, never taking his eyes from Zoey. Each step hissed against the dry grass, searing blackened footprints into the ground, followed by wisps of acrid smoke. Zoey quickly tore her gaze away, breaking the spell.

Dark clouds suddenly appeared in the distance. They were approaching fast, casting ominous shadows across the forest, turning day into night. A shot of lightning pierced the sky, then a moment later thunder rumbled, shaking the earth.

Zoey's hands weakened as fear consumed her, squeezing the air out of her chest. The dragon had stopped a few inches in front of the wolf and seemed to be sizing him up. Still, the wolf didn't budge or take his gaze away from Zoey.

"Please help us," the wolf implored. "Remember, Zoey, who you truly are."

The dragon hushed the wolf's words with a roar that echoed deep into the forest, ringing loudly in Zoey's ears. The roar, it seemed, instantly summoned a downpour of rain that fell hard and fast against the canopy of branches above them.

The dragon leaned forward, almost touching the gray wolf's chest with its nose. Rain pelted against the dragon's hard, scaly skin and slid off, making a slime-covered mess on the ground. To Zoey's astonishment, the rain didn't seem to touch the gray wolf at all.

The dragon took a deep sniff, inhaling the scent of the gray wolf's fur. He began to walk in circles around the wolf, creating a rising mist with each stride. The wolf remained motionless, and seemed to convey a calm whisper of love to Zoey until the mist completely surrounded him, hiding him from view.

The rain got louder, landing with increased force against the bark of Zoey's tree, and her grip started to slip.

Thunder and lightning rolled across the now blackened sky, and a ferocious storm let loose.

The dragon turned on Zoey, revealing a wicked smile. She could see he had crystals on his forehead and chest, too. Only his were solid black. Her stomach churned, and waves of nervous energy crept through her body.

The mist forming around the wolf spun faster and faster, like a small whirlwind.

"What's your name?"

Zoey gasped, startled by the frozen, low voice of the dragon, but she refused to take her eyes off the growing whirlwind surrounding the wolf.

"I said," he repeated menacingly, "what *is* your name?"

Zoey snapped her head around and looked deep into his scalding eyes. A wave of anger rose from her belly. "Leave me alone!" she yelled.

The Komodo dragon pounded his right foot on the ground and the tree shook fiercely, unlocking her grasp and flinging Zoey's legs off the branch. She tumbled backwards, flipping in mid-air, as she screamed and closed her eyes, waiting for her body to hit hard on the ground.

∞

"Zoey, keep it down."

Zoey bolted upright in her bed. Her face was clammy and her breath was quick and heavy. She nervously looked around the room for any signs of forest, the gray wolf, or the Komodo dragon.

There was nothing but the darkness of her bedroom in the pale moonlight.

She sighed in relief. She was only dreaming. And just to make sure, she pressed firmly on the mattress, assuring herself that she was in her own room, awake and safe.

"I'm trying to sleep," her older brother complained.

"Okay, I'm sorry Coda," she said with a heavy breath.

"Yeah, goodnight Zoey, and try to have a better dream or something."

For some reason, unknown to Zoey, Coda was always a little nicer to her in the dead of night, which wasn't always the case during the day. He was thirteen, only a year older than her. But like most older brothers, he didn't like his younger sister following him around everywhere he went, which she tended to do. And, to make things worse, he had to share a room and bunk beds with her. Their parents didn't have an extra room in the house. Only two. They had one room for the kids and one room for the parents. Zoey knew Coda didn't like that, but neither did she.

A drop of sweat trickled down her forehead, taking her away from her thoughts. She wiped it away and poked around the sheets that were wet with sweat. She sighed, realizing she was hot and exhausted because she had just woken up from a frantic dream.

Was it a dream?

It felt real, more real than any dream she'd ever had. The dream terrified her, and yet, in a funny way she felt wonderful at the same time. It was that gray wolf, she thought, that gave her the nice feelings. There was a certain familiarity about him that she couldn't quite place. And that maple tree, and that twisting tree, and the meadow—had she been there before?

Help? She wondered, *why does he need my help. He was so beautiful and calm.*

She quickly shook the thought away. "It's just a dream," she said out loud.

Coda's arm dangled off the edge of the top bunk. "Zoey! Shhh!" The moonlight gleamed through their window and silhouetted Coda's face as he peered over the edge. "Be quiet!"

"Okay," replied Zoey. She knew she couldn't sleep in the damp bed, so she waited until she heard the deep breaths of slumber coming from her brother before she pulled her sheets off and got out of bed. She stretched her arms and legs, letting out a big yawn during the process. There was no way she could get any sleep after that dream.

She tiptoed over to her dresser and opened a drawer as slow and quietly as she could, making sure not to waken Coda. She grabbed dry underwear and a long t-shirt, but as she turned in the semi-darkness she accidentally kicked something. Whatever it was, it smashed against the wall into tiny pieces, scattering all over the carpet. Zoey froze and held her breath.

She waited for her brother to yell or throw a pillow at her, but thankfully, all she heard was Coda's deep breathing. After what seemed to be an eternity of silence, she finally took a breath and moved toward the door, carrying her change of clothes. She crept out of the room, shutting the door quietly behind her.

The hall closet, just outside her bedroom door, stood partially open. A bad latch that hadn't been fixed for who knows how long, prevented it from closing.

She reached inside the closet and grabbed a towel. She took off her clothes, dropping them on the floor, and with the towel wiped the sweat off her body. She rubbed her drowsy eyes and heard her stomach growl. *I'd better get something to eat*, she thought, putting on her dry clothes.

She crept downstairs and into the kitchen. The cold hardwood floors beneath her feet made her shiver, a contrast from the soft carpeting upstairs. Opening the fridge, she grabbed a large, juicy-looking red apple.

At the sink she started her apple ritual. "A," she said as she held onto the stem, turning the apple clockwise; "B," she continued, and with another twist; "C"...

"Zoey?"

Zoey jumped, dropping the apple on the hardwood floor. It was the same voice from her dream. The hair on the back of her neck stood up as she spun around. The gray wolf was standing in her living room, just beyond the kitchen.

"Huh? Yes? What?" She felt tiny goose bumps jumping all over her body.

The gray wolf dipped his head in respect and the violet crystal on his forehead glowed. "Please answer our beckoning."

Zoey quickly bent down to pick up the apple, knowing that her dad didn't like spills. When she stood up, the wolf was gone. She rubbed her eyes and blinked a few times to make sure they were still working properly. How could she see a wolf right in front of her, and then the next instant its gone? And what's more, a wolf from her dream! *I must be totally tired,* she thought.

Zoey went into the living room and switched on the light. On the backrest of a large couch was her favorite blanket, wool with black, white, and purple stripes.

She snuggled into the couch, clutching the blanket to keep warm. On top of a large TV set stood a clock that said 2:38 a.m.. *What's on at this time? Probably nothing,* she replied to herself.

Zoey picked up the TV remote and curled up against a pillow, trying to forget the dream that still stuck to her like glue. She clicked the power button on the remote and the TV suddenly blared in the silence.

"Shoot!" she panicked, frantically pressing the volume button. "Down, down, down. There," she whispered.

On the TV screen was one of her favorite cartoons. It was the one where she always predicted that the cat would never catch the mouse and she was always right. She stared blankly at the TV, not really watching or listening to it, lost in the dream again. *It felt so real.* It felt like she was really there, sitting in that tree, overlooking that strange meadow and the smell of the meadow still lingered...and the wind? *Wow,* she thought, *the wind felt so real, too! And who was that gray wolf, and that mean-looking dragon?*

Her thoughts quickly faded when she heard footsteps coming down the stairs. She hid her eyes under the blanket, half expecting the gray wolf to show himself again. Her dad's voice echoed in the kitchen, "Who's up?"

"Me, Dad." Zoey lowered the blanket and turned to look at him. His hair was disheveled as he stood between the kitchen and the living room in his goofy red boxers.

He rubbed his tummy, yawned, and ran his fingers through his hair, messing it up even more. He plopped down next to her on the couch.

"What are you doing up, Zo Zo?" He put his elbow on his knee, resting his cheek on his hand. He closed his eyes and yawned again.

Zoey put her feet on his legs and stretched out. "I had a bad dream...I think," she mumbled, looking at the TV.

"What?" he said in an irritated voice. "Stop covering your mouth when you talk. You do that all the time and I can't understand you."

"I said," Zoey's voice became louder, "I had a bad dream—I think."

"Oh." He opened his eyes. They were bloodshot from lack of sleep. "How bad was the dream?"

She put her head down as if in thought. "Well, it was a good one *and* a bad one."

"How can you have a good dream *and* a bad dream at the same time?"

"The first bit," she said, with her right hand over her mouth and her left hand holding the uneaten apple, "was good, and the last bit of the dream was bad."

Her dad reached over and gently moved her hand away from her mouth. "Why do you do that?"

"Do what?" She knew what he was going to say, but pretended she didn't.

"I don't teach you to mumble and I don't think your mother does, either."

She shrugged her shoulders. She didn't feel that mumbling was a bad thing, and didn't like her dad pointing it out.

He sighed and stood up. Zoey's feet fell from his legs, onto the couch. He reached his hand toward her. "Come on. Let's go to bed."

"I can't. My bed is all wet."

She had again mumbled, but her dad could make out some of the words. "It's wet? Did you pee in the bed?"

She looked at him with disdain. "No, Dad, it's my sweat and the bed's all wet from it. I'll just sleep on the couch."

Her dad yawned loudly and scratched his stomach again. "See, when you look at me I can hear you." He crossed his arms, continuing, "And, no, you aren't going to sleep on the couch. I'm too tired to make your bed. You'll sleep with us tonight."

Zoey smiled. "Okay." She had hoped her dad would offer that, knowing her parents would protect her from anything and everything, including dreams.

"Thanks for not getting mad at me for watching TV this late, Dad," she mumbled into her hand.

Her dad rolled his eyes, "What?"

Zoey shrugged. "Never mind."

With that, he turned off the TV set, and scooping Zoey off the couch, carried her upstairs. Now being a twelve-year-old, she was getting heavy.

"Goodnight Zo Zo," he said, slightly out of breath as he placed her in the bed between him and her mom, who was sleeping soundly. He kissed Zoey on the forehead and turned onto his side. Within moments, she could hear his quiet, comforting snores. She felt good and safe now. Maybe she'd even get some sleep.

She closed her eyes and took slow, steady breaths, feeling her wakefulness fade as the slippery slope of the dream realm began to take over. Her breaths became deeper and the rhythms of her body gradually slowed, giving her much needed rest.

Suddenly, off in the distance and far below, she saw hundreds of furious animals—tigers, elephants, lions, badgers, coyotes, and more—charging out of a huge, thick forest, toward a gigantic white pyramid.

She saw her brother standing on a platform in the middle of the pyramid. A long staircase led up to it. He was facing the oncoming onslaught. He held both hands in a fist, waiting for what was about to come.

A large, shadowed entrance arched behind him. A white leopard with black spots walked out from the shadows and stood at his side. The leopard had violet crystals, just like the wolf.

Then the leopard nudged Coda's hand with her muzzle, and looked up at him with bright blue eyes. "We must fall back."

Coda looked at the leopard, then back to the oncoming animals. He nodded, placing his hand on top of the leopard's head.

They walked through the entrance, disappearing from Zoey's view. As they did, the hoard of animals raced up the stairs, toward the doorway Coda and the leopard had just passed through.

Just before she could see what happened next, the scene faded into a gray mist and large red eyes appeared in front of her. The eyes made her body feel like ice, shooting fear into her and temporarily paralyzing her.

She wanted to get away from this nightmare as fast as she could, but her body just wouldn't, and couldn't, budge. She felt like she was suffocating, as if someone held her lips together and plugged her nose at the same time. She couldn't breathe! Doing her best to gasp for air, to push away the haunting red eyes staring at her, she frantically struggled against the energy holding her down. She tried to open her eyes, willing her body to move, but nothing. She felt the beat of her heart slow down, pumping heavy, thick beating sounds into her ear. Her eyes started rolling back in her head as she began losing vital life. Her body was being controlled by something, by someone. She wanted to grasp her throat, to do something to get this terrible feeling to go away, but her arms and hands just wouldn't work.

"You don't get off that easy, Zoey!" came a low, growling voice, echoing in her mind. "You stay alive until I say otherwise. You are released!" The red eyes faded, making her go from the dream state to grayness, and then to waking up. She opened her eyes, heard herself scream, "No!" as she broke free from the invisible energy that held her down. Her breaths came quickly and heavily, giving life back to her body, relief flooding her senses.

"Huh?" she said as she sat up. She looked to her mom and dad. They were peacefully sleeping as if nothing had happened. Slowing down her breathing, she told herself it was just another nightmare, one that would never come back. Glancing at her parents once again, she shook her head. *So much for their protection.*

Chapter 2

Coda was asleep in his bed. His head was facing the window and the crook of his right arm rested over his eyes— his favorite sleeping position. He was breathing deeply, as if in a pleasant dream. Suddenly a loud screech, like that of an owl's, filled his ears. Startled, his right arm slammed against the window. The screeching got louder and louder as he clamped both hands over his ears. Then, like turning off a light, it stopped.

He heard a voice in his mind. "The owl's screech will protect you. It's a warning of approaching attackers. Tomorrow your journey begins."

"What the heck?" grumbled Coda as he sat up, rubbing his arm. The mid-morning light poured through the window, making him squint to see what was outside making that screeching sound.

He searched the leaf-covered oak trees growing next to his window, but could only see small finches singing and flying from branch to branch. He looked over the street, half-thinking he'd see a kid playing with a blow horn, but saw the usual kids riding bikes or laughing and chasing each other across green lawns. He shook his head, hoping to get the residual ringing out of his ears.

"Zoey?" he called, wondering if she had heard the loud screech or the calm voice that had spoken to him. He leaned over the railing, peering down at an empty bed. The sheets were off, revealing a bare mattress. *Where is she?*

Getting out from under his covers and climbing down the ladder, he glanced over at his Lego creation he had made the night before. His stomach lurched when he saw the pieces scattered all over the bedroom floor. Coda scowled and bared his teeth. "Zoey! I told you not to play with my stuff!"

He looked at the Winnie the Pooh painting on the wall as

both of his bare feet touched the carpet. It was a picture of Christopher Robin standing next to a tree in Winnie the Pooh's forest. All of the characters were surrounding Christopher Robin, waiting to hear one of his stories. It was his favorite picture and the forested scene always calmed him down when he looked at it, though he'd never tell a soul.

His door opened. "Stop yelling, please." His mom stood in the doorway with a serious expression on her face that soon turned into a smile.

"Don't you look handsome with your hair all sticking out everywhere." She ran her hands through his brown hair and drew him in for a hug.

Coda's blue eyes shone with the love he felt for his mother. He wrapped his arms around her waist and sighed. "Mom, why doesn't she leave my stuff alone?"

Coda's mom looked at the mess on the floor. "You'll have to ask her yourself. She's downstairs eating cereal."

Coda lifted his arms up in disgust. "She doesn't even ask." He rolled his eyes as he walked out of the room, almost dragging his legs in disappointment. He'd spent hours creating the perfect city of houses, buildings, gas stations, and more. It was his best creation yet. Though, in the back of his mind, he always wondered if he was getting too old for this stuff. Maybe this disaster was a good thing...still, she was annoying.

"Be nice to your sister," his mom chided as she followed him, closely behind.

As he walked down the stairs, he placed his hands on the smooth railings of the old staircase to catch himself just in case the stairs decided to collapse, exposing a bottomless pit below. He knew it would probably never happen, but it could. He always wondered how long he would fall down into that bottomless pit. Forever? He could land on floating bottomless pit islands and have adventures with two-headed monsters, battling the evil sword king, who had a screeching voice that...

The screech!

He stopped in the middle of the staircase and turned around to his mom. "Mom, did you hear that loud sound this morning?"

His mom shook her head and tapped her forehead with her index finger, trying to recall if she heard anything. "Loud sound? I don't think so. What kind of loud sound? When did you hear it?"

"Um, I don't know. It woke me up. It was like a scream. A bat scream or something?"

His mom giggled, "I don't think bats can scream, but I could be wrong."

"Well, it scared me. Maybe it was..."

"A dream?" asked his mom. She nodded toward the kitchen, gesturing for him to keep walking down the stairs.

Coda opted to walk backwards, looking behind him as he grasped the railings to make sure he wouldn't fall. Then he continued to walk backwards, even into the kitchen.

"I could still hear it when I was awake," he continued.

His mom sat down at the table in the small dining room that attached to the kitchen. She glanced worriedly at him for a moment, and then picked up a magazine she had left open on the table. She scanned through the pages, stopped, and silently read something that was obviously the utmost of importance. Her lips moved as she read, and a crease formed across her brow. Her focus on the magazine wasn't a good sign. It meant that his mom really didn't think that the screech was a serious matter, and didn't want to hear any more about it.

Deciding it was probably just a crazy dream, Coda shut his mouth and opened the cupboard next to the refrigerator, and looked at the cereal boxes. The chocolate puffs and fruit flakes looked really enticing.

He grabbed the chocolate puffs and placed them on the counter. He saw Zoey out of the corner of his eye, eating cereal and watching a cartoon in the living room. He casually ignored her.

"So, it wasn't a dream then?" asked his mom, still nose down in her magazine.

Surprised that his mom still wanted to talk about it, Coda paused, looking to his left as if remembering the sound. "It was like what I said. The sound was loud, but it rang in my ears for a while after I got out of bed. And then I heard a voice in my head tell me not to fear, or something like that, and that my journey will start tomorrow." He began to feel silly after saying it out loud.

"Oh," said his mom, giving a flicking motion with her hand, dismissing the topic. "Then I guess you shouldn't worry about it. But," she looked up with concern, "do you still hear the ringing in your ears?"

Coda shook his head. "Uh-uh." He opened the fridge and grabbed the milk. "It was so, so loud, though." He poured the chocolate puffs into a bowl on the counter. He picked up the milk and turned to his mom. "Mom, you sure you didn't hear it?"

His mom looked up from the article. "I'm sorry that the dream was scary. I've never heard you talk so much about a dream before. It must have been intense." Her eyes turned back to the article. "And plus, if the dream was correct, you get to go on a journey tomorrow. Wouldn't that be fun?"

Coda knew she was trying to make him feel better, but that just didn't do it.

He took a deep breath and poured the milk into the bowl, grabbing a spoon out of the drawer. *It couldn't be a dream*, he thought.

He sat at the dining room table next to his mom and looked at the clock in the kitchen. "I've slept past eleven?"

"Yup. That's not like you. Zoey has already dressed, been outside, and back again for her second serving of breakfast." His mom closed the magazine and put it down on the table. "You missed Michael, too. He was looking for you."

Coda's mom glanced at Zoey sitting on the couch, eating her breakfast and singing to herself, garbling words as she chewed. "She's at least eating in the morning. That's a relief."

Coda remembered that it was just last year that Zoey had stopped eating breakfast, complaining of stomach aches. *She's such a faker. Always wanting attention.* He had noticed that since that time she was always looking at her skinny figure in the mirror, checking her backside and stomach. He wanted to tell his parents that she just wanted to be skinny, like the fashion models on TV, but he held his tongue. If she didn't like

26

to eat, that was her problem, not his.

A loud clunk from a shutting door upstairs interrupted Coda's thoughts. "Dad's up," said his mom.

Coda's dad came down the stairs still in his rumpled red boxers, and wiping the sleep from his eyes. He yawned out loud, stopping to scratch his back, looking a little bit like a monkey. Then he looked at Coda and his wife before he took a big stretch, standing on his tiptoes, and reaching his arms toward the ceiling. He smiled at Coda. "Good mornin', buddy!"

"Hey Dad," replied Coda.

Coda's dad walked through the kitchen to the dining room table. He kissed the top of his wife's head and reached over to ruffle his son's hair. "It looks like a nice day today. You gonna ride your bike or something?"

Coda laughed, pushing his dad's hand out of his hair. "Well," he shrugged his shoulders, "I don't know...can I play on your computer?" Coda asked, hopefully.

His dad scratched his head. "Uh, okay. Only for about an hour, though, then you're outside."

"No, no," said his mom. "Let him go out and enjoy the sun. It doesn't last forever here, you know?"

"Mom!" complained Coda. "I just—"

"Yeah, come out and play with me," Zoey chimed in. Coda saw that Zoey had already finished her cereal and was ready to go.

"Yeah," said Coda's mom. "Play with your sister for a while. I don't want you playing video games all day."

"Oh, man! Do I have to?" complained Coda. He looked up at the ceiling in distress. "I can play outside by myself or I'll look for Michael."

Zoey's head drooped in disappointment. With heavy steps, she walked toward the dishwasher to place her dirty bowl. Suddenly she smiled and perked up. "Hey Coda, let's go to the forest and build a fort!"

Coda rolled his eyes. Having a younger sister hanging around him all the time wasn't his kind of fun. He sighed, "You're not good at that."

He glanced at Zoey and saw her expression—like her heart

had sunk to the floor. *She's such a brat!*

"Oh, alright," Zoey mumbled. Her shoulders hung like she had a heavy weight on them, but Coda knew she was acting out her disappointment worse than it was. "I'll play in my room, I guess." Her mouth barely opened to get the words out, making everyone lean close enough to understand her.

Coda's dad put his arm around her. "Did you say something about your room?"

She looked down. "Yeah, I said I'll just play in my room, *I guess*." It came out almost as a muffled whisper.

"Zoey," her dad bent down on one knee to look at her. He gently pushed his finger up, under her chin, making her lift her head so he could look directly into her eyes. "What did we talk about last night?"

"I don't know," she muttered again, shrugging her shoulders.

Coda saw sadness in her eyes, and like always, he wondered if it was a real sadness, or the actress inside of her.

"We talked about your mumbling problem. We can't hear you when you speak like that, remember?"

"I don't mumble," Zoey protested, her eyes welling up, "and I don't have a problem!"

Coda could tell his mom was starting to get uncomfortable with the way this was going.

"We're not disciplining you, Zo Zo," she reassured.

She stood up to go and comfort her daughter. "We just want to know how you feel." She put her arm around Zoey, pulling her snugly against her hip. "And we can't understand you when you always have your hand around your mouth when you talk." Coda saw his mom's forehead wrinkle as she added with concern, "We just want to hear you."

Coda took his first bite of cereal. He'd seen this scene play out many times, always with the same ending. The funny thing was that he hardly ever had a problem understanding his sister. He could hear Zoey a mile away if he wanted to, but *wanting to* was never the case.

Zoey looked down again and crossed her arms with the bowl still held firmly in her hand. A tear fell down her cheek and she started to cry. *Here we go again*, thought Coda.

"Zoey?" Her dad peered into her eyes. "Everything is alright, just tell us what the problem is." His voice had picked up slightly when he'd said "problem," and Coda felt a twinge of anger in it. Coda knew his dad wasn't buying this act any more than he was.

"I don't like it when you tell me that I mumble, because I can't help it." She put the bowl on the counter and slowly walked toward the entryway. She opened the door and went outside, forgetting to shut the door behind her.

Coda took another bite of cereal as he watched his parents shake their heads. "I know," said his dad, "let's get that speech therapist on the phone, the one that Susan told us about."

"Good idea," agreed his mom as she started wiping up the table with a damp cloth. "Susan said it helped her son a lot."

Coda's dad walked to the entryway. The sun shone through, engulfing the wood floor and showing some dust that covered the area. He poked his head out of the doorway to see if Zoey was around. Coda looked back at his cereal and dipped his spoon in it for another bite. As he lifted the spoon toward his mouth, he suddenly dropped it on the table, clutching his ears with his hands.

He fell off his chair and onto the floor as the loud screeching sound blasted his eardrums. He closed his eyes tightly as blackness entered his vision, with bolts of electric violet light shooting around. His mom rushed to his rescue, grabbing him, and then helping him to his feet.

Coda opened his eyes. The screeching sound roared in his ears as his mom mouthed something he couldn't hear. Then he felt the large hands of his dad rubbing his back, doing his best to calm him down.

The screech turned into a voice that screamed, "Don't fear! Tomorrow, your journey begins!" and it quickly faded away.

Coda jumped up, yelling at his mom. "Did you hear *that*?"

"I didn't hear anything."

"Hear what?" asked his dad.

"The...well...um...I don't know. The noise, I guess," said Coda, rubbing his ears with annoyance and embarrassment.

"It's the noise I heard this morning, but then it said, 'Don't fear' and something, something about a journey, again."

"Oh boy," said his dad. "I guess we'll need two appointments—one with the speech therapist and one at the ear doctor."

Coda's mom gave his dad a scornful look.

"No, I'm fine," protested Coda. He shook his head, trying to get the last of the ringing out of his ears as he walked upstairs, toward his room. He kept rubbing his ears, not wanting to hear that noise ever again.

Chapter 3

Zoey followed a dirt path that she and her brother had dubbed Abernathy Trail—named after the creek that ran alongside it. She was on the edge of the Cornell Forest, just a block from their house. It was a place where she felt at home, even more than in the house she lived in. She always felt welcome here, and her favorite tree didn't care how she spoke or mumbled.

Walking close to the narrow flowing creek only a few feet away made it all that much better. The creek sent cool air to her body, making it easier to bear the summer heat.

Zoey saw that the sun was at its highest peak, beaming shafts of light between the gaps of maple and oak leaves, mixed with pine branches. She heard the sounds of birds chirping and fluttering from branch to branch, bringing a sense of business amongst the trees.

Zoey looked back down at her feet and kept walking, lost in thought. *I talk just fine,* she grumbled to herself now and then.

As she came around a bend in the creek, she gasped in surprise. The forest ahead of her was completely unfamiliar. There were trees that she knew she'd never seen before, and the surroundings seemed pristine, much more than usual, yet the dirt path next to the creek continued onward. She wondered how long she'd been walking and why she'd never come this way before.

She wiped away a tear, looking more carefully at the woods around her. She noticed a peculiar tree about ten yards away. It was strange looking. Its bark was twisted, spiraling up the trunk, and well-lit leaves that seemed different from all of the other leaves growing in the forest. *The tree from my dream?* She shook her head. *That's silly.* Then the feeling of her dream came back like a surge of rushing water. She couldn't help but think the dream was more real than it should have been.

She looked more closely at the twisted tree. There, at its base, was a rather large knot sticking out. Her eyes widened in delight and she quickly forgot about her dream. *What a perfect stool to sit on.*

She was about to run toward the tree but stopped, remembering her dilemma. *How do I get my mom and dad to stop bugging me about the way I talk?*

Her head drooped, her shoulders sagged forward, and her eyes became teary again. *It's impossible. They don't understand.*

She walked to the edge of the creek and stared at the moving water. She stood in a sad, self-pitying daze.

An abrupt wind picked up, nearly pushing her into the creek. She shrieked in surprise, catching herself from toppling over by stepping into the creek with her right foot, soaking her shoe and sock in the process. Quickly pulling her foot out of the now clouded, muddied water, she crossed her arms in disappointment, making a 'humph' sound. Then she plopped straight down, onto her rump, and sat cross-legged with her wet shoe dripping muddy water onto the ground.

As she sat there pouting, she noticed something very unusual about a green fern next to her. It had a strange, white powder on it.

She looked over at a yellow dandelion and saw the same white powder on it as well. She then realized that the white powder was everywhere—on the dirt, on the flowers, on the bushes, but it seemed to go no further than the edge of that spiraled tree's branches hanging just above her.

Did it fall from the tree?

Zoey touched the white dust on the fern. It was cold and felt like snow. A big grin appeared on her face and she screamed with delight, "Snow!" She grabbed a handful and threw it into the air.

Zoey knew, though, that snow fell only around Christmas time. *It's summer, so how could it snow?* She grabbed another handful and threw it into the air, tucking the question away for later.

"Zoey?" said a woman's sweet soft voice.

Zoey froze. "Who's there?" she called out tentatively.

No one answered. She shrugged her shoulders, continuing to forage for snow. However, it was quickly melting away in the summer heat.

She had an idea. If she gathered the snow fast enough and showed Coda, then maybe he'd play with her. She gathered as much snow as she could, and then paused for a moment. Something jumped in front of her. What was that? The small green creature jumped again.

"Frog!" she yelled, as she dropped the snow and trapped the frog in her hands.

"Hi, little froggy, how are you?" She opened her hands to peek at the frog. "It's okay. I won't hurt you," she said as she tried to pet it.

Too late.

The frog jumped out of her hands and onto the forest floor. She giggled and picked up some more snow.

"You're very kind," said the same sweet voice she'd heard only moments earlier.

Zoey paused. "What? Who said that?" She slowly surveyed the forest to see if her brother was playing a trick on her.

"Coda, where are you?" She walked up to the tree to peer around it. "I see you, Coda," she called out, fibbing, not really seeing her brother or knowing if he was around.

Zoey took a step forward, bumping her knee on the large knot growing out of the tree. "Ouch." Then she remembered. *The knot. It's a perfect place to sit.*

She touched the interesting looking knot. It was amazing. It almost looked as if someone had carved it out of the tree just for people to sit on it.

A squirrel scampered down the tree, stopping midway down the trunk. Its nose and whiskers rapidly twitched and its black eyes stared intently at Zoey. She considered if the squirrel was actually thinking or perhaps examining her. It jumped onto the knot, made a loud squeak, and stared up at her again.

"Hi, little one," said Zoey. She slowly reached out her hand. Frightened, the squirrel jumped up and down on the knot, and

Zoey pulled her hand back. Suddenly, it scooted back up the trunk and then into the high branches.

This gave Zoey an idea. She could stand on the knot and grab the lowest lying branch to climb the tree.

She placed one foot on the knot, then the other. She felt something zap her as she reached for the branch just above her. She screamed and jumped off the knot as fast as she could. Her heart pounded as she stared at the tree. What had zapped her?

She tiptoed all around the tree, but didn't see anything that could have sent a shock through her. She remembered that static electricity would do that to her every so often, so she shook her body to get the sensation to go away and stepped on the knot, or seat, once again.

She stood still, waiting for it to come again.

Nothing happened.

She grabbed the branch above her. A strong tingling sensation vibrated through her, from her head all the way down to her toes.

Startled again, she jumped off.

"It's alright. All of us trees are good trees. I have a seat right here, just for sitting, if you'd like," said the sweet voice.

Zoey stopped breathing for a moment. She put her hand and ear against the bark of the tree, trying to pinpoint where the speakers were located. After a brief period of quiet and hearing nothing, she stepped back, inspecting the tree by its entirety.

Glowing green leaves and twisting bark were the only things different about the tree, so she bent down, feeling the soil dampened from the melted snow that had covered the area minutes before, thinking a speaker might be there.

Is the tree actually talking to me?

"You are merely listening," responded the tree.

Zoey smiled, looking around the forest. "Trees don't talk. Who is this? Coda?" She was convinced a joke was being played on her.

"Come—sit," beckoned the tree.

Zoey rolled her eyes. "Okay, whatever."

She slowly sat down on the knot in the tree. She couldn't relax, wondering what was going to zap her next. She even wondered why she was being so silly, doing what a tree, or whatever it was, had asked her to do. *This is a joke,* she thought. "Who's playing a joke on me?" she said out loud.

As she sat, Zoey felt the wave of tingling go through her body again. It felt weird to her, almost like a tickle and she laughed.

"I'm the Snow Tree."

"Snow Tree?" Zoey snorted. She waited for a prankster to jump out of its hiding place, camera in hand.

"There's no such thing as a Snow Tree. Who's saying that?"

"Oh?" said the voice. "I *am* a Snow Tree." And, as if on cue, the tree started to sprinkle snowflakes onto Zoey.

Zoey jumped up from the seat. "Brrr, that's cold." She glanced up at the Snow Tree to see snow forming on it's branches, and dropping to the ground.

"Wow," said Zoey, "are you really talking to me?"

"You're merely listening," replied the tree.

"Can all trees talk?"

"Yes, most can, and most do."

"Nuh-uh," said Zoey. "Then how come I can't hear them?"

"You've never listened," replied the tree. "You've never paid attention. You were focused on the snow when you heard my voice. The snow is a big part of me, so it was easier for you to hear me."

Zoey furrowed her brow. She didn't understand, and only replied with a lonely, "Oh."

"Just look around," said the Snow Tree.

As Zoey looked at the landscape, she saw what she usually saw in the forest; trees slowly rocking in soft wind with ferns shadowed underneath, wild green grasses off in the distance bathed by the glow of the sun, the sound of the creek flowing against rocks and roots, and birds flying from branch to branch while singing their own tunes.

"What do you see and hear, Zoey?"

Zoey shrugged her shoulders, mumbling, "I don't know."

"You don't see and hear the forest talking?"

"I guess," replied Zoey.

"Good. You're listening. Now, I want to show you something."

After a short pause, the Snow Tree said, "Look at the fern in front of you."

"It's a pretty fern," Zoey said, as if that was what the tree wanted to hear.

"Yes, it is," said the Snow Tree. "Now come and sit back down on my perch."

Zoey shrugged her shoulders and sat down on the knot at the tree's base. "Okay, here I am, now what?"

"When you stop thinking about other things," replied the Snow Tree, "and pay attention only to the fern, then you'll truly be able to see it in a way that the inhabitants of the forest see it."

Zoey rolled her eyes and lowered her head, murmuring, "I see the fern."

"Let your eyes relax. Do you see who's taking care of it?"

"Is it you?" asked Zoey.

"In some ways I'm its caretaker, but I don't care for it like my friends do. If you watch the fern without any thought of yourself, or any thought of what you think I want to hear, then I'll help you find that place within yourself so you can see."

Zoey didn't know what the Snow Tree was talking about, but stared at the fern anyway. She gradually started to feel a different tingling sensation embracing her body. It somehow gave her more focus and concentration.

Zoey's body took a long, deep breath of fresh air without her command. Then her eyes widened in complete amazement.

There, hovering next to the fern was a small pink ball of light. Zoey put her hand over her mouth in surprise, and pointed at the pink ball. "What *is* that?"

"Keep concentrating, Zoey."

Zoey looked straight at the ball with no other thought than what she was seeing. Within seconds, the ball turned into a beautiful, tiny woman with wings. She had her hands on the fern, tending to it, while singing the most beautiful of songs.

Zoey jumped off the knot and ran over to the fern. But,

before she could reach the fern, the tiny woman disappeared.

"What was that?" asked Zoey. She was delighted by this whimsical creature. She'd never seen anything like it, and couldn't stop smiling as she scurried about, looking for the flying woman.

"That is what's called a nature spirit. Nature spirits take care of this forest. There are many different types of nature spirits. That one was a nymph."

Zoey looked around the fern and started calling for her. "Nymph? Nymph? Come here little Nymph."

"She's still there. I wanted to show you that there's more to life than what you see on a daily basis. There is so much more to the world than what you normally perceive it to be. You'll experience more of this very soon," said the Snow Tree.

Zoey had no idea what she was talking about, but ran over and sat on her chair again, hopefully. She wanted to see the nymph. Gazing into the fern for what seemed to be several minutes, she saw nothing more than the fern itself.

"I can't see her."

"But you did, and that's all that matters."

The wind then blew a mighty gust and Zoey closed her eyes. Her thoughts drifted away from the tiny flying woman and onto the wind. "That felt good."

"She likes you," said the Snow Tree.

"Who likes me?"

"Her name is Lady Wind. She'll guide my words on her breezes when you're in need."

In need? In need of what? thought Zoey.

"Now," continued the Snow Tree, "we want to understand why you were crying."

"What do you mean?" asked Zoey.

"You were crying when you first walked into the forest," responded the Snow Tree.

Zoey then remembered what she was crying about and the fire in her spirit erupted. "Because I can't talk right! I get made fun of, or people just won't talk to me anymore because they don't know what I'm saying!"

"You can talk very well, Zoey," the Snow Tree said as she

37

raised one of her branches, letting the rays of the sun land upon Zoey.

"Do you feel the warmth coming from the sun?"

"Yeah."

"That sun, its warmth, and its brightness are like you. You were created just like the sun. You are here to shine. Everyone would see the wonderful qualities of the sun in you if you allowed them to see how bright you truly are. However, you dim your light, hiding it from everybody. This is what happens when you speak with your head down, with your hands covering your mouth. It dims your voice and it dims you."

After a moment, she added, "Your dad gets impatient with you and your friends tease you when you put your head down toward the earth, while covering your mouth when you speak. Your hands and the ground can hear you just fine, but do you think anyone else can?"

"Yeah, sometimes they can."

"Only after they ask you to repeat yourself over and over again. Is that true?"

"Yeah, but my brother can always hear me—when he wants to."

The Snow Tree opened her branches wide and the sun embraced Zoey even more. "The sun is seen by all of us, and isn't embarrassed to show us its brightness. It speaks its truth by giving us warmth, and doesn't worry about what others think about it. It lights our way because it knows that it IS light. That is you, Zoey. You shine like the sun."

Zoey stayed on the chair for what seemed to be hours. The Snow Tree and Zoey didn't speak for a long time. Zoey's thoughts were on the sun. She even imagined herself as the sun. She saw that every time she talked to someone, and looked them in the eyes, she could see a ray of herself shining upon them.

She understood. She saw how simple it was. If she looked in the eyes of another when she talked, they could hear her words more clearly. She imagined herself in the middle of a field of flowers of all different colors, with her chin up and her chest out, yelling to the sun, "I am like the sun!" Then she announced to the sky loudly, "I am!"

"My dear Zoey," said the Snow Tree, jostling Zoey out of her thoughts, "you have mastered your challenge today."

"I have?" Zoey looked around. "Mastered? What's that mean?"

"If a child passes a test by knowing, understanding, and then correctly applying the answers to real life questions, then that means the child has mastered it," explained the Snow Tree. "Today, my child, you have done just that. Tomorrow is another story. Nonetheless, today you've learned a great lesson, and in good time. Tomorrow, you have an important mission to embark upon."

"Embark? Mission?" Looking up, Zoey scanned the limited dictionary she had in her mind. "I don't understand."

"Embark means to get on board or to go somewhere. Mission means that you have an important calling or purpose to fulfill."

"I do?" asked Zoey, standing up and looking around at the beautiful forest around her, which suddenly seemed more bright and clear. The colors popped and the sounds were soft and elegant.

"You both do," replied the Snow Tree.

"Both?"

"You and your brother. You both have an important mission and it will begin tomorrow."

Zoey placed her foot on the knot and grabbed the lowest hanging branch. Then she placed her other foot on a small protrusion, about a foot above the knot, and pulled herself up to the first branch. "I don't think my parents would want me to go on a mission." She tilted her head and continued, mostly talking to herself. "Well, if it's not too long of a mission, then I guess I could go." She gently shifted her body back and forth to feel how sturdy the branch was before putting all of her weight onto it.

"Your mission, like any other missions you may have in your life, is yours, and only yours. You have the choice to answer its call, or to ignore it. There is no judgment," said the Snow Tree. "It's simply what you and The Great Spirit have planned for you."

Zoey looked wide-eyed at the tree. "The Great Spirit?" This was sounding even weirder now. For sure her brother wouldn't have any part of this. He won't think this kind of stuff is real, especially if it comes from his sister. *He'll just make fun of me like he always does.*

"The Great Spirit is the creator of everything you see around you, and everything you don't see. There's nothing that The Great Spirit hasn't touched. It has been here since before the beginning. It's full of truth, patience, and love. All of nature honors The Great Spirit."

Zoey looked around with amazement at the large, twisted branches and bright, glowing green leaves. She suddenly felt important for the first time in her life. She rubbed her hand on the branch, feeling the cracked bark. "Where does the mission start?"

"Do you see the long line of blackberry bushes to your right?"

Zoey twisted around the tree to see blackberries thriving under the sun, just off in the distance. "Yeah, I think I see them."

"There's an entrance where the blackberries grow. You can walk through that entrance and take a peek."

Zoey climbed down the tree and stood on the knot. "Take a peek at what?"

"At your mission," said the Snow Tree.

"You want me to walk through the blackberries? Won't that hurt?"

"The entrance isn't through the blackberries. It's at the beginning of the blackberries. It won't hurt because the entrance is large enough for a human to walk through," replied the Snow Tree. "You'll soon see for yourself."

Zoey nodded. She wanted to ask what it was an entrance to, but for some reason she held her tongue. She felt an odd and happy trust in the Snow Tree that seemed familiar to her, but she couldn't place where the familiarity was coming from, just like in her dream.

With that trust, she walked several yards, feeling the breeze from Lady Wind lightly caressing her as it cooled her off from the heat of the day.

She crossed her arms as she continued to walk, her mind showing images of her mom wagging her finger at her, telling her not to go into unknown places.

Her stomach felt like it had nervous butterflies trapped within it as a wave of uncertainty slowed her movement toward the blackberry bushes. What if this is a joke? What if she gets totally lost, never to see her parents or brother ever again?

Zoey stopped, taking a deep breath. Her mom wouldn't mind if she just took a peek. She suddenly knew, beyond any doubt, that the Snow Tree had her best interests at heart. Her mom wouldn't disagree with that, would she?

"Ouch!" Zoey's leg brushed against a sharp shrub beneath the edge of the Snow Tree's outstretched branches, snapping her back to the moment. She had a mission and she was about to get a peek at it. A sudden feeling of excitement pushed away any doubts, hurrying her along.

There she stood, staring at the opening of a large circle slightly overgrown with blackberries. Peering deeper into the circled entrance, she could see that it was more like a tunnel created by the growing blackberry bushes. The whole blackberry tunnel seemed to be about two school buses long.

She took her first step inside, watching her foot hit the ground, and wondered if she'd feel the tingling sensation that the Snow Tree gave her. But, as she took her second step into the tunnel, nothing happened.

She looked left and right, making sure everything was safe, then cautiously proceeded forward.

As she walked through the tunnel, she noticed that the ground consisted of wilted, dry grass. Her father had once told her that grass can go dormant when it doesn't get enough water, which seemed to have happened to the grass in the blackberry passageway.

About halfway through, the normal sounds of the outside forest became quieter and different. In fact, there seemed to be very little sound at all. Where were the birds she had heard moments ago? The light had even changed. Instead of it getting fainter from the shadows of blackberry vines blocking the sun, the lighting became a bit brighter. The air, too, seemed to have changed. The air felt much richer, and it was a lot easier to breathe. It was as if each breath brought with it a mouthful of pure energy. She took in a long, deep breath. *Yes*, her body screamed! Zoey felt like she had needed this type of air her entire lifetime.

Taking several more paces forward, Zoey paused as she heard someone humming from somewhere beyond the other end of the tunnel. "Snow Tree? Is that you?"

The humming ceased.

"Huh?" said a male voice. "Who said that?"

A rustling of grass and the sound of heavy steps vibrated through the tunnel. Zoey crouched down and stared at the exit of the tunnel nervously, waiting for someone, most likely a young man, to appear.

As she crouched, she placed her fingers on the ground to give her more balance, but felt something cold and soft. *Snow?* She looked down. It was definitely snow that she was touching, but how did it get there? It wasn't there a moment ago. She paused. She had the feeling that someone was staring at her. The hairs on the back of her neck stood up straight and she didn't want to look. But, she had to. This was her *mission*.

Slowly, she lifted her head to see who was spying on her at the end of the blackberry tunnel. When she saw it, her mouth fell open. She wanted to scream, but couldn't.

Chapter 4

Zoey slowly inched her way backward from the enormous elephant staring back at her. He leaned on his front legs to get a clearer look. His eyes looked as wide as hers.

It didn't look mean, but Zoey had only seen elephants on television. She didn't know if it would bite or stampede her and she didn't want to stick around to find out. But, then she remembered what the Snow Tree had told her. She had a mission.

She took a couple of deep breaths and looked into the eyes of the elephant, seeing that they were friendly. But, what does an elephant have to do with a mission? Plus, the voice around the corner she'd heard was from a young man. Maybe this is the young man's pet?

She looked at the elephant's gray hide, seeing a strange beauty in it. Just like the gray wolf, the elephant had a glowing crystal on his forehead, and one on his chest as well. But, the elephant's crystals were orange, rather than violet like the gray wolf's.

A warm feeling of love suddenly washed through her. She straightened up and smiled. She loved animals and wondered how she could ever have felt scared of this one. This elephant was beautiful and seemed very friendly. The young man she had heard from beyond the tunnel exit must have trained this elephant well.

She knew now that this creature was as harmless as a fly and all of her fear melted away. "Aren't you just a beautiful looking elephant?" Her voice was like a child talking to a baby.

The elephant looked to the left, showing his profile, and then to the right, showing his profile again, almost as if he was posing for her.

He turned in a circle, wiggled his rear end, and then turned all the way around again, until his gaze met Zoey's. Then he smiled. Zoey blinked a couple of times to see if her eyes were tricking her.

"Well, thank you for saying so," said the elephant. "I think I'm a rather fine looking fellow, if I do say so myself."

Zoey yelped, dropping to the ground and backing away.

The elephant flinched at Zoey's startled fright, looking confused. "Oh, yeah," he stammered, "sorry about that." He cleared his throat, just like a human would do. "Ahem." He proudly pulled himself up taller and opened his mouth. "Meeeeeeeooooooooooowww?"

If Zoey hadn't been so startled, she would have burst out laughing. *A talking and meowing elephant?* However, this bizarre behavior prompted her to resume her backward crawl.

"Wait, no, no, no." The elephant tilted his head and let out a reasonably convincing, "Moooooooooooooooooooo!"

He looked intently at Zoey, waiting for another compliment. When none came, he asked, "Isn't that the sound I'm supposed to make?" He frowned. "Did I do it wrong?"

But Zoey had bolted, and was already past the halfway point in the tunnel. She looked behind her to see the elephant simply disappear, vanishing into thin air. The shadows from the blackberries were blocking out the sun and the normal air had re-introduced itself. Zoey ran the rest of the way out of the tunnel, back to the Snow Tree, as fast as she could.

Panting, she threw herself onto the Snow Tree's knot, landing with a loud thump.

"What...was...that?" she gasped.

"That was an elephant," replied the Snow Tree.

"Yes, I could see that! But it talked!"

"You had a glimpse of Ohm Totem—the land beyond the Cornell Forest. It's a place, just like this, teeming with life, emotions, lessons, and experiences."

Zoey looked up at the branches. The sun glimmered against the green leaves and the squirrel that she had seen earlier jumped from tree to tree. "Huh? Ohm Totem?" She shook her head. "But the elephant talked!"

"That place is different than this one. The elephant you met is a Being called a PureLight. The PureLights have many human qualities, especially speech."

The squirrel jumped from another branch and glared at Zoey. It made a high-pitched chattering noise, the sound they usually make when annoyed or protecting their territory.

The Snow Tree shuddered, dropping snow onto the squirrel, and on Zoey. The squirrel raced off to a higher branch, busying itself by staring at the cedar tree many yards away.

"That's Dinzy. He was telling you not to climb my branches. I reminded him that it's not up to him."

"Oh," responded Zoey, somewhat bewildered and wanting the Snow Tree to explain more to her about Ohm Totem.

"Ohm Totem," continued the Snow Tree, "can only be reached by going through the tunnel hidden within the blackberry patch. This is the only entrance and exit to Ohm Totem. Otherwise, it's concealed from this land, covered by a thin shroud.

Puzzled, Zoey raised her eyebrows. "Shroud?" she asked.

"Shroud means hidden or covered by something, be it rain, a cloth, and in this instance, spirit. When you saw the elephant, you had walked through the Shroud of Ohm Totem.

"For example, if a waterfall was safe enough to walk through, you could walk through it and see that it actually conceals a rock wall. The water acts as a shroud concealing the rock wall hidden behind it. Does that make sense, Zoey?"

"I think so."

"The waterfall is like the shroud that covers Ohm Totem."

Zoey's attention was momentarily distracted by an unusual beetle crawling toward the tree. "But an elephant talked to me," she persisted. "How did it do that? It meowed, too! How weird is that?!"

"That's something you'll learn about, soon. Remember this—not everything is the same from one place to another, or one time to another. Everything is always changing, sometimes in small ways, and other times in big ways. Before today you didn't know about a talking elephant. Now what you know has changed, and as a result, you have changed, too. Many people fear change, and fight against it. What people must realize, even you Zoey, is that change is the only thing that you can count on in life. Nothing is ever exactly the same from one moment to the next."

Zoey was still having a hard time with the idea of a talking, meowing, and mooing elephant. "But, since when do elephant's talk? I don't get it."

"You will, Zoey. This I promise."

She sat on the Snow Tree's seat and took a breath as the world opened up to her again. She saw the blue, white, and purple balls flying around, dodging each other as if they were playing. She saw the wind's slight breezes nudge the leaves and plants. She saw that all of the forest glimmered with joy, in constant motion, living peacefully under the sun's rays.

"Wow," she said in a whisper. Then she noticed that the sun was starting to drop lower in the sky. It was later than she thought and she needed to get home.

"Yes, it's time to go," said the Snow Tree, as if reading her thoughts. "Tomorrow your mission begins, as does your brother's."

"Okay, I don't know if he'll come, but I'll try," replied Zoey, turning to go home.

"I'll see you tomorrow," promised the Snow Tree.

Chapter 5

"There's no such thing as a talking tree," Coda protested, as he and Zoey entered the Cornell Forest that began at the end of Cornell Avenue, one block away from their home. *She's always making up fantastic stories for attention,* snorted Coda, rolling his eyes.

It was a vast forest rich with 144 acres of trees, such as Ponderosa Pines, Western Hemlocks, and some well-established clusters of Oaks and Cedars.

Zoey jumped onto a large rock. "I swear, Coda." She hopped off the rock and picked up a pine cone off the ground. "She talked to me and she wants you to come with me today."

Coda's blue eyes flashed with anger and he scratched his tousled brown hair. "I know mom talked about the walking trees in Jamaica, but they didn't really walk. It was the way their roots grew that made them *look* like they were walking." He scratched his head again. "Maybe you heard the roots making sounds?"

Coda was tired of his sister creating stories that weren't true. He stopped in stride, pointing his finger at her. "No, you're making this up," he said sternly, sounding just like their dad. "You always make things up."

"No, I don't," Zoey said, stamping her foot on the ground. Then she started walking, following the dirt path that led from the paved street to the creek. At the creek, it forked into three directions. She turned left to follow the same path she had taken yesterday, when she had met the Snow Tree for the first time.

The sun pushed its light through the many branches hanging above, dappling the path with bright shadows from branches and leaves. Today was going to be another hot one, thought Coda. At the triple fork, he planted his feet firmly on the ground. "I'm not following you."

Zoey started to sing one of her made-up songs, clearly ignoring him. Coda frowned. *Zoey's ignoring me?* She had walked away without any hesitation, when in the past she'd always follow Coda, doing what *he* wanted to do when *he* insisted.

Coda shrugged his shoulders and followed her. He wasn't going to let her off the hook that easily.

"Why are we going to see a stupid made-up talking tree?"

"She's real!"

"You don't have any friends because you make everything up," Coda badgered.

"I do not, Coda!"

"Yes you do, Zoey!" he insisted, and laughed obnoxiously to really get on her nerves.

Zoey scowled, but didn't reply. They walked in silence on the skinny dirt path. Coda listened to the sounds of the creek, its water curling around roots and splashing against rocks, making him yearn to jump into the water to escape the heat of the day.

It was too hot for Coda and the last thing he wanted to do was go with his sister to see an imaginary tree. If his parent's hadn't made him go out, he'd be back at home playing with his Legos in his air-conditioned bedroom.

They walked past light green ferns and orange and yellow wild flowers, until they finally came to the spot Zoey had found the day before.

"Right there!" she proclaimed, pointing at the tree.

"What? That's it? It looks like the cherry tree at Michael's house."

Just at that moment, a ray of sunlight lit up the tree.

Looking closer, Coda could see that the tree stood proudly by itself, glowing more brightly than the other forest trees. It twisted in a spiral all the way from the base of its trunk to its top branches. The limbs from the tree dazzled in the light as the wind nudged its bright green leaves, making it look as if the tree was waving at them.

"OK, that's a weird looking tree," Coda admitted. He'd already forgotten about Zoey's story and ran toward the twisted tree to climb it.

This is perfect for climbing, he thought. His legs brushed against a myriad of ferns that covered his path to the tree as he ran.

"Wait for me, Coda!" yelled Zoey, chasing after her brother.

"You can't get me!" called Coda. He looked behind to see his sister closing in on him fast.

"Let's play hide-and-go-seek," said Zoey, as she got closer.

"No, let's play tag and you're it!" Coda sliced through a narrow crack between two large bushes that lined the path. Then he stopped with a quick jolt. He was just a couple of yards from the weird tree when he felt a wave of different sensations running throughout his body. "Whoa!"

Zoey caught up to him and gently touched his hand as she stood next to him. She stared at the tree along with her brother. "What's the matter?" she asked.

"Do you feel that, Zoey?" A tingling sensation started to play with the crown of his head and a soft, almost feathery touch tickled his arms, hands, legs, and feet.

"Oh, that's the Snow Tree. I told you about it. She gives off that feeling."

Coda screwed up his nose, something he always did when he was unsure. He looked up and saw the Snow Tree's branches directly above him. "I d-don't know, Zoey."

"Seriously," said Zoey, walking over to the Snow Tree and sitting on its knob. "It's okay. Come and..." she stopped talking and pointed at Coda, her mouth wide open in surprise. "Oh, my gosh!" She was staring at a spot just over Coda's right shoulder.

"That's his spirit animal. It will be with him for his entire life," said the Snow Tree. "You have one, too."

Zoey pointed over Coda's right shoulder. "Coda, look! That's your spirit animal."

Coda stood perfectly still. He was confused. He had heard a voice talking to Zoey, but where did it come from? He could feel a strange tingling sensation on the right side of his face and ear. He twisted around to look over his right shoulder, but couldn't see anything.

"He's touching you!" yelled Zoey. Her eyes glowed with utter delight. "He's a big black panther!" She laughed, "He's standing on his back legs, with his front paws on your shoulder. He's licking you!"

What's she talking about? Coda nervously whipped his head from side to side, seeing only the forest around him, not a big black cat leaning on him.

"He's purring," Zoey added.

"Who's touching me?!" yelled Coda.

"Your spirit animal. He's always at your side," answered the Snow Tree softly.

Coda froze. He could hear a woman's voice speaking to him, but only Zoey was there. Still, for some strange reason, he didn't doubt that the tree was talking and he didn't doubt that a spirit animal was next to him.

"He's simply you in another form," explained the Snow Tree.

Coda's eyes squinted as he looked off into the distance. "Me—in another form?" A small breeze ruffled the leaves above Coda as a calmness settled over him.

"Yes," replied the Snow Tree. "Your spirit animal will help you with your journey in more ways than you could ever imagine."

Coda looked to the ground, scuffing the dirt with his shoes. "Um...okay." His mind raced as he remembered the voice in his ears from yesterday. It, too, had talked of a journey, but he didn't show any outward sign that he remembered it.

"Who are you?" asked Coda.

"I am the Snow Tree. Come and sit next to your sister."

Zoey scooted over, and then got up so Coda could have the whole knob chair.

"Look around," said the Snow Tree.

Wide-eyed, Coda looked around, but saw nothing but squirrels playing, birds taking flight, and trees all around.

"Close your eyes, Coda, and take a deep breath," directed the Snow Tree.

Coda wriggled a bit, and then closed his eyes. As he took in a deep breath, he felt a tingling sensation surrounding his body. He began to smile as a sense of joyful energy entered him, pushing away the nervousness he had felt only moments before. He opened his eyes to see a completely different world. A world he thought existed only in cartoons.

He saw blue, green, white, and purple balls of light floating over and around trees, bushes, ferns, and everything growing in the forest. Some of them were traveling fast, some were slow, and others were stationary, hovering over large and small plants. He noticed that the stationary balls were beaming white light into the plants.

"Those are the caretakers of the forest," said the Snow Tree. "They're called orbs. Now, focus on an orb and tell me what you see."

Coda had completely forgotten his objections to Zoey about a talking tree as he eagerly put all of his attention on a green orb a couple of feet in front of him. It was hovering over a strange long-leafed plant with purple flowers. Without warning, the image faded into the background and he could only see Zoey sitting cross-legged next to the plant, her face illuminated with exhilaration.

As usual, this annoyed Coda and he shook his head. "I don't see anything else. What am I supposed to see?"

"Relax," said the Snow Tree. "Take a deep breath and clear everything from your mind. It's then that you'll see."

Doubt crept into Coda's mind and he began to feel silly. Is a tree really talking? Is it good to see orbs? Were his eyes and ears playing tricks on him? What kind of a trick was Zoey playing on him?

Coda stood up abruptly and all of the orbs instantly disappeared. He brushed past Zoey with a scowl. "We're going."

"What's the matter?" Zoey asked.

The Snow Tree spoke again to Coda. "There will be plenty of moments to think twice about me. But, right now I need to help you and Zoey get ready for the mission you're both about to go on."

"Mission?" Coda liked the idea of a mission. He stopped and turned toward the tree.

"Yes, a mission. In order to start your mission, I'm going to show you and Zoey how to find your true courage."

"Whaddya mean, our *true courage*?" asked Coda.

"True courage is when you can look at something you fear, and change the fear into love. When you do this, all of life feels safe in your presence and life fears you no more."

"I'm not afraid," Coda asserted.

"Life fears us?" asked Zoey.

"All of nature senses your fear. Animals will respond to your fear with their own fear. Changing your fear into love will change the way nature responds to you," said the Snow Tree. "Fear is the opposite of Love. It is an energy that flows through your body when you have negative feelings and thoughts. Love is an energy that flows through your body when you have positive feelings and thoughts. Both energies are very powerful. Love, however, has more power than Fear. Love comes from the thoughts and feelings of your heart and evaporates fear instantly. You must have the courage to love what you fear in order to fulfill the mission you're both about to go on."

Coda played with a small rock, trying to understand what was just said. "How can you think from your heart?" He dropped the rock and watched it hit the moss-covered ground. "That doesn't make sense." He furrowed his brow, not trusting the words he was hearing.

"It's easy," responded the Tree. "You can practice by closing your eyes and bringing an image to your mind."

"Alright," Coda nodded, "I'll give it a try—even though I'm not afraid of anything." Zoey stood next to Coda as he closed his eyes.

"What's something that scares you?" asked the Snow Tree.

A vision of his mom came to mind, scolding him over something. Next, he saw his school teacher from last year, Mr. Hacklin, and his heart nearly stopped. Coda and his friends thought Mr. Hacklin was the scariest teacher in the history of school teachers. He was a towering, grumpy old man with gray hair and white whiskers that came out of his ears and nose. He would creep up behind someone when they weren't paying attention, and ferociously slap a metal ruler against his own hand or on the desk. More than once Coda had nearly jumped out of his skin at the unexpected noise, and then had to go to the front of the class to explain what Mr. Hacklin was just talking about.

"What do you see?" asked the Snow Tree.

"Mr. Hacklin. He was my teacher last year," Coda said, anxiety wriggling around in his stomach.

A bird landed on the Snow Tree's lowest lying branch, twitching its blue head to the left and right, as if listening to the words being said. Then it flew off, darting to the next tree.

"Before we start this exercise, the bluebird wants me to tell you something. When you're done practicing, she would like you to follow her."

"Huh?" asked Coda. "Follow her where?"

"Wherever she leads you, but I suspect she'll lead you through the blackberries."

"Will I see the talking elephant again?" asked Zoey.

"The talking elephant?" Coda questioned.

"Yeah, an elephant...an elephant talked to me yesterday. I swear, Coda!" Zoey was very animated, waving her hands above her head and tripping all over her words.

Coda gave a sideways glance toward the Snow Tree. "Is that true?"

"What Zoey says is true."

Coda rolled his eyes. He wanted to tell them both that this entire thing was ridiculous, but before he could say anything the Snow Tree asked them both to close their eyes and calm their minds by taking deep breaths. He was intrigued by the idea of a talking elephant, so he closed his eyes.

"OK, let's practice changing fear into love. This is the same practice you use for all Beings in nature, and for all people," added the Snow Tree.

For a few minutes everything was quiet, except for the wind slowly blowing against the leaves and the sound of water streaming in the background.

"Now, Coda, I want you to think of Mr. Hacklin again. When you see him in your mind's eye, imagine him moving down from your mind and into your heart."

Coda suddenly felt very uncomfortable. His whole body had tightened up and his heart felt like it was filled with gremlins trying to scratch their way out. He didn't like Mr. Hacklin occupying his heart.

"Imagine," continued the Snow Tree, "a pink light filling your heart and surrounding Mr. Hacklin. Give him all of the joy, love, and happiness that you can with that pink light. Know that he comes from the same creator that you come from, and know that you are both equally loved. Even though Mr. Hacklin looks like he's always mad, know that he needs love, just like you."

Coda imagined the angry, seething Mr. Hacklin covered in neon pink light. He chuckled as the pink light bubbled and dripped all over his most feared teacher. It looked like he was being smothered with melting cotton candy. Then, for some reason, he thought of his friend Michael and the fun times they always had together, making him smile and filling him with joy.

In a flash, the butterflies in his heart and the tightness in his body disappeared. Feeling very happy, Coda naturally thought of all the things his mom and dad did for him. He knew without a doubt how much they loved him. He even thought of Zoey and how much she loved him, even if she was a bit of a pain sometimes.

"If Mr. Hacklin were in front of you now," said the Snow Tree, "you'd beam that pink light through your heart toward him. At the same time, you might feel him become happy. Since he's not in front of you right now, try to beam that light out into the world, addressing it to Mr. Hacklin. Like mailing a letter."

Coda did just that, instantly feeling tranquil and alive. He felt as though the fear he had for his old teacher was completely gone from his heart and he felt a new sense of freedom.

"Someday soon, Coda, and you too, Zoey, you'll be able to do that instantly without having to do this exercise at all. It'll become a healthy habit. You'll even be able to do it with your eyes open. This exercise will become a part of you in the same way that your hands, eyes, nose, and mouth are a part of you. "

"That's cool!" yelled Coda. "Zoey, you should..."

The bluebird suddenly flew over Zoey's shoulder, interrupting his words. Zoey ran after it and Coda followed. The bluebird dove through the entrance of the blackberry bushes, vanishing from view.

Zoey suddenly came to a screeching halt and Coda zoomed right past her. "Come on, Zoey, let's see where the bluebird is going." Coda ducked just in time to avoid the dangling thorns and vines hanging from the top of the blackberry entrance. He screeched to a halt with his body half in and half out of the entrance, and stared at Zoey. He prodded her to join him.

Zoey looked at him and closed her eyes. She took a deep breath and opened them. "Okay," she said somewhat hesitantly, but forcing a smile.

What's wrong with her? wondered Coda. He turned around and slowly walked through the opening into the tunnel. He saw that the vines shielded most of the light coming from the sun, shadowing the ground beneath his feet. He heard the sounds of birds singing, the sounds of tree branches shaking as squirrels jumped from tree to tree, and felt a cool breeze coming through the bushes carrying the scent of the forest with it.

"This would be a cool fort!" he yelled, then scrunched his nose. He shouldn't have said anything. Now Zoey will want to use this as a fort with him. *And she'd ruin the fort somehow, like she always does!*

Zoey shrugged her shoulders and stared past Coda's head. She looked like she was waiting for something to happen. Coda half-grinned. "What's wrong?" He hoped to goad her away.

"Nothings wrong," lied Zoey.

Coda giggled. *Maybe she's afraid of seeing another elephant. Maybe,* he thought deviously, *if I talk about it she'll turn around and go back home.* "Is it the elephant you saw yesterday?"

"It's weird seeing an elephant that can talk, that's all," replied Zoey. "Aren't you scared?"

55

"No. Well, I don't know. I don't feel much of anything right now." He sighed. He might as well just let her do what she wants to do.

Coda held his hand out for Zoey, which she eagerly grabbed, and he pushed forward, almost dragging Zoey along.

Coda was halfway through the tunnel when he stopped and looked around. "Where'd that bluebird go?"

He noticed something else, as well. The sounds of the forest had changed and everything was quiet. The birds weren't singing and the squirrels rustling in the background had disappeared. The fresh smell of the forest had changed to a more rich and thick aroma, reminding him of the roses that grew in his side yard at home. He loved that smell and gave a huge sniff. "That smells good!"

"I think we've entered the new place now. It feels good to breathe here," said Zoey. She stared longingly at the end of the blackberry tunnel, wondering if the elephant was going to show itself again.

"New place?" asked Coda.

"You'll see," replied Zoey.

Coda took several paces forward, but Zoey didn't move. He looked into her blue eyes. "Well, come on!"

Zoey knelt down, poking at the ground with her fingers. She slowly shook her head no and opened her mouth to say something when a loud pounding sound came from just outside the end of the tunnel.

"Hey, I found you guys," called an elated voice from outside the tunnel's exit. "Why are you hiding in there?"

They heard another pounding, as if something heavy had hit the earth.

Coda looked back at Zoey. Her eyes were wide with astonishment and her mouth gaped. She lifted her hand, pointing in the direction of the exit. "See!"

Coda slowly turned around and jumped back, flabbergasted. "It's an elephant!"

Chapter 6

A large gray elephant was bent down on its front knees in front of them. It was him. He was back.

Again, just like before, the elephant spoke.

"Are you going to come out? We've been looking all over for you two. You had us all a little frantic and worried." A gentle smile appeared on his face, half-hidden by his trunk, and the orange crystal glistened on his forehead.

"The elephant's talking!" screamed Coda, not taking his eyes off of it.

Zoey shrieked. Not because of the elephant this time, but because her arm pointing at the elephant was no longer an arm. It was a wing! It was white and black, with all sorts of brown colors mixed in. Her arm was a wing!

Coda? She looked desperately at Coda, wondering if he could see her wing, as well. But, the moment she saw him she forgot all about herself.

Her brother, the small and skinny young man with brown hair, blue eyes, and buck teeth was now a large black panther with a beautiful red oval crystal glowing on his forehead, with another one on his chest. It looked like the same panther she'd seen licking him earlier.

Before she could utter another sound, the long trunk of the elephant grabbed Coda by the scruff of the back of his neck, and pulled him out of the blackberry bushes.

"Whoa, whoa, whoa!" yelled Coda, as he was lifted over the elephant's shoulder and set upon its back.

"Ouch," said the elephant. "Watch those claws."

Without a moment's hesitation, the elephant stretched his trunk back into the blackberry tunnel and wrapped it around Zoey's little body. She struggled to move, but the elephant's grip was tight, but yet, like his voice, very gentle. In a matter of seconds, she went from inside the tunnel to over the elephant's head and onto his back.

She perched on the elephant's back in shock. Her body trembled as the elephant turned on his haunches and started walking at a quick pace.

"Zoey! Hey! Zoey!" echoed her brother's voice in the back of her confused mind.

What's happening? She stretched her wings, examining them. Her eyes widened and she tucked them back into her side as quickly as possible. She felt gross being something else. *I'm dreaming. I have to be dreaming.*

She tried to pinch herself on the cheek, expecting to feel fingers, but instead, she felt soft feathers.

"Zoey!" called Coda's voice again.

Zoey shook her head and did her best to concentrate. She wasn't dreaming. Her body was slightly tilting to one side for a moment, then to the next side, over and over again, in tandem with the elephant's long strides. *What's happening?*

"Zoey?" asked her frantic brother. "Where are we?"

Zoey looked at him. There he was, a large black panther standing on the elephant's back like a terrified kitten with eyes as wide as saucers. His claws were fastened to the elephant, making sure he wouldn't fall. Her brother's mouth moved. "Why are you a bird?" Coda exclaimed.

"Why are you a panther?"

"And, you have a glowing red rock on your chest, and another on your forehead," replied Coda. "What's going on?"

"I don't know," said Zoey. She looked around, hoping to find some clues. She saw trees of every size all around, glowing in the same way the Snow Tree did. Through the cracks between the trees, she could see a large, rushing river ten times the size of the creek. It dazzled in the rays of the sunlight as it splashed hard against boulders jutting out from underneath its surface. But nothing was registering. Her mind was a ball of nerves and confusion. Where was she? Who's carrying her? This just couldn't be real, could it?

An owl swooped overhead. Zoey wondered what an owl was doing flying around in the daytime. She watched as it arched high in the blue sky, and then turned around for another pass at them.

Zoey crouched down as the owl neared. She noticed that it wasn't far from her stomach to the elephant's back. She was a small bird and her legs weren't the normal size of human legs. This brought her back to her immediate concerns. All she knew was that she was a bird and they were being taken somewhere by a talking elephant. She went to scream, but nothing would come out.

"Good day, Chev. You found them," said the owl, as it flew by the elephant's ear.

"I did," replied Chev. "I'm taking them to Nova."

Coda was freaking out. His panther-face couldn't hide his fear. He was also doing his best to comprehend what was happening.

The owl swooped by Chev's big elephant ear again. "She's just around the trees ahead, next to the Snow Tree."

The Snow Tree? thought Zoey. *But we aren't in the Cornell Forest, are we?*

Chev lifted his trunk and swung it around to pat the top of Coda's head, "Don't worry, you two. Everything will be positively fine."

What was going to be positively fine? Zoey had no idea what Chev was talking about.

"Can you take us home now?" Zoey pleaded with the elephant. "I think we're lost."

"Let me take you to Nova first. Then you can go home."

The elephant picked up his pace as Zoey and Coda held on tighter.

Zoey could see that the trees ahead were beginning to thin out, leaving more space for grass to grow. And what beautiful grass it was—it was the most beautiful green grass she'd ever seen.

Then the trees suddenly disappeared, and they were in an open meadow, sparsely populated with oaks and maples. The sun's rays, no longer shadowed by the trees, had burst into full view, showering them with light. The meadow was gorgeous. It was filled with colorful flowers and long, plush green grass.

Zoey and Coda both "ahhhhed" in appreciation.

Then Zoey gasped. She'd been here before. This was the meadow in her dream where she had met the dragon and the wolf! But, it couldn't be! That was just a dream, *wasn't it?*

Taking in a deep breath helped to shift her mind from the dream to the air. She took another deep breath, instantly bringing a stream of energy into her body, making her feel refreshed and more alive. The air was rich with something, but with what she did not know.

She glanced at Coda and saw him breathing deeply, as well. He wiggled his whiskers in delight as the air brought a smile to his panther face. It was strange, though, to see Coda as anything but Coda. It was almost like he was a fake mechanical panther robot that had the same voice. He looked real alright, but how could he be? He's a big black cat. Coda caught Zoey's eyes with a look that seemed to say he was having the same thoughts about her.

Chev came to a halt. He dipped his head. "Hello, Nova. I've found them."

Zoey peered around Chev's right ear to see a large twisted tree. *The Snow Tree!* Zoey became excited, then curious when she noticed a big white and black spotted leopard sitting at the base of the Snow Tree. It had a violet crystal embedded in its forehead, and one on its chest.

Chev lifted Zoey into the air, carefully placing her on the ground a few yards in front of the white cat.

As Zoey's feet touched the grass, the Snow Tree made a crackling sound that sounded like branches were breaking.

Within the bark of the tree, eyes started to form, then a nose protruded outwards, and lips creaked into place. It was the face of a beautiful woman. The Snow Tree's eyes opened and her nostrils flared, taking in a big breath. A moment later, her mouth moved. "Welcome home, Zoey." A flash later, the tree creaked and the face slowly melted back into bark.

Zoey's head jolted back. She searched Coda's face for confirmation, hoping that he had seen this, too. He stared, motionless, at Nova. He looked bewildered, but she could tell he hadn't seen or heard the tree talk. She looked at Chev, who smiled back at her. Nothing in his face showed her any recognition toward the Snow Tree woman-face, either.

She desperately wanted to talk to the Snow Tree, but before she could say anything the white leopard turned and stared at the Snow Tree, then back at Zoey. The leopard nodded. *Did that big white cat see the talking tree, too, or are my eyes playing tricks on me?*

The white cat bowed her head, smiling. "Welcome. My name is Nova the VioletLight. I'm a PureLight of the Sihu lineage."

Immediately, Zoey's apprehension melted and she felt completely at ease with this creature. And, strangely enough, she felt loved as well, but didn't know why she felt this way. It was a similar feeling that she had received from the Snow Tree.

"Are these the ones?" asked Chev.

"Yes, you found them. Thank you." Nova looked at Zoey and Coda with a calm, light expression. The air around Nova's body sparkled for an instant, taking Zoey off-guard and calming her down even more.

"Are you hurt?" asked Nova.

Zoey and Coda shook their heads, no.

Coda took a step forward. "Um," he said, a little unsure of himself, "we need to get back home." He looked at the vast trees and shrubs that circled this place, adding, "To *our* forest."

"Yeah," responded Zoey. She also took a step forward, which, because of her short legs, only moved her a couple of inches. "It's back in the direction we came from," mumbled Zoey, pointing with her wing, which she quickly hid by her side when she realized, again, that her arm was now a wing.

"I didn't understand you, child," replied Nova.

"She said," Coda replied on Zoey's behalf, "our home is back in the direction that we came from."

"Of course. We won't hold you here against your will," Nova assured them.

Zoey looked over Nova's shoulder for a moment, noticing a small hut. It looked as if it was built out of shining, golden hay.

Nova followed Zoey's gaze. "That's my home," she said with obvious delight.

Nova's serene demeanor instantly softened any residual fear that Zoey was having in this new place, just as the gray wolf had done in her dream. *Can I talk to the Snow Tree?* she thought, but said nothing.

Zoey stretched out her wings, pulling them back again as fast as she could. In a barely audible voice, she asked, "Why am I a bird and why is Coda a big black cat?"

"I'm a snow leopard," Nova said. "Coda, you're a black panther, and Zoey, you're a skylark."

Zoey frowned. "What's a skylark? And why are we these animals?"

"Excellent questions," Nova replied enthusiastically. "And, Zoey, it would be much easier to hear if you spoke with greater force. Trust me when I say this—you're a great force to be reckoned with." She smiled. "Please follow me."

Nova turned and walked eastward, without glancing back.

Chev, sitting on his rump, bowed his head to the children. He gestured with his trunk for them to follow Nova. "She won't bite," he reassured. "She's as peaceful as a ripple in water." Looking thoughtful, and speaking mostly to himself, he added, "Well, is a ripple really a peaceful thing?" He stared off into the distance, suddenly lost in thought.

Coda shrugged his black furry panther shoulders and walked in Nova's direction. Zoey followed along.

They walked on a path that led past the golden hut, toward the curving river. Zoey inched along, having to run to keep up with the long paces of the two cats. The path was wide, soft, and open to the light of day. Friendly birds and large animals of all shapes, sizes, and colors watched as they walked past the few trees that dotted the edge of the path. Some animals simply nodded their heads in kindness and others smiled.

Zoey noticed that the trees around the meadow were sparse, but were as healthy as any tree she had ever seen. They were mostly maples, with leaves of orange hues cascading to bright yellow tips. Colors of the fall, but it didn't seem like fall in this strange land. In fact, it seemed like mid-summer, with a cool breeze. The temperature seemed perfect.

The sound of rushing water, mingled with the sound of trees creaking in the wind, became louder as they approached the river. Zoey paused for a moment and listened. She could hear someone whispering. She shook her head, hoping the whisper would disappear. The opposite occurred. It became louder.

"It's been ages since you've been here. Welcome back," said a female whisper. It didn't sound like the Snow Tree. Was it another tree? Zoey shook her head again, running to catch Coda.

"Did you hear that?" she asked him.

"Hear what?" Coda's shoulders hung low and his long black tail hid between his legs. Zoey wondered if that meant he was scared or nervous. She'd seen cats do that in her neighborhood when a car would drive by. Nova, on the other hand, walked confidently. Her chest was out, her shoulders were strong, her head was up, and her tail reached toward the sky.

"You're a tad late," said another whisper, male in tone.

"She's come, that's what matters. She arrived when she was meant to," stated a third whisper, much softer than the first two. Zoey looked around, but didn't see anyone talking to her. "I hear whispering, Coda." She paused, waiting to hear more.

Before Coda could reply, Nova stopped at the bank of the river and sat next to a giant boulder with a flat top. The boulder had to be as wide as a bus and twice as tall. Zoey and Coda looked at each other wide-eyed, almost to say without words, "What a rock!"

With one giant leap as effortless as a leaf falling to the forest floor, Nova landed lightly on top of the tall boulder, and then turned to look down at the children.

"How did you do that?" asked Coda.

Nova smiled. "It's something that took me many moons to master. As it turns out, it's actually rather simple."

Zoey looked to Coda, whose shrug said *I don't know*. Then she looked at the ground. *I can't do that,* thought Zoey, dejectedly.

Nova nodded. "You don't need to. Spread your wings and

fly, Zoey." Nova sat patiently on her hind legs. "You're a skylark. Like most birds, a skylark can fly."

How did she hear my thoughts? wondered Zoey.

"You're made to fly!," yelled Nova. "Don't think—just do! We have a saying here—*empty your mind and proceed from the heart.*"

Zoey knew that Nova had a point about her being a bird. She might look like she's made to fly, but did Nova know she'd never flown before? *I can't fly!*

"Flying is your nature. It's imprinted inside of you. Once you flap your wings, all memory of flying will come to you as if you've been doing it your entire life. Remember, *empty your mind and proceed from the heart.*"

Just like the Snow Tree, Nova's words made Zoey feel at ease. In fact, her whole body seemed to relax. She made Zoey feel as if anything in the world was possible, even flying. It wasn't *what* Nova said, but more *how* she said it.

With growing certainty, Zoey stretched out her wings. She glanced down her right wing and then down her left, cringing at how strange it felt. Then started flapping them up and down until she knew, deep down in her heart, that she could fly. It was more than a feeling. It was a knowing, just like Nova had said. She could do this.

Nova closed her eyes and a strange wind picked up. It helped lift Zoey off the ground. Zoey felt confidence surge through her feathers as her wings pounded against the air, becoming stronger with each flap. Almost instantly, a huge flow of energy coursed through her wings, lifting her high into the air, above the rock and above Nova.

Zoey looked around at her new view. The river was rushing below, pulsing with white rapids as the water bumped and pushed against the rocks at the river's bottom. She was amazed at how natural and easy it felt to fly.

She looked at the forest where she had entered this strange land, seeing how vast it was. It seemed to go on forever. To the west she saw that it started to thin out into grasslands, slowly disappearing into a white-capped mountain range covered with low-lying white clouds.

Looking to the north she saw a vast forest, with gigantic trees the size of skyscrapers that vanished in the clouds. Slightly turning to the northeast, she viewed rolling hills topped with sporadic green trees and reddish-brown soil, spreading like frozen waves in an ocean, until she couldn't see any further. She wondered how far they had actually traveled.

She looked down at the meadow. It was much larger than she'd thought.

Twisting her body, she eyed the south, feeling the warmth of the sun on the top of her head and the breeze ruffling her feathers. She glided effortlessly toward a large body of water miles away. She thought it must be an ocean. It was turquoise blue and its waves threw ferocious tufts of water into the air, onto the southern cliffs. She peered to the east to see the meadow transitioning into small hills that eventually flattened into a vast, golden ocean beach, with slow moving waves from an ocean tide.

She turned around in mid-glide, facing north, flapping her wings to pick up speed. The freedom and exhilaration of flight thrilled her. Flying even higher in the sky, she imagined she could do this forever. She rolled to her right and went for a dive, but suddenly hovered as she eyed something strange a mile or so beyond the river.

A dark fog, like the one she'd seen rising up from the earth around the gray wolf in her dream, cut straight across the forest, reaching from the ocean on the east end of the land, going west, further than her eyes could see. Spinning around, she saw the same fog miles away nearer to the ocean, stretching across the southern portion of the land, also going from east to west. Before she could investigate, she heard her name being called from below.

Her attention shifted and she flew down toward the large boulder where Nova stood, then hovered inches above the boulder and gently made a perfect landing. Zoey peered over the edge to see Coda staring up at her.

"Did you have fun?" asked Nova.

"Oh my gosh! I had so much fun! Did you see me?" Zoey's excited voice was loud and beautiful. She'd never felt so excited before. Zoey stretched out her wings, adding, "It was so easy."

Coda was looking at Zoey like she was crazy. "How'd you do that?" he demanded.

"I don't know. I just did. It was easy."

Nova turned to Coda. "Now, Coda, would you like to come up here and look at the view?"

"Sure," replied Coda, "but how do I get up there?"

"Yeah, how's he going to get up here?" echoed Zoey.

Nova closed her eyes and took a few deep breaths. Again, sparkles of light filled the air around the snow leopard for a heartbeat, and then disappeared. Nova opened her eyes and Zoey felt her skylark body relax as Nova's appearance seemed to change. It almost looked like Nova was glowing. Her crystals surely were, but even her fur was brighter than before.

Then a sight that Zoey had only seen in movies happened right before her eyes.

What in the world?

Chapter 7

Coda looked down at green moss, watching his paws dangle in the air. He was about five feet off the ground, slowly floating toward the boulder where Zoey and Nova both sat.

What's going on?

He tried to fall back toward the ground, but nothing allowed him to do so. He had no control over the forces carrying him. He felt comfortable, though, almost like he was riding on a fluffy warm blanket.

In his mind he heard Nova speaking, "Empty your mind and proceed from the heart. That's where all knowledge and understanding originate." Instantly, Coda's mind went from fright to the Snow Tree's exercise on thinking from your heart.

He closed his eyes and filled his heart full of as much love and joy as he could, surrounding it with white and pink light. His body started to tingle, and when he opened his eyes he found himself safely lying on top of the boulder.

Coda stood up and sat just like Nova, on his hind legs, tail lying on the flat boulder top and curled around his forepaws. He stared down at the choppy river flowing next to the boulder. He faced north as the sun's light struck the left side of his body, making him squint to keep the bright light out of his eyes. In his mind, the boulder was so tall that it looked like it was a thousand feet to the river below. In truth, it was only about twenty-five feet.

"Um... how did you do that?" he asked.

"I'm considered a PureLight Master. We're called VioletLights for short." She swished her tail in front of her, winking, "We'll get to that later." She walked to the western edge of the boulder and peered into the horizon.

For the first time, Coda saw some of what he thought his sister must have seen from being so high in the sky.

The sun was dipping, closing in on the trees in the west, casting light over the thick forest of trees in his line of sight. Even more to the west was a large, snow-capped mountain range that stretched South to North, sloping drastically in height only miles past a dense smoke rising out of the ground.

Coda also noticed smoke to the north, cutting across the forest in a straight line from west to east.

"That," said Nova, "is The Fog."

Coda padded across the warm boulder top and stood next to Nova. "The Fog? I've never seen a fog like that."

With the flick of her head, Nova gestured for Zoey to come sit beside her. Nova waited for Zoey before she began to speak. "The Fog arrived in our land thousands of moons ago. So long ago that most can't remember exactly when it formed. There's a fog cutting across the land behind us as well, farther in the south. Crossing beyond the North and South Fog takes you into the Dim Lands. It's a place to enter at your own risk."

"The Dim Lands?" repeated Coda.

Nova nodded. "They're as they sound—dim. Diminished of light. The Fog is a boundary that divides the Dim Lands from the PureLight Lands. Right now, we're on the eastern portion of the PureLight Lands." Nova looked down at her paws and Coda could feel a sadness suddenly overwhelm her. "The Dims are the name for the many Beings who've lost their way.

"Both lands, the Dim Lands and PureLights Lands, are on this island, and we call this island Ohm Totem," Nova let out a deep sigh. "The Dims populate most of the island, while the PureLights occupy only the middle portion."

Coda didn't know what to think. *Was there a war going on between the Dims and PureLights? What does this have to do with us? Why are we here?*

"I can't tell you why you're here. It's up to you to figure that out on your own. I can help steer you in the right direction, though."

Coda narrowed his eyes. *How did she know what I was thinking?*

"Yes, there's a war going on," continued Nova. "A war on many fronts. One is a war between the Dim's themselves.

Another is a war between the PureLights and the Dims."

Zoey remained silent, but Coda could almost hear what was going on in her mind. He knew she just wanted to get back home. He felt a little curious, though. Was it the panther in him making him feel curious?

"Why is there a war?"

"The Dims want to control all of Ohm Totem. They started out as a tiny group living in a small portion on the middle-northern part of the island, but quickly spread throughout the majority of it. They defeated many of the PureLight tribes and, in the process, were able to capture and turn many of the inhabitants of the tribes into slaves, warriors, and killers." Nova shook her head. Coda was expecting to see anger in her eyes, but it was just the opposite. They held compassion. "You'll know a Dim by the gray color in their crystals."

Fascinated, Coda asked another question. Zoey suddenly seemed interested as well. "What are the PureLight tribes?"

"There were nine tribes that settled here in Ohm Totem. Each tribe had an individual name, but together we were called the PureLights. We had left a world immersed in war, disease, and pain to come here to Ohm Totem—a place of beauty, peace, and love. We wanted to rid ourselves of all technology, and of all ability to create technology. Here we thrived and shared amongst each other for what seemed to be millions of moons."

Nova paused before adding, "I'm from the PureLight tribe named Sihu. You're on Sihu land right now."

She glanced to the north, going back to her story as if it was very important for them to know. "Thousands of moons ago, a VioletLight—a PureLight Master named Crepus, drastically changed. His mood shifted suddenly, so much so that every VioletLight in Ohm Totem felt it. The island itself shook from the ferocity of the change. He came to us with grandiose ideas; things that he thought would benefit others, but in truth, would cause us to fall from our peaceful, loving nature.

"We challenged his ideas and he lost control of himself, doing one of the worst things that a PureLight can do. Something we hadn't experienced since we had come to Ohm

69

Totem. He took our response to his ideas personally."

Coda was taken aback. *How could taking something personally be the worst thing?*

Nova replied to the unspoken question. "When we take something personally, we become very selfish. We assume that everything in the world is about 'me'. Then we see ourselves as victims."

Shaking her head sadly, Nova continued her tale. "Crepus considered himself a victim when we didn't agree with his ideas. He thought that since we didn't agree, we were against him. However, the opposite was true. We loved him very much, but we saw the error in his thinking that he was unable to see. We wanted to talk it through with him, but he declined. It confused us. We'd never seen him take anything personally before.

"He started to blame others for any mistake that occurred in his life. He thought, and still thinks, that others are the cause of all of his grief, when in truth, he is the only cause. His life went from 'bliss' to 'selfishness'. We watched his crystals slowly fade from a Master's violet color to a gray. It was something we'd never seen before. When his crystals turned black, we could only wonder at what would happen next."

Zoey scratched the surface of the boulder with her skylark feet, but said nothing. Coda sensed that she had something important to say, something she was holding back.

"Yes, Zoey?" inquired Nova.

"Well, I..." she stopped and closed her beak. Her voice was soft as she continued to scratch the boulder. She wouldn't look up at either Coda or Nova.

Nova took a deep breath and focused on Zoey. Coda could feel a warmth surrounding him, causing him to feel at ease in his body. He knew Zoey felt the same thing.

"Zoey, take a deep breath and close your eyes."

Zoey did, so Nova kept speaking. "You have a wonderful voice. It's easier to hear that beautiful tone of yours if you look at me while you speak." She spoke very gently. "When I tell you to open your eyes, I want you to look into mine and take a deep breath. That will calm you, bringing confidence to you in this moment, and dispel your fear. Then tell me what you have to say. I really want to hear it."

Zoey nodded and opened her eyes. She took a deep breath and Coda could see her face muscles relax. She stared into Nova's eyes. "I think I saw him."

"Saw who?" demanded Coda.

"Crepus, the one with the black crystals. He's a Komodo dragon, right? He was in my dream."

Nova looked away, trying to hide her disappointment. "He may already know."

Coda became uncomfortable. He was in a strange land, but now this land seemed to be getting a little stranger at the moment. "Know what?"

"He knows about Zoey." Nova's eyes narrowed into slits and she seemed to be scouring every inch of the land before her. "This is unsettling."

Zoey flinched and said nothing. But her eyes had a thousand questions. Coda could suddenly feel that Zoey wondered why it mattered if Crepus knew anything about her. *How can I 'feel' Zoey's thoughts?*

Nova lay down, stretching her front legs out and resting her chin on them. She gazed into Zoey's eyes. "My dear child, if you only knew who you are. You're more powerful than words could ever describe. You have the ability to change everything." She turned to Coda. "You have to protect her. Forget about the challenges that you have with your sister. This is more important than that. Your *mission* is more important than that. She won't be able to do this without you."

Coda shivered at the word 'mission', and every cell in his body told him that what Nova said was true. He and Zoey were at a loss for words, but deep down, Coda still didn't want to have anything to do with helping his sister. *It's always about her!* Coda grimaced as he glanced at Zoey.

Zoey shrugged back at him. "What? I'm powerful?"

"Yes, once you find that power within you, you'll be unstoppable. If Crepus truly knows who you are, then he knows how powerful and important you are as well. He'll do anything and everything to prevent you from finding your true

71

self."

Zoey screwed her face up in confusion and simply looked away.

Coda shifted his weight from side to side. "Well, why can't the VioletLights just stop him?"

Nova sniffed the air intently. "There are only six VioletLights left in Ohm Totem. We're spread throughout Ohm Totem, connected only by our thoughts. Though, we think we've found the way to stop him, and that way is you two."

"What? Us, stop him?" Zoey laughed uncomfortably. "I don't know about that. I just want to go home."

Coda backed up a step. "*We* have to defeat these bad guys?"

Nova shook her head. "No one's a bad guy. I view the Dims as being misinformed. They've been misguided by someone they trusted—Crepus. Someday you'll see that there are no bad guys or good guys, only the informed and the misinformed. The Dims and the PureLights."

Coda almost laughed in disagreement, but held back. He knew that wasn't true. Bad guys are everywhere. Shifting gears, he asked, "Why does he want to kill you all?"

"I don't think he wants to kill us all. I think he wants something important from the PureLights. He wants the PureLight Order. This, I think, he wants to destroy." She eyed the fog to the north and answered the next question before they asked it. "The PureLight Order is a sacred scroll explaining how to live a successful, loving, and honorable life. It's the most powerful item in Ohm Totem. It has the ability to change a Dim into a PureLight, just by peering into it."

"Then why don't you use that on Crepus?"

"Because we don't have it. The PureLight Order was written on a scroll the moment we arrived in Ohm Totem. It was kept here in the Sihu tribe. Long ago, it went missing."

Coda noticed a peculiar feeling rise inside of him. It wasn't his feeling, though. This he knew. It came at him from his right, where Zoey stood. It was a feeling of confusion buffeted with a twinge of fear. *Why do I keep feeling her thoughts and emotions?*

Nova gave a nod of understanding to Coda, as if she felt the same thing too, but where did it come from? Nova quickly answered his thoughts.

"Here in Ohm Totem, things are different than where you come from. The environment here is healthier. The air you breathe here is untainted and pure, as are the plants and water. If your world was in a state of harmony and health, then it would be much easier for you and others in your world to discover the abilities that lie hidden deep within you.

"What you're feeling, Coda, is your sister's fear to ask me her many burning questions. Feelings, thoughts, and emotions from others are very easy to sense here on the island." With that, she faced Zoey.

"Okay," acknowledged Zoey, "why do we have these crystal things on our head and chest?"

"The crystals are our birthright. They're part of our bodies, just like our bones, muscles, tendons, ligaments, eyes, and organs. They're ingrained in us from the moment we're born. They're just like the large crystals seen on unicorns, but not as pointy."

She walked to the northern tip of the big rock, knowing full well that both Zoey's and Coda's minds were spinning from the mention of unicorns. Even though they were in a land of talking animals, they doubted whether or not unicorns were real.

"I see that the other world has taught you that myths and legends are mere stories thought up from the imagination of poets and story tellers." Nova laughed, and then padded toward the other end of the rock. "Along with the health of this land, which nourishes our bodies, allowing us to have abilities that your world would consider as being abnormal, we have these crystals that grow in us, helping us to expand our abilities even more. It's a gift from the Great Spirit.

"You felt your sister's feelings, Coda. That's an example of an ability that comes much easier in Ohm Totem. With the crystals, your sense of feeling was heightened even more."

Coda groaned. He didn't like the idea of sensing his sister's feelings.

73

Ignoring Coda's dismay, Nova looked at the vast trees growing on the hills to the northeast. "Another example would be our eyes. Here in Ohm Totem, you can see much further into the distance than what you're used to. Your world would consider this an ability that is vastly superior to normal vision. But, for us, we consider our vision to be, well, very normal. That attributes to the health of our bodies, the air, the land, and the water. If your land was as rich and healthy as it should be, your abilities would be nearer to what we have in Ohm Totem."

Nova paused for an instant to allow Coda and Zoey to digest what she had just said, then continued. "The colors that your crystals display tell us what you are. You two are both PureLights, because your crystals shine with a color. The Dim's crystals don't shine. Their crystals are dimmed to gray, where they shall remain until they wise up—so-to-speak."

Nova lifted her chin toward the blue sky and watched a redtail hawk fly overhead. "The hawk above has indigo colored crystals. If she were to gain even more mastery, then the color of her crystal would change from indigo to violet, making her a VioletLight."

"Why is Coda a panther and why am I a skylark?" persisted Zoey.

"Another good question." Nova thought for a moment, trying to think of a way to explain in a fashion they could understand.

"To get to our world, you must enter through the portal that you used. Once here, your body changes from your human form to your animal form, known as your 'spirit animal'."

"Whoa!" Coda's mind was spinning.

Zoey pointed a wing at Coda, saying, "That's what I saw when I sat on the Snow Tree. I saw the black panther next to you, Coda! Your spirit animal."

"First, we all come into being, or into existence, by way of The Great Spirit. The Great Spirit instills gifts in us by endowing us with the special talents and life lessons of a certain animal. Coda, for example, is a black panther. The black panther represents a powerful and fierce guardian. In

74

that aspect, Coda will eventually grow into a protector. If you follow your heart, Coda, you'll always defend the innocent, keep the truth safe, and above all, master the night. In the darkness you'll be able to see what most others cannot: the truth. If you pay attention to your heart, the truth will never slip away from you.

"And Zoey," continued Nova, "you're a skylark. The skylark is associated with the universal song, which is the sacred sound of nature and the universe. Zoey was born with the sacred sound in her heart, allowing her the ability to communicate with nature much easier than most. With practice, all of nature will become Zoey's greatest partner and lifelong friend. If you follow your heart, you'll always be able to sing that sacred song. The question is, do you trust your heart enough to sing your song?"

Nova paused for a moment, looking toward the sun. She nodded in its direction as if agreeing to something.

She bowed her head to the children. "I'm honored to be in your presence."

Zoey and Coda gave each other a funny look, not knowing why she would be honored. Zoey spoke up and Coda could feel that this was her most burning question of all.

"So," said Zoey as she stared toward the river, eyes unblinking, "how do we get back home?"

"You follow the path you came in on. Do you remember the path?" asked Nova.

"Zoey and I were pretty scared when we got here, so I don't think we really know how to get out. I wasn't paying much attention to the path when we were on the elephant."

"Yeah, me neither," said Zoey.

"Ah," replied Nova with a smile. "Well, if you wish to go home, then we must take you there." There was a tinge of sadness in her voice.

Coda sniffed the rich air into his lungs and closed his eyes. He didn't know how to explain it, but if felt energizing here, making him feel stronger, not only in his physical body, but also in his mind.

"I'll ask Chev to carry you back to the portal. You must

hurry, though. The portal closes when the sun meets the horizon in the west."

"We won't miss it, will we?" Zoey replied, her nervous energy very apparent. "Mom and Dad would get mad if we stayed another day."

Nova rubbed her cheek against Zoey's little body in a nurturing way. Zoey relaxed and Nova stood tall, with her tail pointing to the sky. "If you miss the portal, then you'd remain here until the next full moon. It opens only when the energies of the moon are at their peak."

Coda thought for a moment, bringing up a scary image of his parents looking for them all over Cornell Forest, yelling their names, and wondering if they were lost or dead. "Well, Mom and Dad would be panicked and worried if we didn't go home right away."

Nova bowed her head to them again. "You don't have to worry. A day in Ohm Totem is only a few moments where you're from. I won't let you miss the open portal, though. You still have many moments until it closes." With that, Nova jumped down from the large boulder, landing as softly as a cat jumping only a foot or two to the ground.

"Whoa!" said Coda. "Did you see that?"

"And she doesn't even have wings," replied Zoey.

Nova focused her gaze onto the two children. The air around her body burst with sparkles of white light. Instantly, Coda felt his and his sister's body loosen up. They both were lifted from the boulder by the mysterious force. They descended slowly, being gently placed on the ground beside Nova.

Without a second to spare or even a moment to gather themselves, Nova dashed down the mossy path, back in the direction they came from. She called over her shoulder, "Follow me or miss the portal!"

Zoey flapped her wings, pushed off with her small legs, and flew at an incredible speed toward Nova. Coda reared back and dashed as fast as he could, quickly closing in on them. As he ran, he noticed that the green shrubs lining the path were whizzing on by as if he was running at a hundred miles per hour. *Is this how fast a panther can run?*

When he caught up to Nova, Zoey was just above her, flapping her wings with all of her heart. She beamed absolute joy because of her newly discovered ability and she was determined to keep up with the fast pace of Nova.

"Chev!" yelled Nova as they narrowed in on the Snow Tree.

Within seconds Chev arrived at the Snow Tree.

He grinned, "Hello everyone!"

Nova stopped her run as abruptly and as skillfully as she had started, and looked to Chev. "Will you take them back to the portal?"

"Of course I will. Now..." he said, getting down as low as he could, "jump on! We have a portal to catch!"

Chapter 8

Zoey studied the gray elephant. Her wings were still new to her and the thought of landing on something round, such as the curve of Chev's gray back, didn't appeal to her. What if she landed incorrectly and fell off? She imagined that if she did, she'd simply flap her wings and fly up and then onto his back again. She dismissed the thought, noticing that his trunk was lying perfectly still on the ground. *That's the way to go*, she thought.

Chev's orange forehead crystal glowed brightly and his big, blue eyes seemed to shine at her in amusement. So, instead of jumping in the air and flapping her wings, she simply walked up Chev's trunk, walked over his crystal, down between his large floppy ears, and onto his back.

Zoey turned around and faced the back of Chev's head, then sat a little way from the base of Chev's neck. She looked over at her brother. He decided to copy the same route, but did so with all the steadiness of a bear balancing on a slippery wire. One leg would fly out in one direction, keeping him from falling, and then, once that leg landed back onto Chev's trunk, another leg would flail to the other side. Coda did this all the way up, making Zoey laugh out loud.

"Ow!" said Chev. "That's my eye you're putting your paw into."

"Oh," replied Coda, "sorry."

"It's okay," responded Chev. He waited for a minute for Coda to get settled on his back. "Are we ready?"

Zoey was excited to get back to her parents. Enthusiastically, she replied, "Yep!"

Chev stood up and trotted toward the portal. One foot pounded onto the ground and then another, bouncing Zoey and Coda up and down.

Nova's voice boomed behind them, "I hope to see you again."

The kids looked back. Coda waved a paw goodbye and Zoey waved a wing. Nova nodded solemnly.

Zoey felt bad for leaving, but why? Nova was nice and helpful for sure, but Zoey had a home in another land. This is Ohm Totem, not the Cornell Forest where she came from.

"Zoey?"

Zoey saw Coda staring at her, deep in thought.

"Yeah? What is it?"

"I don't know. The Snow Tree said we had a mission. I sort of think we should at least see what the mission is."

Zoey was shocked. "Don't you want to be with mom and dad?"

"Yeah...but, Nova said time is different here or something like that." Coda's tail lashed back and forth, indicating that he was nervous. Zoey shared his nervousness. "I think," said Coda hesitantly, "that we should stay."

"Stay here?" asked Chev as he itched the top of his head with the tip of his trunk. "Okay," he responded, and stopped smartly. He turned around and walked back in the direction of the Snow Tree. Nova was still there.

Nova's eyes widened, as if surprised by their unexpected reappearance. She looked curiously toward the children.

"No, turn around. I want to go home," ordered Zoey. A picture of her parents scolding her for being out too late had flashed into her mind. "Please, please, please take us to the portal, or whatever it's called."

She didn't want to be in trouble. She was tired of being in trouble. She was always in trouble for the way she talked, in trouble for never eating breakfast, in trouble for sleeping in her clothes, and now she might be in trouble if she didn't come home in time for dinner.

"Will do," Chev said agreeably, turning and pointing his trunk at the line of dense trees straight ahead. "We're off again!" he announced.

The sun, dazzling lower in the west, sprayed the trees ahead with its light, welcoming those entering the vast forest. Zoey bounced up and down again from Chev's fast strides, staring at the terrain as it passed by. A breeze whispered in Zoey's ear saying, "Close your eyes."

Zoey startled. "Huh?"

"Are you alright back there?" Chev called back to Zoey.

"Did you hear that?" asked Zoey, as she sat back down on Chev's thick elephant hide.

"Nope, didn't hear a thing," replied Chev.

Zoey turned to Coda. "Did you hear that?"

"Hear what?"

"I heard, 'close your eyes'."

Coda shook his head. Then his panther face grinned broadly. "Let's just stay the night here. Just one night." He looked excited, as if staying the night would be a fun adventure.

"Stay the night?" repeated Chev. "Okay." He was only a few feet from entering the large forest, but he turned around and headed back toward Nova and the Snow Tree.

"Coda! We'll miss the portal if we stay the night!"

Coda laughed, doing his best to get under his sister's skin. "Who cares?" he said with delight.

Zoey could tell that he really wanted to stay in Ohm Totem for a while. She looked back at the fleeting tree line blanketed by low-lying shrubs and ferns. She saw that the mossy path led straight to the shrubs and through them, parting the trees slightly as it continued.

If I just flew off of this elephant's back and followed the path, then I could make it to the portal by myself and I wouldn't get in trouble.

Doing just that, she leaped off Chev's back, flapping her wings against the air. She was determined not to get into trouble.

She'd already been in the forest for several moments by the time she realized that she was flying. Pine needles showered her face and wings, making her drop below the lowest branches to avoid them. The ground consisted of brown soil, low-lying brush, and some scattered pine and green scaly cedar needles. She landed next to the base of a skinny maple tree and looked around. She didn't know where she was.

Uh oh! Zoey was off the path and it was nowhere in sight. *Where is it?*

She hopped as fast as she could to what she thought was south, hoping to run into the path. Passing next to a mushroom growing near an old fallen tree branch, she stopped abruptly, amazed at the sight before her. She was standing in the middle of thousands of mushrooms. They were everywhere, and of all different varieties. Red ones, brown ones, polka-dotted ones, orange ones, and even purple ones.

Something made her look up, away from the mushrooms. She could feel someone or something watching her. An eerie feeling crept down her spine, all the way to her tail feathers. Then it penetrated her like a sharp knife digging deep in her belly, paralyzing and pumping her full of fear. She'd felt this before. But when?

The Komodo dragon!

Shaking her thoughts loose, she scanned the forest, seeing rows of trees that seemed to go on for miles. She turned around and took small baby steps, making sure to be quiet. She didn't want to disturb who or whatever it was that had bothered her.

"Welcome to our land, young lady," said a low-pitched, malicious voice directly behind her.

Jumping and turning a full 180 degrees in the air by flapping her wings, she could see him staring at her. It was the Komodo dragon. His angry red eyes penetrated her soul, making her recoil. She looked away.

A red-hot burning sensation suddenly surrounded her.

"What do you think of this place?" he asked.

Zoey pushed against her fear. "It's kind of weird here," she replied uncertainly. The burning sensation deepened. Her stomach felt like someone was scraping it with a fork. A moment later the sensation passed. *Was the sensation from the Komodo dragon?*

The Komodo dragon hissed, showing sharp teeth and a forked tongue behind his green, scaly mouth. "Don't you like this land?" His tongue slid out of his mouth like a snake, splattering saliva onto the ground.

Zoey shrugged her shoulders and looked down at her feet. "I don't know," she mumbled, "I just got here."

"I see," he retorted.

Regardless of the heat surrounding her, Zoey abruptly felt ice grip her spine, making her head snap up to stare directly at the Komodo dragon, as if he had willed her to do so. Between his eyes was a lifeless, black crystal.

The creature glared at her, completely still amongst the mushrooms that surrounded him. His head slowly lowered, revealing his crystal more clearly, showing his small, unflinching black pupils as well.

"I've asked you this before, young lady. What's your name?"

Zoey was stunned. She remembered the part in her dream where he did ask for her name, but that was just a dream. Wasn't it? *No! It had to be real!* Her beak, however, would not move to form her name. She knew she shouldn't tell him, but didn't know why. Again, the breeze blew across her body, whispering, "Close your eyes."

"Don't!" yelled the Komodo dragon with a ferocity she hadn't felt before. She winced as the circle of heat around her body rose in temperature. Abruptly, his tone became soft as a pillow, simultaneously lowering the temperature around her. "If you know what's good for you, then don't close your eyes."

His angry expression sharply changed to a soothing calmness that made Zoey feel somewhat at peace.

"I'm sorry I frightened you," he continued, still speaking more gently. "I only want to help you along your way. Sometimes I get a little pushy. Old age, I guess." A crooked smile showed his many sharp teeth.

"It's okay," replied Zoey, shifting her eyes to the ground. She felt composed now, suddenly and strangely, but she also had a nagging feeling there was something wrong about her feeling okay.

"The lies are endless in the Sihu Tribe. Be cautious and aware of that. That's why I must point you in the right direction, away from Sihu's evil."

He pointed due north with his front right leg, portraying

green, scaly reptile skin wrapped tightly around strong muscles.

"Isn't that where the Fog thing is?" asked Zoey.

"Yes," the dragon said, looking away in sorrow. "The Sihu Tribe punishes us for not following their rules. They banish us to live behind the fog forever, making us live in misery and turmoil."

Zoey shook her head. "Everyone here seems nice, though. They wouldn't do that."

The heat around her picked up. For a moment, she thought her feathers might catch on fire. She drew back. Her insides felt like they were being clawed, scraped, and eaten with sharp teeth. Then again, a moment later everything ceased and she felt better. How strange, thought Zoey. A second ago I hated this Komodo dragon for creating the pain in my stomach, and in the next moment I feel grateful to him for taking it away.

"You have a lot to learn," said the Komodo dragon. "Trust me. I wouldn't have risked my life to come here if what I told you wasn't true." He glanced to his left and right, to be sure no one else was around. Then he whispered, "The Great Spirit sent me to tell you a secret shared only amongst the most courageous and wise. It's something you, and only you, can fulfill. It's your only way back home. And," he said with a loud hiss, "it'sss part of your missssion."

Zoey's eyes opened wide in astonishment. "How did you know I had a mission?" She was becoming suspicious. The only ones who knew about her mission were Nova and the Snow Tree. Was the Komodo dragon spying on her, or reading her mind? *I've got to get home. This is creepy.*

The Komodo dragon's eyes narrowed and a pleased smile peeled back his skinny, reptile lips, "Isn't that what they told you?"

Zoey nodded.

"Then," he asserted, "you can't go the way you came. The portal to your home can only be opened once you fulfill your mission. Once you fulfill the Windstorm Prophecy."

Zoey was baffled by this new information. "The Windstorm Prophecy?"

83

"Yes, yes, yes. The Windstorm Prophecy." He recited: "The prophecy says, 'Two children from a forgotten land, lost to the Island of Ohm Totem, one being of the night walkers and the other being of the sacred heart, will purify the energies, bring to us the old ways, and deliver us from the evil clutches of the Sihu Tribe, continuing the everlasting Shiver.'"

"Gibberish and untruths," scolded a familiar voice behind Zoey. She turned, relieved to see Nova standing just a few yards away. Nova closed her eyes and the heat around Zoey's body vanished. *How did Nova take the heat away?*

Nova opened her eyes. "You've changed the prophecy, Crepus Dim."

"I speak..." Crepus Dim paused, looking at Zoey and bowing his head to her, "I speak only the truth, my friend."

The sound of a small twig breaking behind Zoey startled her. There was Coda, walking toward her. His panther body was shiny black like the night. He stepped smoothly, easing over fallen branches, slinking through the bushes without disturbing a leaf. He did look like a night walker, just as Crepus mentioned in the prophecy—if it was real.

Nova took a step closer. Her eyes were glued to Crepus. "This is a prophecy that came to the Sihu tribe and evil isn't a term we use here. It doesn't serve us."

Crepus hissed, "Evil serves you quite well, Nova."

"It doesn't." Nova sat on her hind legs, curling her tail around her front paws. "And I was the one who interpreted the Windstorm Prophecy shortly after you created the Fog."

She looked up at the canopy of trees. "It says, 'Two children from a forgotten land, ancestors of the Island of Ohm Totem, one being of the night walkers and the other of the sacred heart, will purify the energies, bring back the old ways, and unite the PureLights once again, putting an end to the coming Shiver'." She eyed Crepus. "The Shiver is almost amongst us, Crepus. The prophecy is accurate and the Shiver won't last."

"I wouldn't be too sure of that," Crepus snorted.

Nova lifted her head and raised herself to her full height. In a calm voice she appealed, "Find your heart, Crepus."

Zoey felt anger consume Crepus again and fear stung her

heart. She didn't move. She couldn't move. She looked at Nova slowly advancing on Crepus. Nova mouthed again, "Find the heart within." Her eyes were like stone, unmoving from Crepus, and her violet crystals glowed brightly.

Crepus stomped and a smoky gas crept out of the soil and started to surround his body.

He cackled, glaring at Zoey, who backed away, bumping right into her brother.

With a curl of his mouth, Crepus whistled. It sounded like a high-pitched flute, but ten times as loud.

Zoey and Coda fell to the ground, paws and wings pressed over their ears trying to block the horrid, deafening noise. The soft grass and ground cover shook, and then as quickly as it came, the whistling stopped, leaving only a ringing in Zoey's ears.

Zoey stood up. Needles and soil sprinkled from her feathers. She stared at where Crepus was only moments before, but he was nowhere to be seen. He had disappeared. Charred grass and singed mushrooms only remained. Nova sedately faced the now scorched earth next to her paws. "It's fine now. He won't be coming back."

A screech filled the air, not as loud as Crepus's strange whistle sound, but nearly so. Nova's eyes widened and she looked skyward, past the thick tree cover. Nova yelled, "Get them to the portal!" and sprang off toward the meadow.

Zoey looked at Coda. He was alarmed. That was the same screech that woke him yesterday morning. He wanted to say something, but was cut off by Chev's large gray elephant trunk grasping his body and lifting him onto his back. "Hey, you two!" said Chev, "to the portal we go."

Zoey jumped up and spread her wings, flapping them hard and fast to get onto Chev's back as quickly as she could. Something was going dreadfully wrong here and she wanted to get out, and get out now.

"What's going on?" she asked Chev, landing on his back.

Coda interjected before Chev could respond. "Look up!"

Zoey looked up and saw a shadow cast across the sky. At first it looked like a cloud, but then she realized that clouds didn't move like that. Thousands of birds covered the sky like a heavy blanket. They flew chaotically from the north, perhaps from where Crepus lived. Chev broke into a run. The scenery of cedars and pines quickly became darker and darker, until everything became covered in pale dusk.

"Whoa!" yelled Coda, pointing with his tail. "Look at that!"

Chapter 9

To the east, hundreds of different birds came into view, forming a wall against the darkened sky. *The wall of birds must be the PureLights*, thought Zoey. They faced the oncoming flying Dims. It was apparent that the PureLights intended to stop them.

Zoey wanted to close her eyes, but didn't. Chev picked up speed, then stopped abruptly. Zoey tipped backwards, sliding sideways, and falling toward the ground. She spread her wings and glided softly to the green moss. She looked at the darkness above—at the battle about to ensue.

"We're here," announced Chev.

Zoey's heart pounded hard and fast, sinking into her stomach. She knew that the wall of birds were from the Sihu Tribe and she didn't want such nice animals to get hurt. *What if they lost? Would the PureLights be gone? Would we be stuck here in Ohm Totem forever?*

Unable to watch, she shielded her eyes with her wings. Shaking her head, she cried out, "Let's go home, Coda. Let's go home. Please, let's go home! I'm scared. I want to go home!"

All that returned to her was silence. Still clasping her wings over her eyes, she took a deep breath, waiting for Chev or Coda to respond, but heard nothing. Something was different. Something had happened. Where was she?

She took another deep breath and the soft, rich air filled her lungs, giving her trembling body a calmness she very much needed, bringing more vitality to her muscles. She suddenly felt strong, peaceful, and loved—loved in a way that felt like a long overdue hug was offered and received.

The silence suddenly filled with the soothing sounds of ocean waves. It was as if everything drifted away from her and she was back in her bed, waking to an early morning sunlit glow. *But, at the beach?*

"Coda?" she said, still covering her eyes.

"Coda doesn't play in this realm, child. You do"

"Snow Tree?"

"Open your eyes, Zoey."

Zoey lowered her wings, slowly lifting her eyelids at the same time.

She was standing on a beautiful beach that stretched ahead of her for miles. The sand was the color of ivory, soft and warm under her feet. Sparkling, luminescent blue waves broke, splashed, and foamed against the sand.

A few feet in front of her sat something shiny and golden, surrounded with an aura of moving colors. It reminded her of the Aurora Borealis, which she'd seen on TV. She took a step closer, realizing it was a thick book. It had a cover of pure gold.

In its center were words etched in white. The Golden Opus. Embroidered around its edges were spirals. They looked a lot like the DNA strands she'd seen in her science book at school.

She tentatively glanced around, wondering if she was alone.

"Hello?" she said aloud, hoping that someone kind and helpful was there. She felt a little bit stranded for the moment, but not really afraid. In fact, she felt pretty good here. Somehow this place felt familiar to her, like home. *Where's the Snow Tree?*

A short, soft breeze picked up, slightly ruffling Zoey's feathers. "I'm here," said a whisper in the wind.

Zoey looked all around, but didn't see the Snow Tree. Taking in a deep breath, she imagined herself inside of her heart, surrounding herself with beautiful pink and white colors. She took in another breath and cleared her mind.

"Where am I?"

The wind picked up, blowing against her feathers. "You're in the heart of Ohm Totem."

Zoey furrowed her feathered brow, somewhat baffled. "In the heart of Ohm Totem?"

"Yes, it's the most sacred of places."

This looks more like the beach than the heart of anything, thought Zoey.

"Snow Tree?" she asked.

Just then snow started to fall all around Zoey, and then quickly stopped. "This is the Snow Tree. Lady Wind carries my words on her back."

Zoey smiled. She was excited that her friend was with her.

"Why am I here?" she asked.

"Follow your heart, Zoey. It will answer your question. It will tell you."

"What will it tell me?"

After a long pause, Zoey looked to the left and right, expecting the Snow Tree to be standing in all of its beauty somewhere. "Tell me what? Snow Tree?"

All was silent. Zoey sat down, examining the white sand.

What am I supposed to do here?

A tingling sensation tickled up and down her spine. *The book!*

She excitedly half-walked, half-flew over to the book, flipping open the cover with her beak.

Empty.

Not only empty, it was hollow. It had a perfect rectangular hole cut out of it, and sand at the bottom of the hole.

She was disappointed. *Now what?*

As if in response to her question, the sand at the bottom of the book slowly moved up and down and left and right, like swells in the ocean.

Placing her wings on each side of the book, she drew her beak in closer to observe the moving sand. There had to be a reason it was doing that, but how? And why?

As she observed the movement more closely, she noticed the swells were getting bigger and bigger, becoming more active in the process. The swells smashed against the sides of the book, splattering sand every which way. The swells grew even higher, until the sand transformed into a volcano.

The volcano grew so quickly that Zoey had to step back to get out of its way. She heard a loud 'pop' and the volcano erupted a geyser of sand twenty yards into the air.

Zoey's beak gaped open. She'd never seen such a phenomenon. Suddenly, three books flew out of the geyser, landing side by side with a thump, thump, thump right in front of her. Within seconds the geyser began to die down, until it completely stopped.

Except for the beach, air circling around her, and the crashing of the waves, quiet filled the beach once again. *What just happened?*

She sat on her haunches, tail feathers in the sand, and curled her wings around her cheeks. She wasn't sure if she was waiting for another explosion or if she was just getting her wits about her. She looked around, hoping for some help to arrive, but realized once again that she was alone on this beach.

"Snow Tree?"

She sat quietly for another minute, waiting for a reply.

Nothing.

"Snow Tree?" she called, raising her wings in exasperation, "what do I do?"

Again, nothing.

She looked at the books, noticing that they were slightly smaller than 'The Golden Opus', but had identical designs, except for the titles.

The title of the first book read, *The Opus of the Mind.*

Confused, she looked at the middle book, hoping for a better understanding.

It was called, *The Opus of the Heart.*

She slowly shook her head. She was puzzled, not knowing what that title meant, or even what the word 'Opus' meant. She looked at the third book's title: *The Opus of Fear.*

As she read the title of the third book, a hazy, violet light began to appear around the letters of the title.

Tentatively, she inched closer.

The book seemed to be coming alive. She saw a blueish-white electric energy form around the hazy, violet light. The electricity danced around the light, slowly spreading itself around the rest of the book, dancing over the spirals, through the book, and around the sides.

Zoey was transfixed. She wanted to move away, but the dazzling lights seemed to be sucking her in. She was in a placid, deep trance that she couldn't, and didn't want, to get out of.

And then it stopped.

Coming back to herself, she took a deep breath and sat on her tail feathers.

The book opened up and the pages rapidly turned, stopping smack dab in the middle of the book.

Zoey was flabbergasted. *What now?* She stepped forward, peering into the book to read what was inside:

Aria: "Fear persists."
Bienra: "How is that?"
Aria: "The energy of 'what you fear' follows you where ever you go. 'What you fear' will continually repeat itself as a lesson in your life, until that lesson is learned. Once the lesson is learned, then 'what you fear' is transformed, and no longer has the ability to frighten you. Therefore, fear persists until it is transformed."
Bienra: "Transformed?"
Aria: "Yes, transformed—that is, when you change your fear into love. Most of the time we're afraid when we don't know or understand what is going on. But what we're afraid of isn't necessarily scary, we just think it is because it is new to us. When you embrace the fear of the unknown, then what you fear is transformed into love."
Bienra: "How do you do that?"
Aria: "By emptying the mind, which is where all fear exists, and facing 'what you fear' with your heart, which is where all love exists. Therefore, fear persists until it is transformed with your heart into love. Thus, you will truly love what you once feared. That's the path to follow. The path of the heart. When you follow the path of the heart, nothing in life can harm you. You have found peace."

Zoey stared at the page, wondering what it all meant. *Isn't that what the Snow Tree was talking about?*

She wanted to keep reading, but she knew if she were to turn the delicate page with her beak, she'd probably rip it. So, she gently touched the page with her wing, feeling the silky texture of the paper against her soft feathers, and attempted to turn it.

Her wing slipped. She tried again. It slipped a second time. This wasn't going to be as easy as she thought.

She tried again and again with her feathers fumbling all over the page, slipping off its smooth, silky texture. Soon she realized that feathers weren't at all like fingers, making this once simple task nearly impossible.

She paused and scratched the top of her head with her wing. There had to be a better way to do this.

She placed the strongest, most hardy part of her left wing on the page and pushed down on it, crinkling it to the left, allowing her longest right wing feather to slip under the crinkle.

Aha! she boasted loudly in her mind, as she easily flipped the page over, uncovering the next.

Fear persists until it is transformed with your heart into love.

Those words again.
Now what?

"Fear persists..." echoed a gentle voice. Zoey looked up. A gray wolf with a violet crystal stood in the distance next to reeds and grasses that grew out of the soft sand. She knew immediately that it was the wolf in her dream. He smiled as he continued, "Until it is transformed with the intelligence of your heart into love."

He walked toward Zoey, stopping just a few feet away. He bowed his head, gazing into her blue eyes. "I remember going through the same book many, many moons ago. The writer of that book is a very special spirit animal."

"Who are you?" asked Zoey boldly, all of her fear vanishing. It was a question that had been on her mind ever since she had the dream. She felt she knew him very well, but how?

"I'm Lao. It's nice to see you again, Zoey."

"Nice to see you again, too." It was a habitual response, rather than a true statement. She wasn't entirely sure if it was nice to see him.

"Thank you for answering my call and coming to Ohm Totem. I must ask, will you stay and help?" beseeched Lao.

Amidst the deep chasms of emotions in a place hidden in her gut, Zoey felt a strong energy wash through her. She felt an overwhelming sense that she must stay in Ohm Totem. She didn't understand why or even where this knowing came from, but it was rooting her feet into the ground, making her feel strong and brave. She knew what she must do. She must stay and help these wonderful creatures.

She closed her eyes, trying to shake the feeling away. It didn't budge.

"How do I know you?" she asked again. As she said these words, an image popped into her mind. She saw Lao and her sitting in a forest with gigantic trees. The trees were the width of houses and the height of skyscrapers. The sun was brilliant, shining in a blue sky. He was playfully laughing at something she had said. This image, however, felt as if it was something that happened long ago. The scene then faded and she saw the wolf staring directly at her. He smiled.

"We've traveled together before. You've known me for many moons," he answered.

"I've just met you. How could I have known you for many moons?" Zoey puzzled.

Lao sat on his hind legs. "Remember, Zoey."

A little frustrated by Lao's response, Zoey asked, "Remember what?"

"Who you are."

"But I..." Lao vanished, just before Zoey could protest anymore.

A light wind touched upon Zoey's body and a whisper in her ears said, "Open your eyes."

Chapter 10

Even though the sun hung low in the west, it shouldn't have been this dark in the green forest. The shadows from the confrontation in the sky blanketed the land drearily. Coda flinched, shivering as a cold, southern wind blew against his fur.

He looked up to the northeast, watching the storm of birds fight in the air. He felt unnaturally still about this, almost as if he'd seen this picture a thousand times before. He looked at Chev to ask him why he felt this way, but yielded. He could tell that Chev had his mind on something else.

Chev grunted, shaking his head in disbelief. His long trunk scraped the ground, lifted up soil, and tossed it over his back. He was disgusted.

"Why does he continue to attack us?" asked Chev, speaking his thoughts out loud.

Chev hung his head low, dragging his trunk, pacing back and forth. "We leave him alone, but he doesn't leave us alone. We do this, he does that. We defend ourselves, he attacks us repeatedly. We drive him back, he comes right back at us. He..." Chev caught himself, realizing he was having a little fit in front of Coda. His orange forehead crystal glowed. He gathered himself and cleared his throat. "Shall we go to the portal?"

Coda looked toward the sky again. He saw the wall of Sihu birds moving forward as the attacking birds moved back. The attackers were fast, but the dance like movements of the Sihu birds were too much for them. The attackers were thrown left and right, and many of them fell out of the sky like limp, dead birds.

Dying birds? A sudden shock hit him and he looked over at Chev, then Chev looked at Coda, understanding his unspoken question.

"They're alive, don't worry." He pointed with his trunk at the ongoing onslaught, "Pay attention to one of the PureLight birds and see what they're doing."

With great focus, Coda peered into the dark sky. He could see so much farther here in Ohm Totem, and in the distance he spied a white swan. He saw an indigo colored crystal on the swan's chest and forehead.

"I think I see one," Coda said, pointing his tail toward the battle in the sky. "It's a white bird, just over there. I think it's a swan."

"Yes, watch her."

The swan ducked as an eagle's talons swiped at her head, barely missing her. If the swan hadn't ducked, the eagle would have sunk his talons deep into the swan's skull, maiming her, or worse. Instead, the eagle passed on by, clearly surprised at his sudden miss.

The swan flipped on her side, nimbly turning and circling to face the eagle. The eagle also flipped on its side, turning just as nimbly as the Swan.

"Watch this. I can tell she has something tricky planned for the eagle," said Chev.

The eagle and swan flew at each other, both with skill and determination. It almost looked like a head-on collision in the making, until the eagle rose slightly, widened its wings, and turned over with his outstretched claws reaching toward the oncoming swan.

The swan, seeming to expect this, straightened her body, pointed her feet toward the ground and her head toward the sky, fanning her wings out wide. To Coda, she looked like a winged angel in the sky.

In one swift movement, the swan twirled at lightning speed, causing the eagle to miss yet again. However, what Coda wasn't expecting was the precision in that twirl.

One of the swan's wings pushed the backside of the eagle with an incredible force, directing the flailing eagle toward a target that the swan had picked out with pinpoint accuracy.

The eagle slammed head-first into a dark brown hawk that

seemed to be having its way with a defending Sihu owl. The hawk and the eagle tumbled toward the ground, appearing in and out of Coda's view between the obstruction of trees and branches.

Coda crouched low, inching forward to give himself a clear view of the falling birds. He saw the two birds continue to fall to the meadow floor, until finally, they flapped their large wings only a few feet before hitting the ground. They flew off toward the sky, unharmed.

He detected, however, that the owl and swan were waiting for them. They dove and landed on top of their attackers. In a flurry of feathers, the hawk and eagle fell motionless to the ground.

Coda gasped, and Chev, feeling the surprise that pounded at Coda's heart, touched the top of Coda's head. "They're stunned, not dead. They'll be out cold for a while."

Stunned? How did they stun them? wondered Coda, but withheld the question, knowing that he didn't have much time before they needed to get back to the closing portal.

Remembering Zoey, he looked at his sister a couple of yards away. She was as still as a statue, with her wings covering her eyes.

"Zoey, let's go!" he yelled, then glanced again at the fight in the sky. The wall of Sihu birds was still advancing its line. He could see that the attackers were falling out of the sky, hitting the grass, moss, and ground cover in the meadow below.

"Coda?" Zoey rubbed her eyes with her wings and took a big yawn. She seemed to be as calm as a sleeping baby, unlike a few minutes before when she wanted to get home as fast as she could.

"Zoey?" questioned Coda, wondering why her composure had changed.

Zoey said in a clear voice, "We're staying," and stomped her right foot on the ground, letting him know that she wasn't budging or changing her mind.

Coda stared at her in disbelief. "Are you crazy? I didn't want to go at first, but look at what's happening here."

"He's right, Zoey," added Chev. "It's time we got you away

from here and back home."

Zoey, as if not hearing a word Chev had just said, jumped up and flapped her wings. She rose into the air, landing on a strong cedar branch about ten feet up.

Coda lashed his tail back and forth impatiently. "What are you doing, Zoey? We gotta go!"

"No," was her only reply, and she turned her head away and stared off toward the meadow.

Coda and Chev looked at each other. Chev shrugged, "Well, she's like a rock you can't move."

Coda was about to yell at Zoey, but gasped instead. Below Zoey stood a large lion, with eyes that burned with fury. He was much larger than any lion Coda had ever seen. He had a big, brown mane, and dark yellow matted fur covering the rest of his body. He slashed his forepaws on the ground, flinging dirt to the left and right, flexing giant muscles that looked like they were going to pop out of his skin. The lion's crystals were gray. Coda knew that this creature was one of those dreaded Dims.

The lion let out a massive roar, momentarily stunning Coda with pulsing fragments of fear, as if he'd just been hit by shrapnel from an explosion.

"Oh, boy," said Chev, "they got through the Fog."

Coda's taut muscles screamed of panic, and he slowly shuffled his paws backward, not taking his eyes off the lion. He stopped once he felt he was beside Chev's big body.

"What do we do?" whispered Coda, hoping not to rouse the already angry lion.

Chev shrugged his shoulders again. His face was grim and twisted in concern. "I don't know. I've never done this before." His voice cracked and was barely audible.

Coda's eyes widened. "You've never done *what* before?"

Chev's voice shook, "I've never fought a lion."

The lion twitched its tail as if motioning to someone. In response, two smaller and even less friendly looking coyotes stepped from the bushes, out from behind the lion. The coyotes had gray crystals, just like the lion.

Coda's tail, as if acting on its own, went right between his legs and his stomach turned upside down. "Chev? Have you fought any coyotes before?"

"Well," Chev shifted nervously from side to side, "I'm really not much of a fighter. You see, I'm a singer, a poet, a nice guy, and an all around charming elephant once you get to know me." He looked at Coda with concern on his face. Then his face brightened. "Maybe I can charm them?"

Oh no, thought Coda. *We're doomed.*

The lion and the two coyotes moved closer.

"Oh boy," said Chev again, as he stepped in front of Coda, doing his best to shield him from an attack.

The lion, just ten yards away, let out a low, menacing growl, yelling, "Separate!"

At first Coda didn't know if the lion meant them or the coyotes. Noticing that one coyote walked to the right and the other coyote to the left, he knew it was meant for the coyotes. A moment later, the lion roared, jumping straight at Chev with his claws bared, ready to dig into his opponent.

Chev shrank back, closing his eyes, waiting for the inevitable pain from the sharp claws.

Coda, watching the lion as it jumped, saw a blur of something moving fast out of the corner of his eye. First he thought it was one of the coyotes, but realized that it was Zoey, flying at an incredible rate of speed.

"Wait!" cried Coda as he suddenly realized what she was doing.

She was flying head on, straight toward the lion.

With a confidence he'd never seen Zoey display before, she did a half-flip in mid-air, aiming her feet at the lion's eyes, screaming, "Leave them alone!"

The lion's outstretched forepaws went from attack mode to protecting his eyes, but a second too late.

Zoey's heels planted firmly against the black pupils of his eyes, immediately coursing pain through him. He yelped and tumbled over, landing in front of Chev, bumping his back against Chev's front leg. Zoey, not realizing the full force of the inevitable impact, ricocheted backward, landing hard against the ground.

The lion, now succumbed and writhing in pain, twisted and turned on the dark soil, crushing grass and brush in the process. Finally, he stood up in a daze on unsteady legs, but his eyes wouldn't focus, no matter how many times he blinked.

Before Coda could run over to help his sister, Chev shifted to his left and threw his body in front of Coda just as a coyote lunged at them. The coyote bounced off Chev's big right flank, skidding across the forest floor, until he dug his claws into the ground, stopping himself.

The coyote slowly shook his head and forced a low, long growl, saying without words that he wouldn't let the elephant get the best of him again.

Suddenly, remembering the second coyote, Coda glanced behind and saw the second coyote only ten feet away and charging toward Coda at full speed. Coda had never seen such menace in another's eyes; eyes that told a thousand killing stories. Coda knew this coyote wanted to rip him apart.

Before Coda could yell for help, the coyote, now only five feet away, sprang into the air and opened his mouth, baring sharply-pointed, saliva-dripping teeth.

Coda, without knowing how he did it, reacted in a way that he himself couldn't explain. His whole body relaxed. In an instant that seemed to pass in slow motion, he assessed the situation like a trained soldier and immediately knew the weaknesses and advantages of the coyote's plan of attack:

One - The tree to the right was precisely three-and-a-half feet away.

Two - The coyote's jump was very risky. It allowed a trained defender more time to evaluate the attack.

Three - The coyote only extended his left front leg, leaving the right portion of his body unprotected.

Coda could use the coyote's left leg against him. This meant two things; that the coyote was going for the immediate kill by using his teeth as a weapon, and that he had underestimated Coda's skill.

In the quickest move the coyote had ever seen, Coda jumped straight up, meeting the leaping height of the coyote, and caught the coyote's left leg with his mouth. Still in the air,

Coda flipped while clutching the coyote's leg, then let go at the perfect moment. A moment later, the coyote slammed against a tree.

Coda landed, facing the coyote. He saw that the creature was slumped on the ground, shaking his head violently, trying to make the stars in his eyes go away. Coda stood on all fours with his head level and chest out. He flared a new aura of confidence, more so than any defender the coyote had ever been up against.

Slowly getting up, the coyote eyed Coda. For the first time, the coyote saw something in Coda that he'd missed only moments ago. "It's him!" the coyote barked.

The lion, who could see a little more clearly now, hesitated and stepped back. "He's returned!" he echoed. Swiftly, the attackers turned and ran, retreating from their failed attempt and heading north, disappearing among the trees and foliage in the forest.

Coda, sitting proudly amongst the maples, cedars, and pines, glanced at his sister and Chev, who sat uncomfortably under the branches of a maple tree.

"That was...it was... incredible. You saved our lives, Coda. How did you learn to defend like that?" asked Chev.

Coda wondered the same thing. He hadn't the faintest clue. It had come to him as naturally as sleeping. It was easy, just as easy as it was for Zoey to fly.

But that, however, wasn't what racked his brain and heart the most. It was the words, *he's returned!* Who is "he" and what has "he" returned from? Perhaps they mistook Coda for someone else? Yet, they feared every ounce of him, tucked tails, and ran.

Then something, some memory of defensive skills, scratched at the back of his mind. He saw himself training thousands of spirit animals, but he knew it was from the past. But how? He suddenly heard the words "the Art of Defense" echo in his mind. *What's that?* His thoughts evaporated a second later as he sensed his sister. She was trying to understand what he just did as well. She eyed him seriously.

"We must get to Deer Meadow," said Chev. "The battle in

the sky has ended."

Chapter 11

Dusk had settled and the sun hung just over the vast trees in the west, washing the horizon with gold and purple hues. The few clouds in the distance were like dark moving shadows with interwoven pink outlining their form, giving them more life. Zoey could see that they floated toward the western shores.

The last few hours had been a blur for her. She was standing in the meadow on a large circle of soft, minty moss. The battle in the sky had been fought above this meadow, known as Deer Meadow, less than fifteen minutes ago. Along with her brother, she had followed Chev here, and upon arrival saw hundreds of other animals standing around in a half-circle, mostly in silence. She didn't know what to make of all these animals. She felt like she stood out like a sore thumb.

Some of the animals looked at Coda and her with curiosity, wondering who the newcomers were, but most smiled, nodding in appreciation to them. What she was appreciated for she didn't know, much like the myriad of things that she didn't know about this land. Maybe it was because Zoey and Coda had stood up to three of the invaders?

She tried to calm herself down by taking a few deep breaths. Her emotions had been a roller coaster during the fight. She'd been nervous, then calm, then back to nervous, and then scared, and then determined and focused. Up and down, left and right her emotions went, merging into a state that was numbing to the body, and dizzying to the mind.

She had stopped the lion from hurting Chev and Coda by mustering up a courage she never knew she had. She knew it was love that had driven her actions. What would she do without Coda as her brother any more? She had to do what she did! She had risked her life to save his. The moment was quick and she hadn't given much thought to it. She only remembered diving straight for the lion's eyes, and then hitting hard against the earth.

Then it was Coda who shocked them all, including the coyotes and lion. He had moved with grace and precision when the coyote attacked. His lightning-quick actions had turned the tables all at once, making the intruders fall back, running north, through the Fog.

Where had he learned to fight like that? Was it something he learned at home?

No, it couldn't be. He'd never taken any karate classes or had any lessons in wrestling. His reaction was amazing, though. Zoey sighed, looking around at the disheveled animals in the gathering. Some licked their wounds; others seemed to be patiently waiting for something.

Chev pointed toward the river with his trunk. "There are about fifty PureLights just beyond the River Ohm standing watch near the Fog, just in case the Dims come back for another attack." He'd been standing silently between the two of them for some time. He, like the others, was waiting for something.

"Don't worry," he said, lowering his voice to a whisper. "The Dims won't show their faces any moment soon." He winked at Zoey, adding, "We PureLights of the Sihu Tribe whipped 'em good. Everyone is calling this conflict 'Sky Battle,' and it will be spoken of for many moons. It's being recorded in the tablets."

Sky Battle? Tablets? Zoey didn't know what he was talking about.

Chev continued to recount details about the conflict, and Zoey was very sad when she heard that several PureLights had died. They were apparently outnumbered by the Dims five-to-one. Still, she had anticipated that most of the PureLights would've been massacred. She was thankfully proven wrong.

Yet, on the other side of the confrontation, some of the Dims were killed as well. Not many, but nonetheless, this blew Zoey's mind. How could such a small tribe take on that massive Dim army and not get slaughtered? She had noticed several Dims lying on the ground on her walk over to the meadow, but she didn't know if they were knocked out or truly dead. She saw some blood, but did her best not to look. She was told that some of them were "stunned", whatever that meant, but knowing that some of them were dead put a knot in her stomach. She didn't count on this mess when she decided to stay here and help. Help with what? The PureLights seemed to be doing just fine dealing with these Dims on their own. And the Dims who were stunned? What about them? They're lying there on the outskirts of the meadow right now. They've either been forgotten by the attackers or left there to die, or perhaps to find their own way back to the Dim Lands. And, why weren't the PureLights paying much attention to them? Don't they want to put them in jail or something?

None of this made sense.

Zoey looked around at the crowd, and then focused on Coda. He was still looking quite stunned by what had just happened.

Nova was now standing regally at the head of the half-circle, facing the gathering, and beaming a calm energy to everyone. Her eyes were clear, while reflecting the concern in the spirit animals she surveyed.

"I'm saddened," Nova addressed the assembly, jolting Zoey out of her thoughts, "just as you all are." She surveyed the crowd for several minutes, seeming to make eye contact with each and every member of the gathering.

"Remember," she continued, "that this, too, shall pass, much like a giant wave hitting the shore. The wave pounds and disrupts the sand while it's there, then recedes back into the ocean to be whole again. The Dims are like that wave. Right now they're on the shore, slowly receding. One day they'll be pulled back into the ocean, and into the source of it all—The Great Spirit—and find peace. When this happens, they'll realize that doing harm to another is no different than doing harm to oneself. They'll understand that they're all part of that same source, the vast ocean of The Great Spirit, and that we're all the same."

Zoey noticed that Nova bristled, as if she felt something unspoken from the crowd. "Yes, I understand your dissatisfaction with the war. Remember, it's a war they brought to us. It's not your fault."

She then frowned, saying, "I know you detest violence. All decent beings detest violence. And yet, we're forced to protect ourselves and this land. This, my friends, is our biggest dilemma.

"Though, how may we be content?" Nova asked, looking toward the northern Fog. "How can we be content in each and every moment, knowing that behind the Fog live the Dims? Knowing that they can attack us at any moment?

"I'll tell you how. We remain content because we look at the Dims, not as demons, but as Beings like ourselves. If we see them as something other, something less than us, then we'll slowly fade into the reality they have created for themselves. We'll forget that we're all connected and we'll become one of them. Our crystals will fade to gray, our memories will be forgotten, and our love toward all things will diminish."

For a moment, Nova's head dropped and she was silent. Then, with a powerful breath, she raised her voice. "We'd even fight amongst ourselves."

The crowd murmured in agreement. Nova stood up, taking a step forward. "However, we won't become the Dims. We'll defend ourselves and this land properly. No one knows what the outcome of this war will be, but I can tell you this—the tides are changing and we're the reason it's doing so. I honor you all for your courage and skill." Shouting toward the Fog, she declared, "We will never be driven out of Ohm Totem!" The crowd cheered and Zoey cowered at the blast of energy that swirled within the half-circle. Then she noticed that Coda still had his head down. *Was he even listening?*

When the cheering died down, Nova resumed. "Many can say that we were victorious today. However, do not rejoice in this victory. There's no delight in the slaughter of our friends and companions. There's no happiness in the war between two great tribes."

She padded toward the front of the gathering and walked along the front line of the half-circle. She calmly paced back and forth before speaking again. "Send your love to the Dims, and to those who have fallen. This will help them along their way. And, in so doing, keep your heads high. All of you. You protected this land. The land that has been granted to you, not by Crepus Dim, not by me, and not by you, but by the Great Spirit. You defended this land and your lives with composure and compassion for your attackers. I'm very proud of you all. I bow to you and thank you for being the brave souls that you are. I pray that our land will continue to be full of love, abundance, wisdom, and a place that serves others. May this conflict be the last." Then she raised her head, cheering, "To the River Ohm!"

The assembly shrieked with joy and ran toward the River Ohm. Coda and Zoey looked at each other, wondering if they should join the run as well. Chev nudged them, "The water won't hurt. It's for cleansing and healing. The River Ohm is sacred."

"Okay," replied Coda, looking in the direction of the river, watching the many pattering paws and flying birds splashing delightedly into the water.

Zoey giggled. "Look at them run. It's like they've won the lottery or something."

"Won the lottery?" Chev asked.

"Oh, I don't really know. It's something my dad says sometimes when people get really excited over something," replied Zoey.

Chev was about to respond, but was interrupted by a sweet voice coming from behind them. "Hi Chev. Who are your friends?"

Turning around, they saw a raccoon smiling and nodding a welcome. Her crystals were emerald green, like her eyes.

"Numee, meet Coda and Zoey."

Numee leaned forward, touching her nose to the ground. It looked to Zoey somewhat like a feminine bow or a curtsy.

"Welcome and nice to meet you two," she said. She gestured toward the River Ohm. "You coming?"

Zoey looked to Chev, wondering if he'd answer for them, but Coda took the lead instead and shrugged his shoulders. "I-I don't know."

Numee narrowed her eyes, pursing her lips, almost prodding them along toward the river with her thoughts.

"Well," she said, "I'll be waiting for you."

And with that, she waddled past them, humming, and then stopped, looking closely at Coda and Zoey. "Thank you for saving Chev's hide today."

Zoey didn't think she had done enough, but nodded anyway. Coda looked at the ground and flicked some dirt to the side with his tail, clearly uncomfortable.

"How'd you know that, Numee?" asked Chev. He narrowed his eyes as he looked down at her, pretending to be suspicious.

"Well," she chuckled, "I saw two wild-eyed coyotes run out of the forest, and then a lion who was bellowing orders to get the news to Crepus. I didn't hear what the news was, but it sounded like it would have been most interesting to know. Then I saw you three walk out of that same spot moments later."

She chuckled. "My guess," she shrugged nonchalantly, not even considering for a moment that she might be wrong, "is that a poet like you didn't drive three angry, muscular, sharp-toothed, sharp-clawed, ego-maniacal, mouth-frothing animals out of the forest."

"Yeah, you know me all too well." Chev's trunk touched Coda's back. "Coda saved us all, actually. And, if it wasn't for Zoey's bravery I'd have teeth marks in my side."

"Yeah, probably," Numee responded. "You're such a goof. You should have thrown the attackers off by singing them some tunes."

Chev scratched the top of his head with his trunk and closed one eye, pondering the idea. "You know? That would actually be a good idea." His trunk waved with excitement. "Yes, that's a great idea! I'm going to do that next time. It will throw them off, and maybe even make a fan out of them."

Numee rolled her eyes. "Okay, I was just kidding, but you go ahead and do that, Chev."

She walked away snickering, calling over her shoulder, "I'll see you all in the water!"

Coda grinned at Zoey and Chev. "Let's go jump in!"

Zoey nodded in agreement, then stole another quick glance up at the sky. It was getting even darker as the sun slid past the horizon, making everything a little more difficult to see. It's probably almost eight in the evening, her time, she thought.

"Well, I can't wait to jump in. Let's go!" Chev exclaimed.

At that moment, Nova called their names. Turning, they saw her sitting by the Snow Tree, gesturing with her tail for them to come to her. They immediately went to her side.

A calm whisper came through the wind and landed in Zoey's ear. It was a message from the Snow Tree. *Thank you for staying, Zoey.*

Zoey glanced at the Snow Tree, and saw the Snow Tree's face take form in the bark. She winked and smiled at Zoey, then vanished. Zoey smiled back.

"Chev?" asked Nova, "would you be willing to take them to the Circle of Elders? We'll be meeting in five nights passing."

Zoey sensed a mixture of anxiety and frustration coming from Chev. But why?

"Yes, I'll do that," replied Chev solemnly.

"Are you sure?" asked Nova, who noticed the shift in Chev as well.

Chev nodded affirmatively.

"Thank you, Chev." She stood up and waved her tail. "Bless you both for saving our friend here."

Nova turned toward her golden hut, then paused, and looked up at the moon.

"The full moon is ending and five nights passing will come shortly. This will give you several moons to observe and understand many of our ways," she remarked to Zoey and Coda. She then dipped her head and turned on her heels, disappearing into the hut.

After several moments of silence, Zoey asked Chev, "What's the Circle of Elders?"

Chev shuddered and sat on his rump. "We have to pass through the southern Fog to get there. I've done it once, but am not keen to do it again." Looking forlornly at the river, he added, "There's a lot of important talk at the Circle of Elders. A lot that I don't understand—" He changed the subject. "I think perhaps it's best to get you all acquainted with your sleeping arrangements, instead of the river. You'll be here until the next full moon, so you'll be able to enjoy the river another fine evening."

Zoey shifted uncomfortably. *The next full moon?* She wondered if her decision to stay was a good one.

"Let's get you settled in," said Chev, pulling himself up. "You ready?"

Coda grinned. "Ready for what?"

He seemed ready for whatever adventure awaited, thought Zoey.

The big, bulky gray elephant pointed his trunk south. "First stop, Spruce Hollow!"

Chapter 12

Dim sunlight peered through gray clouds and into an eastern bay window, bouncing off a flat rock floor to a gray, smooth wall on the west side of a rock room. A fire roared in the fireplace on the northern wall, glowing brightly, and replacing any darkness in the room with much needed light.

The room was empty, except for a large floor rug strung of red and gold, emblazoned with the image of a Komodo dragon clenching a lightning bolt in its fangs. It stood triumphantly, as if winning a major battle.

On the north side of the room stood a massive door. It was carved out of redwood and outlined in hardened silver. A latch, the shape of a half moon, occupied the middle.

Two knocks and a loud creak echoed within the quiet room. The door slowly opened. Wispy, yellowish-red light curled from around the door.

"Yes?" came a voice from inside of the room.

An ape, large and muscular, stepped through the doorway. The crystals ingrained in its forehead and chest glowed a light gray color. He bowed, and then looked up, searching for his master. "Lord?" he called out as he shut the door behind himself.

"What is it?" Crepus hissed, stepping of the shadows. His tough green scales rippled and his claws tapped the ground loudly.

The ape lowered his eyes. "Yes, my—"

"Do tell me why your lack of manners has interrupted my meditation!" growled Crepus.

The ape's eyebrows arched in surprise.

Crepus ambled toward him, stopping in the middle of the rug. He sat down on the emblazoned caricature of himself and glared at the ape with cold, piercing eyes. "Don't you know what manners are?”

The ape nodded contritely.

“Knocking during a time of meditation is one thing, but walking in without an invitation is another!”

The ape averted his eyes and nodded again, hiding a wry smile. “Yes, Lord.”

“So, what is it?”

“Yes,” replied the ape. His eyes stared at the smooth, gray rock flooring beneath his feet. “We've just been given some information I think you might want to hear.”

“And?”

“A group from the invading party has returned with a message.” Waiting for a response yet not hearing one, the ape continued, “They think Orion, the black panther, is back.”

For a moment, Crepus looked alarmed and his shoulders drooped. The ape had never before seen a sign of weakness in Crepus and he stiffened in surprise.

Recovering quickly, Crepus drew himself up and asked in a voice low and soft, “In Sihu Tribe?”

“Yes, my Lord. Inside the Sihu Forest, in Sihu territory.”

Crepus rolled his eyes. “Yes, you bumbling ape, I know where the Sihu Forest is.” He remembered seeing a black panther standing next to the skylark earlier in the day. The black panther was a little too skinny to be Orion. “That wasn't Orion, but you did well to bring the message. It will be noted.” He shooed him away with his foot. The ape turned to leave.

“Stop,” Crepus sniffed. “What's your name?”

“It's Maldwyn of Gwenfree, my Lord.”

Crepus hissed and the ape flinched.

“You fool! Your name does not end with Gwenfree, it ends with Dim now. I rightfully took over your land of Gwenfree. You either call yourself Maldwyn Dim, or you'll never be seen alive again. Understood?”

Maldwyn nodded. “Yes, of course, my Lord.”

“Good.” Crepus's eyes narrowed in suspicion. “In Gwenfree, did you know Aderyn the VioletLight?”

“Yes.”

“Did you know her well?” Crepus already knew the answer.

111

"Yes, my Lord. I knew her well."

"How well?"

"We were close."

"Was her death gruesome? I imagine it was." Crepus searched for a response in Maldwyn's eyes.

Maldwyn's breathing hastened. He clinched his fists as fury rose in his belly. He took a deep breath, letting his fingers relax. "I did not witness her death."

Crepus snorted. "You have control over your emotions. That's impressive." He sauntered over to the fireplace and stared into the fire. "Where did she die?" he asked.

Maldwyn shrugged. Crepus could feel the ape's discomfort, so he pushed even harder.

"I said," hissed Crepus, the fire mirroring in his eyes, "where did she die?"

"I don't know, my Lord," replied Maldwyn. "May I leave? Or do you need anything more from me?"

"I heard that they clawed her eyes out, and picked her bloody feathers off her body. I think that would be a rather terrible death, don't you?" Crepus cracked a sinister smile. "Did you hear how we used her body for food the next day?"

Maldwyn clinched his fists again. He spoke through gritted teeth. "I heard, Lord, that she single-handedly killed a hundred Dims before she fell."

Crepus gave a hearty laugh. "VioletLights don't kill. They're so predictable." Crepus cocked his head. He felt a twinge of deceit from Maldwyn. What was he hiding?

"Maldwyn. Look at me."

As Maldwyn lifted his head, Crepus' black forehead crystal started to pulse. It turned from several shades of gray to black, over and over again, until Maldwyn's eyes locked onto it. A moment later, Maldwyn fell back, against the door. He folded over and gasped for air.

Crepus had gotten what he wanted—the truth. Aderyn the VioletLight was still very much alive.

Crepus lunged and clamped his fangs into the ape's shoulder. He pulled the ape hard to the floor, ripping coarse black hair and skin. He spat the hair onto the ground, and then put one foot on Maldwyn's back. "You've betrayed your VioletLight, Maldwyn. I thought you had better control than that."

Pushing himself up, Maldwyn looked the dragon squarely in the eyes. "I've betrayed no one. Now, do with me as you wish!"

Crepus sniffed the air, hissing, "Leave my quarters! I still have use for you."

A little dazed, the ape opened the door.

"And Maldwyn?"

Maldwyn glanced back at Crepus with sadness in his eyes.

Crepis continued, "You're my messenger. From now on, where I go, you go. Don't think you can get out of this life that easily."

Maldwyn gave a nod and shut the door.

Crepus slowly shook his head, pondering how the PureLights could be so foolish. Naive, in fact. VioletLights, the sages of the PureLight Tribes, had power, but very little intelligence. They steered their tribes wrong and because of this, only two PureLight tribes remained intact. His ways had shown that there was no use for the PureLight Order. *It only gets you so far*, thought Crepus. *Those who think for themselves will eventually think themselves into trouble. They'll collapse under so much freedom.*

He walked over to the bay window and surveyed the large trees below, dimmed by the evening dusk. Snow, he could tell, was on its way. It's funny, he mused, how the thoughts of the masses can be manipulated to create change in a positive way—or in Crepus' claws—a negative way. The negativity tainting Ohm Totem had not only changed most of the lives on the island, but the weather, also. The once warm and plush island was about to experience snow for the first time. A massive shift was occurring. The darkening consciousness on the island was bringing forth a period of freezing, a period where most would shiver. *Good*, he thought. *The Windstorm Prophecy was wrong. The Shiver is amongst us and here it will stay.*

Staring at the scenery below, he watched the snow starting

to fall, engulfing the land with icy flakes. Without warning, the thought of a particular VioletLight entered his mind—Nova, the Snow Leopard.

How fitting.

A memory came forth from long ago. It opened in his mind like an exploding star and Crepus saw Nova sitting next to him on a sandy stretch of beach along the River Ohm. She was laughing with him. Crepus' heart, for an instant, leaped with joy at the memory.

He searched the gray clouds above with a single thought. *What made us laugh?*

But, like most of his memories, the joy faded as quickly as it had arrived, and from the recesses of his mind he heard a voice that wasn't his own.

You must stop Nova. She must fade into the ethers like smoke in a heavy wind. Finish what we started!

Chapter 13

Ten yards away, Chev, Zoey, and Coda stared at a gigantic tree—the Spruce Hollow. It still amazed Chev, no matter how many times he'd seen it. It was as wide as five large boulders, and as tall as five trees stacked on top of each other. It stood at the southern region of the Sihu Tribe, next to the southern Fog.

Knowing she was going to stay here, sleep here, and do whatever else there was to do here; Zoey wasn't excited, nervous, or anxious about it. She was numb. Too much had happened to her in one day, and to top it off she wasn't certain what to expect with this big tree. Really, what was it and why was it so big? During the walk from Deer Meadow, she did, however, feel amazement when she first saw the Spruce Hollow standing way above the forest canopy.

Looking at the large spectacle up close, she saw that it had a grayish, brown bark covering the length of it, and light green moss scattered in the cracks. At the base of the northern side of the tree stood a golden door with a brown wooden latch to open it. A peephole was just above the latch and three silver bells hung over the door frame.

"I hope you like your room. I hear it's nice and comfortable inside," remarked Chev. "Don't get too comfy, though. You still have your place in…um…" he scratched his ear with his trunk and looked off into the distance. "Well, where did you come from?"

"The Cornell Forest," said Coda. "It's in the town of Gladstone, where we live."

"Okay," replied Chev, continuing to scratch his giant ear. He patted the top of Zoey's head and grinned. "You still have your place in Gladstone. I suppose you'll be going back as soon as the next full moon comes around." He blinked his eyes, and then said seriously, "Thank you, again, for saving my skin back there. You're a brave bird, you know."

Embarrassed, Zoey looked down. Chev would have seen her face flush red if she hadn't any feathers. She shrugged her shoulders. "Thanks." The truth is, she didn't really plan on flying at the lion, but sometimes when love is involved, things just happen.

Coda playfully nudged his sister. "Don't get too scared of sleeping *all* by yourself."

"I'm not scared, Coda," Zoey rolled her eyes.

"So, where do I get to go, Chev?" Coda asked excitedly.

Chev pointed with his trunk. "See that large lump of dirt topped with grass way off over there?"

Zoey looked in the direction he was pointing and saw a trail leading up to a big mound, with a rather large hole. The hole looked like it went deep into the earth. It had hazy white, bluish light beaming inside of it that seemed to stop at the entrance of the hole, going no further. *How does it do that?* thought Zoey.

"That's the Marble Burrow. It's for the Paws."

"The Paws?" asked Coda.

"You're a Paw," Chev said, tapping the top of Coda's right foot with his trunk. "And Zoey's a Wing," he said, tapping Zoey's wing with his trunk. "Paws and Wings train in different ways, so there are two different living quarters for two different types of students.

"I've never trained," Chev sniffed. "Well, I did for a day. I slept in the Marble Burrow with my classmates, but they quickly realized that my talents lay elsewhere." He grinned, "Still, I found my home with the bards at the eastern beach."

"Oh," said Zoey softly, "I've never heard of bards."

"They're the poets, storytellers, and singers in the Sihu Tribe. Some day I'll sing you a little tune."

Coda twitched his tail and Zoey felt a twinge of anxious energy from her brother.

"Zoey and I are students here?"

Chev stepped back, astounded that Coda would ask such a question. "Well, yes. You're both young, and haven't been trained in the Art of Defense."

Zoey's blue eyes shone brightly. "Why would we train if we're going home soon?"

"Oh yeah, that's true." He thought for a moment. "Well, of course, you don't have to train. It's your decision, but most of us here do it anyway. It's actually fun and you'll learn a lot of important information and skills." He added, winking at her, "I'd say do what I did and give it a try."

"Sounds like fun!" said Coda.

Zoey squinted her eyes at Coda in a way that he knew meant, h*ow would you know?*

Coda responded with a shrug that said, *I don't know.*

Chev's brow rose. He'd never seen a brother and sister act that way with each other. He decided that brothers and sisters probably communicate much differently in Gladstone.

"Coda, I'll take you to the Marble Burrow so you can get a good night's sleep. You'll need it to help to prepare you for your training sessions, which will in turn help to prepare you for the Circle of Elders."

Again, a wave of anxiety crashed over Chev when he said Circle of Elders, but he caught himself right away, and did his best to hide it. "Okay," he said with forced cheer, "it's time we said goodbye, for the moment."

With that, Coda and Chev bid Zoey farewell. Coda gave her a friendly flick on her cheek with his tail and Chev did his usual patting of the head with his trunk. Zoey watched them head toward the Marble Burrow. Then she turned and stared at the door of the Spruce Hollow. She took in a deep breath, exhaling, "Here we go."

She walked up to the door and did what Chev explained to do on the way to the Spruce Hollow. The secret knock. She gave three knocks with her beak, then paused, then knocked two more times, paused again, and ended with one knock.

The peephole slid open.

"Who goes there?" came a high-pitched male voice.

"Umm... Zoey?" she said.

"Umm-Zoey? Is that a question or a name?" replied the voice.

"It's a name."

"How do I know it's a name? What if you're a skylark posing as a name or a name posing as a skylark and trying to spy on us? You know, the Dims attacked us earlier and you could be one of them trying to be one of us." There was silence, and then a shuffling of paper or something behind the door, "If you want to come in, then answer this question." There was more shuffling and then Zoey heard the voice hum a song. "Aha!" he yelled. "I got it. What's the square root of 18,324?"

"Uh, I don't know," Zoey frowned.

"That's close enough. It's 135.36617007214173."

The peephole slid shut. Silence.

Zoey stared at the door, wondering what to do next. She took another deep breath and exhaled, waiting.

Waiting.

And waiting.

And waiting some more.

She looked around worriedly. *Am I not supposed to be here or something?*

She jerked back when she heard a loud clank, and bells jingled as the door slowly opened to reveal a white crane about five heads taller than her, and standing in the doorway. There was no expression of welcome on his face, or any gesture of hello. He didn't even give any indication that she was supposed to be there. In fact, he looked puzzled for a moment, then became all business-like, as if he had a million things to do.

"Well, what are you waiting for?" He waved her in, gesturing with his wing for her to hurry up. "Don't just watch me, let's move those legs. Come on, come on!"

Entering Spruce Hollow, Zoey noticed immediately how bright it seemed, despite the fading dusk outside. The walls were round, and had many lights shining from them. Zoey could tell they weren't light bulbs, though. They didn't glow the same way. They looked more like jagged rocks sitting in little indents made in the wood wall. The color of the light coming from them was exactly the same color she had seen being emitted from the Marble Burrow. The dark red wood was glossy, as if someone had sanded and stained it, like her dad did to the doors at home. Zoey followed the wall all the way up with her eyes, fifteen floors or so, where it stopped, and opened up to the sky.

There's no roof, thought Zoey in wonder. It was a large, wide, open, windowless skylight.

Looking at the very top of Spruce Hollow, she panned down from floor to floor, noticing that each floor had a balcony going all the way around it with a gold railing along the edge. At every fifty feet or so, doors were set slightly back from the railings and against the wall. Each door was red with a gold latch, and had numbers on it.

The floor where she stood was made out of the same beautiful red wood that covered the walls. Several huddled masses of young birds, many seeming to be her own age, or just a little older, mingled in front of her, laughing and talking amongst each other.

The crane cleared his throat, startling Zoey out of her Spruce Hollow trance.

"Are you done enjoying the view?"

Zoey nodded absently. "Oh, yeah. Sorry."

He gave her a stern stare that seemed more sarcastic than serious. Then he turned, looking at a tablet that stood erect about five feet to the right of the entrance door. The tablet was gray, and resembled a gravestone that arched at the crown. It had a perfectly round green crystal embedded in the middle of it that was pulsing with light.

The crane observed Zoey eyeing the crystal. "That's an emerald, my dear." Quickly changing the subject, he asked, "You say your name is Zoey? Or is it Um-Zoey?"

"Just Zoey," she mumbled.

"Humph," snorted the crane. He bent down and peered into the tablet. Suddenly Zoey saw a beam of green light eject vertically out of the emerald, projecting a three dimensional image just above it. The image contained writing in her language as well, but she couldn't see exactly what was written.

"Ah yes, there you are." The crane turned back to Zoey and the image instantly disappeared. "Do you know what your name means?"

She shook her head.

"Well, it means 'life'. It's a good meaning, so don't forget it."

"I won't," she nodded.

The crane searched deep into Zoey's eyes for several seconds, then closed one eye, leaning in a little closer. His beak nearly touched hers. He smiled. "Nope, you won't. You've got something in you that you don't even know about..." he paused, standing straight up, only to bend down to look at her again, "...yet."

He stepped back and held his wing out to her. "Pleased to meet you. I'm Taregan."

Zoey looked at the wing, but didn't know what to do with it.

He sighed, "Just touch my wing with your wing. It's called a wing shake."

She held out her wing and touched his. The wing shake was short-lived because something quickly distracted him. His eyes widened in surprise. "A bag? Why do you have a bag?"

Zoey followed Taregan's line of sight and saw an orange suitcase with wheels and a handle to pull on. It stood right between them.

Zoey was just as confused as Taregan. *I don't know*, thought Zoey

"What were you going to do?" he asked. "Bring a party dress? I don't think so." He leaned toward her with one eyebrow raised and the other cocked low. He whispered into her ear, "You have quite the imagination, young lady." Then he winked. "And orange? I like your style. It's my favorite color."

"Okay, moving on," Taregan said, all business again.

As the crane gestured Zoey to follow him, she glanced toward the suitcase and saw—nothing!

"Where's the suitcase?" she cried out.

"Suitcase?" Taregan replied. "What suitcase?"

"The one that..."

His laughter interrupted her and he slapped his white feathery hip with his wing. "I got you!" he smiled. His smile was infectious, but his humor was lousy, which made Zoey smile even that much more. It eased her nerves. She suddenly liked this Taregan fellow.

"The suitcase disappeared once you took your eyes off of it. Like I said," his tone became serious again, and his voice low, "you have quite the imagination. And in Spruce Hollow, imagination creates things almost instantly."

"It does?"

"Well, sometimes. Depending upon who you are, you know?"

"Well...but...how do you..."

Before she could finish, Taregan spread his wings out and spoke in a loud voice.

"Let me have your attention, please!"

Birds of all kinds shuffled out of their rooms and stooped on the railings. The birds that were gathered in front of her stopped chattering, turning to look at Taregan. They were wide-eyed in wonder, curious about the newcomer.

"I have a new student!" Taregan shouted. "Treat her with respect, which I know you'll do. Treat her with patience, which I know you'll do. And treat her with love, which I know you'll do. So, thank you for doing what I know you'll do!"

For a moment the Spruce Hollow was silent, then a roar of applause erupted, nearly toppling Zoey over.

One of the birds, a female cardinal with mostly brown feathers, red accents, and a sharp red crest, flew from one of the middle levels, landing right next to Taregan and Zoey.

She pecked lightly at Taregan's tail feathers. "Me, me, me, me," she sang. By then, several other birds were landing beside her, trying to catch a closer glimpse at the newbie.

Taregan feigned irritation. "Yes, San? What's this, me, me, me, me about?"

She tilted her head, pulling on his wing feathers with her beak. "You know," she said, rolling her eyes.

"Yes, she can, but first I have to ask her a question." He turned to Zoey and smartly asked, "What's your favorite number?"

Uncomfortable being put on the spot, for a moment Zoey's favorite number slipped her mind, but closing her eyes tightly for some reason brought the number from the depths of forgetfulness to the front of her brain.

"My favorite number? My favorite number is 3."

He then asked San, "Is your favorite number 3 as well?"

She slowly shook her head, and with wide puppy-dog eyes she said, "No, it's 1."

"Okay, okay, okay." Taregan looked thoughtful for a moment, resting his chin on his wing, trying to hide a smile.

"You two..." he said, pointing at San, shaking his wing back and forth a couple of times, "can room together, but only if Zoey agrees."

San broke into a huge smile and shook her head up and down toward Zoey. "Say yes. Say yes."

Zoey, seeing the excitement in San's face, said, "Yes."

"Zoey, you're on the ninth floor, in room eighteen with San."

"Yeah!" cheered San, lifting off and flying toward the ninth balcony. "Follow me, Zoey!"

Zoey looked at Taregan. He calmly nodded to her and said, "Time to fly."

She jumped up and flapped her wings, zooming past balcony after balcony, until she landed on the railing next to San.

"Are you ready to see your new room?"

"Sure," said Zoey. By now, Zoey was more and more curious about this place. San, for one, was very nice for picking her as a roommate. She wasn't used to being picked for much of anything, especially by her brother. He always left her out of any game he and his friends played. He never wanted her to sleep in his room either, even though it was both of theirs and she had no other choice. For some reason, he always claimed it as his own. And to top it off, he always did his best to walk as far as possible from her on their way to school in the mornings. Zoey wondered why she was never good enough in his eyes.

San hopped off the railing, taking Zoey away from her thoughts, and landed in front of a door that had a gold 18 engraved on it. Pulling the latch with her beak, San opened the door, beckoning for Zoey to come in.

The room was simple and small, but roomy enough for the both of them. The room was shaped like a crescent moon, with a nest of feathers on the left and the same type of nest on the right. Zoey guessed that the nest on the right was San's. There were feathers thrown about.

San smiled her big smile. "Are you ready for the Art of Defense training tomorrow?"

"I don't know," replied Zoey. She didn't. She didn't even know what it was.

San threw up her wings, high toward the ceiling. The ceiling was tall. It looked to be about ten feet up, which was quite high compared to the size of their bodies. "Well, I'm excited!" cried San.

Is she ever not excited? wondered Zoey. Why was the Art of Defense so exciting in the first place? Zoey began to feel a little apprehensive. She didn't like not knowing what was going to happen. "What do we do in training?"

"First, let's see who you're training with tomorrow." San hopped to the middle of the room and said, "Sacred tablet." A tablet, like the one Zoey had seen downstairs, rose from the wood floor in the middle of the room. "What's Zoey's training schedule tomorrow?" she asked.

The tablet radiated a green light that shot vertically, much like the tablet on the main floor. San waived Zoey over, pointing with her longest wing feather at the words: "The Art of Defense" with Kaya.

"Wow," replied San. "We're in the same training!"

"What's the Art of Defense?" asked Zoey.

The tablet disappeared back into the floor.

"The Art of Defense has something to do with defending yourself. I'm not exactly sure about it. It's not like you're actually learning how to hurt anyone or anything like that. Well," she paused, looking down in deep thought, "I guess you could get hurt, but it doesn't matter. They'll teach you how *not* to get hurt when the Dims attack. You'll also learn how to not hurt them, you know, when you throw them across the meadow."

"Oh," yawned Zoey. Her body was tired all over from all the

stress and mayhem she'd been through recently. She wanted to lay her head down, but wasn't sure if that's what she was supposed to do.

San focused on a crack midway up the wall directly opposite from the door. "Open," she muttered, and just like that, the crack slowly opened into a perfect circle. The night air drifted in and Zoey was able to see the evening sky in the east.

"The breeze is nice," San exclaimed.

Zoey yawned once more. "Yeah, but I'm tired."

San pointed to the nest where Zoey was to sleep. "You'll like those feathers. They're so soft and perfect for sleeping."

"Is it okay if I go to sleep now?" Zoey asked, as she collapsed into the feathery bed.

San looked disappointed, as if she wanted to keep talking all night, but Zoey couldn't wait for a response. She closed her eyes in what she thought was a blink, but her heavy eyelids remained shut and she drifted off into a dream.

∞

Zoey opened her eyes to see a wolf's gray paws and legs standing on thick snow. She was lying on her stomach, on the frigid ground. A chill went up and down her spine. She exhaled a puff of steam. Wherever she was, it was cold.

Placing a wing on the ground, she pushed herself up, into a sitting position. *Where am I?* She glanced at the wolf. It was Lao, his violet crystals beaming brightly as he stood before her. A thin strand of trees encircled them and the sky above was almost as gray as his fur.

"Can we talk?" he asked.

"I guess." Zoey looked around, finding nothing that looked familiar to her. "Where are we?"

Lao looked around. "I don't know. I've not been in this forest before." The air around his body suddenly sparkled with bright white lights, then faded a moment later. *That's just like Nova*, thought Zoey.

Zoey smiled, feeling the tranquil, gentle energy. She spread her wings to stretch, and as she did she felt the earth under her feet momentarily shake. She eyed Lao. He dipped his head, "Don't be afraid, Zoey. Remain calm. Crepus knows we're here."

Zoey's stomach fluttered nervously. "What do we do?"

He sat on his hind legs. "We talk."

The earth shook again, this time more fiercely, and Zoey barely kept her balance. Her body, however, felt a sudden panic. She wanted to get out of this place.

She spread her wings, flapping them hard, lifting herself into the air. She glanced upward, spotting a branch she could land on a few yards away.

Lao saw her panic and blew softly in her direction, instantly steadying her nerves. She peered down at him and landed back on the ground. "How do you do that?"

"Do what, Zoey?"

"Make me feel so calm all over."

"It's the calmness inside of me that you feel. When you feel my calm energy, it reminds you of who you truly are. Who we *all* are. It helps you to find your inner peace."

"But," replied Zoey, "how did you not freak out when the earth shook? I mean, really, how do you do that?"

"I do it by letting things take their course. It's a practice, a discipline, and a remembrance. This allows me to remain composed in any situation."

"Remembrance? What are you remembering?"

Lao sat down on his haunches. "I'm about to give you a lot of information. I'll be planting a seed in your mind. The seed will eventually grow. Once it grows, then and only then, will it make sense to you. Are you ready for this?"

Zoey nodded tentatively. She wasn't entirely sure about getting information from this gray wolf. It's still strange, though, how he felt so familiar.

"Okay," continued Lao. "I remember self-control. If something in my life goes awry, then self-control stops my negative emotions from taking over. If I were to allow my negative emotions to take over, then I'd react with fear, disrupting the fabric of the flow, and I don't want to live my life living in fear. Instead of emotionally reacting to the things

I fear, I take a deep breath in that moment when I am afraid. This makes me stop, allowing me to feel what's truly happening in the moment before I react. To negatively react changes what's truly happening to me—makes it worse. It forces me to repeat the lesson of fear until I learn not to repeat it. Does that make sense, Zoey?"

Zoey shook her head no. Lao dipped his head. "When you emotionally react to a situation, you tend to blame your reaction on something or someone else. When in truth, it's you who created your own reaction, your own feeling, and your own disharmony. You're the only one who makes you feel afraid, happy, or angry. No one else does that for you. Do you understand?"

Zoey slowly shook her head again in disagreement. "My brother can make me mad. He does that all the time."

Lao saw that Zoey was doing her best to comprehend. "In a way, that is true. However, does he go inside your mind and tell you to be mad or be sad or, better yet, be happy?"

Zoey chortled. "No way, that's impossible."

"Then, Zoey, is it you who goes inside your mind to make you feel a certain feeling?"

Zoey thought for a moment, remembering a time when her brother insulted her. She was happy the moment before her brother insulted her, but not after. Lao can't be right about this, she concluded. "I don't think so. One time I was happy before my brother made fun of me in front of his friends and then I was mad and sad after he did that. So, he made me feel that way."

"Let's look at it another way, okay?" Lao moved closer to Zoey and spoke calmly. "When you're with your brother and he's playing a game by himself, does he get mad when you want to play with him?"

Zoey nodded an emphatic yes. "He never wants to play with me. When I sit down and play with him, he always gets angry. Then we get in a yelling fight." Zoey paused, and her wings slouched. Her voice became soft, mumbling. "I bug him, I guess."

"And, did you make him angry and make him yell at you?"

"I don't think so."

"When you yelled back at him, did he go inside your body, control your mouth and make you yell back at him?" asked Lao.

Zoey laughed, "No, he can't get into my body and move my mouth."

"Would you then agree that you didn't control his body, his mind, or his emotions either?" Lao's voice was calm.

Zoey put her wing to her beak, deep in thought. "I don't go in anyone's body and control things."

"If that's the case and if that's the case for most healthy beings, then would you say that he didn't make you say, think, or feel something? And that you were the one who said, thought, and felt it?"

"I guess so."

Lao raised her beak with his paw to look into her eyes. His blue eyes imbued a deep stillness around her. He spoke again.

"Right. It's up to me how I react to things, and the same is true for each of us. Taking a deep breath allows me to remember this. Then I can remember another discipline. The discipline of the flow. I've disciplined myself to go with the flow of life, no matter what happens. I accept it just as it is. If someone insults me, I continue to go with the flow of life, not being bothered by the insult. I have a life to live. If I stop and pay attention to the insult, analyze it, and dissect it to see if it's true or not, then I've interrupted the flow, causing harm to my mental and emotional state of being. I'd get angry or sad, causing myself stress." He paused, blinking. "Going with the flow is the greatest aspect of all. In this, I know nothing can harm me. Everything drips off of me like rain."

Zoey was a little uncertain. "How can nothing harm you?"

"I've learned that life is nothing more than a dream. I'm a VioletLight and VioletLights have woken from the dream. We go with the flow of the dream."

Zoey really didn't understand this. "Woken from the dream?"

"Yes, woken. I know beyond reason or doubt that everything is connected and that we're all partners—you, me, the rock next to your feet, the snow covering the land, the rain hitting the river, everything—and we're all co-creating this life together. Those who haven't fully realized this are still dreaming."

Lao layed down, resting on his forepaws, looking up into Zoey's eyes. "Again, we're all creating this together. We're all pieces of the same puzzle. We're all aspects of the Great Spirit and we're creating this dream as we go. The challenge is this: When are you and the rest of the dreamers going to wake up? When are we going to go with the flow of it all? When you do, you'll understand the most important facet of the dream. That life is about the choices you make, determining where you'll be in the flow of life."

Snow crunched behind Zoey, taking her attention away from Lao's words. Lao sat up and Zoey quickly turned. Coming straight toward them was a Komodo dragon.

Crepus Dim.

He stopped. His eyes were like slits and his brows were drawn downward in anger. "What are you doing, Lao?"

Lao bowed his head. "Greetings Crepus. What brings you this way?"

Zoey was slightly taken aback. *Greetings?* At first, Zoey thought he was kidding, but Lao's body language showed sincerity.

"Zoey? You don't really think life is a dream, do you?" asked Crepus.

His cold voice, and the way Crepus said her name, made her feathers quiver. Zoey dropped her head, stammering, "I...I don't know."

Lao nodded to her. "In moons to come, Zoey, you'll begin to understand what I speak."

"Silence!" yelled Crepus. The ferocity of his voice shook the trees, dropping snow from the branches and on top of her. Zoey shook her body and flapped her wings, knocking most of it off. She noticed that the falling snow had somehow missed Lao.

Crepus hissed and the black crystal sparkled. "She is naive, Lao. You use that against her. You trick her. You use your calm to bring her closer to you and closer to your precious PureLights and VioletLight Masters. You're no better than Nova." He looked down upon Zoey. "They're running you straight into a trap, Zoey, and there's only one way out."

The black crystal between Crepus's eyes gleamed. Zoey tried to look away, but her eyes wouldn't budge. She tried to move her body, but even her body wouldn't cooperate. She was paralyzed.

She tried to take a deep breath, just like the Snow Tree had taught her. But she couldn't breathe. She wasn't breathing! She heard sinister laughter echoing all around her. It was Crepus. He frightened her, and at the same time, pulled her inside of his darkness. She felt trapped as if someone was slowly squeezing her between two walls. Her thoughts spun back to her breathing, but still, she couldn't breathe. *Why can't I breathe?* It was as if she were underwater, with no way of reaching the surface to gasp for air. She gulped and gulped, doing her best to inhale. But, nothing happened. The paralysis had her. Crepus had her in his fierce mind grip and he wasn't letting go.

She wanted to bring her wings over her eyes to block Crepus' black crystal from her vision. Her wings wouldn't budge. Her legs became weak and she dropped to the ground. Her body started to lose its life, fading away into the breathless confusion of it all.

"Breathe! Focus on the flow!" bellowed Lao, instantly shifting her awareness to the gray wolf's presence.

Zoey gasped for air. Her energy quickly returned and she jumped back from Crepus, hiding behind Lao.

The wind suddenly picked up and the trees slowly leaned to the side. Their limbs flapped in the wind. Large snowflakes fell to the ground, instantly sticking and building upon each other.

Lao stood tall with his gray chest puffed out. "You're not welcome here, Crepus."

"You're telling an old friend to leave? That's not very VioletLight of you, Lao. I thought all were welcome around you."

"Yes, in my life you're welcome to come and go. I'd like that, as old friends do. However, I'm not a spirit animal that you can harm, but Zoey is." He sniffed the air. "The tenth suggestion of the PureLight Order, if you remember Crepus, states that we must serve, cherish, and protect the weak, and those who are oppressed, and all beings that suffer wrongdoing." His violet crystal glowed brightly, "Crepus, I'm protecting Zoey from you."

Zoey felt herself relax and her breathing slowed. She knew now, beyond doubt, that this wolf would not let anything harm her. At least, not when she was in his presence.

Crepus' eyes became sad. "You don't realize what she's going to do to us, do you?"

"I do realize. It's what we've been waiting for," replied Lao.

Zoey searched Lao's eyes for a hint of what he meant. But she saw nothing that gave it away.

Crepus retorted, "No, it's what the PureLights have been waiting for, not anyone else. You're a fool, Lao! You're going to ruin everything!"

Crepus moved closer until he was nose-to-nose with Lao. His black crystal flashed and he stomped his right foot on the ground. The earth shook, knocking Zoey over. She squawked as a crack formed between her and Lao. She scrambled away from the crevice, putting even more distance between her and the wolf.

Looking up in horror, she saw that Lao remained still. He hadn't moved. Lao turned his head to check on Zoey who now stood behind him. Zoey screamed, pointing over Lao's shoulder with her wing, "Watch Out!"

Lao turned just as large, razor-sharp claws struck full force on his face. He fell awkwardly on his side, splattering blood against the snow, staining it red. He lay still for a moment, then calmly shook it off. He stood up gracefully, as if nothing happened, which surprised both Zoey and Crepus. Clearly, Crepus wasn't expecting Lao, or anyone else, to be able to get back up, let alone survive such a harsh attack.

Crepus attacked again, growling, causing the earth to shake yet again. Zoey instinctively wanted to jump in and help her friend, but she slipped, falling on her back as the ground shuddered heavily beneath her.

Zoey watched with dread as Crepus' claws were about to slice into Lao a second time, but suddenly something changed. Zoey heard and felt what she thought was static electricity cracking in the air around her. Crepus stopped in midair, just out of the reach of Lao. There, Crepus remained, looking as if he was hanging from an invisible rope. He swung his claws furiously at Lao, spitting and hissing.

"Let me go!"

Lao watched with soft eyes but showed no emotion. Zoey could see that his left cheek had four slash marks that slowly dripped blood off his fur to the snow covered earth.

"You left yourself open, Crepus."

Crepus stopped flailing his forepaws, knowing he couldn't get to him. "Fight like a warrior, Lao!"

Lao bowed slightly, allowing Crepus to slowly descend until he was standing motionless before him. Zoey could see the Komodo dragon's powerful muscles twitch, wanting to attack, but Lao had some type of power over him that she didn't understand.

"A true warrior doesn't fight, Crepus. Fighting only brings violence. A warrior rises above all violence, finding another way to resolve conflict."

"How are you going to resolve this, Lao?" Crepus hissed.

"You're beyond resolve. That's a reality that the PureLights must face. We've lost hope in you, Crepus. Now, you must leave this forest and never return to Zoey's dreams. If you do, I'll be waiting." With that, Lao blew a gush of air toward Crepus. Crepus disappeared right before them.

"Are you alright?" Lao asked Zoey.

Zoey nodded yes, but looked at Lao's face with worry. The claw marks looked deep and she didn't understand how he wasn't moaning from pain. He nodded in understanding and closed his eyes. As he did so, the claw marks slowly healed and vanished, showing clean and healthy fur.

Zoey's eyes widened. "How did you do that?"

"I've woken from the dream, Zoey." He leaned forward, whispering into her ear, "Zoey, wake up."

Zoey opened her eyes and looked around. She was safely snuggled in her bed of feathers. San slept across from her, whistling a sweet chirping snore with every breath. Good, it was only a dream. This time, though, she knew the dream was more real than she wanted to think.

What did Crepus mean by ruining everything and why did he say that Lao doesn't realize what I'm going to do to them?

Zoey stared out the window. The stars twinkled through the light wispy clouds that quickly moved across the sky. It wasn't quite night time yet, telling Zoey that she had only been asleep for ten minutes at most. Taking a deep breath, she calmed her nerves. *I don't know,* she thought. *My dreams are strange lately!* She closed her eyes and drifted off into a nice slumber.

Chapter 14

The entrance of the Marble Burrow was large. It looked as if Chev could easily fit through it, even though he didn't attempt to when they arrived. He introduced himself to the caretaker, Honani, a wise old badger with indigo colored crystals. Chev nudged Coda toward the entrance. "Goodnight, Coda."

"Goodnight, Chev." He looked at Honani, then at the descending tunnel, and then back again at Chev. "What do I do now?"

Chev yawned, stretching his trunk out toward the fading sky. "You follow Honani to your room. I'm getting me some much needed shuteye." Chev winked at Honani, "Take good care of my friend here."

Honani nodded, "Of course." With that, Chev patted the top of Coda's head and turned toward the east. Coda watched him until he disappeared into the darkness of the trees beyond.

Coda suddenly felt a little scared and, in some way, abandoned. Alone. But before he could sulk, Honani brushed his small tail against Coda's side and started walking down the tunnel. Coda followed.

The tunnel of the Marble Burrow went deep underground. It wasn't anything special, either. It was simply dirt. Dirt walls, dirt ceiling, and a dirt floor. He thought how lucky Zoey was for staying in what was probably a luxurious big hollow tree. *She always gets the best.* A sinking feeling came over him, just like the times when his mom and dad gave her a bigger Christmas gift. It wasn't the first time he had felt like this. *She's such a spoiled brat.*

Coda walked side-by-side down the tunnel with Honani, who hadn't spoken a word yet, giving Coda somewhat of an uncomfortable feeling. He was rather used to Chev's friendly and playful demeanor. So Coda remained quiet, too, thinking this was probably best.

On each side of the tunnel, lights were positioned in the wall every twenty steps or so. Coda wondered how they lit up like that, since Ohm Totem probably didn't have electricity. As Coda passed one of the lights, he gave it a close inspection. He saw that the lights were actually two rocks, lit up, and set in a cavity dug into the wall. The cavity looked to be about a foot deep, a foot wide, and a foot high, making a nice, snug fit.

Coda wanted to ask what they were, but looked to the ground instead, and walked at a faster pace to catch up with Honani. *Am I not supposed to talk?* wondered Coda. *Probably not.*

"You can talk," said the badger, turning his head to Coda. "I'm not as uncomfortable to be around as you think. Sometimes silence is the greatest company you'll ever have. Try it for several days sometime. You won't regret it."

"Sure," replied Coda. His reply was enthusiastic, but deep down Coda thought it would be boring to be quiet all day long.

Coda's reply didn't fool Honani. Honani stopped, prompting Coda to do the same. He looked into Coda's eyes and spoke slowly. His eyes sparkled wisdom, much like Nova, and his demeanor was strong, composed, and innocent. There was a sense of genius to the way he articulated his words.

"Sometimes being quiet can be a bore, especially for the first couple of days. However, if you say nothing for a couple of days, you'll start to see your thoughts for what they truly are— nonsense and noise. During those first couple of days, you'll notice that your thoughts will become louder and louder. They'll scream for you to speak. Finally, your thoughts give up screaming all together when they realize that you aren't going to speak at all. Then, stillness enters the mind. When that happens, you realize what it's really like to be truly calm and present. You find joy in everything. You find inner peace and happiness for the first time since you were a baby."

"Oh," said Coda. He didn't know what else to say. He didn't think he would ever stop talking, so this wouldn't matter to him anyway.

Honani shrugged his shoulders in a way that said he knew

someday Coda would benefit from silence. Then he nudged Coda, changing the subject. "Come over here, my friend." They walked over to one of the cavities in the wall. It held a pair of glowing rocks.

"I'm curious, do you have anything like these where you come from?" asked Honani.

Eyeing the rocks, Coda twitched his whiskers as a peacefulness enveloped his body. This peace seemed to come from the soft glow emanating from the rocks.

Both rocks had slightly different shapes and were translucent. At the point where they touched each other, they emitted a bright dot of light which then dispersed, radiating a soft, serene glow over all the rocks.

"We have light bulbs, but nothing like these," replied Coda.

"Light bulbs?" queried the badger.

"Yeah, they give off light, but they're a little brighter than these rocks. You can't look into the light bulbs like you can these rocks."

"Why is that?"

Coda stared deeply into the glowing rocks. "Because staring at light bulbs can hurt your eyes. They can probably ruin your eyesight if you stared at them too long."

"Ahh, I see. These lights won't hurt your eyes. They'll strengthen them, along with the rest of your body. Do you feel the soothing energy?"

Coda nodded, not taking his eyes off the rocks for just that reason—the light soothed him. It felt good.

"They're crystals. These two illuminate when partnered with each other," explained Honani. "The crystal on the left is a large Calcite crystal. You find those deep in the caverns of Sango Mountain." Coda saw that the Calcite was long and hexagonal in shape. He noticed the one next to it was more rectangular and much wider.

"The one on the right," continued Honani, "is called a Quartz crystal. They're found in the clay beds at the base of the Mosazi Mountain Range. Together we call them zytes. A forming zyte must be okayed by the caretakers inside of each crystal in order for them to produce light."

Surprised, Coda asked, "Someone lives inside the crystal?" *No*, he answered himself, *I must have heard that wrong.*

Honani nodded his head, smiling as he did so. "Oh yes, each crystal in Ohm Totem has a caretaker. They live within the crystals." Noticing Coda's confusion, Honani explained, "If you were to merge into one of those crystals, you'd see a large crystalline palace—the home of the caretaker—somewhere amidst a beautiful lake, forest, or whatever place is of interest to the caretaker. They have a very busy job in keeping the crystal healthy. They have a responsibility to clean, guard, and energize the crystal. They're very important beings in our world."

"Wouldn't you need a microscope to see them?"

The badger tilted his head. "I'm sorry, Coda. I don't know what that is."

Coda playfully rolled his eyes, thinking how silly he was for bringing up such a word in a world that obviously didn't have microscopes. "Where I come from, a microscope is something you look through to see things that you normally can't see."

Honani still looked bewildered, so Coda tried again. "Well, if you want to see something smaller than what your eyes can see, you look through a microscope. Like...water. Water looks clear. It looks like nothing but water is inside of water. But nope, water has little squirmy things inside it that you can only see through a microscope."

Honani frowned. "I've never heard of such a thing. Well, here in Ohm Totem, you can perform a special breathing technique that allows you to merge into the crystal. You'll learn that someday in your training. When you merge into the crystal, you'll see that everything within the crystal is the same proportionate size as you. It would seem no different than here. And there, you'd meet the caretaker."

Coda tilted his head curiously. "What does a caretaker look like?"

Honani pursed his badger lips. "Well, they look like you or me, I guess. Depends what their spirit animal is. Maybe a hawk, a cougar, or a giraffe. Just depends."

"And they light the crystals?"

"Yes. In order for a zyte to form, you must consciously ask both caretakers of each crystal to partner up and work together. If they agree, then touching them together creates a zyte."

"What if they don't agree?" asked Coda, thinking how clever he was for asking such a question.

"That rarely occurs, but if they don't agree, then a zap of electricity, much like a mini-lightning bolt, will ignite between the two crystals, pushing them farther apart from each other."

"How do you push them together, anyway? You don't have hands...I guess you could use your paws?" Glancing at the zyte again, another question popped into his mind. "How did you even lift all the zytes into these holes in the first place?"

"You can move anything you want with a single thought, or a sound."

Coda's eyes widened. "Oh yeah, Nova lifted me onto the Large Boulder. It was a little scary."

"She's one of the most enlightened Beings you'll ever meet. Consider yourself very lucky," Honani said solemnly.

Coda thought for a moment. "But, I can't lift anyone with a thought or a sound."

Honani winked, "Perhaps one day you will. Most spirit animals in Ohm Totem can no longer do this. It's become a lost art. Imagination, with an unshakable confidence in what you're doing, is key in this process. It allows the spirit animal to move objects, or to do incredible feats with thoughts and/or sounds. Imagination is everything."

This was something very new to Coda. "VioletLights are probably the only ones who can move objects with their thoughts, right?" asked Coda.

"Every being is capable of doing this, but as I said, most have forgotten. The VioletLights have not forgotten, though. Neither have some of the spirit animals with indigo crystals," explained Honani. "Some of the Dims can, too. Otherwise, it does take a lot practice to perfect this ability."

Honani walked forward and gestured with his head for Coda to follow. "You'll learn all about this stuff soon enough. Let's continue to your room, now. I think you'll like it there."

The tunnel continued along a slight decline, going even deeper into the earth. Coda thought for sure he was fifty feet underground by the time they stopped, when in front of them stood a large marble disc surrounded by a solid wall of dirt. It blocked them from going any farther.

"This is the door to the sleeping quarters of Marble Burrow," said Honani. "To open the door, you need to slowly blow onto it. It will record your scent, allowing you to open it each time you blow onto it. However, I must give it permission to record your scent." He turned his head toward the door. "You ready?"

Coda didn't know if he was asking him or the door, but when Honani looked back at him, Coda realized that Honani was talking to the door. Honani smiled. "The door is ready for you."

"Ready for what?" asked Coda, doubtfully.

"For you to blow onto it."

Coda took a small breath in and exhaled at the door. He waited and waited. And, waited. But, nothing happened. He looked at Honani, who simply nodded. "My friend," he said, "it has been recorded. Now, blow again."

"Oh," replied Coda. He looked at the door, wondering what was behind it. He curled his lips and softly blew.

The door silently shuddered, then slowly rolled to the left, causing a coating of dust on the ground to fly up.

Coda could see bluish-white light curling around the door and filling the tunnel. Within several more seconds, the door was fully open and the light from inside was so bright that Coda squinted and looked away. When his eyes adjusted, he saw the source of the light.

Lighting up the gigantic room was an immense, glowing crystal. It was by far the largest crystal he'd ever seen. It must be a hundred feet wide and a hundred feet tall! Coda wasn't great at measurements, but he knew this crystal was huge. It stood in the middle of the room, surrounded by marble ceilings, marble walls, and a marble floor. It was beautiful. It was magical. It was like a picture from the most gorgeous of paintings.

Honani giggled. "I know. It's quite unique, isn't it? There's no other place like it in all of Ohm Totem. It was here before we arrived. Someone created this room long ago, but we don't know who."

"Really?" asked Coda. His eyes widened with curiosity. "You don't know who?"

"We don't know. There's a large tribe of Yeti on an Island to our east. We've always wondered if they built it. They're a mystical race, with magical abilities much like our own. They may have created this long ago."

"You mean, Big Foot?"

Honani frowned, "Big Foot? I don't know Big Foot. Yeti have big feet—if that's what you mean." He gestured toward the opening in the large room. "Shall we go inside?"

Coda bobbed his head up and down several times enthusiastically. Stepping through the entrance, he could see spirit animals of all sizes walking around, talking amongst themselves. A tiger, having a conversation with a deer, nodded his head at Coda, calling out, "Hey, young one." Coda happily nodded back, and then stared at the large crystal. It was hard to keep his eyes off of it. It came out of the ground like a giant iceberg thrusting out of the Arctic Sea. It had to be several stories high. It peaked like a mountaintop, just below the large, marble domed ceiling.

Honani brushed his shoulder against Coda's leg to get his attention. "Are there crystals like that where you come from?"

"I don't think so. That's huge!"

Honani pointed with his nose to a hallway in front of them. "You'll be staying in a room down there. This is where new students live. You'll be sharing a room."

Coda walked into the hallway and saw zytes lining the walls. To Coda's left and right stood several more disc-like doors.

"Your room is right here," said Honani, stopping in front of a disc door that had a glowing, translucent 9 at the top.

"Are you ready?" asked Honani.

Again, Coda's thought was that Honani was talking to him, but he quickly realized that Honani was speaking to the door.

Honani turned to Coda. "Now, blow."

Coda blew and nothing happened, which he expected this time.

He blew again, and as before, the door shook and rolled to the left, slowly revealing what was inside.

A squirrel sat on one side of the room. A pale, reddish color emanated from the it's crystals. He seemed to be in deep thought. His face was screwed up in worry until he glanced at Coda. He gasped and clasped his paws over his mouth.

Did I startle him? worried Coda.

The squirrel skillfully recovered from his start and dropped his paws. Honani entered the room, gesturing for Coda to follow.

"Sorry to disturb your thoughts, Skint." Honani twitched his ear in Coda's direction. "This is Coda. He'll be your new roommate for a while." The badger smiled. "Coda, this is Skint." Suddenly the badger paused, looking off to his left as if something disturbed him. He nodded and took in a deep breath. "I'm needed in the main hall," he said matter-of-factly. Honani whispered to Coda, "You have a lot to teach him." Honani walked out and the door rolled shut behind him.

Teach him? What could I possibly teach him? Coda looked around the room. It was silent, but Skint's stare nearly screamed at him.

Skint's mouth seemed permanently fixed in a drooping frown, but Coda sensed the squirrel was more shocked than sad. *Why would he be shocked at seeing me?* Coda shuffled his paws, not knowing what to do next. Was he supposed to make polite talk? He didn't want to, but the silence continued and so did Skint's stare and frown.

Coda looked up. "Hi."

"Hi," replied Skint.

"I'm Coda."

"I-I-I know," Skint's body tightened. "I mean, I-I-I know 'c-cause he j-just t-told me."

"Oh." Coda felt a strange nervous energy pulse through him. It wasn't his nervousness, so it must be Skint's. Something was amiss with this squirrel. Coda nosed around the small, round room, doing his best to hide how uncomfortable he was starting to feel.

The room was covered in marble, just like the main hall. The ground, though, looked like soil, but felt like soft cushions. Coda sat on his haunches and studied his paws. He forced a smile and conversation. "Nice to meet you." But as he spoke, his stomach felt like he had just fallen ten stories.

"N-n-no. D-d-don't feel that w-way." Skint stood up and smiled, but something didn't seem genuine about it. "I used t-to be a D-d-im. S-s-so I have some things t-to get over."

"Oh," was all Coda could manage to reply. Truthfully, though, Coda didn't understand at all.

Coda furrowed his brow. *Hey, how did Skint know what I was feeling?*

All was silent again, and Skint blinked his eyes a couple of times. Then he yawned and lay down, curling up into a ball. He closed his eyes, and to Coda's amazement, the squirrel fell fast asleep.

Coda felt relieved and continued his inspection of the room. Zytes hung from the domed ceiling, lighting the room. Next to the zytes was a green blinking light, pale like Skint's crystal, being reflected off of the marble ceiling. Coda stared curiously, wondering what it was, or better yet, where it came from. He searched the walls, but couldn't see anything that would explain the source of the mysterious blinking light. Then, on the dirt floor, he noticed a long, rectangular depression with something gray in the middle of it. In the depression, a green hue blinked off and on. Coda wondered what it was, and then jumped back in fright.

The gray object in the depression had suddenly risen, and now Coda could see the source of the green light. A blinking green emerald, about the size of a baseball cut in half, sat embedded in the middle of a gravestone-looking thing. As it reached its peak and stopped rising, the emerald stopped blinking, radiating a solid green color.

Coda paced around it, wondering at its purpose. He sniffed it, which was odd since he'd never felt the urge to sniff anything before. He sat down in front of it. Nothing happened. Curious, he blew on it. Again, nothing.

Remembering that you have to blow twice, he blew on it again.

Still, nothing.

He twitched his whiskers and shrugged his shoulders. Giving up, he yawned and went over to the opposite corner from Skint. He lay down, comforting his chin on his black forepaws. He peered around the room again. Nothing was happening. It would be good to have a TV about now, thought Coda. I'm bored.

He sighed. Nothing to do.

I guess I'll lie here until I close my eyes and fall asleep.

"I'm bored, I'm bored, I'm bored, I'm bored..." he said in a soft voice. He stopped when he heard Skint make a slight movement. Good, thought Coda. I'll talk to Skint.

Skint, however, only had an itch and fell right back to sleep.

He looked around again until his eyes came to the gravestone-looking thing. He stared at it for several minutes, until an idea popped into his mind. He stood up, and after a long, deep stretch, strode over to it. Tilting his head, he touched the green emerald with his paw.

Coda flinched as a green light shot toward the ceiling, hovering several feet above Coda's head. The light turned into a map. It was a map of an island in the middle of a vast sea. Underneath the island read, 'Ohm Totem'.

Coda wondered where he was on the map and instantly the green light zoomed to a portion on the right side of the map that read, 'Marble Burrow'. He sat on his hind legs, curiously surveying everything. He saw where Spruce Hollow was, and the Large Boulder. To the left was a hut labeled 'Yellow Hut', which must have been the golden hut that Nova lives in. He then noticed that the portion of the map he was looking at was called the 'Sihu Tribe'.

Oh yeah, Nova told us that we're in the Sihu Tribe, thought Coda.

Again, the green light responded to his thoughts, and in the matter of a second, words formed in the light, displaying more information:

"The Sihu Tribe arrived in Ohm Totem 9,363,213 moons

ago. The Sihu Tribe maintained a population of 1,800 spirit animals until a change occurred. The change occurred 187,264 moons ago. Since then, the population of the Sihu Tribe has been decimated to 801 inhabitants. The Sihu Tribe is known to be the home of Nova, a highly evolved VioletLight and the wisest, most accurate interpreter of The Great Spirit. The Sihu Tribe's goal is to maintain the balance and harmony of all life, and to live under the PureLight Order. They are in service to all. The Sihu Tribe is one of the two, out of nine, remaining PureLight Tribes left in Ohm Totem. The rest of the inhabitants on the island have become Dims."

The last of the writing disappeared as soon as Coda finished reading the last sentence. The light continued to beam, but nothing else formed. He wondered what this gravestone-looking thing was and again, words appeared in the light.

"I am a tablet. I keep the record of Ohm Totem. I record information that passes from moon to moon in order to keep accurate knowledge of the past and present. The future, though, is not set in stone, so it isn't recorded until the future becomes the present. My function is to answer your questions based upon what is stored in my records. I am all-observing and mistake-free. Nothing passes through Ohm Totem without passing through me."

That's cool, thought Coda. He looked at Skint still sleeping quietly on the soft dirt. He eyed his soft dirt bed longingly. He was tired. He eyed the zytes above him and thought, *how am I supposed to sleep with the zytes on?*

The tablet then formed new words: "Zytes will help you sleep. They don't affect or disrupt your sleeping patterns like the sun would, if the sun remained here all day and all night long. Instead, the zytes emit a glow that penetrates whatever cycle is present in your brain. For example, if you're sleepy, then it promotes the sleeping cycle and you fall asleep quickly after you close your eyes. If you're awake, it will energize your wakefulness, giving you more energy throughout the day. The zytes, once sleep has been attained, will lower their glow, or sometimes turn off all together."

Good, thought Coda. He stared at the green light, waiting

for more words to appear. After several moments of nothing, Coda wondered what he should do next.

The light flashed and words quickly formed. "I'd suggest that you fall asleep. You have a big day scheduled tomorrow. Once asleep, your soul will re-energize your mind and your body. You'll need your energy, because tomorrow you'll start your training bright and early."

"Whoa," whispered Coda. The green light flashed off, leaving the air still and calm. Coda wondered if this place, Ohm Totem, could get any weirder. He walked over to his bed, then walked around it in a counter-clockwise circle three times. With his right paw in mid air, he stopped, perplexed by what he had just done. *Walking in circles? I'm just tired*, he told himself. *That must be why.* Letting it all go, Coda lay down and closed his eyes. In one breath, he drifted off to sleep.

∞

The zytes were off when Coda abruptly awoke. A sound in the room woke him and a sudden wave of nervous energy struck him in the gut like an arrow hitting a bullseye. However, it wasn't his nerves. It was someone else's.

He lifted his head and peered around the room. He could see everything. Unlike home, it was easy to see in the dark here. Maybe because he was a panther.

There was a sound near the door, taking his mind away from his newly found night vision.

Skint was up, staring upward, toward the middle of the door. The energy coming from Skint quickly changed from nervous to suspicious. Coda, sensing this, laid his head back down and closed his eyelids into small open slits, giving the impression that he was asleep. And just in time.

Skint spun around. He appeared upset and angry. He cautiously walked toward Coda.

Coda closed his eyes completely, once Skint was only a few feet away. He felt Skint sniff him up and down.

"C-coda?" whispered Skint.

Coda didn't move or make a sound.

"He's asleep," whispered Skint. "I can go."

He can go? Where's he going and who's he talking to?

"Yes. I'm positive. He's asleep," whispered Skint again.

Skint walked to the door and Coda cracked opened his eyes, seeing that Skint was definitely the only one there. He blew on the door, and quiet as a mouse, the door slowly rolled to the right. Skint stepped halfway out and checked to the left and right, making sure no one was around. Seeing it was clear, he walked into the hallway and the door quietly shut behind him.

Coda got up to follow him. He took a step forward and nearly lost his balance as his legs wanted to go back to sleep and recharge. He took another step, and fell on his side. It was a hard fall, but thanks to the cushion-like soil, he wasn't hurt at all. Coda groaned as he pulled himself back to his sleeping area. He closed his eyes, and again, with one breath, drifted off to his dreams.

Chapter 15

A knock on the door woke Zoey from a much needed night's sleep. She heard San yawn and stretch her wings. She looked over at Zoey, saying brightly, "It's time to get up. I'm excited!"

You seem to always be, thought Zoey.

Zoey got out of her nest to answer the knock at the door, but stopped when she heard San laughing. "It's just to wake us up. No one will be there."

"Won't Taregan be?" asked Zoey.

"No, it was the Spruce Hollow who knocked."

"The Spruce Hollow can knock? How?"

San pursed her beak in thought. She had never wondered about that before. She grinned and fluttered her wings. "I don't know. It's just what happens."

Mystified, Zoey hopped over to the open window. The dream echoed in her mind. She heard Crepus' voice hissing, *You don't realize what she's going to do to us, do you?* Her feet tingled with fear. Then she realized her feet were sore, bringing her back to the present. She shook them, hoping to relieve some of the pain, but it didn't help.

Zoey gazed out of the window to take her mind off of her hurting feet. The sun was rising just over the horizon and the blue sky looked as cheerful as ever. The green grass and foliage below held morning dew and the wind lifted the scent of flowers and herbs to her nostrils. There were animals of all kinds walking north, to who knows where, and birds flying in the same direction.

"Yup!" yelled San, startling Zoey. She tore her gaze away from the beautiful view.

San hopped over to Zoey, wrapping a wing around her. "They're off to training," she chirped, pulling Zoey toward the door. "We've got to catch up with them. We can't miss it. This is amazing!"

San opened the door and birds of every kind—hawks, eagles, robins, blue jays, and many others—flew from the railings to the beautiful red wood floor. "Follow me," sang San. She spread her wings, gliding effortlessly toward the ground.

Zoey opened her wings, then hesitated and closed them. *What if I forgot how to fly?*

"I'll catch you if I must," echoed a voice from below. It was Taregan. He stood next to the entrance with his wings folded in front of him, tapping his foot impatiently against the floor. "Well, what's the hold-up?"

Zoey spread her wings out. "I'm coming," she said in a faint whisper.

Taregan cupped his wing near his ear. "What? You better start speaking up or you won't start speaking up! Some day you'll find yourself in a singing predicament. And you don't want that! You'll think, 'should I sing or should I not?'"

What does that mean? I think, maybe, he's a little crazy.

Zoey cleared her throat, lifted her wings, and called out with false confidence, "I'm coming!"

She jumped over the railing, and to her astonishment, glided easily to the ground, next to Taregan. San was there, waiting impatiently for her.

That was easy.

"Well," Taregan beamed, unfolding his wings, "that was easy."

"That's what I just said," replied Zoey.

Taregan tapped his temple a couple of times. "No, that's what *I* said. You only thought it."

Zoey was puzzled. *Did I only think that?*

"I'm not as crazy as I seem," Taregan quipped, tapping his foot again.

"Let's go," San said eagerly. She grabbed Zoey's wing, rushing her out the door.

Outside was refreshing, filling Zoey's body with energy after just a few deep breaths. She was awake, happy, and vibrantly alive again. She let out a contented sigh, then focused her attention to the east. Many animals were walking from that direction, but far off in the distance she could hear spirit

147

animals singing the most beautiful of melodies. *Is that over at the beach where Chev lives?* Her wings longed to take her there. She felt she belonged in the melodies of that music. She wanted to sing with them, but decided it would be best to follow San so she didn't get lost.

She took a couple of steps and found the ground to be a little wet, but refreshingly so. Zoey walked northward, feeling the drops of dew soaking into her feet, making her once sore feet feel good again. They walked in blissful silence behind the many spirit animals in front of them.

San broke the silence by confiding in Zoey, "I'm going to do my best to be like Nova someday." She took a deep breath, lifted her beak, and puffed up her chest. "San the VioletLight!"

Zoey simply nodded. She had no desire to be anything in this land. She just wanted to do her mission and get home. *I miss Mom and Dad.*

"How come you hesitated before you flew down from the balcony?" asked San. "You acted as if you had never flown before. I acted that way when I first started using my wings, but you're older than I am."

Zoey was a little embarrassed. "I'm not from here. I've only been here for a day."

"Where are you from? The Dim Lands? That's okay if you are. Some of them come over here and become PureLights once again. I've seen it. But," she peered into the crystal that was ingrained in Zoey's forehead, "you don't have Dim colors. Are you from the Zola Tribe?"

Zoey shook her head. "I'm from the Cornell Forest."

"Huh?" San skipped over a small rock. "Is that near Zola Tribe?"

Zoey looked to the west, pointing toward the Sihu Forest. "It's through a portal, or something like that. The portal is over there."

San flapped her wings and lifted off. She hovered high above Zoey.

"What are you doing?" asked Zoey.

"I'm looking for the portal. What does it look like? Does it look like a door?"

"It's through the blackberry bushes." Again, Zoey pointed to the west.

San looked toward the west. "I don't—" She abruptly closed her eyes and her body went limp. She began spinning toward the ground, but then suddenly opened her eyes again and started flapping her wings. She brought herself into a hover.

Shocked, Zoey ran underneath San, just in case she needed to catch her if she fell again. "Are you alright?"

"Yeah." San slowly floated toward the ground. "I don't know what happened. I was just—" And for the second time, San's eyes unexpectedly shut and her body plummeted. Zoey gasped, expecting to have to catch her, but just before she landed in Zoey's outstretched wings, San regained consciousness and recovered.

Shaken, San slowly lowered herself to the ground. Her legs gave way and she fell straight on her rump, ruffling her tail feathers.

Numee, who had witnessed the whole thing, rushed over to San. Numee's raccoon eyes were worried and suspicious. She looked around wildly, as if trying to find a certain someone in the crowd. Not finding what or who she was looking for, Numee touched San's back with both paws, then closed her eyes, slowing her breathing to long, deep breaths.

Zoey then witnessed something strange. Something she'd never seen before. A slight haze of white light came down from the sky, entering the top of Numee's head. The light surrounded both Numee and San. It wasn't bright, but yet she could still see it. Numee's green crystals started to glow brighter and brighter, creating a green halo effect around Numee's chest and head.

Numee took one last breath before the white light receded back up into the sky. "There," exclaimed Numee.

San opened her eyes. She looked refreshed. "What happened to me up there? It felt like all my strength was sucked out of me, and then a few moments later, my strength would come back."

Numee scanned the passers-by warily. "We have a traitor in our midst." She walked around Zoey and San, surveying more, then stopped. "I've seen it before. It's a tactic the Dims use. They steal your energy, taking it as their own. However, it's very rare when someone can take your energy to the point that you pass out and then regain your composure a few moments later. That means someone is stealing and giving back. Very odd." She glanced around again. "Whoever it is, he or she is very, very powerful."

Numee turned toward Zoey. "You're Zoey, right?"

Zoey suddenly felt a pang of insecurity, being put on the spot like that. She wondered if Numee thought she caused this. Was she in trouble? Zoey looked to the ground and murmured, "Yeah, I'm Zoey."

Zoey felt a paw underneath her beak. It gently lifted Zoey's head. She saw Numee's motherly gaze. "Zoey, here in the Sihu Tribe we enjoy being spoken to." She nodded once to Zoey with reassurance, asking, "Do you understand?"

Zoey nodded as Numee continued. "You are one of us. There's no need to feel shy or insecure around here. Your voice is beautiful—speak up. So, in every moment from this point forward, you have our permission to feel secure, compassionate, and strong. Practice that every day." Numee gazed into Zoey's eyes. "I want you to tell yourself, 'I'm secure, compassionate, and strong'."

Zoey mimicked her, saying, "I'm secure, compassionate, and strong." She felt a little weird and hoped no one else was listening.

"Wonderful," replied Numee. Her eyes were proud, like a mother watching her child successfully perform something new. Zoey felt drawn to her, just like she did with her own mother.

"Okay you two," Numee pointed to San and Zoey. "Follow me. I don't want you flying right now. Not until we can get you to the Wing's and Paw's training meadow."

They followed Numee to Deer Meadow. On the way, Zoey noticed a large zebra standing next to a small maple tree. The grass was lush all around him. She saw the zebra's feet shift slightly when he glanced at them. A squirrel stood next to him. The zebra leaned down to the squirrel and whispered

150

something. Zoey sensed, and she could tell Numee did as well, that these two were holding a secret.

The zebra realized that Zoey, San, and Numee were staring with interest and quickly hushed the squirrel just as it was about to speak. They looked at Zoey with sullen eyes and fake smiles.

Numee laughed, "Don't mind them. They spend their time trying to recruit other spirit animals. It's silly."

"For what?" asked Zoey.

"They want to create a government. They think it will be the best way to stop the Dims." As they walked past them, Zoey sensed another feeling. She didn't know what it was, but it didn't feel right. She looked back at them with innocent eyes. The Zebra smiled even wider, but the squirrel, for some reason, looked baffled.

"Why are they looking at me like that?" Zoey asked.

"Who knows?" replied Numee.

San flapped her wings wildly, but kept her feet on the ground. "We're about there!" She nudged Zoey, "Are you ready?"

Zoey didn't reply. She felt apprehension run through her body. *What am I getting myself into?*

Up ahead was Deer Meadow and they were heading straight for the Snow Tree. Sitting near the Snow Tree were what looked to be forty or so animals of all types and sizes. They must be some of the students, waiting for something. And there, right next to the tree, stood a tall elephant. Was it Chev? When she saw her brother next to him, she knew it was Chev.

"Coda!" screamed Zoey. Her excitement startled both San and Numee. She flew ahead of them, forgetting Numee's orders not to fly, landing happily next to her brother.

Coda grinned, "Hey Zoey." He dug his claws back and forth into the soft earth. "What do you think of all this?"

Before Zoey could answer, Chev patted her back with his trunk. "Hey little lady! How are you this fine sunny morning?"

She looked up into Chev's friendly eyes, "I'm good." And, it was true. It felt good to be with her brother again.

"It's your first day of school. Are you nervous?" asked Chev.

Zoey shrank back a little. She disliked the sound of "school." "I don't know. What do we do?"

"Well, you walk over there where the other animals and birds are. You know, the Wings and the Paws. You take a place among them and viola! You learn."

"Learn what?" asked Coda.

A woman's voice made Zoey twirl around. "The Art of Defense. I'll be leading the Paws today." It was Nova. The sparkle of lights glistened around her as she bowed. "Are you two ready to start?"

"I am!" came a voice behind Nova. It was San. She was walking with Numee.

Numee looked serious. "Nova? Can I talk to you after the training?"

"What's the matter, Numee?"

Numee nodded, "Nothing we can't handle."

"Shall we talk now?"

"It can wait."

Nova brushed her tail against Numee's fur. "Keep calm, Numee. The children are safe because of you." Nova gestured her tail toward the Snow Tree. "San! Coda! Zoey! This way, please."

∞

"The Art of Defense has nothing to do with fighting," began Nova. She sat on a small mound in front of the Snow Tree. "It's a non-violent technique to keep you from being harmed, and to guide your opponent away from you."

Zoey watched from the back row of animals as Nova gave the lesson and her thoughts began to wander. Coda sat to Zoey's left and San sat to her right. Chev was nowhere to be seen. She had no idea where he'd disappeared to. Still, he's a bard and no doubt had different things to do. *But really, what's a bard again?*

Nova made eye contact with each of the students as she spoke. "The Art of Defense is a form of calm, self-control. It allows you to control your opponent, or several opponents, at

152

once. It allows you to control a situation before a severe or deadly incident may occur. If your opponent does perish, even after you've mastered this Art, know that it came only as a last resort in the defense of your own life. That's your right as a living Being according to the PureLight Order—the right to protect yourself."

Nova paused. She closed her eyes, turning her head toward the sky, as if receiving information from an unknown source. Then, opening her eyes, she continued by saying, "I'm here to teach you how to master this art. You all have it within you, having been placed in your heart the moment you were born. It's a form of love, and even the Dims are born with this, but they have forgotten how to use it. I'm here to give you the directions to find it within yourselves, and instructions of what to do once it's found."

Zoey could feel the hearts of many spirit animals around her tighten when Nova mentioned the Dims. She sensed that none of the students had ever faced a Dim. To them, the Dims were unknown—something to be scared of. Zoey's heart clutched when she remembered the lion and the two coyotes. *They were scary.* She realized that she also feared the Dims.

"The Dims never develop this art," continued Nova. "Instead, they learn fear and become fighters. The love inside of them gets lost. Forgotten."

Zoey looked around at the many animals and birds in the gathering. They were all attentive, looking pleased to be receiving this knowledge from Nova. Some even looked grateful. Then, a sudden urge rose in Zoey's heart, pulling her in the direction of Nova, who was staring benevolently at her, as if waiting for her mind to wander back to her direction. Nova nodded at Zoey when she made eye contact, and continued the lesson.

"If a severe incident develops, then you've momentarily lost control. We'll teach you how to gain it back.

"Your opponent," continued Nova as she gazed off into the distance, toward the northern Fog, "deserves neither punishment nor death, no matter what the situation." She looked intently at her students. Everyone was quiet, and all ears were pointed in her direction.

Zoey shook her head. That didn't sound right.

No injuries? Then what were all those dead and knocked out birds lying on the ground doing if they weren't injured? They fell from the sky and hit the ground. That had to hurt. Zoey, again, wondered what she had gotten herself into.

"Sometimes injuries, and even death, can occur." Explained Nova, as if reading Zoey's thoughts. "But if it can be avoided, then do so. Never, and I repeat, never do we end the life of a Dim unless it's absolutely unavoidable. Remember, war is unpredictable. Death occurs on both sides, even if the intent is otherwise."

After a moment, she continued by saying, "There is no winner and there is no loser in the Art of Defense. If you think you've won or lost, then you've entered into the minefield of your own thoughts—the minefield where doubt, judgment, and competition live. Once entered, the Art of Defense disappears from your heart, and fighting enters. Our goal is to avoid fighting. Fighting only brings more fighting, creating a never-ending circle of pain and fear. Our goal is peace. And peace may never be attained by being the aggressor."

Nova paused again, scanning the students. "Fighting cannot eliminate fighting, period, and never has. Only peace can. Just like darkness cannot give light to darkness. Only one thing can give light to darkness—light. Fear cannot eliminate fear. Only love, the most powerful force in the universe, can. Don't expect to heal a spiteful person by returning spite. It doesn't work that way. Peace, love, and forgiveness are the most powerful weapons you possess. If you don't continually use these powerful weapons, then you'll have an angry attitude with a short lifespan.

"We use these weapons like a dance. Your opponent is your dance partner. You simply lead the dance, not because you're a better spirit animal, but because you know the dance steps and they do not."

Zoey was bored and nudged Coda's shoulder. "What is she talking about? This is dumb."

"Shush. I'm listening."

Zoey shuffled her feet back and forth, giving her something to do.

"Zoey?" called Nova's voice, arching over the crowd in front of her.

Zoey's head jolted up and pang of anxiety hit her chest. Did she do something wrong?

"Do you have a question?"

Zoey held her breath, quickly shaking her head "no".

San raised a wing.

Nova grinned, "Yes, San?"

San stepped forward and puffed her chest feathers. Zoey could tell she wanted to feel powerful and confident in front of Nova. She wanted to impress her. San cleared her voice with a couple of 'ahems'.

"Zoey's a little shy, so it's hard for her to speak her thoughts in front of other people." San then pursed her beak, "No, no, no. That's not right. I think she doesn't speak her mind to older people. I think she's fine with her friends—those who are the same age as her."

San nudged Zoey, whispering, "Come on. Tell her."

Zoey, feeling singled out as all eyes in the audience were now on her, nudged San back. "What did you do that for?"

San seemed puzzled, as if suddenly realizing that Zoey didn't want San or anybody else talking about her. "Didn't you just ask the black panther kid over there, 'what's she talking about?'"

Zoey nodded, "Yes, but you don't need to tell everyone."

"Okay, sorry," San whispered back, then gestured with her wing to Nova. Then she said to Zoey, "Anyway, ask Nova your question and she'll explain it to you in a way you'll understand."

Zoey, embarrassed, looked down at the ground. Her cheeks flushed red, but her feathers hid the fact. "I...um...I don't understand what you're saying."

Her voice was quiet and, like usual, she mumbled.

Nova leaped off the mound. "Everyone, speak amongst yourselves. I'll be but a moment."

Nova approached Coda, San, and Zoey with a determined

look. She padded around the crowd, glancing over her left shoulder. "Chev!" Chev came bounding around the Snow Tree, tripping over a large root, falling hard onto his chin. He skidded to a halt a couple of yards away from Nova.

The crowd paused and silence filled the meadow, then laughter erupted and cheering ensued. Chev's brows rose, surprised by the sudden cheer. He gathered himself and stood up, shaking off the dirt, simultaneously bowing for his audience. "Thank you all. Thank you all. The entertainer has arrived, but must keep it short. I have other duties to attend. Mingle amongst yourselves." With that, he dipped his head and held it there for a long applause. Once the cheering dissipated, he walked over to Nova.

"Was that a nice entrance?" he asked her.

"As clumsy as ever," Nova replied. "It changed the energy of the students and for that, I thank you, even if it wasn't your intent. Now we need to help the energy of one of our friends here. She's comfortable around you, so I thought your presence would help her."

Zoey almost gasped out loud when Nova pointed a paw at her. Zoey blinked a couple times. *What did I do?*

"Zoey?" Nova tilted her head like most spirit animals did in Ohm Totem. "San made a wonderful point. She noticed that you talk liberally and confidently amongst friends, but not in front of elders."

San beamed from Nova's recognition and Zoey shrugged her shoulders. *What's so wrong with that?* With that thought, the Snow Tree entered her mind, saying, *Remember, Zoey, that the sun's warmth and brightness are like you. You were created just like the sun. You are here to shine. Everyone would feel the wonderful qualities of the sun in you if you showed them how bright you truly are.*

"That's true," said Nova.

"What's true?" wondered Zoey.

"What the Snow Tree says."

"Oh," Zoey innocently looked up at Nova, "can you hear her, too?"

"I can, but most here in Ohm Totem can't. There have been

many moons of struggle and they've forgotten how to listen. You, however, will always hear. You were born to listen. It's a gift."

Zoey looked at Coda. He was sitting quietly next to her, watching Zoey and Nova speak. Chev and San remained quiet as well. She had the feeling that she was being ganged up on. A flame of anger rose in her belly and she eyed her feet. "Well, Coda can hear the Snow Tree, too." Her voice was low, barely audible.

Nova slowly shook her head. "Only when you're around. You enhance that ability in him."

Coda's eyes widened, "Really?"

"Yes, really. Now, Zoey, I want you to close your eyes and focus on your heart," Nova continued.

Zoey closed her eyes. She felt anger welling up inside of her, but with a couple of more breaths it slowly started to fade away. She focused her thoughts on her heart, and felt it pumping and pulsing blood through her veins.

"Do you feel that?" asked Nova.

"Feel what?"

"Your heart."

"Yes," replied Zoey, keeping her eyes closed.

"What do you feel?"

Zoey shrugged, murmuring, "Um... it's pumping kinda fast."

Zoey could feel Nova nod, prodding her to explain more.

"I think..." she tightened her eyelids in concentration. "Yeah, I feel the blood flowing to my wings and stuff."

After a brief pause, Nova spoke. "Concentrate a little more."

Zoey squeezed her eyes even tighter.

"Take a slow, deep breath," instructed Nova.

Zoey slowly inhaled, and on the exhale, her eyelids eased up, relaxing the rest of her body. Zoey could feel her brother and friends around her watching with intense interest. She pushed that feeling away, realizing it was taking her away from feeling her body. Then she took another deep breath, and as she let it out she felt the blood coursing through her veins, down to her feet. But, it didn't stop there. She felt it flow from

157

her toes into the ground, like roots reaching deep into the earth and soil. There she followed cracks in the earth's crust, going down, deeper and deeper. Then everything opened up. *Clouds?* She was floating downward, descending slowly through a mist of clouds. *Where am I?*

Passing through the clouds, she could see that the sky was blue all around her. Beneath her was a beach. The ocean slammed waves against the shore. Peering down, she noticed an object lying on the beach shining a golden light back at her. *What's that?*

Instantly, her vision expanded, showing her what it was— The Golden Opus.

She now knew where she was. In the heart of Ohm Totem.

Zoey glanced around as she continued to descend, and felt the wind lightly touching her feathers. It felt good. "Look up!" she heard a voice say.

Zoey looked up, but saw nothing but clouds and more blue sky. Then she noticed something peculiar off in the distance—a stairway!

The stairway was set against a large red cliff, built out of the cliff's own rock. The cliff was so immense that the clouds hid the top of the stairway from view. Below, the stairs vanished into the canopy of lush forest that went on for miles. A large patch of snow covered a thicket of brush and trees way off in the distance as well, reminding her of the snow dream with Lao last night.

Why am I here?

With that thought, a rush of energy went through her and she inhaled sharply. She opened her eyes, and there standing before her were Chev, San, Coda, and Nova. Coda looked a little concerned.

Zoey blinked her eyes several times, asking, "How did I get down there?"

"Get down where?" asked Coda. He looked at Nova. "Is she okay?"

"Yes. She just went to another place."

Coda had no idea what Nova meant. Zoey gawked at everyone, and then stammered, "H-how did I do that?"

158

"It's called listening. Many spirit animals take thousands of moons to learn what you just did in one attempt. You have the ability to listen to all of life. And, you do so by listening to your heart, and then expanding your awareness outwardly. It's an ability within everyone. However, you just know how to do it, without practice. It's quite amazing."

"Oh," replied Zoey. She didn't know what else to say.

"Your ability doesn't stop there, Zoey." Nova's blue eyes shone, lighting up her beautiful fur. "Your voice is enchanting, but you hide it. Why?"

"Enchanting?"

"It's delightful, with a touch of magic."

Zoey replied while covering her mouth, "I don't know about that."

"Maybe some day you will know," replied Nova. "Until then, I must get back to the students. We'll be splitting up. The Wings will go to the Sihu Forest and the Paws to Deer Meadow by the Large Boulder." She licked Zoey on the cheek. "Thank you for allowing me to help you today."

"Sure," Zoey muttered. She didn't know how any of that helped. She felt very uncomfortable. She felt as if something was being expected from her. But what? It was something that she felt she didn't have.

Why do they care about how I talk, anyway? Who cares! A wave of frustration overcame her. She suddenly just wanted to be left alone.

Nova gestured for Coda to follow her. "Come with me. I'll be training the paws today." Coda nodded. "And Zoey, I'd suggest taking the day off. Go back and rest in the Spruce Hollow, if you feel you must."

Zoey liked that idea and nodded.

"Stay and train with me, Zoey!" San was standing with her wings pointing to the sun. "We can train together. We can be training partners."

Zoey shook her head no. She wanted to be left alone. She wanted to think.

San persisted, "Come on, Zoey, I need a partner."

Zoey looked at Nova for approval. Nova tipped her head to

the left, indicating for Zoey that it was okay if she left the training. Zoey looked down and twisted her foot back and forth in the dirt. "I'm sorry, San, but I just want to go back to Spruce Hollow. I'll be your partner tomorrow maybe?"

San's wings sunk and her head dropped. "Okay, I understand." She sulked off toward the Sihu Forest for Wing Training.

Zoey felt bad. She wanted to help her friend, but she also felt she should do what Nova suggested. She watched San disappear into the crowd, then turned back toward the Spruce Hollow. A pang of sadness spread through her. She suddenly missed her mom, her toys, her dad, and watching her brother build Lego cities. She missed everything that was familiar to her.

She turned around and watched Coda. He stood proudly next to Nova. He seemed to be in his element, and was strangely interested in this Art of Defense. He was interested in Ohm Totem, a world she knew nothing about. They did everything so differently here. They talked to her like she was equal to them. They could move things with their thoughts.

Turning back around, walking toward the Spruce Hollow, she heard Nova bellow, "Wings, follow Kaya! Paws, follow me!"

Chapter 16

Coda landed hard on his back. He twisted to his left, dodging a swipe. A thud sounded next to him, telling Coda that the bobcat missed, but was inches from hitting him. He slowly backed away from his opponent and crouched low, waiting to spring at any moment. The bobcat swiped at Coda's face. Coda ducked, and put up his paws to block the next swipe, only to feel the bobcat gently slap him on the side. She was tricky and fast.

"Stop!" called Nova.

The students surrounding Coda and the bobcat took several steps backward as Nova wove her way through the crowd of students, stepping between Coda and his opponent. "Coda, you're fighting. The Art of Defense has nothing to do with fighting. It's a dance."

She circled around him, saying, "Remember, the tactics in a fight are linear." She brought one paw up in front of her, moving it forward in a perfect line, indicating 'straight ahead'.

"The tactics in a fight are clawing, tackling, wrestling, biting, and blocking, none of which are the Art of Defense. When you block an attack it interrupts the force of your opponent. That may sound like something you would want to do, but that's not so." She moved her paw in a circle to demonstrate. "The Art of Defense is circular. You want to use the full force of their own movement against them." She put her paw down. "When they come at you, dance with their movement. Help them move past you. Do what we've been practicing."

She nodded her head to the bobcat. The bobcat nodded back and Nova crouched slightly, readying for an attack. In a flash, the bobcat dashed at her, extending her claws for what looked to be a quick and deadly strike. As the force of the attack came toward Nova, she moved to the side, circling both front paws down upon the bobcat's swiping paw, sending the bobcat somersaulting forward at twice her attacking speed.

Coda couldn't help but join in the "whoas" coming from the rest of the students. That was amazing, he thought. Before he could form another thought, the bobcat leaped at Nova with her claws out, teeth bared. Nova quickly moved backward, circling to her left, letting the bobcat land on nothing but grass and weeds.

Determined, the bobcat twisted, jumping at her again, but Nova was ready. In a crouched position, Nova waited until the bobcat was almost on top of her before she fell softly onto her back, allowing the bobcat to pin her front legs on the ground. Before the bobcat could plant her hind legs on Nova's belly, Nova let the full weight of the bobcat's front paws land on her before kicking the bobcat's hind legs toward the sky, hitting her just under the belly, flipping the bobcat onto her back.

In what seemed to be faster than a blink of an eye, Nova was now standing on top of the bobcat, holding the bobcat's forepaws against the ground.

Nova turned to the students, and then at Coda. "At this point, I'd use an advanced technique to stun my opponent."

Coda furrowed his brow. *Stun the opponent?*

"You haven't learned how to stun an opponent yet. That comes later," Nova said.

Nova looked around the clearing at the many students waiting their turn to spar. "The Art of Defense is fluid and powerful, much like a whirlpool," she instructed them.

Coda remembered when he and his sister had walked around the edges of a swimming pool, doing their best to create a whirlpool. He quickly realized that analogy didn't help him. *How can a whirlpool defeat anyone?*

Nova climbed to a higher position a few yards in front of the Large Boulder. "Now, begin your practice!"

They practiced holding a low, balanced stance and moving out of the way when the opponent attacked. If the opponent attacked left, the defender dodged right. If the opponent attacked right, the defender dodged left. It was simple. Basic.

They were taught to avoid the attack, rather than block or fight back. To Coda, it all seemed the opposite of what you're supposed to do. You're supposed to fight back and stand your ground. But not here with the PureLights. This all seemed too wimpy. Cowardly. He wanted action. He wanted fun.

Nova eyed the bobcat from her high position. "Muna, your act as a Dim is excellent. Keep it up."

"Thank you, Nova." Muna bowed.

Coda had learned that Muna was also a teacher. Today, she was helping Nova. Nova said that Muna was one of the best defenders in all of Ohm Totem, a master at the Art of Defense. Coda wanted to prove Nova wrong.

Coda came back to the moment when Muna's indigo crystals brightened and she scuffed the grass with her claws, ready for another sparring practice with Coda. She was the opponent, acting as a Dim and he was the defender. This is how it had gone all day.

He looked into her eyes and Muna stared back intently. He could see anger in them, and even though it was only an act, it was still intimidating.

She growled, and then leaped. Coda's stomach about fell out and his eyes practically popped out of his head from fright. He jumped to his left, spinning around as she passed him. Surprised that she missed, and even more surprised that he was quick enough to move out of the way, Coda swiped with an outstretched paw, glancing the bobcat's nubby tail.

Muna spun around, narrowing her eyes. "Do that again and I'll be feeding you to Crepus!"

"Huh?" stammered Coda. The words were cruel. He never thought PureLights talked like that. It caught him off guard and Muna jumped at him, pummeling him to the ground, pinning his forepaws above his head. She growled at him, showing her sharp, white teeth.

"Stop!" Nova ordered, as she strode over to them. She studied Coda as he lay pinned on the ground. "Do you see what's happened?"

Coda nodded a yes.

"You're fighting again. You danced for a moment, but the

moment didn't last. Swiping at Muna used your energy against yourself. It slowed you down. It helped take your focus off the opponent's moves, onto your opponent's words."

She glanced at Muna. "Thank you for the demonstration. You can release him now."

"Oh, yeah," replied Muna. She grinned at Coda. "You're a tough one. Once you get this down, everything else gets a little easier."

"I hope so," Coda said with uncertainty as he slowly stood up, shaking the grass and dirt from his fur. He took a deep breath and sat on his hind legs.

Nova addressed all of the students. "The Art of Defense is not about strength. The smallest bird who has mastered the art can take down a bear with a single move. Keep in mind that it's about controlling your opponent and, inevitably, about controlling the situation. If the situation is out of control, then violence can occur.

"Coda, please join me for a conversation. The rest of you, please keep practicing."

The students nodded and Coda padded toward Nova with his head hung low. He was a little ashamed. Why couldn't he just dodge and duck instead of fight? He was quick, but his reflexes became reactionary. He seemed to punch and block, without doing it on a conscious level.

How did I defend myself so well against the Coyote?

The River Ohm raged next to the Large Boulder, bringing a heavy breeze that ruffled Coda's fur. He stood in front of Nova with his head down.

"I'm right here, Coda. I'm not the grass under your paws."

He looked up with an embarrassed grin and saw that Nova was smiling. This relaxed him. He felt like an equal in the moment, not beneath her. She gestured for him to follow her. They walked to the edge of the river and stared into the wind. The twinkle of light danced off the water rapids in front of them.

As they sat in silence, Coda thought about the coyote that had fled from him the day before saying, 'It's him!'

Nova peered across the rapids. "Yesterday, Coda, you were

focused."

Coda nodded. *I was focused? How does she know?*

"When you're focused, Coda, not even a coyote, a lion, nor Crepus Dim has a chance against you." She shook her head at the river. "The river is high today."

"Why did the Coyote say, 'It's him'?" asked Coda.

"What do you mean?"

"When the coyote ran away, he said 'It's him'. They were talking about me."

"You look and defend like Orion. You do a lot of things that remind us of Orion. He was a black panther, just like you."

"Who's Orion?" A splash of water landed on Coda's nose, tickling it.

"Orion was one of the few VioletLights in Ohm Totem, just like me. He had mastered his life, and was very aware and awake to The Great Spirit. He was the first to see Crepus for who he really was. Orion and his tribe were the first to challenge Crepus." Nova pointed her nose toward the north. "It ended in bloodshed."

"What happened?"

"Orion's tribe, the Ionna Tribe, was destroyed, caught off guard by the Dim's violent techniques. Orion came out unscathed, but his tribe was lost. Many were taken and turned into Dims. Many others died under the claws of Crepus and his minions. Orion came to me shortly afterwards and explained everything that happened. He taught us the Art of Defense. He knew it was one of the only things that could help us, but he hadn't fully learned it until after his tribe was decimated to nothing. He claimed he had learned it from The Great Spirit.

"He vowed to protect the rest of the tribes in Ohm Totem. He ran from tribe to tribe, doing his best to teach what he knew. Those tribes that fully learned the technique were the only ones who survived—the Sihu and the Zola Tribe. However, before we mastered the Art of Defense, many of our tribe-mates perished in battle."

Nova looked down at her paws, saddened by this memory. "Orion left Ohm Totem nearly five thousand moons ago. Crepus claimed that he killed Orion, but it's not true. I know

165

that Orion left, but for what reason, I don't know. He was there the night I interpreted the Windstorm Prophecy. I didn't see him, but found his fresh tracks next to the Sihu Forest. I looked for him for many moons, but I couldn't find him." Nova looked intently at Coda. "Until now."

Wow, thought Coda. He wanted to meet this amazing VioletLight. "Where is he?" asked Coda.

"He's done something none of us have done before, but how he did it and why, I don't yet understand."

Confused, Coda asked, "Done what?"

"He entered life as a human, rather than as a PureLight." She shook her head, "How he did that and what he sought as a human is a mystery to me."

She peered deeply into his eyes. "What I do know is that his name is now Coda."

Coda's head snapped back. *Me?*

"Yes, you. And if Crepus finds out, you'll be targeted. He's intelligent. He'll figure it out some day. Hopefully, not soon. We must get you to remember what you once taught us. You remembered your teachings when you faced the coyote. Just tap into that memory and go from there, alright?"

Coda was stunned. "Me? How could I be Orion?"

Nova didn't reply. Her placid demeanor didn't lesson the shock that ran through his veins as his mind went in circles. This couldn't be. Could it? He tried to remember his life back at the Cornell Forest, but his mind was too hazy, too amped up with excitement and bewilderment.

Coda shook his head, "I don't know. I think I'm just Coda."

"What if you did know?"

"Huh?" replied Coda.

"What if you did know? What if you knew you were Orion? Then what?"

Coda's brows furrowed and he bit his lower lip, "I guess I'd know how to do the Art of Defense?"

"Yes, you would."

Coda looked at her with a blank expression. "Well, I don't know the Art of Defense."

Nova tapped her tail on his back. "You do."

"But, if I was Orion, then I'd remember it, right?"

"That's right."

Coda nodded, "Okay. But I don't remember it." He giggled. He was beginning to think this conversation was silly. He wasn't Orion. That much he knew. "So, I'm not Orion." How could Orion become him? That didn't make sense. Was Nova playing a game with him? A game he didn't know how to play?

"Are you sure you don't remember the Art of Defense?" Nova's tone was a little sarcastic, but not in a way that poked fun, but in a way that stated she was a little surprised. She curled her tail around his shoulders.

He began to speak, then stopped. He was going to tell her that he didn't remember anything and never would, when suddenly a memory flashed in his mind. It wasn't a memory of Orion. It was a memory of yesterday, when he had faced the coyote. He remembered how he'd turned into something more confident and more skilled than he'd ever been before. The Art of Defense was an extension of himself. It was easy. He controlled every aspect of his opponent, turning the situation from certain death into a group of fleeing Dims.

Nova slowly nodded her head. Coda could tell she knew his thoughts. Coda's expression changed and he lit up.

"Yesterday!" he blurted out. He dug his claws into the grass. "How did I know how to do that? I've never done anything like that before."

"Ah, but you have," Nova smiled. "Just remember who you are, and everything will make sense." She turned and strode away, leaving Coda to stare at the river alone.

The water danced with the rays of sun as it sparkled off the rapids. *Remember who I am? What does that mean? I'm just Coda—aren't I?*

A gust of wind blew and the long grass beside him brushed his fur. He took in a deep breath and stood up. He froze. *What was that?*

He glimpsed movement in the tall grass on the other side of the river. A second later it stopped.

He sat back down, narrowing his eyes. There it was again. The grass rippled, as if someone or something moved through it. He wondered if it was the wind, but none of the grass on the other side of the river moved. It was just this clump.

Coda focused on the clump of grass some more. A fluff of fur emerged. Was that a tail, or some type of plant he'd never seen before? A plant that only grew in Ohm Totem? An instant later, the fluff of fur disappeared inside the clump, hiding it from view.

Coda lifted himself by standing only on his two hind feet to get a better view. Still, he couldn't see what was in the clump of grass. He gave up. What harm was it anyway? He gently dropped back down on all fours. As he turned to walk away, he heard a loud rustling sound over the churning rapids. A pitter-patter of small feet ran through the grass. He was still amazed by how well he could hear as a panther.

Quickly glancing back, he watched something shuffle and violently shake the grass. It was running north, directly for the Fog. A loud owl's shriek filled the sky and several owls lifted out of the trees that bordered the Fog. They flew down toward the shape, and Nova, as quick as a jet, ran past Coda, leaping over the wide river, landing softly on the other side.

How did she do that?

She dashed forward, in pursuit of whoever was running through the grass. Her reflexes and speed outmatched the small creature. Nearly to the Fog now, the small figure zigzagged through the long grass, trying to shake Nova. It wasn't working. Nova seemed to know its moves before it even knew its moves. She drew closer.

The owls dove, but did something that shocked Coda. They attacked Nova. Three of them grabbed her fur while the others fluttered in front of her, blocking her from the Fog. One owl was on her tail, another on her shoulder, and one on a hind leg. A moment later the Fog lifted and the small retreating figure was gone.

But Nova! She was being attacked, forced down by the owls. *Why would the PureLights attack a PureLight? Especially Nova?* Coda looked back at the meadow, hoping that Muna and the rest of the students were on their way to stop the owls. He saw that they were practicing the Art of Defense and had no idea that Nova was in trouble.

"Hey everyone!" yelled Coda. All heads turned. "Nova needs our help!"

Muna's eyes widened. She gestured for everyone to follow her, but Muna and the students were too far away. If Coda didn't do something now, then Nova might get hurt. He gazed over the river and saw Nova lying on the ground. Her head in her paws. She was facing the Fog. The owls stood around her.

Is she dead?

Coda jumped into the river without hesitation, splashing into the running rapids, feeling the warm water soothe his body. It was surprisingly warm, giving him a rush of energy that he didn't know he needed.

He soon realized that looking at the rapids from the shore was much different than being in the rapids. They seemed huge. As they bubbled around him he kicked his feet, doing his best to keep his head above water. A wave smashed against his head, pulling him under. He accidentally took a large gulp of water, and when he resurfaced a second later, let go a ferocious cough, only to go under again as another rapid pounded on top of him.

His back paws hit the bottom of the river and he pushed off, allowing him to lift higher than he would have. He took a deep breath, then raised his arms just as another wave crashed on top of him. He realized, however, that he didn't have arms. He had legs and paws and he wasn't used to using them as tools for swimming. Regardless, he doggy-paddled toward the opposite shore, determined to help Nova, but the river's current was too strong for him. His heart sank when he realized the current was taking him downstream. Then he heard yelling from the shore. It was Muna and the students.

Coda started to panic. Was he going to get out of here alive? He kicked hard with his back legs, but the water was relentless. It was pounding and it surged, pushing him further and further downstream. He paddled and paddled and closed his eyes, wishing himself to the other side.

That didn't work either.

Panic took over his body. His throat closed up and his

nerves shot icy adrenaline into his muscles. Instead of pushing him onward, the cold adrenaline anchored his thoughts to death. He wasn't going to make it. He felt his energy quickly draining with each struggling movement. There was no way to make it to the shore. He was stuck in the middle of a large, fast-moving river.

A splash against his face forced his eyes to open. He glanced left and right, realizing that he was gaining ground on the opposite shore, but hopelessly out of sight from Nova and the attacking owls. Determined, he pushed onward. *I've got to get to the shore!*

A slight change in the current pushed him to the left. And, under his hind paws, he felt the rocky river bottom. It was shallow and he was able to hold his footing. He slowly made his way to the shore, making sure that every paw step was steady before he took another.

"Do you need any help?"

It was Muna. Coda was surprised to see her, to say the least. She was standing on the shore a couple of feet from him.

"What? How..." Coda was too tired to say anything else as he stumbled onto the shore.

Muna gestured upstream. "It's very shallow just past the boulder where the rapids begin. I just walked across." She smiled and held out her paw. "Need a paw?"

Coda heard the crunch of pebbles beneath his paws, then shook his head no. He was on the shore now, inching his tired body toward the grass a few yards away. Reaching the grass, he fell on his side, and looked up at Muna. "Did you help Nova?"

She looked over her shoulder, then looked back. "Did she need help?"

Coda lifted his head, and stood up on shaky legs. "Yes. That's why I yelled. We've got to go. She's being attacked." His words were tired and barely audible.

"Let's have you rest, Coda."

Coda shook his head furiously. *Doesn't she care about Nova?*

Coda tried to stand up, taking several shaky steps forward.

A worried Muna followed his halting steps.

"Coda? Nova's just fine. You rest now, alright? I'll bring in some extra Prana so you can get your energy back."

Prana? wondered Coda. He shook his head. He must not have heard her clearly.

Muna gestured for Coda to sit down. He ignored her, deciding to drag himself further up the riverbank anyway. He was determined to find Nova.

Muna padded up to his side. "Please sit. You're not going to get far if you don't let me help you."

Coda's tail dragged on the rocky shore. "Nova's in trouble. We have to help her," he pleaded. His legs shook. He was drained of energy. Each breath felt like ice stabbing at his lungs. Panting hard, striving with each weak muscle at every step, he took a couple more steps. Finally, his legs gave out and he lost balance, falling flat onto his chest. He hugged the rocks in desperation, doing his best to push himself up. His eyes were half-closed with weariness.

Muna sniffed his head. "Good. Still alive." She smiled and gently admonished, "I warned you, Coda. If you let me bring some helpful Prana to you, then I could take the heavy burden of weak knees and shaky muscles away from you."

There was that word again, Prana. Curious, Coda turned his eyes toward Muna. "What's that?"

"What's what?"

"Prana?"

Muna seemed surprised by the question. "Are you serious?"

Coda gave a limp shrug. "Uh-huh."

"Good joke, Coda. You should be a bard. You're a good actor," she giggled.

Suddenly realizing that he was taking up valuable time in getting to Nova, he nodded his head in agreement. "I guess, give me some of that Prana? Where do you get it?"

Muna laughed again. "Yeah, you're in the wrong training. The Bards are definitely for you." She sat down and closed her eyes. She put her front paws on his back and took several deep breaths. Coda felt heat, and a lot of it, coming from Muna's paws. A moment later, he felt a tingling sensation accompanied by a feeling of calmness washing through him. He reactively took a deep breath, filling his body full of vibrant energy. His muscles strengthened, his mind cleared, and his body reacted with a couple of jolts. It was literally electrifying.

Muna took her hands off of him. "There. Feeling better now?"

Coda pushed up with one front leg, and then the other. He tested his back legs, bending them several times, then pushed them up as well. Standing, he bent both legs several more times. Good as new. In fact, everything felt better than ever!

He jumped up and down. "Whoa!" His eyes glowed with a joy and energy that he didn't have only moments prior. "How did you do that?"

"How do you think?" She pointed with her tail up shore. "Aren't you forgetting your heroic adventure to save your queen?"

Coda's eyes widened as he remembered Nova and dashed off as fast as he could. He rounded a corner, quickly turning, kicking up dirt behind him. He headed into the tree line, hoping to reach Nova quickly, if she wasn't dead already, and to cut off the owl attack where they wouldn't expect it.

The tree line was thick. In fact, if it weren't for the Fog only a few yards to his left, he'd think this tree line was more of a forest. It probably went on for miles on the other side of the Fog. In front of him was thick brush that crossed north into the Fog. It wasn't tall, so he sprinted as fast as he could, flexed his hind legs, and took a powerful leap over them.

"Argh!" he yelled. His front legs were extended, but instead of falling. he continued to ascend. He was twice as high as he imagined he'd be before he started to descend. *Is this how high Nova gets?* Then he wondered how he was going to land without hurting himself. The thought quickly diminished when he realized he was heading straight for a moss-covered tree. He curled his body in a fetal position, and closed his eyes. Moments later he heard a loud thump and saw lightning streak across his darkened vision. His legs went numb, then pain scorched through him. His limp body slid down the tree, making a big thud when he hit the forest floor.

Dazed and shaken, he opened his eyes to see Muna standing over him, again. She rolled her eyes, "Come on, hero. Let's get you up."

"How did I do that?"

"Yeah," Muna said, "I saw that. It was quite impressive. I've only seen Nova jump that high."

"Nova!" he remembered. He turned and ran, ignoring the sheering pain that engulfed his body. He had to get to Nova.

The trees blurred by him as he moved with precision and speed he never knew he had. He dodged large ferns, twirled around trees, and zig-zagged his way forward. He could tell he was outrunning Muna by far, even with pain stabbing at him.

Up ahead he could see a small opening in the trees and white fur through the gaps of foliage. *Nova!*

Coming closer to the opening, he could see her lying on her back with her forelegs stretched out wide. She wasn't moving.

Oh no!

He skidded to a halt, hiding behind a large tree as he stared at her. Her eyes were closed and the owls were gone. He looked up, just to make sure none were watching over her. He saw massive tree limbs, and light peering through the gaps, but no owls. Everything was silent, except for his aching body.

His heart started to beat faster. He'd never encountered anything that was dead, or at least up close, other than the usual bug here and there. He froze, not knowing what to do.

Suddenly he was shoved from behind, pushing him forward until he fell next to Nova. He landed on fresh fallen leaves.

"Sorry," came Muna's voice, "I came around the corner and didn't see you." She was standing over him, panting from trying to catch up.

Nova stirred. "Blessings."

She's alive?

Muna quietly giggled. "I think Coda here thought you were attacked by the Wing Watchers."

Wing Watchers? wondered Coda.

Nova stood up, looking at Coda blandly. "What would make you think that? I was just lying still and enjoying nature's silence."

Coda shrugged sheepishly. "I...I don't know." He felt embarrassed. She was fine. Of course she'd be fine. She's Nova.

Nova smiled in understanding. "The owls were holding me back from going into the Fog. They saw my determination and knew I wasn't going to stop. They were right."

"I thought they were attacking you."

"The owls are our Wing Watchers," replied Muna, "they'd never harm us. They warn us if Dims come through the Fog and they stop us from going through the Fog, as well. They protect us."

Nova walked over to the water's edge. She gestured with her head for them to follow. "A Dim snuck over to Sihu land and the Wing Watchers somehow missed him. He spied on us, then managed to escape. That's a powerful Dim. Nothing usually escapes the Wing Watchers' eyes."

"A Dim was here?" Muna repeated, somewhat mystified. She sniffed at a rock. "I don't smell a Dim."

"We spotted the Dim over there." Nova gestured upstream with her tail.

"Did you see who it was?"

"I didn't. It was fast, and disappeared into the Fog before I could get a good look."

Coda pushed a rock back and forth with his paw. "How come nobody else came when the owls shrieked?"

Nova walked near the river's edge. It was noisy and the water seemed full of rage, splashing against logs and branches and hitting boulders in the middle of the river. She bent her head and lapped some water. "The shriek was low-pitched. They were calling me. A high-pitched shriek means that we all get ready." She took another lap of water. "Coda, come and have some."

Coda walked over and lapped some water with her. Instantly, more life filled his bones, taking away the pain from hitting the tree.

Muna told Nova about Coda and his attempt to outmatch the rapids. Nova nodded, drinking some more water. She grinned, "You can't fight against nature and expect to win.

174

Next time you're fighting the rapids, just let go. Go with the stream. Something will always appear to help you, such as a rock, a log, a large branch hanging from a tree, one of us, or something else. The Great Spirit always lends a hand in moments of necessity, unless you choose otherwise."

Confusion pulsed through Coda. *That's impossible to do. How can you not panic in a time like that? It's natural. Everyone does.*

Muna joined them and lapped some water as well. She leaned against Coda, rubbing her fur against his. "I'm off to the students. And, Coda, what Nova says is true. Go with the stream. Keep in mind that it takes practice. It takes discipline to not panic." She sighed, "I'm always taking the words from you, Nova, but here's another one, 'When you panic, you choose otherwise.'" She licked both Coda's and Nova's cheek, then with a thrust of her hind legs took off along the shoreline. Looking back over her shoulder, she yelled, "Coda, you've got more Art of Defense to learn, so don't be long."

"I won't!"

Coda drank again and thoughts flooded his mind. How can he be calm when his friend is in trouble? He felt frustrated. He couldn't have gotten to Nova if he had let the stream take him all the way down the river. What if a rock didn't appear to help him? What if nothing came? Then he'd be going down the stream forever, probably drowning under the force of the rapids.

Nova, as usual, answered his unspoken thoughts. "The river always has a calm to it. It's not always rapids, you know." She scooted away from the river's edge, licking her paw. She rubbed it against the top of her head. "The 'what ifs' will drain you of experience and life. The 'what ifs' stop you from walking the path. They take you away from The Great Spirit and away from your mission in life. If you die, then you die, and the 'what ifs' did nothing to save you. They never do. They only hold you back, until you eventually die from a 'what if' like event."

She looked to the river. "We all have a mission in life, and a mission's greatest ally is knowing—knowing that everything will be fine, even if or when you die. Once you get that down, nothing will stand in your way. As I have told you, you and your sister are powerful Beings. If you follow your mission, and act with knowing, then nothing can stop you."

Coda's heart felt otherwise as his claws dug into the earth. "I'm not that powerful," he protested. "I couldn't get to you even though I was paddling as fast as I could."

Nova nodded. "I know what you did and thank you for that. I'll always remember your courage." She patted the top of his head. "And, I was trying to help you as well."

"You were?" The air sparkled around her and he felt the tranquility of calm energy flow from her to him. Instantly, his body felt at ease. *How does she do that?*

She leaned in and whispered into his ear. "It's very rare that I go after a Dim the way that I did today. I was trying to stop it from relaying a message."

Coda looked up from lapping some water. Little droplets dripped from his chin and back into the river. "What message?"

"That Orion the VioletLight is back."

Chapter 17

"I'm secure, compassionate, and strong," chanted Zoey as she walked to the Spruce Hollow. "I'm secure, compassionate..."

"It sounds like you've been talking with Numee."

The zebra stood under the same maple tree where Zoey had seen him before. The squirrel still sat next to him, and a large weasel was now with them.

Zoey stopped, squinting her eyes. The sun was high, beaming brightly, slightly blinding her from getting a better look at the three. She nodded her head, giving a barely audible 'yes' to them. They all leaned in to listen. The squirrel's eyes widened as he ran over in a fit of excitement, "I-I-I'm S-skint. I h-have a speech p-p-problem t-too!" He looked as if he wanted to jump into Zoey's wings to give her a big hug.

Zoey didn't think she had a speech problem. Or, did she? Regardless, she gave a friendly nod to Skint. He smiled and grabbed her wing, practically dragging her over to the zebra and weasel. He looked funny as he walked. He had three of his feet touching the ground and one pulling her wing.

The Zebra looked down at her calmly. He seemed like a dad—a stern and calm one. His voice was thick and heavy. He had an air of charm about him that drew her nearer. It was hypnotic.

He lowered himself, looking her square in the eyes. She noticed he had indigo crystals just like Taregan. "I'm Tasunke, but call me Ke." His eyes were determined, hard, almost as if he'd lived a tough life. "Does Nova think you have a speaking problem, too?" He looked over at Skint, "She's pegged him as having one. Right Skint?"

Skint vigorously nodded his head up and down, "She sh-sh-sure d-d-did." He stood on his back legs and folded his arms.

His eyes became heavy and rebellious, "I-I talk how I-I'm s-s-supposed to!"

Zoey felt a little odd, especially with that weasel staring at her. He seemed uncomfortable in the group, but at the same time, he made her feel the same way. He gave off a sense of anger, almost like a bully at school does. He spit on the ground. "I'm Piv. Call me Piv, okay?" His crystals were red like hers.

"Uh, okay." Zoey wanted to leave, but Skint gently held her wing. "We are n-n-nice."

Zoey nodded again. She didn't think that was entirely true.

"Don't take everything Numee and Nova say to heart," said Ke. "They may have an issue with your speaking problem, but they don't mean any harm by it." He stood up, towering over her.

"They have an issue with my speech?" this took Zoey off-guard. She just thought they were trying to help her speak more clearly.

"Of course. Why would they continue to bother you about it?" Ke shook his head, looking disgusted. "They act like they want people to live their own life, but if that were so, then wouldn't they leave you alone, and not worry about how you speak? It's simple logic."

That makes sense, thought Zoey. "I guess so, but I think they're trying to help."

"D-do you even n-need help?" replied Skint.

Zoey leaned in to listen. She wanted to hurry up his sentences, but didn't know why. She shouldn't even consider it. *Poor guy. It's just how he was born.* A quick twinge of anger nudged at her. *It's true*, she thought. *This is how I was born. Why should I try to fix myself if I was born this way? I should be left alone! Speaking this way doesn't bother me, why should it bother them?*

Piv was staring at her, looking her up and down. "You wanna join?"

Zoey frowned, "Join?"

"Yes," replied Ke. "We're forming now."

"Forming what?"

Ke winked at her. "I'm glad you asked, young one." He added in a quiet voice to Skint and Piv, "It's the young ones who aren't brainwashed yet." He paused as if a thought had just entered his mind for the first time. "Do you know what brainwashing is?"

Zoey shook her head. She'd heard the word before, but didn't know exactly what it meant.

"It's when a spirit animal, or a group of spirit animals, convince you to change your thinking to fit their own ideas. They want you to help their agenda, and steer you in the direction they want you to go. They use special techniques. Nova's doing it to you already. Don't get me wrong, I love Nova, but she got to me when I was young, too. She brainwashed me extremely well. I've overcome it, but most here have not. She means the best, but tends to steer you where she wants you to go, rather than where you want to be." He thought for a moment, "Does that make sense?"

Zoey shrugged, mumbling, "I don't know."

"What was that?" asked Ke, leaning in to listen to Zoey. Piv leaned in as well, aiming his ear in her direction.

Skint gave Zoey a friendly nudge. "I-I-I heard y-you. She s-said, 'I d-d-don't know'." He smiled at Zoey, giving her a look that suggested they were now equals because he understood her.

He's weird, thought Zoey. *Ke's nice.* She didn't think she was brainwashed, though, and shook her head. "I'm not brainwashed."

Ke's browse rose, "Really? Well, not all of us know right away." He stepped a couple of inches forward, his hooves made a clopping sound. "Anyway, we're forming a government."

"Oh yeah," replied Zoey, "Numee told us."

With the mention of Numee, all three bristled with annoyance.

"She's been a pain," said Piv.

Ke gently nosed Piv's side, pushing him to the left. "She's not a pain. She's just brainwashed like the rest of them." He turned to Zoey, changing the subject, "Everyone's been talking

179

about how beautiful your voice is."

Zoey lifted her wings in surprise. "They are?"

"Yes, it is beautiful. Voices like yours have a unique ability to sing in rhythm with nature. I bet you're a good singer." Ke lifted his shoulders, puffing out his lower lip. "Mind if you share a little song with us?"

Skint stood on his hind legs and waived his hands in front of his face. "No, no, no." Startled at his own reaction, he hugged his arms in and crouched on the ground.

"Why is that?" asked Ke, looking a little peeved.

Zoey, relieved that she didn't have to sing, also wondered why Skint was so adamant about her not singing. *And why would Ke want me to sing for him? I don't even know how to sing.*

"B-b-because I know that she d-doesn't know how to s-sing," Skint stammered.

Piv walked between Ke and Zoey. He looked up into the zebra's eyes. "Yeah, I can tell she doesn't know how to sing. Plus, she has a speech problem."

Ke lifted a hoof, carefully pushing Piv out of the way. Piv scooted to the right, irritated by the interference. Ke bent his neck to look eye to eye with Zoey. "Is this true? You don't have a good singing voice?"

"I-I guess not," replied Zoey. *Why do they care if I can sing or not?*

"Well," said Ke, "alright. Then that's that." He turned and walked to the maple tree only a couple of feet away. He scratched his right side against the white, smooth bark. He grinned. "You want to join our cause to right the wrongs in this world?"

Skint put his arms in the air, and for the first time, Zoey saw a gray crystal on his forehead. Her eyes narrowed just as the crystal turned red a second later. *That's a Dim! But, how did it turn from gray to red? Dim's can't do that, can they?* Zoey didn't care. She knew he was a Dim. She started to back up, getting more and more worked up about being so close to a Dim. She started fluttering her wings to escape, but they weren't lifting her off the ground like they should. Someone was holding her down. She looked behind her to see who it was, but saw no one. Did she simply forget how to fly?

"Hey!" came a yell a short distance away. Zoey felt the weight holding her down suddenly let go. She lifted off the ground and hovered at a height level with Ke's eyes. He looked genuinely concerned. "Are you okay, Zoey?"

Numee ran over to the group. "Who held her down?"

Piv and Skint both shrugged their shoulders. Zoey landed on the ground as Numee crept forward. The sharp raccoon eyes darted from Piv to Skint to Ke. She pointed her paw at the zebra. Her voice turned into a low growl. "You and your group keep your paws and hoofs off the students! Understand?"

Ke nodded his head. "I understand, Numee. What I don't understand is why you are pointing your claws at us. We did nothing."

"Y-yeah," said Skint. He put both paws up in an 'I don't know' fashion, stuttering, "W-w-we didn't d-do anything."

Numee pointed her tail at Zoey. "Then how do you explain what just happened? She couldn't get off the ground. Someone had her in an energy clasp!"

Piv grunted as he walked away, rolling his eyes as he walked by Numee. Ke watched him, then turned to Numee, "Again, I don't know. I saw what happened, but I don't know who did it."

Numee locked eyes with Ke. She nodded, "You aren't lying. Thank you, Ke." She looked around. "Then who was it?" She glanced at Skint, peering deeply into his eyes. She nodded again, "It wasn't Skint and I doubt it was Piv." She looked off into the distance.

"Numee?" asked Ke, startling Numee out of her detective work, "can you do me and my small group a favor?"

She tilted her head, a little confused as to what the favor might be. "What is it, Ke?"

"Would you stop spying on us? We have the right to our own opinions, you know?"

"You do, Ke. I agree. However, I don't agree with your ideas on this government stuff you keep talking about, that's for sure, and you must not accost the students." She glanced at

Zoey, who was following the discussion intently.

Once again, Zoey felt like she had done something wrong somehow. She could see that Skint was glaring at her. *Why is he staring at me like that?* He had both eyes fixed on hers. They were intent and unblinking. *Is he making me feel like this?* Her heart started to race and her body started to perspire. *What's he doing?* She started to feel paralysis creeping over her, a feeling she was getting a little too used to. Anger rose from her belly as she narrowed her eyes on Skint. He mimicked her. She screamed. "No!"

A moment later, Skint tumbled backwards about five feet, landing with a thump on the grass behind him.

Zoey fumed, breathing heavily. Her body tingled everywhere and her heart felt as if it was on fire.

Numee's ears twitched furiously. "What was that?"

Zoey snapped back into the moment. *Did I do that?*

Numee turned to Ke. "That's why I spy." She pointed her nose at Skint, who was taking his time getting back up. He was clearly dazed. "I think your group likes to do things a little too controlling."

Bothered, Ke's brows drew down, though his voice was soft. "Around us, she is safe. I assure you, Numee." He bowed, flicking his head to the right, telling Skint and Piv to follow him. They walked west, toward the large Sihu forest.

Numee rubbed her fur against Zoey's feathers. "Are you okay?"

Zoey didn't respond. She was still in a daze. Her body wobbled as she did her best to keep upright and balanced.

"Zoey. Zoey. Come back," Numee sang, waving her tail in front of Zoey.

Shaking her head, Zoey stretched her wings wide and voiced her question. "Did I do that?" She pulled her wings back in to her side, realizing that she was exhausted.

"Yes," responded Numee. "I've only seen a VioletLight do that sort of thing."

Zoey yawned. "Really? How did I do that?"

Numee slowly shook her head, "I don't know. Can you remember exactly what you felt before Skint went rolling backwards?"

Zoey closed her eyes tight, doing her best to remember. "Well," she said, "He was making me feel terrible and I didn't want to feel that way anymore. I felt like I couldn't move. It made me mad and then all my anger and frustration built up inside of me."

"Anything else?"

Zoey's voice quieted as her energy drooped even more. "I was stuck and couldn't move, but I wanted to move so badly that it felt like my anger was about to burst out of my feathers. I think I yelled 'no' to get it all out. Then he tumbled backwards." She opened her eyes, astonished. "But I was looking at him when I yelled it. I..." Zoey started to feel dizzy. Numee was becoming blurry in her vision. Then she fell on her tail feathers, and with a big yawn closed her eyes, saying, "I'm tired."

Numee softly leaned her cheek against Zoey's head. "You're drained. You used your own energy against Skint. I think you accidentally gave your energy away."

She placed her paws on Zoey, just like she did on San earlier. Zoey started to feel better within seconds. Her mind stopped spinning, her legs stopped wobbling, and her body strengthened. It felt like a flood of water slowly flowing into her head, down her back, through her feathers, and into her legs. She stood up. Her vision was normal again.

"You see, Zoey? If you use the energy that I just used, that of the Great Spirit, then you'll find that it's a well that never empties. It's there for everyone's use."

Numee padded forward, heading in the direction of the Spruce Hollow. Zoey followed, hanging her head in thought. The grass was soft, and every step felt pleasant. *How do you use the energy of the whatever-you-call-it? The Great Spirit?*

Coming around a tree, Numee stopped. "You have to remember that Skint has been here for only a few more moons than you. He's still a Dim. He gives off a strange energy when he's around, and sometimes he does strange things. He hasn't gotten it out of his system yet."

"If he's a Dim, then why is he here?"

183

"He snuck over from the Dim Lands, then found Nova and asked her if she'd help him, which, as you see, she granted."

"Help him with what?"

Numee turned her head to the forest, as if looking for Ke and Skint. "He wants to become a PureLight."

Zoey felt a cool breeze flow through her feathers, taking some of the heat of the day away, making it a perfect afternoon. She followed Numee's gaze. "How can Skint be turned into a PureLight?"

Numee gestured with her tail to follow her. "Let's continue to the Spruce Hollow. I want to check something out."

"Okay," Zoey agreed, walking after her.

Numee furrowed her brow. "To answer your question, there's a rumor that the PureLight Order can turn a Dim into a PureLight instantly. I think that's why Skint is here. He heard about it and didn't want to be a Dim anymore. So he crossed over." She shook her head in disgust, "I can't imagine being a Dim. Yuck!"

"Then," replied Zoey, "why is he still kind of a Dim if the PureLight Order can change him so quickly?"

Numee stopped, prompting Zoey to do the same. "Didn't Nova tell you?"

"Tell me what?"

Numee frowned. "That the PureLight Order went missing eons ago. We think Crepus stole it." Numee started to walk again. "So, without the PureLight Order, Skint must work hard to find the love in his heart to transform into a PureLight."

They rounded a large tree, then stopped. In front of them stood the Spruce Hollow. It was magnificent, and even though Zoey had been inside and slept there, it amazed her again. It practically took her breath away.

"Yeah, it's spectacular, isn't it?" asked Numee.

Zoey nodded her head. There really weren't any words to describe it.

Numee's crystals glowed as she smiled. "Race you!" Without warning, she took off toward the giant tree.

Laughing, Zoey jumped into the air and flapped her wings. She gained speed, soaring over the head of Numee, landing softly in front of the door of the Spruce Hollow.

A moment later Numee arrived. She was beaming. "You did it!" She brushed her fur against Zoey.

Zoey raised her wings in celebration. "I know. I won!"

"You sure did," replied Numee. "What I'm talking about, though, is even better than winning."

Zoey scrunched up her brow. "What's that?"

"You, Zoey, with your beautiful voice that will be spoken of in legends, stories, fables, and myths to come..." her grin grew larger "...didn't mumble or murmur once on the way here."

Zoey shrugged. "It's not that big of a deal."

Numee nudged her with a paw. "It's bigger than you can imagine." She turned and walked up to the door. She knocked three times, then stopped. Two more times, then paused. One more time and the peep-hole slid open.

"Who goes there?" asked Taregan.

Numee rolled her eyes. "Just let us in, Taregan."

The door slowly opened with a clunk and the clang of the bells. The old crane tapped his foot up and down, wings folded. "Follow the rules, Numee." He gestured his beak to Zoey, then looked at Numee, "And don't make me look bad in front of the students." Glancing at Zoey, he gave her a wink. He turned to Numee, sighing. "Yes, what is it?"

"You know what it is," Numee walked in, almost forcing her way passed Taregan. Taregan motioned for Zoey to follow. The door closed with a thud behind her.

The place was empty, echoing every step throughout the tree.

"Numee, why are you involving Zoey?"

Numee became very serious. "You know why."

Taregan looked up at the sky. Although they were inside, Zoey remembered that there wasn't a ceiling in the Spruce Hollow. She glanced up as well. A small white cloud slowly moved by, almost as if it was painted against the blue sky.

He tapped his foot again, glancing at Zoey with one brow raised. "There's change afoot."

Zoey put both wings together. "There's change afoot?"

Numee looked around, making sure no one was within

earshot. "There are some real Dims living in our tribe. We haven't discovered who, as of yet." She sniffed the air and then paused, again, making sure no one else was around. She eyed Zoey, "And, no, we aren't speaking of Skint."

Taregan looked worried. "I think some are learning the Art of Defense here. When they complete the training, they'll most likely find their way back to the Dims and teach them what they've learned."

Zoey didn't have much of a reaction to this. She hadn't learned the Art of Defense. She didn't know anything about it. She replied with a simple, "Oh."

Taregan tousled her head feathers, just like her father tousled her hair. "Well," he said, "we're entering the era of the Shiver, so we should expect this sort of thing. The combined thoughts in Ohm Totem have declined significantly. The thoughts have become fearful. It's spreading to the PureLights."

"What's the Shiver?" Zoey inquired, faintly remembering she had heard this word before.

Numee padded next to her. "The Shiver is a change in weather. We're quickly turning from warm weather to cold weather. This happens because of the change in the mass thought patterns in Ohm Totem. When the thought patterns change, the weather responds in kind. The more erratic and violent our thoughts, the more erratic and violent the weather behaves." She sat on her rump. "Soon, snow, ice, storms, and tornadoes will be common occurrences."

Taregan walked next to Numee and sat on his tail feathers. "And," he explained, "we know the Dims have infiltrated the Sihu Tribe. That's the only way that the shiver-inducing consciousness could have spread through our tribe so quickly." He scratched his head, now talking more to himself than to the others, "how they hide among us and produce a colored crystal to deceive us is beyond me."

Zoey was about to speak, but a loud bang interrupted her. All three looked up to stare at the balconies above.

"Was that a door?" asked Numee.

Taregan continued to watch the balconies, slowly moving

his eyes left and right. "That was a door."

Again, a loud bang and Zoey's heart raced. She accidentally flapped herself off the ground from the sudden start.

Taregan motioned to Zoey and Numee to be quiet. He spread his wings, gesturing for Zoey to do the same. He jumped and flew faster than she'd ever seen a bird fly before. He landed on the ninth railing and waived his wing for Zoey to join him. She stared in uncertainly. Taregan had been as stealthy as a mouse. *And he expects me to do the same?* She nodded, flapping her wings anyway, doing her best to be quiet. She flew up to him, landing awkwardly on the railing, almost losing her balance. Taregan steadied his wing on her back, making sure she didn't fall.

"How graceful," he whispered. He pointed to the twelfth floor and whispered again, "It came from that balcony." He nodded to her, asking her if she understood. Zoey nodded back.

He flew to the eleventh railing and Zoey followed. They jumped off the railing, and walked as softly as they could to the wall. They planted their backs against it, listening.

Another bang. Zoey's stomach twirled. She did everything she could not to jump off the balcony to wait it out with Numee below. She didn't know what else Ohm Totem had in store for her and she didn't want to find out.

Zoey heard a scuttle of feet from the balcony above, then a door slam.

She glanced at Taregan. He had one eyebrow raised, the other lowered. He was doing his thinking thing. He put his wing under his chin. "Who is trying to get our attention and why do it in this fashion?" He spread his wings. "Follow me, but stay ten crane lengths behind. I can deal with a surprise attack. You can't, as of yet. Understand?"

Zoey did, but didn't want to go. Nonetheless, she followed Taregan to the twelfth railing.

There they perched. She looked to her right, where Taregan was, realizing she was only a couple of crane lengths beside him. She moved several paces to her left.

The balcony floor was as polished looking as ever, reflecting

187

the light from above. The crystal lights were off and all the doors were shut. She saw nothing suspect.

Taregan pointed at the door with the number twenty-seven on it. "In there," he whispered.

He slid off the railing, gently tiptoeing to the door. Zoey waited.

She wanted to yell for Taregan. She wanted to tell him to wait for Nova. *Just don't open that door*, she thought. Still, she bravely slid off the railing and crept forward. She heard a creak, and saw Taregan opening the door. He hid behind it as it opened.

She hopped, softly landing about five crane lengths away from Taregan. The nerves in her body tingled up and down her spine. She didn't want to walk any farther, and was happy when Taregan gestured for her to stay put. *Why does he want me here anyway?*

The door and the room behind it seemed silent. Taregan peered around the door, peaking into the room, and then ducked back behind it. He took a deep breath and closed his eyes. Zoey didn't move. She watched him for several moments, until he opened his eyes. He motioned for Zoey to come closer, "Whomever it was, is gone."

He walked around the door, but Zoey hesitated. *What if there actually is someone in there?*

"There's not. He, or she, escaped out the window," said Taregan. His voice echoed loudly in the room. "It had to be a bird."

Zoey felt annoyed. *How do they always know what I'm thinking?*

From below, Numee called out, "Is everything alright up there?"

Zoey peered over the railing and saw the raccoon staring up at them.

"We're fine!" called Zoey.

"Did you find them?" asked Numee.

"Zoey," Taregan's voice was a heavy whisper, "look at this."

Zoey shook her head 'no' to Numee, then went to investigate Taregan's find.

As she entered the room, she noticed that the room was much like hers. An open window, two nests, and a tablet in the center. Not much else, except whatever it was that Taregan was standing over.

His face was solemn as he crouched down to peer deeper into something. Zoey walked around him to see what it was.

It was an open scroll. It was golden in color, thickly outlined in black.

He pointed to it, asking, "Can you see writing?"

She looked closely. It had words, just like the words in her books at school. She nodded a yes.

"Then it's written for you," he replied. "Because I don't see anything."

Zoey was befuddled by this new mystery. "Huh? Why not?"

"To me, the writing is invisible. Whoever wrote this wanted you to see it, and only you." He stood up, placing both wings on his hips. "Whoever wrote this has the touch and expertise of a VioletLight." He continued to stare at the scroll. "No one else but a VioletLight can do something like this." He turned to Zoey, asking, "So, what does it say?"

Zoey stared at the scroll. She mouthed the words. Then frowned. She was confused. "That doesn't make sense to me."

Taregan became anxious. "Read it out loud."

"Alright," she sat down to take a closer look. "You who walk the path of the sacred heart must stand alone in the eyes of the shaded crystal, and wait for the protection of the ghost shadow. Fear not, for she will be there."

Zoey hoped Taregan could translate this for her, but he didn't seem to know either

"Pick up the scroll, Zoey. It's yours. Take it into your room and study it. Sing with it if you have to," he winked. "The meaning may come to you tonight, or in several moons to come. I have a feeling it's to help you."

"Sing with it?"

He nodded. "Sing with it. In the meanwhile, I'm going to do my best to figure out who the messenger of your scroll was."

Zoey picked up the scroll with her beak as she hurried out of the room. She jumped on the railing and looked back at

Taregan inspecting the open window. "Get, get!" he shooed her along.

Clutching the scroll in her beak she thought, *I should at least say goodbye to Numee.* But before Zoey could wave a goodbye, Numee blurted out, "I'm going to get Honani," and dashed out the main door.

Who's Honani?

Zoey took a deep breath and allowed herself to glide into a landing on the ninth railing. She glanced at her door, perched in thought. *How can I be the only one who can read this? Mom and Dad could probably read it.*

She suddenly felt a sadness she wasn't expecting. Her insides seemed to slump with the thought of her parents. She missed them. It's been two days since she's seen them. When will she be able to go home? *Oh yeah*, remembered Zoey, *at the next full moon.* Her heart wept and a tear fell from her eye. *I want to go home,* she moped. For several moments, she wept. Her wings folded forward in melancholy and she hopped onto the wooden surface of the balcony.

She dragged herself to the door, wiping a tear with her wing. Her heart felt empty as she walked into the room and sat on her nest and stared out through the window. The leaves and branches of the Spruce Hollow stirred from the wind, sending a nice cool breeze that caressed her feathers. The sky was blue and the tops of trees danced with the fading wind.

For an instant, she no longer felt sad or empty as she stared at the canopy of dark green needles just outside her window. She was lost in the sound of pines swishing back and forth against each other and the rhythm that came with it. Then she became aware that she was holding something in her beak.

The scroll!

Dropping the scroll on the floor, she opened it up and stared at the words. There they were. *I'm supposed to sing?* She rolled her eyes, then peeked around the room. It was empty. She was sure no one would ever hear her.

She opened her mouth to sing a song that she liked back home. The chirps of a bird filled the room. *Where did that come from?* Curious, she opened her mouth to sing a second time. Again, the chirps echoed around her. *Is that me?* She began to sing again and the same thing happened. Zoey realized it was her making those sounds.

She giggled. This place continued to surprise her. She turned her attention back to the scroll as she made one more attempt to sing. She chirped.

"Ugh!" Frustrated, she pushed the scroll forward with her beak and looked outside at the moving branches. She quickly became lost in them. She felt herself swaying back and forth, mimicking their movements.

Why did she stop singing? It was so beautiful, flowed a whisper into her ears.

She looked around. She didn't know where that came from.

It came from us, Zoey, the trees, the branches, the roots, the very essence of us. Please sing.

There was no ending to the strangeness of this land. Instead of questioning where the voice really came from, Zoey decided to chirp a song into the scroll.

Here I go, she thought. She opened her mouth and cringed at the first couple of chirps that came out, but soon realized that it felt really good to chirp a song. She continued on and on, moving her head back and forth in rhythm with her music, almost forgetting about the scroll. When she looked down she nearly choked.

The words on the scroll were moving, like a ship in the sea. Back and forth, up and down. She watched hypnotically, until the words slowly disappeared as a fog enshrouded the scroll. Her eyes wide and unblinking, she continued to sing.

Within the fog, three sets of eyes started to form. Gray crystals were set in between the eyes; one, however, was completely black. *Crepus?* The eyes glared with an anger that seemed to penetrate the very depths of her soul.

She continued to sing. She wanted to look away, but knew she mustn't. She held fast against those eyes, until they started to fade. An owl's hoot filled the room, then a shadow covered the fading eyes. The shadow closed in on the eyes, becoming smaller and smaller, until she could see that the shadow was an owl.

The piercing eyes vanished and the penetrating feeling in her body left. But the shadow remained, and in a flash it changed into the talons of an owl swooping at her. Zoey lurched back and stopped singing. For a second she took her eyes off the scroll. When she looked back, the images were gone.

Her heart raced. She'd never experienced such a thing. Heck, she'd never experienced most of what Ohm Totem had to offer. She closed her eyes and saw only blackness. But in that blackness, the scroll slowly appeared, as if it was already part of her. And a chorus of female and male voices read the scroll prophecy aloud, saying, *You who walk the path of the sacred heart must stand alone in the eyes of the shaded crystal, and wait for the protection of the ghost shadow. Fear not, for she will be there.*

Chapter 18

The sky was dark, but the moon was bright, casting a shadow of the Large Boulder over Coda. His black fur hid him well. At a swift glance, no spirit animal would ever see him.

Coda didn't care. His day had been a long one. His mind was in a daze.

The stars blanketed the night sky, something he had never noticed back at home. A shooting star streaked high above him. It lit up the night for a split second.

The wind was still and the air was silent, which made the night warmer. He brought his eyes forward and his ears back, as he listened to the sound of the river behind him.

He lay down, chin on his forelegs. He'd been sitting here for what seemed to be an hour. The constant practicing tired his muscles and ached his spine. After training, he couldn't find Zoey anywhere in the meadow. He wanted to know how she was, and boast to her about how well he did in training. Nonetheless, he drifted into deep thought.

Orion? It's weird. I'm not Orion.

He shook his head. He couldn't be Orion. If he was Orion, he wouldn't have created the Art of Defense in a way that made you practice so much. It was exhausting. Although, throughout the day, they did take breaks, and drink water. He was grateful for that. Though, they never stopped to eat. He thought that was strange. He shrugged his shoulders. He wasn't hungry anyway.

Wait a minute. Hungry? I haven't been hungry ever since I got here. He thought about that for a moment, then dismissed it. He was too tired too care.

From the east came the familiar sound of heavy hoofs hitting the earth. Coda lifted his head, "Hey Chev." His voice was weary.

"That tough today?" Chev appeared concerned. "I can carry you back if you want. Or," he smiled, "I can easily toss you all the way back to the Marble Burrow. It's not far." Chev stopped a few feet from Coda. He started to pose for him, flexing his muscles. He grunted, "You see that?"

Coda managed a half-smile. Chev was funny, but he was too tired to laugh.

Chev relaxed, whisking his trunk in front of Coda. "Yeah, I've been practicing sitting at the beach all day. It's hard work." He flexed again. "You see those rippling muscles? See the tone in them?"

For a moment, Coda thought he was serious, then Chev laughed. "I'm just kidding with you. I admire your hard work. You deserve some rest, and..." Chev bent down a little closer to Coda, "...seriously, do you need me to carry you? I'm going in that direction."

Coda shook his head. He didn't want to be babied, though it would be nice to be off of his paws for a while.

"I'm okay. Thanks."

"Can I walk with you?" asked Chev.

"Sure."

Coda stood and padded toward the Marble Burrow, which he could easily see just to the south of them. The light blueish, white light glowed from the entrance, inviting him to come and rest.

"Have you seen Zoey?" asked Coda. After his question, he realized that the first few steps he took did the opposite of what he thought would happen. Instead of making his paws ache even more, the grass seemed to soothe and massage them.

Chev looked down at him. "Doesn't that feel better?"

Coda nodded, "Yeah."

"Walking on the grass always calms the nerves and eases the muscles." Chev placed his trunk on Coda's back. "And, yes, I've seen Zoey." He patted Coda's back, "She's back in her room. She had a tough day too, although different from yours." The elephant sounded somewhat gloomy.

Coda's eyes showed his alarm. "What happened?"

194

"Numee said that she was attacked by a Dim, and..."

"What?!" Every muscle in Coda tensed. He wanted to get to the Dim, any Dim for that matter, and defend his sister. He glanced toward the Spruce Hollow, but saw only the blackness of the night, deepened by the heavy shadows of trees.

He narrowed his eyes. His vision then became clearer, showing him the Spruce Hollow beyond the shadows.

Coda was about to run, but was held back by Chev's large trunk across his chest. "Hold on, Dim Killer."

Coda's eyes flashed anger. "I want to see if she's okay!"

"She is. She's asleep," Chev assured him, releasing Coda from his grip.

"I want to see my sister!" Coda growled.

Chev let out a breath. "I know. I'm sorry Coda. She's sleeping right now. She wasn't hurt. No one was hurt." He smiled. "Right now your emotions and energy are violent. You'd disturb her sleep. Plus, Taregan's a stinker on these things. He'd sense your energy and turn you away. And you don't want to mess with Taregan." He chuckled. "Come on. Let's get the hero to sleep."

Begrudgingly, Coda followed Chev to the Marble Burrow.

I better not see a Dim, thought Coda. *No one touches my sister!* His fur bristled, standing on end in frustration. He clawed the grass as he walked, then wondered why he was so angry about someone harming his sister. He sniffed the air, realizing he was just in a bad mood. It had been a long day.

"We're here," said Chev.

"And you are," replied a calm, wise voice.

Coda dipped his head in greeting. He hadn't seen Honani since last night and his mood lightened a bit when he saw the peaceful badger. Honani stood at the entrance with his head bowed. "It's good to see you Chev, and you, Coda."

Chev patted Coda affectionately. "I'll see you later, okay?"

Coda faked a smile. His heart felt heavy, but he couldn't understand why. Was he mad at what happened to his sister?

As Chev walked away, the badger turned and slowly walked down the tunnel. Coda took a step inside, placing his paw on cold, dry soil. A much different feeling than the grass. He noticed that instead of soothing his feet, each step felt like pinpoints of pain. Every step was accompanied by a small pebble pain here, and a tiny dirt clod stab there.

Honani counseled, "Fully allow each step to take its course. If you step on a rock, the rock is there to mend a wound in your body, whether that be in an organ, muscle, or vein. There are thousands of nerve endings in paws. Each nerve that receives pressure will send a signal to a corresponding point in your body and relax that area."

Coda's mind wasn't on Honani's instructions. He just wanted to get to his bed and rest. He wanted to fume over the unjustified actions that the Dims inflicted on his sister. The last thing he wanted to worry about were these pebbles under his paws or any nerve endings in his feet. He simply nodded and did his best to maneuver around any hard objects.

Then something occurred to him. Why was he so mad at the Dims? He loved his sister, but he'd never reacted this way before. She was annoying for sure, but he wanted to protect her more than anything. He now felt that he needed to be by her side at all times. *Why was that?*

For a while, there was silence between them as they padded down the tunnel. This didn't help matters any. Coda was imagining throwing Dims across the forest, or sending them hard against the grassy meadow. *That'll teach them to put their filthy claws on my sister!*

"Coda?" Honani's voice was soft, easing Coda back to reality.

Coda looked at Honani. The badger's eyes mirrored his soft voice. "When you look at things from a higher perspective, you can see the whole picture. Right now you're seeing just a sliver of the picture."

Coda's whiskers twitched. *Sliver?* "What picture?"

"The pictures and images you hold in your mind right now are just a sliver. This sliver, or piece of the picture, is what angers you. The sliver in your mind takes you away from what's real."

Coda looked up at the ceiling highlighted by the zytes that lined the walls. He looked at Honani, almost forgetting about his anger. "Oh? Well, what's real then?"

The badger stopped and slapped the ground with his right forepaw. He twisted his foot left and right, making a small impression in the ground. He pointed to the ground, then looked around, pointing to everything around them, then pointed back at the impression. "This point in the ground is what you're focusing on. But look around. There's more to this dirt than just this point." They continued walking in silence. "Do you understand, Coda?"

The only thing Coda understood is how different they talked here compared to where he came from. They talked of moments and of the heart, and other things like that. Coda shook his head, "I don't know."

"I'll make it a little easier," said Honani. "If you were swimming in the River Ohm and you saw the rapids in front of you, then what do you see?"

Coda thought for a moment, "I guess I see the rapids."

"Correct," replied Honani. "If Nova lifted you out of the rapids, carrying you high above the land, looking down, what would you see?"

Coda pictured himself high above the rapids. He saw the River Ohm below. He saw the Large Boulder. He saw Deer Meadow. He saw as much as he could remember in his short stint here in Ohm Totem. He glanced down at the impression in the dirt. "I'd see a lot more."

"Right. You see, Coda?" Honani pressed his paw against Coda's chest. "You saw more than just the rapids. There was an entire life going on around you. If there was a waterfall just beyond those rapids, you'd see the waterfall. If there was a widening in the river, you'd see that as well. You'd see that there's more to the river than just the rapids."

Coda nodded. He understood the point of Honani's example. This didn't soften his anger any, but it made sense.

Honani smiled. "When you drop into your heart and replay what you're angry about, you see more than what you're currently focusing on." Honani shifted on his paws. "You're angry about what happened with your sister, aren't you?"

Coda's eyes raged, his fur prickled with anger.

197

"I see," said Honani. "Perhaps your sister needed this lesson as part of her training. And, if she learned from the lesson, then it advanced her experience in some way." He paused, taking in a long breath. "When you can see beyond your anger, then the anger slowly recedes into something a little more tangible and helpful. You see the big picture. You see the lesson in all of this."

Coda absently kicked a large rock in front of him to the side as his pace quickened. "Tangible?" He'd never heard that word before.

Honani hurried to catch up. "Yes, tangible. It means 'real'."

Coda walked even faster. He didn't necessarily want what's "real". He wanted to help his sister, here in Ohm Totem—to be by her side at all times so she'd never be hurt again. *But why do I suddenly feel that way?*

Honani tried again. "When you go into your heart, you'll see the bigger picture. You'll understand that everyone has something important to learn. Your anger about your sister tells you that you love your sister so much that you don't want anything to happen to her. Perhaps protecting her is your goal in life, I don't know. However, your anger isn't helping her any. It's creating the opposite effect. That's just how life works. You're whipping up more drama, like a whirlwind, by fuming over her lesson." Honani suddenly stopped, making Coda skid to a halt. He was surprised and a little impressed that Honani could stop so fast. "Has Nova shown you how to go into your heart?"

"The Snow Tree did," replied Coda.

"Yes," nodded Honani. "The Snow Tree is a very reliable source. A master teacher. When you go into your heart, you might see the lesson in your anger and what you're truly angry about. So, it's a good idea to practice as much as you can. Your heart holds all the answers. I'd suggest that you go to a silent place, bring that anger into your heart, and cover it with love. Then rise above the image and look around. You might see something you need to know."

Coda was too tired to practice, and simply nodded his head. He just wanted to go to sleep. Maybe that would help him let go of being angry. It usually did.

∞

The number nine glowed on the disc door to his room. The door quietly opened with a blow of his breath, revealing the soothing light of the zytes. Skint was there, lying down, seemingly in deep thought. He glanced up as Coda walked in, then resumed his ruminating

"Hi Skint," greeted Coda, walking over to the right side of the room. He elegantly collapsed on his bed, curling his tail around his forepaws.

"Hi C-coda." Skint looked disinterested. Or, rather peeved that Coda was there.

Coda was ready for sleep, but then remembered a question he wanted to ask Skint. "Hey Skint?"

Skint turned, placing the left side of his face in his paws, facing away from Coda. He faintly replied, "Y-y-yes?"

"Where did you go last night?"

There was a long pause, then Skint turned his head in Coda's direction. His eyes betrayed a mysterious and firm displeasure. "W-w-hat do you mean?" His ears perked in alertness, waiting for the answer.

"Oh," Coda replied casually, looking at his paws in front of him and twitching his ears. Should he not have asked that question? "I thought I heard you leave last night."

The squirrel lifted himself up with both front legs and remained silent for a moment. He looked at the door. "R-r-really? I was here all-all-all night. You m-must have d-dreamed it."

Coda narrowed his eyes in thought. *Why is Skint lying?* Still, Coda didn't want to make Skint feel any more awkward. Maybe he had to use the restroom, wherever that was, and was embarrassed? Closing his eyes, Coda mumbled, "Yeah, I must have been dreaming." He took in a deep breath. "Good night, Skint."

"Y-you too."

He heard Skint rustle with the bed for a moment, then felt

himself drifting off into a welcome, deep sleep.

∞

The sound of small feet slowly pattering across the dirt floor woke Coda. He opened one eye, making it a tiny slit. Skint stood across the room near the disc door. His pale outline was very discernible in the darkness. His bushy tail wiggled back and forth, as if waiting for Coda to wake up. Coda almost opened his eyes in surprise. *The tail! The tail in the grass today looked just like Skint's!*

"C-coda?" whispered Skint.

Coda could clearly see Skint now, but he could tell Skint didn't have the same ability with night vision as he did. Coda remained silent, faking sleep.

Skint whispered his name again. Coda didn't respond. He kept one eye open, doing his best to push the heavy, sleep-deprived eyelids from shutting.

"He's asleep," said Skint, as if talking to somebody else in the room, but like the last night, no one else was there.

Skint faced the door and quietly blew on it. Coda saw the door open, but fell asleep before he could see it close.

∞

Then, again, something startled him, waking him up. How long had he been asleep? He looked up. Standing over him was Skint. He was snarling, peering closely into Coda's eyes. His eyes revealed a hatred Coda hadn't seen before.

Skint's red forehead crystal changed into gray and started to fade in and out. For an instant, Coda felt peculiar, as if a heavy weight was descending on him. Then Coda felt a stir in his heart, and almost instantly, Coda felt peaceful. It was as if Coda had somehow flipped a light switch, changing his fear into something else.

Skint's eyes widened in alarm. Coda lifted his head. He somehow knew what Skint was doing and words came out of his mouth that he'd never said before. "Your Dark Arts don't work on me and never have, Skint."

Skint backed up slowly toward his nest. He trembled in fear, wondering why his trick didn't work. He kept his eyes fixed on Coda until he reached his bed. There he relaxed. His frown melted. "I-I'm sorry, Coda. I-I still h-have s-some D-d-dim left in me."

Coda nodded with understanding, then closed his eyes, knowing he needn't worry about Skint the rest of the night. Sleepy thoughts drifted through his mind. *Dark Arts? What in the world was I saying? Was he the one who hurt my sister?* Coda fell fast asleep before he could think about it any more.

Chapter 19

"Knock-knock," said a voice, waking Zoey from a heavy sleep. Opening her eyes, she saw San sitting in her nest, smiling at her. "I've never seen someone sleep so long, and so deep. You've been asleep since I got back from training yesterday..." San lifted her wings in the air, "and the moon wasn't even up yet!"

Zoey rubbed her eyes with her wings and yawned. She was still drowsy. "What time is it?" She stretched her wings out and stood up.

"Time?" replied San. "What does that mean?"

Zoey cocked her head. "You don't know what time means?"

San shook her head. "No, I've never heard of it." San hopped out of her nest, gently landing on the wood floor. "But, you should have seen me yesterday. I wish you had stayed." Her red crystals glowed brightly as she exclaimed, "I was brilliant!"

San spread her wings and imitated flying. "I was coming this way," she said as she quickly ran toward the window, then stopped, "and he—my opponent—was coming this way." She turned around, acting as if she was 'him' flying toward her from the opposite direction. She turned around and twirled. "I spun in a circle and he whizzed right by me! He twisted around and I was ready for him." Her eyes widened. "Then he tricked me."

She turned, facing Zoey, who was watching intently. All of this looked exciting, or was it just that San was exciting? Either way, Zoey was rather enjoying the display before her, even though she was still waking up from her long night of sleep.

San put her wings out in front of her. She wiggled the left wing, "This is me." She wiggled the right wing, "This is him." Then she brought both wings slowly together and dipped the right wing and said, "He acted as if he was going to go down, so I fell for it." She dipped the left wing, quickly bringing up the right wing. "He went really high after he faked me out and attempted to come down on me from above." She shook her head, narrowing her eyes, "I knew what to do, though. I faked him out by making him think I wasn't too sure where he was, but when he was about a wing's length from me I did a somersault and he missed me again!" She imitated her words with the movements of her wings. She was now above 'him' and her left wing came down on top of her right wing.

Her eyes lit up. "I ended it by landing on top of him and stunning him." Laughing, she said, "He fell to the ground like a lump of dead leaves."

"Was he okay?" Zoey asked, with concern.

"Oh yeah. I actually didn't stun him. We haven't learned that yet. He acted as if he was stunned, and he did fall, but landed on his feet just before he hit the ground."

"Well," responded Zoey. "Great job, San!" She clapped and San danced in a circle in the middle of the room.

Three abrupt taps at the door stopped the dance cold. They looked at each other as if someone suspicious was about to intrude.

"We don't have all day, children." It was Taregan's voice. Zoey realized that they were supposed to be going to training and jumped out of her nest and opened the door. No one was there.

She peered around the doorway, looking at the balcony, thinking that Taregan would be walking around the railing or knocking on someone else's door. He wasn't there. Was it really Taregan, or another spirit animal wanting to drop off another mysterious scroll? She looked to the floor and peered around.

"Remember, Zoey, I can fly. I swooped down here after I knocked. I don't have all day to wait all day and I don't want to be saying this every morning."

She peeked over the railing. Taregan stood with both wings folded, tapping that foot again. "Let's get going, you two." He touched his head with his wing. "Is your brain in there or do I have to flap your wings for you?" He gave a wink, but his tone was flat serious.

Huh? thought Zoey.

San walked over to the railing. "Sorry Taregan, I was just telling her how I beat my opponent yesterday."

Taregan put both wings on his hips. "You beat someone?"

"Yeah," her eyes gleamed with pride, "I stunned him."

"We'll have to define 'beat' when you get down here. Which, by the way, I'm still waiting for!"

Zoey and San looked at each other. San shrugged and hopped onto the railing, then glided down, landing next to Taregen. Zoey followed, landing beside the two. San and Taregan were already in a deep conversation.

"But I did," said San.

Taregan shook his head, his indigo crystal brightened. "You aren't in the Art of Beating, San. You're in the Art of Defense." He sighed. "I'm getting very impatient with you and I don't understand why."

He said to Zoey, "When you get to know me, you'll know that I'm usually a pretty patient bird." And just as he said this, his expression changed from perturbed to peaceful.

Zoey looked at San. Her expression did the opposite of Teragan's. She went from happy to sad. Her wings drooped. "But I did, though. I beat him."

Taregan took a deep breath. "I'm sorry, San." He patted her back. "I lost myself for a moment there." She lifted up, resuming her usual happy manner. He continued, "The Art of Defense doesn't deal with beating anyone. Beating implies several things such as punishing, violence, forcing something or someone against their will. Now, the Art of Defense," he leaned in, "which you're taught here in the PureLight Lands, deals with defending your space, your life, and your friends. You do so with the utmost compassion and understanding that you don't hurt, beat, or win anyone or anything." He nodded to Zoey, and then at San. "You use your opponent's own force against them. Do you both understand?"

Nodding their heads, Zoey and San agreed with the white crane. The lesson over, he called out to everyone, "Okay! Get going!"

Dozens of students stood around. They were waiting to exit the tree. Zoey didn't know how she missed them or missed their chatter. She must have been too focused on Taregan and San.

As they flocked out, Taregan tapped on Zoey's wing. Looking over her shoulder, she saw Taregan mouth the words, "Be careful," as he indicated to San with his eyes. San's back was to them, so she didn't see Taregan's warning.

Be careful with San? Does he want me to stay away from San? Be careful about what?

Shaking the thought away, Zoey spread her wings and jumped into the air. San was already many yards in front of her, so she flapped hard, doing her best to catch up. When she did, San had her attention on the Snow Tree way up ahead. She was ready for training, seemingly wanting to get to the Deer Meadow as soon as possible. She looked determined.

Zoey was about to say something, but noticed Chev and Coda walking to the meadow. She veered off course, leaving San without a word, gliding just over the top of a pine tree. Its glowing green needles tickled her toes as she eyed her brother and friend below. She smiled as a breeze swept against her feathers, bringing her back to the joy and freedom of flight. It felt so good to fly. For the first time that morning, she saw the blue sky and the sun shining its warmth upon the land. Glancing north, she saw the gray clouds beyond the Fog's borders. *You'll never catch me over there.*

"Hey neighbor," yelled Chev from below.

Zoey saw Chev and her brother looking up at her. From her vantage point, they seemed like small toys. She circled them once, feeling gentle air flowing against her chest, then descended quickly. She untucked her legs and spread her toes, landing nicely on Chev's back.

"Well, I don't mind if you do," said Chev with a laugh. His trunk lifted high, blaring a loud trumpet sound.

Zoey looked over Chev's large rump, eyeing Coda below. He smiled up at her, saying, "Hey Zo Zo. I'm glad you feel better."

Feel better? She frowned, *why is he being so nice to me?*

"I'm fine." She sniffed the air, breathing in the sweet fragrance coming from the meadow a short distance away. "Did Chev tell you what happened?"

Coda looked at Chev, giving a faint look of disgust. "He wouldn't tell me."

Chev let out a snort. "Ooh, you should have seen your brother. He was ready to take on the whole Dim Lands after I told him that a spirit animal hurt you."

Inside, Zoey felt a happy tingling sensation fill her small body. She'd never really thought that her brother cared for her, at least not that much. She loved her brother more than anything in the world and she glowed knowing that Coda might feel the exact same about her; even if it was just for a moment.

"Thanks Coda," she called down.

Coda rolled his eyes. "Yeah."

Zoey felt a jostle and a bump against her back. Startled, she looked over her shoulder, expecting Chev's long trunk. It was San, grinning, but her eyes weren't the normal, innocent eyes that usually stared into Zoey's. There was a bit of mischief in them. Zoey thought for a moment, wondering how she could see mischief in someone's eyes, but she knew for a fact she saw it there.

The pause between the two was long, until San broke the silence. Her eyes returned to normal as she nudged Zoey with her cheek. "I looked and you were gone."

"Yeah," replied Zoey. "I saw these two and wanted to say hi." Her words were slightly mumbled.

San opened her beak to say something, but whatever it was, it would have to wait as Nova's greeting interrupted them.

"Welcome, you four."

Zoey looked up to see Nova up ahead of them, standing on the tall green grass with her head held high. She reminded Zoey of a kind queen looking out for her children.

Chev stopped and bowed. "Greetings, Nova."

"I see you've taken some passengers for a ride," said Nova.

Zoey could see the meadow just beyond a small strip of trees. There she would see the Snow Tree. She got excited, but quickly became withdrawn. *The Snow Tree doesn't talk to me much, here in Ohm Totem*, she remembered sadly.

"San?" asked Nova, "can you lead Coda to the Snow Tree? I have some things to discuss with Chev and Zoey."

San bowed as well. "Of course, Nova." She looked very disappointed, but did her best to hide it. She probably wanted to be the one that Nova wanted to talk to.

San flew off Chev's back and above the trees, heading toward their destination. Coda took a giant leap over a large fern, slightly rustling the top of it with his hind leg, and landed in the meadow. Zoey was shocked to see him leap so far. Coda peered over his shoulder, wondering if the others saw what he just did. He seemed as astonished as Zoey.

"Zoey?" Nova's voice was soft and happy. "I was shown something about you while I was in my quietness last night."

Quietness? thought Zoey.

"It's a state of being where you spend several moments sitting in solitude. Well, last night I had a vision. A scene appeared before me." She paused, making sure Zoey was following her. When Zoey nodded, Nova continued, "The vision showed you walking to the beach with Chev at this very moment of the day." Nova glanced up at the round sky. "I asked the vision if you were to come back and train after the walk, but that's not what I saw."

Zoey waited for Nova to keep talking, but there was only silence.

"What did you see?" Zoey finally asked.

"Nothing scary," assured Nova. She turned and walked toward the meadow, then stopped just before she passed the last line of trees. "Nothing is set in stone, Zoey. Today, however, I ask you to go with Chev. Does that feel right in your heart?"

Zoey didn't feel any twinge of fear. She actually felt a tiny amount of eagerness. She didn't want to sit and listen to another lesson from Nova. It's not that she didn't like Nova, in fact, she felt a love for her. She just wasn't into this Art of Defense stuff.

Zoey nodded yes, and Nova bowed in acknowledgement,

then leaped forward, running toward the Snow Tree.

"Chev?" asked Zoey, "can we do absolutely nothing today? I just want to relax." She stretched her wings to get her point across, and added some grunting sounds for effect. She'd seen her grandpa do that every so often.

Chev chuckled. "Sure, Zoey. I have the perfect place."

Zoey rode on Chev's back as they walked due east. They passed several large trees, the Large Boulder, and a nice badger that sat at the entrance of Marble Burrow. He had indigo crystals and seemed very comfortable just sitting there. She could tell by Chev's body language that he knew the badger well. Zoey wondered if the badger was the caretaker of the Marble Burrow, and quietly envied Coda. He didn't have to deal with Taregan. The crane was nice and all, but a little confusing and strange, too.

Taregan never makes sense, thought Zoey.

Zoey could hear waves crashing a short distance away. The landscape was starting to change from heavy, dense grass and large trees, to sparse clumps of long, tan grasses surrounded by sand here and there. There was a short, sandy hill in front of them, hiding the sea from view. But she could smell the sweet, salty air of the beach as Chev climbed the hill.

Chev reached the top. "Here we are, little lady!" Zoey took in the majestic beauty of the waves tumbling end over end. The wind brought the smell of the ocean and the sun was fully out of the sea, looking only inches away from dipping back in. It was still early morning.

"Wow," said Zoey, under her breath. The beach was wide, seeming to go on forever to the north and to the south. Several spirit animals stood on the sand a good distance away. They were in a circle, singing. She couldn't quite make out what they were singing about, but it sounded gorgeous. A giraffe stood in the middle, nodding his head up and down, which looked to be in unison with the melodies coming from their voices. In fact, he looked to be the director.

"If you want some relaxation, we could go over there and you could just listen," Chev suggested. "Does that sound enticing?"

Zoey shrugged. "Sure." She didn't want to sing, but listening would be fine.

Chev ambled toward the circle of animals. His soft steps made it easy for Zoey to relax. As he approached, several spirit animals looked in their direction. They continued to sing, but greeted them with kind eyes.

Chev sat in a large space that was probably designated for him within the circle. Zoey jumped off his back, landing on the cool sand. She sat on her tail feathers, simply listening.

For a while, they all sang in perfect unison and didn't let up. Their crystals pulsed and glistened with each note sung. Zoey noticed that they all had different colored crystals. The giraffe had indigo crystals, Chev had orange, a rhinoceros had green, and a large bird had blue crystals.

What kind of bird is that? Zoey wondered. It had a long, tan neck and stood tall. Its fat body was covered in black feathers. As she stared at the creature, it looked back at her. Zoey could somehow tell that it was a female. She could see it in her large golden eyes. Suddenly it came to her—*ostrich*. The ostrich dipped her head, as if reading Zoey's thoughts. *Does everyone read your mind here?*

Zoey shifted her attention to the ocean. She watched the waves. The longer she stared, the more the ocean started to change. The water started to twinkle, as if there was glitter spread throughout it. She'd never seen this in an ocean before and couldn't peel her eyes away.

For what seemed to be hours, she watched the water dance. Then she heard a voice. It was the Snow Tree. It was one word, but a word that would change everything.

Sing, said the Snow Tree.

And Zoey did.

She sang and sang. She closed her eyes, swaying her head to the rhythm of her own voice. Her feathers tingled, her wings fluttered. She felt as if she was floating, but the touch of sand beneath her feet told her that she was planted firmly on the ground. In the darkness of her closed eyes, she saw things starting to change. A pulse of energy, electric blue in color, swirled in her vision. It then changed to violet. She noticed that the louder she sang, the more intense the swirling became. Suddenly, like a burst of an exploding star, the violet color turned into rainbows, covering her entire vision, until she felt something peculiar.

Silence.

Then she heard it. She heard the stillness and silence around her. There was no way she could describe the way it felt. She felt as if she was the only spirit animal on the beach.

A female voice slowly faded in and out of her mind. Zoey tried to hear the words, but couldn't make them out and she focused as intently on the words as she could.

It was a fleeting sound that repeated over and over again, *Welcome*. Then, like a scream, she heard, *Welcome, Aria!*

The voice startled her and her eyes shot open. More than a dozen spirit animals were staring at her, their mouths gaping from utter astonishment.

Did they hear the voice, too? Zoey wondered.

Chev was astonished as well, his eyes betraying his happiness for the moment at hand. She withered, wishing she could hide under her feathers, knowing that would at least give her some comfort, something to hide her embarrassment.

All the spirit animals sighed in unison when Zoey became silent. Some gestured for her to go on, but she looked down, shaking her head no. That familiar, uncomfortable feeling of being on the spot had her stomach rolling in knots. "Sorry," she mumbled.

"Nothing to be sorry about," Chev beamed. "That was the most beautiful singing we've ever heard."

"Huh?" Zoey slowly looked up to see if he was being genuine. She peered into the eastern horizon. *Where's the sun?* When they arrived at the beach, the sun was peeking slightly above the water. Now, it's not there. How long had she been singing? Glancing up, she noticed it was high above her and creeping more to the west.

"Chev? How long have I been singing?"

"You sang from the sun's eastern rise to its tipping point to the west. But, I wish you would've sung for moons on end." He gazed at her as if she was a queen. "I wish you had your eyes open, not that you needed to, but you would have seen what you created."

Zoey tilted her head, completely baffled. "What did I create?"

The giraffe walked toward her, peering down into her puzzled eyes. "The sea was moving with your voice." He gestured with his head toward the sky. "The sky was turning into a rainbow of colors with each note that you sang." He lowered his neck to get a better look at Zoey. "This was all because of you." He bowed. "I'm pleased to meet you, but, what we all undoubtedly want to know is," he paused, taking in a deep, happy breath, "who are you?"

It seemed to be more of a question for Zoey to contemplate. The giraffe acted like he knew exactly who she was.

"I'm Zoey."

"Zoey, is it?" The giraffe shook his head. "No, I think not."

Perplexed, Zoey looked at Chev. He bowed slightly, "We've been waiting for you. For many, many moons. I didn't know it was you at first, but now I'm sure. Nova always knew." His shoulders jiggled as he chuckled. "I guess you can call me one of those "see it" kind of spirit animals. You know, I have to see it in order to feel that it's true."

Who I am? I'm Zoey! Do they think I'm somebody else?

"Zoey," called a male voice from the crowd. Zoey lifted her head, gazing toward the crowd. She saw that it was Taregan. He smiled at her and came closer. "You are the voice of the sacred heart. You're destined to spread the light and unite the PureLights once again. Your voice is your greatest gift, and thus, the greatest present The Great Spirit could offer us."

My voice? All she did was sing. It wasn't something she was particularly good at. Or was she? She was used to singing wherever she went. It was something that always annoyed her brother, so she knew her voice wasn't that special. But singing always calmed her down, making her feel good. And, it was something easy for her to do.

Taregan stopped in front of her with his wings folded. This time his foot wasn't tapping. "Your voice sends beautiful chills up and down our spines. There's only been one before you who

211

did what you just did. If you remember who she was, then you'll remember who you are."

Again, this made no sense to Zoey. *I'm Zoey,* she repeated in her mind. *Why do they insist on getting me to remember who I am? I'm me!* A sudden stir of anxiety tugged at her heart. *Is this a riddle?*

Numee walked from the circle and stood next to Taregan. Seeing her instantly made Zoey feel better. Wait, thought Zoey. *When did Taregen and Numee arrive at the circle? I don't remember seeing them when I got here.*

Numee mouthed the words, *you're secure, compassionate, and strong.*

Zoey shuffled the sand under her feet. Right now, she didn't feel that way. Not at all.

Help me understand, Snow Tree!

Chapter 20

Coda watched Nova standing in the middle of the meadow. The Wings had gone to their training and he'd been practicing the Art of Defense with the Paws for what seemed to be hours on end. He looked to the east, observing that the sun was barely showing over the hills. He sighed. He apparently hadn't been in the meadow for as long as he'd thought.

He knew his skills were much better today than the day before, but he still didn't trust himself with this Art of Defense. Yesterday he was a loose cannon, frightened one moment, surprised the next. He blocked paw swipes, even though he was well aware that he wasn't supposed to, and he attacked even though it was drilled into his mind to do otherwise.

Nova's words interrupted his thoughts.

"Remember, the Art of Defense is less physical and less mental than you would think. It comes from inside of you." She pointed to her chest with her long tail. "It comes from your heart."

Pacing back and forth in front of the Large Boulder, Nova addressed the students. "The heart claims victory over no one. The only victory the heart and the Art of Defense claims is over the self—yourself. Once you've mastered the Art, you'll move with fluidity—more than you could ever imagine. You'll become one with your movements. In that state, no opponent can force their will upon you."

She slowed her pace, then walked toward them, eventually coming to a halt in the middle of the circle of spirit animals surrounding her. "Close your eyes," she instructed.

Coda closed his eyes and listened to the words coming from Nova. "Bring your awareness to your feet." She paused. "Now, take a few steps."

Coda took a few steps. The grass was soft, and a little damp. There wasn't much sound with each footfall.

"Good," said Nova. "Do you feel the grass beneath your paws?" Coda nodded, trusting that the rest of the students nodded as well. This wasn't so hard to do.

"Bring your awareness from your paws and into the grass around you."

What? How do I do that? That's not possible! Coda could feel his heart close a bit. He never heard of bringing your awareness to anything except to yourself, which is perfectly sane. Now, bringing it to the grass? That just can't happen.

"If you can't feel the grass, then imagine that you can feel the grass," directed Nova.

Coda relaxed a bit. It was easy for him to imagine just about anything. So, he imagined that he was a sharp blade of the grass flowing in the breeze. After a few short minutes, he decided he didn't want to be just one blade of grass, he wanted to be the entire patch of grass around him. The more he imagined it, the more it felt real.

"Take a deep breath," continued Nova, "and listen."

Coda's ears twitched as he heard the sound of the wind coursing through the air. The river, which roared behind him, sounded even louder. His ears perked to the sides as slow, steady footsteps came near. In fact, he felt them in his space—in his area of grass.

He flinched when he felt something near his head. He opened his eyes, discovering Nova standing next to him. She had her paw inches from his face.

"Did you feel that?" she asked.

Coda nodded.

"I invaded your aura," she said, putting her paw down. "When you pay attention to the subtle things in life, then something as simple as placing my paw just a couple of paw lengths away from your head will be something you'll sense immediately. It will be as if I had actually touched your physical body."

"Oh," replied Coda, "that's neat." He didn't really know what an aura was.

Nova sensed this and continued, "The aura is the energy field surrounding your body. It's an extension of your soul."

That sounded weird to Coda.

Nova padded around him, making sure to keep her voice down so as not to disrupt the others. "The main part of an aura widens and spreads from two to three panther lengths in all directions from your body. From there, it sends energy that extends much further.

"Its shape is oval, and composed of many ethereal colors, much like the colors of our crystals. The mood of the spirit animal indicates the color of the aura. It's something that VioletLights, like me, can see around all beings on a constant basis." She gazed into his eyes. "I know what you're thinking and feeling before you tell me. I even know if you are or aren't telling me exactly what you're thinking or feeling, because I can see and feel your aura." She grinned.

That's how she always knows what I'm thinking! He shifted on his paws, a little uncomfortable knowing that she could know this about every spirit animal, especially him. Nova gently touched his pelt with her tail. "Don't worry, Coda. I don't judge others, nor do I allow anyone's thoughts or feelings to affect my emotions. It's not a healthy habit to allow others to get under your fur."

She walked to the other side of him. "Now, close your eyes."

He closed his eyes and felt Nova move her paws toward his head again, but this time he ducked. *Why did I do that?*

Confused, he opened his eyes.

"Good," said Nova. "You ducked just as I swiped my paw over your head."

"How did I know to do that?" retorted Coda.

"You felt it, and reacted. Your body moved with fluidity," she brushed up against his pelt. She whispered, "Orion did that all the time. In fact, he could defend against many others with his eyes closed. He claimed it was much easier. He didn't have the distractions of the eyes to deal with."

She told him to close his eyes, and as he did, he immediately ducked. He looked at her.

"Very good." She stiffened. "Again."

Closing his eyes, he took a deep breath, then dodged and jumped to his left. He opened his eyes, observing that Nova had pounced on the spot where he was standing only a moment before. She looked at him. Her face was hard and her voice loud. "Again!"

Tightening his eyelids closed, he took another deep breath. This time, he felt a sharp chop come down forcefully to the left side of his face, but before she made contact, Coda rolled to the right, easily escaping. A moment later, he felt a jab in his hind leg.

His eyes popped open in surprise and he grunted.

Nova stood over him. "Don't assume your opponent is finished. Most of them aren't." She exhaled. "Okay, now close your eyes and focus."

Coda nodded, tightly shutting his eyes. "I'm ready."

He leaped backward as he felt a swipe coming directly at his chest, then he somersaulted left. Once again, he felt another blow coming. Ducking, he felt the whiff of air from Nova's paws passing over his ears. His movement was lightening fast.

The more Nova missed, the more Coda felt a rhythm taking control of him. Then a sudden change occurred. He felt confident, but more than he'd ever felt before. This was a dance and he was, for some reason, really good at it. His body tingled with affirmation, and as the next paw came, he caught it under the pit of his foreleg and barrel rolled to the right. He landed on top of Nova and opened his eyes. He stared at her with a bold determination. He pressed his front legs firmly against her chest.

Nova grinned widely. "That's how I remember you."

"Did you see that?" whispered a student.

"Yes, and he did it with his eyes closed."

Coda looked around, seeing Muna and the other students surrounding him. Muna dipped her head, more in honor to him rather than anything else. Everyone was wide-eyed and impressed by the display of skill they had just witnessed.

Stepping off Nova, Coda looked away from the many stares. He felt like he was being gawked at instead of admired. He didn't like the sudden stardom. Nova stood, pressing her pelt against Coda. "The Art of Defense will become more natural the more we practice. You'll start to remember what you taught us many moons ago."

Again, it felt strange to be thought of as Orion. He didn't feel like he was anyone other than Coda. *How could I have been Orion?* Shaking the thought away, knowing it got him nowhere, he rested on his haunches, thankful for a short break in practice. Glancing at Nova, he knew right away that the break would be short-lived.

Her eyes were glued to the eastern sky. Coda started to turn to look at what she was seeing, but something distracted him. The ground was covered in the colors of the rainbow. *That's weird!* Turning around, he saw why.

Hazy colors of swirling lights filled the sky. There were reds, greens, yellows, purples, pinks, and all of the colors that he'd ever seen before. Even colors he'd never seen, nor even knew existed.

"Come," yelled Nova, beckoning the students to follow her as she raced toward the east. And, one by one, the students passed him as he stood transfixed, feet planted firmly on the green grass, enjoying the peaceful and gorgeous display above.

"Are you coming, Coda?" called Muna, flicking his nose with her tail as she sped by.

Coming out of his trance, he flexed his muscles and bounded off to the east, passing Muna, flicking her back.

The grass thinned as he reached a sand covered hill where Nova and the rest of the students had stopped. They were staring intently at something to the right of them. Coda slowed to a walk, surveying the area. He'd never been in this direction before. Muna padded up to him, her tan fur glistened in the light, and sat by his side. Her ears perked up. "What's that?"

On the other side of the hill, Coda could hear someone singing. His heart softened from the magic of this spirit animal's voice. It was a female voice and he'd never heard anything so beautiful.

Muna nudged Coda with her nose. "Let's go up the hill to see who it is. That's the most beautiful voice I've ever heard."

He started to follow Muna, but felt something behind him. Something intruding and malevolent. He turned to see what it was. It wasn't long before he spotted him—Skint.

Skint stood next to a cluster of trees about a football field length away. He was with a weasel and that Zebra character. They took their eyes off Coda to view the sky, and Coda felt the uneasy sensation instantly disappear, as if a boulder had just been lifted off of him. He turned around and stared at the sky as well. The colors danced next to the sun, which slightly peered over the horizon, outlining Nova and the audience of students who sat on the peak of the hill.

Coda suddenly heard wings flapping loudly in the wind. He ducked, thinking they were only a few lengths away from his head. Crouching, he looked over his shoulder. Hundreds of birds were flying toward the hill. He could see San in the lead. She was elated.

Looking ahead, Coda noticed Muna was already at the base of the hill. He ran to catch up. As he reached the crest, Coda literally fell over backwards because of what he saw. Zoey sat in a circle, with her back to him and the other onlookers. She was the one singing! Coda's ears twitched in amazement as his sister's voice reached notes he never knew she had in her. In fact, looking around, he could tell by the audience's faces that Zoey's voice was lifting them all into to a state of bliss.

Muna whispered, "Is that your sister?"

Coda could only nod. He didn't want to talk. He didn't want to interrupt the miracle taking place before him and he didn't want the colors in the sky to stop. They were more exciting and more superior than any fireworks display he'd ever seen. They transcended almost everything.

Birds of every kind were sitting on the long hill that formed just before reaching the beach, as were the students Coda had just been training with. Then, coming out of the small forest of trees just before the hills, was Honani. He seemed to have brought the rest of Ohm Totem with him. They walked slowly, gawking at the sky.

Nova appeared from the crowd of onlookers, padding toward Coda. When she was a tail length away she spoke quietly, "Crepus will see this display. He won't need to guess about Zoey anymore. He'll know that you've both returned. There will be no doubt in his mind. He'll come at full force now." She smiled. "This makes things more interesting."

Nova stood up to leave, saying more to herself than anyone else, "I need to ponder on this." She trotted down the hill, calling over her shoulder, "Coda, bring Zoey to the Yellow Hut when you get a moment." When Nova reached the base of the hill, she took off as fast as a jet. How she moved so fast, Coda figured he'd never know.

∞

The sun had risen to its highest peak and Zoey was still singing. Everyone was in a happy trance, including Coda. When she finished, Coda watched her converse with several spirit animals in the circle. He couldn't hear what they were saying, but Zoey definitely looked uncomfortable. A few moments later, Chev lifted Zoey onto his back and walked toward the massive crowd sitting on the hill. The crowd must have sensed Zoey's discomfort and started mingling amongst themselves.

"Did you hear that, Zoey's brother?"

Coda looked down to see San peering up at him. He raised his brows in amusement. "I'm Coda."

San jumped up and down, clapping her wings. "Did you hear her?"

Of course he heard her. How could he not? He gave San a polite smile. He didn't know her very well at all, but her excitement was contagious. "I did. It was beautiful."

"And, that's your sister." She spun around clutching her wings to her heart, saying, "I wish I had a sister like that."

"So do I," said Chev, as he trudged up the sandy incline toward Coda, with Zoey riding on his back.

Coda beamed. "That was pretty awesome, Zoey."

Stunned by her brother's compliment, Zoey grinned back with an embarrassed smile. "Thanks," she muttered.

"Come on," Coda tipped his head to the west. "I'm supposed to take you to the Yellow Hut."

Chev nodded in understanding, raising his trunk to trumpet. "Off to the Yellow Hut!"

"Can I come? Can I come?" shouted San.

Coda shrugged. "I don't care." He looked at Zoey, but she was lost in thought, staring at Chev's gray, round back.

The terrain changed from a sharp decline to sandy patches. They walked slowly and Coda noticed things that he had missed before. The boulders to his right outlined the southern portion of the River Ohm, and turned into the Large Boulder way up ahead. The foliage to the left was dense and grew high. Higher than an elephant. It looked as if there could be a large house in there.

"That's where some of us Bards live. We call it Melody Hutch," said Chev.

Coda nodded. He had wondered where they stayed.

Once they got into the trees, everything was familiar again. They followed a path to the entrance of Deer Meadow, stopping when they saw a deer waiting for them. Its eyes were closed, as if in deep, quiet contemplation. It had indigo crystals pulsing gently.

They waited in silence until the deer opened her eyes. "Greetings, everyone." She bowed her head. "I'm Isi and I'll be taking Zoey and Coda to the Yellow Hut."

Surprised, Coda looked at Chev and San, wondering why they couldn't join. Chev simply nodded in quiet understanding.

San raised a wing, as if waiting for Isi to call on her.

Isi nodded.

San frowned. "But I want to come," she whined, heartbroken not to be included.

"It's my task to take them, and only them," calmly replied Isi.

Zoey jumped from Chev's back and spread her wings, landing lightly on the ground. She walked over to San, putting her wing around her. "It's okay, San. I'll tell you all about the Yellow Hut when I get back."

San nodded dejectedly. Coda couldn't understand why this would hurt her feelings so much, but thought that perhaps the Yellow Hut was something that all PureLights wanted to see.

"Well, get going, you two. I'll see you tomorrow at sun up,"

Chev said cheerfully.

"Come," said Isi, as she walked on the path to the Yellow Hut.

The sun was moving closer to the western horizon, shining its glow into their eyes. The meadow was quiet at the moment. There wasn't the usual chatter and comings and goings of spirit animals.

Coming around a corner, Coda could see the entrance of the Yellow Hut just ahead.

"Why couldn't they come?" Zoey asked Isi.

"That's for Nova to explain." She beckoned for them to walk through the entrance of the Yellow Hut.

Coda felt a little nervous as he proceeded forward through the door-less entryway. He wondered if Nova had bad news for them. Did they have to go home now? Do they have to go into hiding so Crepus didn't get them, or even worse—so Crepus didn't kill them?

Nova sat at the farthest end of the hut, staring at the ceiling. She peered into a light that trickled through the top of the hut. At further glance, Coda could see a round hole in the middle of the roof. *What a nice place to sleep at night*, he thought. He could lie on his back, staring at the stars for hours.

The rest of the hut, he noticed, was very basic. The ceiling and walls looked like straw and the ground was simply dirt. There wasn't anything that would make you think it would be a place that all PureLights would want to visit.

"I had to limit the visit to just you two," said Nova, as she softly padded toward them. She sat between them, brushing her long, thick tail against Coda's fur and Zoey's feathers. "Loyalty to the PureLights isn't a top priority to some of the tribe members these days." She crept to the doorway and peered furtively outside. "You can never be too safe."

Satisfied they were alone, Nova turned to Zoey and looked deep into her eyes. "You put on quite the show today." She gave the customary slight bow, and praised, "I'm proud of you. It was more than I ever imagined it would be."

"What did I do?" asked Zoey.

"You sang, Zoey. You sang from your heart."

"Yeah," replied Coda. "I've never heard you sing so beautifully before. And," he asked, now looking to Nova, "why was the sky all lit up in colors when she sang?"

"Because of who she is," replied Nova.

Coda could feel a sudden pulse of anger shoot out from Zoey. "Why does everyone talk about me like that?" She crossed her wings defiantly. "I am Zoey. That's who I am."

"You are Zoey, but you're here to remember who you truly are," replied Nova.

Again, Coda felt another twinge of anger from Zoey. "That doesn't make sense! I remember who I am all the time. I'm Zoey." She let out a loud sigh.

Coda was uncomfortable. He didn't like Zoey being all fired up in front of Nova. She barely knew Nova, yet she's talking to Nova like she's her best friend or something. Coda then felt an instant understanding come over him. He knew he could talk to Nova that way as well. She wouldn't care or judge him. Zoey probably knew it was the same for her.

Lowering her voice, Zoey asked, "Then why can't you just tell me who I am?"

Nova put her tail under Zoey's beak and lifted her head. "If a baby bird just hatched, would it be wise of the mother to push it out of the nest, asking it to fly?"

Zoey shook an emphatic no.

"That's why you'll learn at your own pace. Not at my pace. Not at Coda's pace. You'll learn in the way that's best suited for you. This will bring back your memory. The memory of who you really are." Nova winked. "You can't expect me to push you into something you aren't ready for, can you?"

"I guess not."

"If you were to learn everything there is to know about you this very moment, then your mind wouldn't be able to handle it. You wouldn't understand it. You'd fear and run from it," Nova said wisely.

Zoey simply looked away. Coda wondered if she even understood any of that. He sort of did, but then he was a year older.

"I've asked you both to come here because of the rainbow

display in the sky. Crepus will know for certain that you've both arrived. I've felt he's just been guessing about you two thus far," she said to them both, but pointing her nose to Zoey. "And, there will be no holding back from now on. He'll do everything he can to stop you."

"Stop me from doing what?" asked Zoey, recoiling at the thought of Crepus.

"You have the power to end the Dim's reign in Ohm Totem and he knows this. He'll do anything to halt your learning. He doesn't want you to find out who you really are."

"So, then what do I do?"

"You listen to your heart. It will keep you safe. Remember, there's always safety no matter what happens, and no matter where you are. Always be aware of that."

Nova took a deep breath, staring vacantly past Coda and Zoey. "I can't guide you your entire life and I can't always safeguard you, either. There will be times when I won't be around, but there will usually be someone to protect you. That's the way of it. And, if by chance you find you're without protection, you have the skills seeded deep in your hearts to protect yourselves."

Nova turned to Coda. "You are your sister's guardian. Again, you can't always be with her, but when you are, it's your duty to keep her safe."

Coda's mind was spinning. He didn't like the idea of guarding his sister, but understood the danger she faced. The longer he was in Ohm Totem, the more he was having those types of feelings. If he could help it, no one would hurt a single feather on her body. He eyed his sister. She was gathering her thoughts. His sister was the secret to Crepus's defeat. He didn't really understand how, but he admired her for it. It wasn't a feeling Coda was used to having for his sister.

Nova asked if they had any questions. Feeling overwhelmed, Zoey slowly shook her head. Coda shook his head as well, then stopped. He did have a question, but it was way off topic.

"How come I'm never hungry?"

Zoey nodded vigorously. "Yeah, and I never see anyone

eating."

"Ah, yes. A good observation." Nova explained, "That's the way of things in our world. You won't see anyone foraging for food, because it's not needed in our bodies. This is because of Prana. It's an energy that sustains all of life and is all around us at all times, even in your world. It's deeply connected to our breath. It's in the air, it's in the rays of the sun, it's in the glow of the moon, it's in everything. It provides the life force that we need to live."

"So you don't eat?" asked Zoey.

Nova shook her head. "Our bodies are at such a high state of vibration that if we were to eat, our energy levels would plummet. Our thoughts, moods, and physical bodies would soon follow." She paused and took a giant breath as if to demonstrate, and then exhaled. Her eyes lit up with vibrant, vital life force. "We live off the air we breath. It's something that all beings can do instead of ingesting physical food."

"So," replied Coda, "I still don't understand. I won't ever be hungry?"

"Not in Ohm Totem. The health of our world is untainted, and therefore it's easier for your body to access Prana. Your crystals also help. Once the air in our world touches the face of your crystals, it triggers your body to receive Prana immediately."

"Oh! That's why it feels so different when you breathe. It's richer than the air we breathe at home," said Zoey.

"Yes," said Nova. "The air here has a quality that makes it seem richer. Make no mistake though, it's the same type of air you breathe at home. It's just like I said, it's untainted, plus, there's more of it here than in your world because of the trees. Here, our forests and trees are sacred and numerous. In both our worlds, the forests are the lungs of the planet."

Coda raised his brows in question. "Don't you miss eating?"

Nova shook her head knowingly. "Before we arrived in Ohm Totem, food was a necessity, but a nuisance. It was always on our minds, from sun up to sun down." She thought for a moment. "To tell you the truth, this is the first time I've even thought of food for thousands and thousands of moons. It's

224

just something we live without. We have more energy without it."

An abrupt rap on the side of the entry way prompted Coda to spin around.

"Nova, Ke would like a word with you," announced Isi.

Nova raised her paw. "Just a moment, Isi." She looked at the children, "Anything else you'd like to ask?"

They both shook their heads and Nova bid them farewell with some final words of wisdom. "Empty your mind and proceed from your heart."

∞

Nova's sweet scent hung over Coda and Zoey as they walked to the meadow. The day was getting a tad bit darker as the sun started to fall closer to the western beaches. Coda noticed dark clouds that clung to the borders of the Dim Lands, looking as if they were too frightened to wander into the land of the PureLights. How strange that was, he thought. The wind never seemed to beckon the dark clouds over to the Sihu tribe.

They followed a path that exited the meadow and wound into a clutch of small trees.

"Let's stop here," said Zoey, as she pointed to a soft stretch of grass.

They sat down and Zoey spoke with a heavy heart. "Coda, you don't act like you miss Mom and Dad."

The words hit his heart like a punch. It was true. He hadn't thought much about his mom and dad. He hadn't had time. Everything was so haywire around here, but he nodded in agreement, "I know. I don't know why." He felt like a bad son and sadness began to trickle over him.

"It's okay, Coda." Zoey patted his front foot with her wing. "I miss mom and dad enough for the both of us and you've been so busy practicing, you're probably too tired to think."

"Nah, I just like it here. It feels familiar to me, like I've been here before. I guess that's why I haven't thought of them much." Coda rested his head against his forelegs. "It's like I've been here my whole life and everyone seems like family."

225

Zoey's eyes widened like saucers. "You want to stay here?"

Coda shrugged, "I don't know." He pondered for a moment, thinking of something to say to his sister that would settle her down. "I probably wouldn't want to stay. I'd miss our parents too much. I guess I could visit Ohm Totem every so often, after we go back home."

"Yeah, I thought of that too. And," she whispered, "it feels like I've been here forever as well. Even when I dream, it feels like I've known Lao forever!"

Lao? Coda wondered. "Who's Lao?"

"He's the wolf that helps me in my dreams. We came here because he asked us to," she said matter-of-factly, as if he should have known this already.

"What? I thought the Snow Tree asked us."

Zoey shook her head. "I met the Snow Tree after I met Lao. He asked for our help and the Snow Tree just showed us how to get here."

"Oh, okay." Lao, the Snow Tree, Nova the VioletLight, Chev the friendly elephant? This new experience here in Ohm Totem had been thrown at him without him asking for it. It landed on him like a ton of bricks. Coda sighed, watching Zoey. She had drifted off into thought, staring at the western sky.

For a while they sat in silence. It was peaceful, even though spirit animals occasionally walked by them. For the first time in a long time Coda didn't want Zoey to go away and mind her own business. He actually felt fine around her. He didn't know why, or if that was such a good thing, but he wasn't annoyed by her presence. He frowned. *What's happening to me here?*

The breeze was low, bringing with it the fragrance of beautiful flowers. The sun was almost gone, dipping much lower in the west, soon to awaken the moon from its slumber.

Coda took a deep breath and stood up. "How long have we been sitting here?"

"For a long while, I think," replied Zoey, stretching her wings. "Let's go to bed."

Coda nodded as Zoey lifted her wings and flew , in the air. They were only a short distance from the Spruce Hollow, but

Coda raised his tail gesturing for Zoey to wait. "Get on my back and I'll walk you there."

"It's only right there, Coda," she protested, pointing with her beak. "I can make it just fine."

"No!" Coda stamped his foot. "I'm your guardian from now on and I'm making sure you're safe. Yesterday I wasn't around to help you when a spirit animal almost hurt you, but now I'm with you. I'm not letting anything bad happen to you again!" His face was stern, much like his father's when he'd discipline them.

Zoey smiled. She felt comforted by his words. She flew over to Coda, hovered above him, and gently landed on his back. "Okay, let's go then!" she shouted.

The journey was short, but Coda liked the feeling of his sister on his back. He didn't want to let her go, but when she jumped off and landed next to him, he softened. She was grinning with gratitude. She waved a goodbye, saying, "I love you, brother."

Coda about fell down. That was the first time she had ever told him that. They always knew they loved each other, like brothers and sisters usually do, but they'd never voiced it. Coda looked down, a little embarrassed and muttering, "I love you, too."

He watched her walk to the door and knock the secret knock that let her in. The door opened with the clang of the bells and the high-pitched voice of Taregan.

"Well, it's nice to see the lady of the day!"

As the door shut, Coda strolled to the Marble Burrow, hoping to catch an uninterrupted sleep, which he highly doubted would occur if Skint had anything to do with it.

Chapter 21

The zytes were nearly drowned by the dark when the pitter-patter of small feet awakened Coda again. For an instant he was irritated with his sister. She had a habit of getting up at night, waking him while on her tiptoes, thinking that she was silent on the carpet. He was about to tell her to go back to bed when he realized he wasn't at home. He was at the Marble Burrow.

He heard the door roll open. Glancing toward it, he saw Skint scampering out into the hallway. Curiosity poked at Coda. He'd had enough of Skint's sneaking around. He wanted to find out where the squirrel was going.

He sat up, shaking himself awake. His heavy eyelids responded well, but his body felt stiff. He jumped up and down a couple times to loosen everything up, but that didn't seem to do the trick. He walked to the door anyway. It was closed.

He blew on it and, just as it should, it opened, revealing a bluish-white glowing hallway. The zytes were in full glory as he headed down the hallway, hoping to catch a glimpse of Skint.

Past the hallway and entering the large hall of Marble Burrow, he noticed Skint's bushy tail slinking passed the main door. It shut silently behind him. Coda gazed at the massive crystal that stood to his right. He took in the magic of it for a moment, then headed toward the main door.

"Hey," came a voice behind him.

The tiger, the one who said a friendly hello to him on the first night he had entered the Marble Burrow hall, walked toward him.

Coda smiled and bowed. "Hi."

"What are you doing?" the tiger snarled.

Coda stepped back, a little stunned at the tiger's disposition. "I-I'm going outside."

The tiger eyed him suspiciously. "And, why?"

Coda shrugged. He wanted to hide. He felt he had done something terribly wrong, but what? Was he not supposed to go out at night? If not, wouldn't Honani have told him so? He looked at the tiger's eyes. They were fierce and unmoving. He didn't want to rat out Skint, saying that he left, nor did he want to tell the tiger that he wanted to follow the squirrel to see where he was going, so he made up something. "I just wanted some fresh air."

The tiger slowly shook his head. Coda could see that he had blue crystals on his chest and forehead. He knew this tiger could rip him apart with one bite and for some reason, Coda couldn't stop himself from imagining him doing so. He prepared himself for an attack. The tiger, instead, took a few steps toward the door, then sat in front of it, blocking Coda's exit. "Why are you lying to me, young one?" asked the tiger.

"Because you've frightened him, Sigun!"

Coda turned to see Honani approaching them. "I've not ever seen you act like this, Sigun. Why are you blocking our friend from leaving the Marble Burrow?"

Sigun relaxed and blinked his eyes a couple of times. "I'm merely doing as Nova asked."

The badger padded up to Coda's side. "I'm not aware that Nova had asked you to do anything. What was it that she asked?"

Sigun dipped his head, his eyes narrowed. "She asked me to protect this young panther friend of ours." He looked over his shoulder at the closed door, and then back at Honani. "If I let him out, then he will have no protection."

"Oh, I see." Honani eyed Sigun for several moments. "However, I ask that you let Coda leave at his own will. His protection is the night. He is a master in that realm. He'll be safe."

Sigun shook his head again. He let out a low growl. "I can't do that."

Honani turned to Coda and put out his paw, showing Coda his way to the door. "Proceed," he said.

Coda looked at the tiger's hostile eyes, then back at Honani. "I'm okay, Honani. I can just go back to bed and get some air in the morning."

The tiger grinned. "That's a good little boy. Now turn around and go back into your room."

That angered Coda, stirring up an aggressive energy in his belly. He didn't know where it came from, but it made him feel like fire was flaming off his black fur. He lowered his eyes and body as he slowly crept toward the tiger.

Honani stepped between them, calming the situation. "It's not your place to impede the comings and goings of any Being." He took a step toward Sigun. "I've explained that Coda needs no security. He'll be safe. You have my word, Sigun. Now, let Coda proceed!"

Sigun stood his ground, letting out a throaty growl, which practically shook the hall. Coda crouched, waiting to pounce if Sigun attacked Honani. Honani simply held his paw up, indicating for Coda to stand back.

The tiger leaned downed, glaring into Honani's eyes. He sniffed the badger in contempt, letting out a frustrated grunt. "At sun up, I'll let Nova know about this." He walked cautiously around Honani and padded off down a hallway on the other side of the big crystal.

Honani watched Sigun leave. Coda was puzzled.

"It seems there's more to Sigun than I thought," said Honani. He smiled at Coda, then turned and blew on the round door. It rolled open. He gestured for Coda to walk through.

Coda bowed his head in thanks, then thought for a moment. "Will Nova get mad if I go? Sigun said she wanted me to stay."

Honani shook his head no. "Nova would never control another being. Your will is your own, not hers. Plus, I haven't heard the screech of an owl warning us that the Dims are coming, so you'll be safe. You have the freedom here to do as you please, so long as it doesn't harm another." His indigo crystals glowed and he nodded. "And so long as it doesn't go against the PureLight Order."

"The PureLight Order?" asked Coda. His whiskers twitched and every cell in his body vibrated when he said those words. He'd heard about the PureLight Order before, but where?

"Yes, the PureLight Order. You'll learn about it soon." Honani beckoned Coda to go through the main entrance. "You may get some air, if you wish."

Coda walked into the long tunnel that led in and out of the Marble Burrow. He looked behind to see the badger staring back at him. Honani exuded a calm confidence. Coda didn't. It felt like he was doing something wrong. It was the first time he had felt guilty here in Ohm Totem.

He walked on, noticing the hazy glow of the zytes. They weren't bright so late in the evening; *good thing for those of us who are sneaking out*, thought Coda. The farther he walked, the deeper his thoughts went. He remembered feeling fine when he first decided to see where Skint was going. It felt good even when he was almost to the main door of the Marble Burrow. It was only when the tiger told him that he couldn't leave the burrow that these feelings of wrong started creeping in. Was he trying to slow Coda down in order to give Skint a longer lead?

Skint! Coda halted, crouching down, trying to disappear within the shadows of the tunnel.

Up ahead, Skint sat at the top of the dirt tunnel. He glanced nervously from side to side. He was low to the ground as well, as if doing his best not to be noticed. Staying low, he scurried forward, until he was out of Coda's sight. Coda inched forward as quietly as he could, until he reached the lip of the dirt tunnel. He peeked out, but only saw the forest trees, the grass, and foliage. Coda narrowed his vision and surveyed the land. Coda remembered what Honani taught him about being able to see the whole picture.

The moonlight lit up the forest, casting shadows of trees across the land. *Movement*, thought Coda. Out of the corner of his eye, he saw Skint scuttling quickly toward the Large Boulder. *What's he doing?*

Coda lowered his hind legs, silently pushing forward into a slow run, matching the speed of the small squirrel. His vision again narrowed, and the confidence of a skilled and stealthy panther took over. He moved with careful steps, allowing each paw to cushion itself quietly, but quickly, on the ground. He didn't know how he could be so quiet, it just happened. As Coda followed, Skint ran up a large fir tree, and out of view.

Coda stopped, searching the many trees in front of him. He wondered if he should climb a tree, but then noticed movement on a fir tree next to the one Skint had climbed. Taking a closer look, Coda realized that Skint had jumped from one tree to the other.

As the trees moved and shuddered, Coda knew that trailing Skint would be easy. Skint jumped from tree to tree, clumsily clinging to branches with his front claws, spinning his back legs, as if he was on a bicycle, to grab hold with his entire body. His movements were noisy and disruptive. Coda wondered how all of Ohm Totem didn't hear him.

Coda suddenly froze. The movement in the trees had ceased. He could see Skint looking right at him from the base of a tree. It was about ten yards from the Large Boulder. Even though the moonlight lit the ground brightly, the ground still held shadows from the trees. Coda was lucky to be in one of the shadows. His black fur masked his body well and Skint merely gazed over him. Not seeing anything that might be troublesome, Skint turned and ran up the tree again, clumsily jumping from one tree to the next.

Coda almost gasped out loud and his heart clutched when he saw Skint attempting a long jump. It was too long. A jump that Coda knew the small squirrel couldn't make, but flexing his back leg muscles, Skint attempted the leap anyway. Skint hit the branch of the tree with his outstretched paws, but lost his footing a second later. He careened down the tree, hitting one branch after another. Coda ran toward him, hoping to catch Skint before he could get hurt, but Skint was too far away. He landed with a loud clunk, stopping Coda in his tracks.

Skint lay motionless and Coda crouched low, watching.

For many long moments, Skint didn't move. *Is he okay?* A panic came over Coda. *Is he dead?* Just then, Skint sat up. He was alert. He wiggled his legs and body, then stood up and ran toward the Large Boulder.

Coda followed.

When Skint reached the boulder, his eyes darted around, checking to see if anyone had followed him. Coda shrank into the shadows. *What is he doing?*

Skint extended his front squirrel paw to something that Coda couldn't quite make out and a portion of the rock opened. Skint tiptoed inside the opening and the rock shut behind him.

Stunned, Coda wondered how Skint knew about the boulder. *Do all of the spirit animals here know about the boulder? Why didn't Nova tell me that it opened?*

Coda looked around to see if anyone was watching. He saw and heard nothing, other than trees moving in the wind. He ran as fast as he could to the Large Boulder, hoping that the door was still partially open. When he got there, it was closed. He stared at the rock face, searching for the way in. He didn't see a button of any kind anywhere.

He placed both front paws on the boulder, feeling for something that Skint may have touched to open it. He found nothing. *Maybe, it's right—*

"Coda!" said a voice from among the shadowed trees.

Startled, Coda whipped around, his whole body tensed for a fight.

Chapter 22

Why can't I sleep? Zoey wondered with agitation. So far in Ohm Totem, she'd been able to go to sleep every night just after she'd close her eyes. *I'm too wound up,* she thought.

The day had been a long one and she'd spent half of it singing in front of all those spirit animals on the beach. It must have stirred her up, making her antsy, because her skin crawled with goosebumps as her mind raced with thoughts of singing. She had enjoyed it so much. It's so different here in Ohm Totem.

Maybe it's that Prana stuff making me feel like this?

She sighed and closed her eyes again, listening to the sound of San snoring triumphantly across the room. A moment later Zoey opened her eyes and shook her wings. *I can't sleep.* She stood up and walked over to the open window. *Maybe I'll just stare at the stars.*

Looking out of the window, she noticed that everything was perfectly still. She gazed out into the twinkling night sky and saw the glow of the moon. Its light was bright, spreading across the forest floor below. She took a big sniff. The sweet fragrance of the flowers that grew everywhere filled her senses.

It's so peaceful here, she thought. *I don't blame Coda for wanting to stay.*

A movement out of the corner of her eye caught her attention. She saw a black shadow creeping slowly toward something. It was Coda! His belly grazed the ground and his focus never wavered from whatever he was stalking, but Zoey couldn't see any other movement. Coda was heading straight for the Large Boulder. *What's he doing that for?* Then she lost him in the shadows.

Was she just imagining that? She blinked her eyes a few times, thinking she was just too wired tonight. *I must be seeing things.* She walked back to her nest and burrowed in.

She closed her eyes a third time. She tried to force herself asleep by taking in several deep breaths. Then she heard a whisper.

Coda needs your help.

Zoey's eyes popped open. She jumped up and peered out of the window again. She didn't see anything or anyone who might have whispered to her. She gazed at San. She was fast asleep. *Was that the wind? Snow Tree? Was that you?*

There was no response to her thoughts. It didn't matter.

She glanced over at San again, making sure she was really sleeping. She was. Good, thought Zoey. She felt that San was a wonderful friend, but tended to be a little loud. Zoey didn't want a loud spirit animal tagging along with her.

Knowing that the window was too small for her to sneak out of, she moved quietly to the door and opened it. She looked all around, seeing that the balconies were empty, or at least the ones she could see on the left side. The view to the right was blocked by the door, so she closed it a crack, peering around it. The coast was clear.

Over the railing, she saw Taregan fast asleep on his little perch. All she had to do was sneak past him and she was free to find Coda.

She stretched her wings, gliding down to the main door. She landed silently. She was confident no one had seen or heard her, not even Taregan. She held her breath as she tiptoed forward.

She then remembered something. The door had bells on it, and would definitely jingle if she opened it. How was she going to get out without making a sound?

"Just open the door, Zoey, and be on your way."

Zoey jumped back. It was Taregan. He had hopped off of his perch and walked over to her. He leaned in, whispering, "Empty your mind and proceed from your heart."

Did he mean to follow her heart and help Coda? Or was it something else? What did he mean? Zoey looked quizzically at him.

He flung his wings all about. "Oh, dizzle dazzle, just go! I don't have all night to explain the comings, goings, and proddings of your heart."

He hurried her over to the door, swinging it open. The bells clanged and he gently pushed her outside. "Now, follow that heart of yours. Get, get!"

Zoey heard the door shutting behind her. A moment later, the door opened. She twisted around to see Taregan's head sticking out. "Be careful! And remember, danger isn't so dangerous if you're prepared for it. Keep your eyes peeled and your mind clear. Pay attention to everything and, by all means, pay attention to your heart! It'll steer you to safety."

Taregan shut the door, leaving Zoey wide-eyed. *Am I heading into danger? Why would he say all that?* Shrugging it off, she realized that Taregan was just an old kook. He probably just wanted to be helpful in some way.

Zoey shivered, bringing her back to the present. It was chilly out and the sudden wind ruffled her feathers. The trees above rocked back and forth, doing their best to keep the cold breeze away from the ground below. How quickly it had changed from just moments ago.

Opening her wings, she jumped and flew toward the last place she had seen Coda. She stayed beneath the canopy of trees, just in case it was too windy up there. She didn't want to try her new flying skills in a challenging wind.

As she flapped, she again felt the freedom and joy of flying. She wanted to do some somersaults and twists, but knew she must get to her brother. Flying over the Marble Burrow, she saw him pressing his paws up against the Large Boulder to the north. *What the heck is he up to?*

She glided in his direction, landing on a tree's thick, outstretched branch. The bark and needles were cold, something she wasn't used to in Ohm Totem. She smiled as she watched her bother. *He's always getting into adventures and mischief.*

"Coda!" she called in a loud whisper.

Coda whipped around. His eyes and body froze, then relaxed when he saw her. "Oh, it's you." Don't scare me like that!"

"Oh, sorry," replied Zoey.

Coda quickly turned back to the boulder, pressing on it here and there with his paws. He looked over his shoulder at Zoey. "Well, don't just sit there. Come and help."

Zoey shrugged. "Okay." She spread her wings, gliding effortlessly through the air, landing next to his hind legs. "What are you doing?"

"Skint," murmured Coda, as he continued to press one different jutting outcrop after another. "He's in here and I want to see why."

"What? Skint's inside the boulder?" Zoey thought her brother was bonkers. He'd finally lost it. *Is he sleepwalking?* She put her wings on her hips. "Please tell me you're joking."

Coda shook his head as he frantically looked for something that would open up this big rock.

"Why is Skint in the Large Boulder?"

Coda stopped and said with exasperation, "That's what I want to find out." He was panting and sounding desperate. "He's been sneaking out every night and I want to find out where he's going. I have this feeling that I must find him. It's weird."

"He's probably just meeting with the weasel, Piv, and that zebra, Ke."

Coda rolled his eyes. "Yeah, they hang out. I forgot."

"They're probably planning their government stuff," thought Zoey out loud. She remembered Skint and shuddered, "That Skint is mean. He put me into something that Numee called an energy clutch."

Alarmed, Coda turned, frantically trying to find the latch that must open the door. "We have to see what they're up to. I'm not letting him do that to you again."

"What's going on, you two?"

Zoey and Coda about jumped out of their fur and feathers. Behind them stood San. She was yawning and her wings were stretched out wide.

Coda looked at Zoey with a glare that said, *Why did you bring her?*

Zoey shrugged her innocence. "What are you doing here, San?"

"I saw you leave. So, I followed." She ran toward the boulder, looking up at Coda. "Can I help?"

Coda frowned, "Help with what?"

"I don't know," San replied, suddenly confused. "Well, what are you looking for?"

"I'm looking for the dang entrance to the boulder," retorted Coda.

Coda was getting impatient, so Zoey stepped forward, "Do you know how to open the Large Boulder, San?"

San shook her head. "I can help you find the way in though!"

"Alright," replied Coda.

San raised her wings in the air, screeching, "Yay!"

"Shhhh," Zoey and Coda whispered in unison.

Together, they searched the rock wall, pushing and pulling on everything that protruded in or out, but they were getting nowhere. Nothing seemed to open the boulder. Then a click sounded, prompting Zoey to stop what she was doing.

The base of the boulder abruptly collapsed upon itself, revealing a small entrance wide enough for them to get through.

"I did it!" hollered San, as she hovered in the air.

"Shhh!" exclaimed Zoey.

"How did you do that?" asked Coda.

"Well, I saw the indentation right here to the right and it looked like it needed something in it, so I tried pushing a rock into it, and then the door opened. That was easy!" she added gleefully.

Without waiting for the others, San glided through the newly created hole, disappearing into the Large Boulder.

"Me first," ordered Coda.

Zoey watched Coda slowly squeeze himself through the gap in the boulder. If it was a tad narrower, then he'd be waiting outside. A moment later, Coda gave the OK.

Shaking her wings, she folded them into her sides. She wasn't confident enough to fly into the hole like San. She walked, instead. The entrance was thin, taking but a mere second to walk through.

"Welcome," echoed Coda's voice as Zoey entered the Large Boulder. Her eyes glowed with amazement. It was gorgeous inside, with marble floors, white marble walls, and white marbled arched ceilings. Beautiful columns, just like the Greek architecture that Zoey had seen in schoolbooks were spread throughout and the area was lined with tablets.

"The columns," said Coda, as he looked up and around at the ceiling, "are holding up the ceiling." He grinned from ear to ear. "The Large Boulder isn't a boulder at all. It's something else."

"Guys?" interrupted San, as she flew into a room to the north. "Do you want to come and check this out?"

Zoey and Coda followed her to the separate room. On the way, they passed lines and lines of tablets. Each had its own engraving with a rolled up scroll attached to it. How the scroll was attached, Zoey didn't know. She stopped to inspect one. "Whoa! Look at this Coda."

Coda padded next to her. She pointed to the scroll, "It's floating just above the tablet. It's not being held by anything. How does it do that?"

"I don't know," said Coda. "A VioletLight's magic?"

"Yeah, probably." They moved on and Zoey noticed that all of the engravings stated that they were prophecies. One read, "The Prophecy of the Elders." Another read, "The ThunderBird Prophecy." She knew that she could press a green emerald on a tablet and it would shoot off a green light, showing them the meaning held within. She was tempted to press one, then thought better of it. *We should find Skint.*

They entered the room San had beckoned them to. It was massive. It was the center room of the Large Boulder, and had four other rooms jutting out from this one. One to the north, one to the west, one to the east, and the one they just came in from—the one to the south.

This room was circular and had high, arched marble ceilings, much higher than the first room they were just in, but there weren't any columns in this one. On the wall opposite and diagonal to Zoey hung a large plaque with an empty frame underneath it. She felt compelled to look more closely. She lifted off and flew to it.

As she landed, Coda arrived at the same time. Coda read out loud, "The Purelight Order." Then glanced curiously up and down the frame. "It's not here."

"It was stolen by Crepus many, many moons ago," said San. Zoey looked toward San, who stood in the middle of the room. Just below San was an incredible design set in the marbled floor. San realized what Zoey was looking at it and jumped up and down. "See! Look, look!" She pointed beneath her feet.

The entire floor displayed an intricate design or symbol of some sort. Zoey had never seen anything like it. It kind of looked like a snowflake, or a flower. It was composed of multiple, evenly spaced, overlapping circles that started in the middle and radiated outward. The pattern covered the entire floor. Zoey didn't know what this pattern meant or why it was there.

"It's the Flower of Life," said San in wonder.

Zoey and Coda weren't as impressed. *What's so neat about that?* mused Zoey.

Reading their body language, San added, "It's the symbol of the creation of life. It's how The Great Spirit created us all, from the smallest atom to the biggest tree. It's a sacred symbol."

Zoey still didn't understand why that was impressive. She'd never heard of a sacred symbol.

"You don't understand," continued San. "Crepus said that he destroyed all of these. But, this one is here, fully intact. Maybe there's more of them in Ohm Totem." She scratched her head. "It's considered a pathway to a better life. It holds the instructions on how to be a VioletLight. These symbols used to be everywhere, until Crepus started crushing them. But this one is still untouched." She put her wings over her heart, singing out, "There's still hope!"

"Shhh," growled Coda. "Now, what's that have to do with hope?"

San started moving back and forth, whispering under her breath. "But he told us he destroyed it. Why would he lie? No, no, this flower of life in front of me must be a fake."

Back and forth she went, until Coda barked, "Stop!"

She stiffened. "Sorry." Her head drooped. "I was told that Crepus destroyed these and that we had no hope and..." she suddenly stopped herself, as if she was going to say something she shouldn't.

"And...what?" Zoey prodded.

San ignored Zoey. She walked over to the middle of the symbol and blew onto it. Nothing happened. She paused, then blew again. The sound of rock scraping against rock started to envelop the room. Zoey lost her balance, staggering backward. The floor was moving.

Getting back on her feet, she watched in amazement as the middle of the floor opened up.

"Skint probably went this way," San murmured.

The floor stopped moving and Zoey pondered for a moment, then eyed San with suspicion. "How did you know we were looking for Skint? We never told you we were."

San looked up at Coda and Zoey with dismay. She sighed, closed her eyes and fell forward, disappearing into the darkness below.

Zoey sprinted forward with outstretched wings. "San!" She peered over the lip of the hole, into the opening. Her heart started to beat faster as she scanned below. *Where is San?* Zoey blinked several times, hoping to see through the darkness. It didn't work. She only saw blackness. "San? Are you there?"

Chapter 23

The thick rock stairs were cold. In fact, the entire castle, including the forest that grew beside it, was starting to freeze from the sudden change of temperature. Crepus wondered if this coming Shiver was such a good thing after all. Then, taking another step down the stairs, he erased the thought. The negative thought patterns in the Dim Lands was one of his goals. He had to change the attitudes of the spirit animals in order for the weather to change, bringing in the Shiver. The Shiver would reduce the population, making it easier to control everyone.

The stairs circled around a main pillar. Crepus took slow, deliberate steps. He didn't want to hurry himself, or his three ape companions who walked behind him. He needn't exude too much energy to meet his spy. A spy he disdained. In fact, he disdained all spies. They weren't the easiest creatures to trust.

"Is that fur-ball runt here yet?" asked Crepus.

"Yes, my Lord. He's waiting at the bottom of the staircase."

It was Maldwyn who replied. His tone was solemn and his posture stiff as he followed Crepus.

Crepus hissed, "You should be grateful I kept you alive, Maldwyn. I'm your savior, you know."

Maldwyn stiffened even more, but remained silent as they continued the long trek down the stairs. The two apes behind him snickered. They didn't like Crepus paying so much attention to this new recruit, and anything negative tossed Maldwyn's way was a plus for them.

As they descended, the stairway grew darker. Crepus stopped and looked at the unlit torches lining the walls. He closed his eyes, and instantly a reddish yellow flame topped each and every torch, giving much needed light.

"Take that as a lesson, Maldwyn. I could put a flame on top

of your head if I wanted to." The two apes behind Maldwyn laughed outright.

Crepus took another step forward then halted, checking over his shoulder to see that the three apes were tailing closely behind. They carried long, wooden spears and no-nonsense expressions. Maldwyn, though, eyed Crepus guardedly.

"Keep your eyes straight ahead," growled the dragon.

Crepus turned, not caring if Maldwyn obeyed or not, and slowly continued toward the bottom of the staircase. Over twenty steps later, he touched the cold, frozen dirt and eyed his spy. The spy stood across from Crepus, snickering as he leaned against the stone wall of the tunnel.

"What news do you have?" asked Crepus.

Maldwyn reached the bottom stair and stood beside the dark reptile. The other apes took watch a few lengths away.

The spy stepped forward, holding his head high. "The Skylark has shown her true colors. She is who you say she is."

Crepus rolled his eyes, "Yes, yes. I saw the display in the sky." He rolled his head from one side to the other. "How amusing it was," he droned, closing his eyes, doing his best to control his anger. "Now, do you have anything important to tell me?"

"Yes," replied the spy. "Nova is being more protective over them."

"I'd do the same if I were her. I wouldn't let them out of my sight. Anything else?"

The spy searched his memory. "They changed the meeting of the Circle of Elders to tomorrow. It's not at full moon like usual and..."

"And," interrupted Crepus, "it's customary to have new students join them." Cruelty dribbled from his smile. "That means the skylark and panther will be there. Good. That's the best information you've given me thus far, Skint."

Skint bowed. "Thank you, my Lord."

"And Skint, we can't converse through thought patterns anymore," added Crepus. "I felt the black panther listening before you left the other night." Crepus paused, closing his eyes as if sensing something. Opening his eyes, he snapped his head toward the squirrel, hissing, "Were you followed?"

Wide-eyed in protest, Skint shook his head. "I made sure I wasn't."

Crepus narrowed his eyes and slinked away, walking with short strides down the underground tunnel, making sure each step was silent. "I feel several beating PureLight hearts." He sniffed the air. "They're not here yet, but they'll soon arrive."

Chapter 24

Zoey and Coda stared into the black hole. Zoey's eyes adjusted to the darkness, allowing her to faintly see steep stairs leading down into a tunnel. She knew Coda had keen eyesight in the dark, but he didn't see San either. Then a small glow of light suddenly appeared, revealing that the steps were marble leading to a dirt floor.

Coda pointed with his paw. "Zytes just turned on."

"San?" called Zoey.

Silence.

Zoey looked at Coda. Both were terrified. The worst went through Zoey's mind. *Did San get hurt? Why did she fall into the hole like that?*

Coda poked his head farther into the hole. "San!"

A crunching sound echoed in the tunnel. It sounded like someone stepping on rocky soil.

"I'm down here."

"Why did you scare us like that?" Coda scowled.

San came into view at the base of the staircase. She shrugged her shoulders. "I don't know. I wanted to get down here, I guess. I wasn't trying to scare you."

Zoey puffed up in indignation. "Well, don't do that again. You scared me—" she glanced at Coda, "and you scared Coda, too."

"Okay," San pouted. "I won't do that again."

Coda slowly crept down the stairs, being careful with every step. "It seems alright down here," he said, giving Zoey the OK to follow.

"Okay," replied Zoey. She flapped her wings and landed next to San. A light, chilly breeze blew against her and she shivered from the sudden change in temperature.

"Where are we?" asked Coda.

They were in a large tunnel that went on for what seemed to

be miles. In front of them and behind them, the tunnel went as far as the eye could see. San pointed to the zytes that lined the walls. "There are zytes everywhere, so for sure spirit animals have been down here before."

Zoey noticed a large round boulder. It was red in color and looked too smooth to be a rock, but nonetheless, it was a rock. Coda saw it as well, walked over to it, and touched it with his paw. Peering around it, Zoey saw another one by its side.

San leaned forward, inspecting the ground. "Over here," she called out quietly.

Zoey flew next to San and Coda bounded to their side. They were looking at an indentation in the ground. "So," said Coda, "what's so neat about that?"

San straightened, explaining, "I find it curious that there are two boulders to our left, but an empty space here with an concave shape in the ground. The shape is the size of a boulder."

Zoey looked at the other boulders. They seemed to be heavier than a house, but they were perfectly round, as if carved out of a mountain. *You'd need a tractor to move one of those, or something even bigger.* She stared back at San blankly. "What's so curious about that? There couldn't have been a boulder there. No one, except a VioletLight, could move it. Especially not someone as small as Skint."

"Oh yeah," replied San. She looked away, lost in thought, and then confided, "There are stories about tunnels that were created long before the PureLights came to Ohm Totem. If I remember correctly, when the PureLights found them they learned how to use them. The tunnels were part of a system of travel that involved these boulders here!" She pointed at the closest boulder with her wing, "They're called Zolts. PureLights used to travel from tribe to tribe in them. Instead of taking ten moons to get somewhere, it'd take half a moon, or even less."

Coda and Zoey still didn't quite understand what she was getting at. And for some reason, San suddenly sounded much smarter than normal. Pushing this thought away, Zoey glanced at the Zolts.

Coda was standing on his hind legs next to one, touching it again with his paws. "I bet a VioletLight could make one of these and they could probably get it down here by moving it with their minds."

San shook her head. "Like I said, they were here before the PureLights arrived."

How does San know all of this? Zoey wondered.

Before Zoey could ask, San spread her wings, jumped and flew to the closest Zolt. She paced around it and blew on it. Instantly, the side of the boulder pressed inward, then a piece of it rolled open. To Zoey's surprise, the Zolt had a door.

"Whoa! How did you know to do that?" asked Coda.

"I thought it, so I did it," replied San as she peered around the inside.

Zoey flew over to Coda, who whispered in her ear, "She's been in that boulder before."

"How do you know?" Zoey whispered back.

"Because you have to blow twice if—"

"Check this out!" interrupted San.

Zoey walked toward her, hopping onto the edge of the opening.

Inside the boulder was a large empty space, surrounded and lined by a perfectly smooth and concaved rock. It could easily fit all three of them inside and, to Zoey's surprise, that's precisely what San had in mind. She beckoned them to join her, and they complied.

The floor was nice and warm, but there wasn't much else to the Zolt. Just smooth, rounded rock above, below, and all around them.

"What exactly is this thing?" asked Coda.

San ignored him, then blew again. The door to the Zolt closed, and everything became pitch black.

"Hey," said Zoey, "what's going on?"

A loud clunk startled them. The boulder started to move, or at least it felt as if it did. An instant later, a screen blinked on in front of them, flooding the darkness with new light. The screen was like a window, allowing them to see right through the rock. And, they were indeed moving!

"Destination?" asked an indistinct male voice coming from the Zolt.

"We're moving!" exclaimed Zoey.

"That's not a destination I recognize," replied the Zolt.

Coda shrugged at Zoey, trying not to grin too widely. He was rather enjoying this. If he was alone, Zoey pictured him putting his paws up in the air, joyfully screaming, "Yeehaw!"

"Zolt, please respond," said San. "Where was the last Zolt's destination?"

"Yes," retorted the boulder. "Please be more specific. Do you want this Zolt's last destination or the Zolt that left prior?"

"The Zolt that left prior," responded San.

"Yes," replied the boulder. There was a brief pause and a thousand thoughts went through Zoey's mind. One of her thoughts was the summary of them all—*how does San know what to do?*

"It traveled course one-one-seven. Would you like the same route?" asked the Zolt.

San gazed ahead, narrowing her eyes. She was determined. "Yes, I would like the same route. Thank you."

The Zolt shuttered for a moment, and rolled forward at a slightly faster pace. Zoey realized that although it rolled, the cabin of the Zolt remained stationary. How it did that, Zoey didn't know.

They passed well-lit zytes reminding Zoey of the lights on the freeway that flashed passed their car at night. Though, in Ohm Totem, the zytes gave off a soft white-bluish, pleasant glow, while the freeway lights seemed glaring.

Coming to a fork in the tunnel, the boulder veered to another tunnel on the left.

San leaned back, pressing her feet against the floor, bracing herself for something. She warned Zoey and Coda, "You better get ready. We're about to change speeds."

Zoey and Coda copied San, and an instant later the Zolt shuttered again, zipping off at an alarming pace. The force slightly pushed them backward for a second, then let up a moment later. Zoey saw that the zytes weren't glowing anymore. The boulder was going so fast that the zytes were now a thick, hazy white-blueish line against the rock tunnel wall.

Coda's tail lashed back and forth with nervous energy. "Wow! This is crazy!"

Zoey, on the other hand, wanted to know how it was that San knew how to work one of these things. San acted as if she'd never been down to the tunnel before, then somehow was able to control and command a Zolt? Her actions told Zoey that San wasn't telling them the whole truth. But why?

Zoey eyed San, watching her confidence as she kept her eyes on what was ahead.

Up ahead stood a Zolt on the left next to the tunnel wall. They were coming up to it at break neck speed.

"That's got to be Skint's Zolt," announced San.

"Destination reached," said the Zolt as it slowed quickly then came to a halt.

"Open," said San.

The door opened and Coda jumped out. Zoey didn't move, blocking San from leaving. Zoey asked suspiciously, "How did you know how to do all of that?"

San put her wing to her beak. "Shhh. Quiet."

Zoey scrunched her face up with annoyance, then turned and hopped out. San followed her.

"This way," whispered San. This portion of the tunnel was dark. The zytes came to an end a few yards back and unlit torches took their place.

Why would someone take the zytes away? thought Zoey.

San nudged Zoey, gesturing for her to get against the tunnel wall. Coda was by San's side and crept low, being as silent as he could.

A hiss shot against the dark and one by one, the torches flamed on. Zoey about jumped out of her feathers with fright, then ducked lower and tightly hugged the wall. Coda merely flinched, but ducked down as well. For some reason, San didn't budge at all.

They crept forward until they came to a change in the tunnel. It forked again and San tilted her head to the right, indicating they'd go that way. A sound picked up and San put her wing up signaling for them to stop. Being as quiet as they could, they listened intently. A conversation was taking place around the corner and pinged against the walls. It wasn't loud, but they could make out words here and there. San poked her head around the corner, doing her best not to be seen. She looked back and whispered, "Skint's talking to someone."

"Do you know who?" whispered Coda.

San shook her head.

They stood there for many moments. Then Zoey looked to the left in thought. She whispered to Coda, "Doesn't Skint have a stutter?"

Coda nodded a yes.

They listened a bit longer and Coda whispered back, "Apparently he doesn't."

Coda silently trod forward, nicely nudging San out of the way. He gave San a look that asked if he could look as well. San looked alarmed and frantically shook her head no. "I shouldn't have taken you guys here." Appealing to Zoey she declared, "Let's leave."

Coda peered around the corner, then abruptly hid back behind the wall.

"Show yourselves!" ordered a voice.

Frightened beyond fright, Zoey slowly retreated backward toward the Zolt. Coda hadn't moved an inch. *Why isn't he coming?*

Zoey saw San pull Coda's tail with her beak, trying to get him to move. Coda wiggled his tail free, then realized himself that he needed to get going. The realization was a moment too late.

Around the corner came a loud hiss.

Crepus!

Zoey felt pure panic run up her spine. They had to get out of there and they had to get out now! She knew how dangerous Crepus was and didn't want to see her brother or San get hurt. She ran toward Coda, pulling on his fur with her beak. "Let's go!"

Up ahead, Crepus poked his head around the corner, glaring at them. Zoey froze. His eyes burned with rage. He growled as he stepped around the corner, exposing his entire body. Zoey looked back at the Zolt. They were about fifty yards away. "Come on!" she yelled to San and her brother.

As Zoey fell back, she continued to look at the Zolt and then back at Crepus. He was walking at an arrogantly slow pace. Finally, checking where she was again, she saw that she was mere steps from the Zolt.

She intended to enter the Zolt, ready to roll away, but the Zolt's door was closed. She gasped and looked over her shoulder. She saw that Crepus was still taking his time walking toward them. With each step he pounded his tail against the dirt.

Zoey turned and blew on the Zolt. Nothing happened. She blew again. Nothing moved. "Coda!" she screamed, "I can't get it open."

Coda stood like a sentinel, about ten yards from her. He was ready to block any attempt that Crepus might make at getting her, though Crepus was still a distance away from them.

San? Where is she? Zoey spun around, but couldn't spot her. Then she realized that San was in front of Coda, pushing him with all her might. Coda wasn't budging.

San ordered, "Help me get him to the Zolt."

Zoey flew over to her brother. Coda's eyes were narrowed at the oncoming dragon. He had Crepus locked in his sights. Coda was clearly ready for action.

Crepus's tongue zig-zagged out of his mouth like a snake, hissing, "Welcome, children."

Zoey twisted back around, eyeing her brother. Yes, he was in another realm or something, and she had to snap him out of it. She pushed and pushed with everything that she had, but he wouldn't move. He didn't even take a single step backward. She finally let up.

"San!" screamed Zoey. "He isn't moving. Maybe if you get the Zolt open, we—"

Too late.

San screamed. Her wings flailed backwards as Crepus grabbed her, then threw her hard against the tunnel wall. Zoey jumped back as Coda lashed forward, jumping on Crepus. For

251

a moment, Coda had Crepus pinned on the ground until an invisible force pushed Coda upward, slamming him against the ceiling. He bounced off the wall, landing back on his feet, seemingly not fazed. He looked at Zoey, making sure she was okay.

"I wasn't expecting you so soon, San," said Crepus as he stood on all fours, staring at the spot where she laid. She was limp.

Is she dead?

"Oh, poor, poor San," said Crepus without any emotion, as he nudged San's limp body a couple of times with his claws. "I guess it's over for that one." He glanced at Coda, who stood between Crepus and Zoey. "Are you next?"

Coda responded with a defensive crouch, but was suddenly lifted off his feet again by another invisible force. He smacked against the wall a second time. This time, however, he wasn't so sure-footed on the fall. He hit the dirt floor at an awkward angle, making a loud grunting sound behind clenched teeth. He lay there motionless, just like San.

"Coda!" came a petrified screech from Zoey. He was the one person in Ohm Totem she loved the most. He can't be dead! She went to fly over to him, but her feet felt like they weighed a hundred pounds. She flapped, but didn't lift. She tried harder, but her feet remained planted on the ground.

Then she saw Skint. He stood next to Crepus. They both were glaring at her. Were they holding her down?

Zoey checked for her brother again. Her heart jumped for joy when she saw that he had started to get up. He was dazed and Zoey could tell he didn't know where he was. She was about to yell his name, but her mouth was pinned shut by the invisible force. Suddenly, she felt an even heavier weight pressing on her, and looked back at the squirrel and dragon. Their eyes were malevolent slits as they approached menacingly in her direction.

Her heart pounded as she frantically looked around. She desperately wanted to move, but her feet were suctioned to the cold earth. Her eyes widened when three apes suddenly walked around the corner. They stood behind Crepus and

Skint. Two of them looked amused, but one of them, standing slightly a ways off from the others, silently mouthed, *proceed from your heart.*

The instant she read his lips, her body started to tingle and her eyes abruptly closed against her wishes. She saw a large violet ray of light shine in the darkness behind her eyelids. It calmed her, filling her with color. She felt as if she were expanding, floating. She felt wonderful.

She opened her eyes.

Directly in front of her, not more than two paces away, stood the two apes. They were both leaning over, swiping their large arms toward her in an attempt to grab her, but just before they did, she commanded, "Get out of my space!"

And like the sun itself, Zoey beamed a flash of energy at them. It seemed to come from every atom of her body. The apes flew upward and against the ceiling. An instant later, Skint tumbled head over tail across the tunnel as if a ferocious, heavy wind blew him. Crepus, though, remained stationary.

"Good," Crepus looked around at his fallen comrades. "I like your spirit, child." He tipped his head to the side. "Guards!"

The two apes rose to their feet and lunged at her. Zoey leaped backwards as their outstretched fingers barely missed her. A terrifying growl filled the air. It was Coda.

He leaped in front of Zoey, clamping hard on an ape's arm. He ducked his head, somersaulting, flipping the ape head over heels. Letting go of his arm, Coda twisted around to see the other ape take a heavy swipe at him. The ape was too slow, allowing Coda to easily dodge the blow. Coda rolled to his right. The ape jumped at him with both hands clenched in a fist. However, Coda jumped higher. He was a step ahead.

He placed both paws on top of the ape's head, pressing down. The ape plunged to the ground and Coda landed on top of him. With a hasty counterclockwise swirl against the ape's forehead crystal, the ape went limp. Coda had stunned him. That ape was going to be out for a while.

Zoey watched from a safe distance. She had unknowingly backed up against the side of one of the Zolts. She saw that

Coda was just as surprised by his actions as she was. *Did he learn how to stun in the Art of Defense classes?*

Zoey gasped and yelled, "Watch out!"

Coda leaped to the side as an ape pounded a double-handed punch against the ground a whisker length away, just missing Coda. Coda was suddenly lifted off the ground by that same unknown force. It hurled him to another wall. Zoey could see that Coda was flying through the air at a speed that would surely kill him.

Coda closed his eyes tight, expecting the worst. Zoey screamed. She was about to lift off when Coda suddenly stopped two head lengths away from the wall. Then he floated gently to the ground.

"Enough!"

Zoey, startled by the familiar voice, turned around.

Nova stood a few bird lengths from Zoey. Next to her were Numee, Taregan, and that badger fellow that sat at the entrance of Marble Burrow.

Nova bowed formally to Zoey, and then walked toward Crepus. He let out a disgusted snort, and then gave a mocking bow. "To what do I owe the pleasure of your visit?"

Coda eased over to Zoey, rubbing his cheek against her feathers. "Are you okay?"

Zoey simply nodded, not taking her eyes from Nova, who was followed by her three companions. Zoey suddenly felt safe, but then remembered her fallen friend, San. Safe wasn't the right word. A deep sadness plucked at her. She hadn't known San for very long, but she was a good friend and tried to keep them out of harm's way. A tear welled up in her eye. Her gut felt empty.

"Crepus," replied Nova curtly.

Skint scurried next to Crepus, his head hanging low. He'd been caught red-handed. He was working for Crepus.

Nova merely glanced at him, dipping her head in greeting as well.

"You're too kind," said Crepus.

"That's how I live. With kindness," responded Nova.

Numee, Taregan, and the badger remained calm and quiet,

but kept their eyes locked on Crepus.

Crepus's expression contorted. "That's a lie." His mighty tail swished back and forth in anger. "You give a good act, that's for sure, Nova," Crepus hissed. "Kindness you say? It was you VioletLights who shunned me, ignored my genius, and tried to destroy any semblance of the wonderful life that I had. You still do!" His eyes were like flames sparking with anger. To Zoey, it seemed like Crepus's feelings had been hurt, somewhere, somehow. A pain from long ago, perhaps?

Nova sat serenely on her hind legs, wrapping her long tail around her forepaws. "When you blame others, there's no limit to your blame. You're in a pattern, Crepus, blaming everyone and everything for the mistakes you've made. Remember, you create your own reality." She paused. "Learn from your past, Crepus. Remember what it was like to be a VioletLight."

She touched her tail to his shoulder. "VioletLights are accountable to no one else but themselves, and because so, they correct their own mistakes in life, and don't expect others to do it for them. VioletLights do what they need to do and require nothing from others. Remember this and all your anger will disappear."

Crepus closed his eyes, and for a moment Zoey could tell that he enjoyed Nova's touch. The calm moment changed in a flash, however. As Crepus suddenly lashed out, driving his fangs into Nova's tail. He wrenched his head back, taking a giant chunk out of her tail. Zoey gasped, recoiling in horror as Nova's blood splattered all over Crepus's face. Zoey flew toward Nova. She didn't know what she was going to do when she got there, but Nova needed help anyway.

But something wasn't right. Nova and her companions remained calm. *How could they possibly be peaceful at a moment like this?* Zoey reached Nova and saw that the end of Nova's tail was fine. Mystified, she began to wonder if she was just imagining it all. Crepus's face told her she wasn't imagining—blood stained his face and he had a tuft of fur caught in his teeth.

Crepus spat it out, eyeing Zoey. There was emptiness in his eyes. *Was that sadness, too?*

"Nova," Crepus hissed, "one day very soon my power will exceed the skylark's power." He glowered at Zoey and she shrank away from him.

Zoey suddenly jumped. *What in the world is that?* Above Crepus hovered two shadows. They looked like dark smoke rising behind him, but they were too thick to be smoke. A moment later they disappeared.

Crepus glanced at San and then turned back to Nova. "I must be getting on my merry way." As he passed the limp cardinal—Zoey's good friend—he grabbed her in his jaws and walked around the corner, disappearing from view. His entourage, including Skint, followed. The last ape, however, looked intently into Zoey's eyes. She could feel his compassion and warmth.

"Who...?" asked Zoey.

"That's Maldwyn of Gwenfree," replied Nova, before Zoey finished her question. "He was, and apparently, still is a good friend."

Numee poked her nose into Nova's side, looking over at Coda. Everyone turned to see an exhausted panther lying on the floor struggling to get up. His eyes were half-closed and he looked as if he was trying hard not to fall asleep.

Zoey hurriedly flew over to him. He was breathing rapidly, and his head was jostling back and forth. "Coda?" His eyes locked on her when she said his name, but then drifted away.

The badger reached him next, placing his paws on Coda's stomach. "He's been drained. It's a trick the more advanced Dims do to the PureLights. They drain your energy, taking it for their own. It's a Dark Art." The badger closed his eyes and his indigo crystals started to brightly glow. In a matter of a few breaths, Coda was standing up, revitalized.

Looking around, he eyed everyone like they were crazy. "Why are you all staring at me like that?"

Numee wrapped her tail around his shoulders. "You've been drained by Crepus. Let's get you back to the tribe."

Coda shook his head. "Not without San."

Zoey then remembered. Her friend and roommate. Gone. She wasn't coming back, no matter how hard she wanted her to.

Zoey started to cry. All of her emotions, missing her mom, her dad, almost losing Coda, and now losing her friend flooded in as she wept. She eyed Coda. "She's dead."

"She can't be. She's right there," Coda said, pointing behind him with his tail. His tail dropped when he saw that San was gone. "Where is she?"

"Didn't you see?" asked Zoey.

"But, I thought I saw her breathing over there."

Numee still had her tail wrapped around Coda's shoulder. They started to walk toward the Zolts.

Nova spoke, "Crepus took her life, Coda. We'll honor San when we get back to the Sihu Tribe. Don't worry, you two. This isn't the end for her. In life, there is no end. All she did was change form from the energy of a cardinal, to the energy of her spirit."

Chapter 25

The next day came and went like a blur. Coda had spent most of the day on the beach, and by now the sun was falling to the west, beckoning the night.

Coda heaved a heavy sigh as he sat on the sand, watching the waves crash on the shore. He still felt drained, and couldn't figure out why. He'd been like this all day, no matter how many times Numee placed her paws on him to bring in Prana. He'd get filled up with healthy energy, then quickly fade into the doldrums with low energy.

Crepus had done something to him that he couldn't quite escape.

He leaned on his side, sighing again, feeling the fresh air against his fur. It was the one thing that felt good. He looked around. All of the spirit animals, except for some Wing Watchers, were enjoying the day at the beach.

Earlier, Nova had explained to Coda and Zoey that the best way to assimilate information effectively at school or at training is by learning for three days, then resting for the next three days. Which, apparently, he and the rest of Ohm Totem were doing right now—resting.

This way, according to Nova, the student's minds wouldn't overflow with too much information. One more day of training would've been too much and 'brain fog' would've trickled in. Plus, a spirit animal's body needs rest as well, and for the PureLights the beach was a perfect place to do just that.

"I think I got it," said Numee, as she turned to Taregan.

Taregan cocked his eyebrows. "Well, I hope so. This kid can't be the guardian of guardians, or the famous night walker, or whatever label we want to put on him, if he can't stay awake."

Numee had seen an energy anomaly in Coda's aura earlier in the day. It was placed there, somehow, by Crepus. She'd never seen such a thing, but it continued to steal Coda's energy no matter what they did for him.

Chev and Zoey sat to his left and Taregan sat several bird lengths in front of him, watching Numee do what she did best—find the discomfort and heal it. And the way she did it almost made Coda laugh.

She'd put a paw near his fur, then wave it in a certain direction, and clap her paws above another area of his fur. She did this for what seemed to be hours. If Coda wasn't in Ohm Totem, he'd think that Numee was nuts.

She clapped next to his left ear. "Got it!" she said with satisfaction. "It's gone."

And it was. In a matter of a second, his energy came back to full strength. He'd almost forgotten how good it felt, here in Ohm Totem. He breathed in the rich air, relishing the tingling sensations splashing throughout his body. He wanted to stand up and run around the beach, but felt a tap on his back just as he was about to sprint away.

"Are you feeling better now, Coda?"

It was Nova. Coda hadn't seen her since this morning. She had spent much of her day in quietude, next to the Snow Tree.

"Yeah. I feel much better. Thanks." He paused as a question popped into his mind. A question he'd had since they discovered the Large Boulder. What exactly is it?

Just as he was about to ask, Zoey had a question. "How's the Snow Tree, Nova?" She had sadness in her voice, not for the Snow Tree, but because she'd been thinking about San all day.

Nova smiled. "She's wonderful."

"Oh," Zoey said, looking forlornly at the sand. "How come I don't hear her much anymore?"

Nova sat between Coda and Zoey. There was compassion in her eyes. "This is your experience. Her job was to point you to Ohm Totem, which she did, and that's all she was to do. She may speak to you here and there, but it would interfere with your lessons if she spoke with you too often. You must learn from your own experiences. It's the most effective way."

Zoey didn't reply. She was too depressed. Nova wrapped

her tail around her as Coda stared into the distance. The Bards sat in a circle, singing and carrying on.

Everything was happy that day, except for Zoey. Coda could feel sadness swell all over her. He knew she wanted to just go home and fall into Mom's arms, crying the day away. Coda didn't know San too well, but she must have made a big impact on Zoey. Coda sighed to himself. *I wish she didn't have to go through this.*

He looked up and realized the stars had come out. He smiled as Chev gently prodded him with his trunk, saying, "We're going soon."

"Going where?" Coda wondered.

"To the Circle of Elders." There was a hint of fear in Chev's voice.

"In a moment," said Nova. She turned to Zoey, continuing a conversation they were having. She leaned over, brushing her cheek against Zoey's. "One ability that a VioletLight has is the power to help a deceased soul move on. We help lead them to the light. It's a way that we honor our loved ones."

Zoey didn't completely understand where Nova was going with this. Coda perked up his ears. He was intrigued.

Nova continued, "I spent many moments today searching for San in the after-realm of The Great Spirit. I found nothing."

Zoey and Coda exchanged befuddled glances. They didn't know anything about an after-realm.

Numee interjected, "She wasn't there? Do you think Crepus did something with her soul?"

"No. I think something else."

Zoey's eyes lit up. "That she's alive?"

"Yes," Nova nodded. "Those were my exact thoughts."

Taregan hopped up and stood in front of Nova. "But, she was clearly dead."

Nova shook her head. "I'm not so sure about that."

Numee paced back and forth. "I knew Crepus was growing stronger. He brought her back to life I bet! But why?"

"The answer will come to us shortly," replied Nova. "We must go now. The Circle of Elders awaits."

They stood in front of the southern Fog, only a stone's throw from the Spruce Hollow. Gathered with them were the nine elders, all with indigo colored crystals, except for Nova's violet crystal.

Coda was a little surprised to see that Taregan was one of the elders in the circle, but wasn't surprised to see Honani—the badger he admired above most.

Ke eyed Coda, giving him a wry smile. "These next few steps aren't like the joy ride in the Zolt you had last night."

How did he know about last night? Did Nova tell him?

Ke winked, then walked directly into the Fog. It swirled around him, until the thickness of it completely hid him from view.

That's not hard, thought Coda.

Chev nudged Coda forward. Coda looked over his shoulder to see Zoey standing on Chev's back. Her thoughts were far off and her eyes were welled with tears. *She must still be thinking of San*, thought Coda.

Nova walked up and stood beside Coda. Isi, the deer he had met a day ago, stood next to her. Nova dipped her head to both children. "When you walk through the Fog, stay true to yourself. Don't react to anything. Do you understand?"

Coda drew back. *What was inside the fog? Was that why Chev was so scared?*

Coda simply nodded, then eyed Chev. He crossed his eyes, making a face at Coda, doing his best to lighten things up. It didn't work. Coda's mind was filled with dread. What was he getting himself into?

Nova brushed her fur against his and assured him, "I'll be by your side."

The red-tailed hawk he remembered seeing above him the day he was on top of the Large Boulder jumped up and flew through the Fog. A puff of mist flared as the hawk went through, vanishing.

Next came the giraffe—the one who leads the bards in song.

His head bobbed back and forth as he slowly walked into the Fog. He, too, quickly disappeared into the thick mist. Then two more, a hummingbird and a black bear, walked through, leaving the ones Coda knew best waiting behind.

Honani tapped Coda on the shoulder. "I'll be on the other side. I'll see you there. And Coda," he said solemnly, "remember when entering the Fog, walk with focus. Focus onto the other side, and do not look at anything else." He added, "Think only that you have already made it through the Fog as you enter it. Exiting the Fog on the other side is the goal. Make that your sole focus. Understand?"

Coda merely nodded. Honani turned and walked through the Fog, vanishing in an instant, just like the others.

"My turn," said Taregan. Coda felt a swoosh of air over his head. Looking up, he saw Taregan dive into the Fog, then get swallowed up by the swirling mist.

Nova repeated, "Empty your mind and proceed from your heart." She and Isi took several steps forward, beckoning Coda to follow. Chev and Zoey were a tail length behind. A second later, he felt small talons dig into his back.

"What?" Coda twisted his head to look over his shoulder. He was relieved to see that it was only his sister.

She grinned. "I want to go with you," she said, pressing the side of her head into his neck. "I trust my brother more than anyone in the world."

Nova nodded, then raced forward into the Fog. Isi was just a step behind.

"Well, here I go." Chev did a little dance, cracking a large smile, waiting for applause. When none came, he shrugged, then closed his eyes, chanting, "This is only temporary. This is only temporary." He blathered all the way into the Fog.

For a long while, Coda stared into the Fog. Fear pulsed through him. He didn't know what to expect and didn't want to find out. He was jostled to his senses when Zoey asked, "Why aren't we moving?"

"Um, I'm scared," admitted Coda.

"Me too," said Zoey.

"What should I do?" Coda looked up and down the fog. It

swirled, but didn't look too threatening. But why couldn't he move?

Just then Nova emerged out of the Fog. Her strong shoulders flexed as she held her head high. The most delicate, gentle smile was on her face. She walked toward them and touched their heads with her long, white tail. "It's okay. I promise."

Instantly, Coda felt lighter and full of confidence. The fear had, for the moment, vanished into thin air. He padded forward, stepping steadily into the Fog. The last thing he heard just before entering was Nova shouting, "That's how you do it. Fear only resides in your heart. The fog doesn't determine our lives, we do!"

Coda felt a sudden thickness surround him and a deep chill engulfed him. The Fog seemed endless and empty. Coda felt Zoey shift on his back, clutching his fur more tightly. She remained silent, as if waiting for something terrible to happen.

Then it began. The Fog rushed around them like a swirling tornado. It felt like water rushing against his body mixed with horrendous winds. A penetrating, jet engine-like sound pierced his eardrums. He lowered his head, pushing forward, pressing his strong paws hard against the earth. His eyes were open just a slit as the rushing fog tortured him like a sandstorm.

"Coda!" yelled Zoey above the torment of wind. "Are you okay?"

He pushed himself to take step after step, though it seemed he was merely walking in place. "I don't know if I'm getting anywhere!"

A vile laughter shot through the Fog. It was Crepus. His image appeared to their right. He flashed in and out from the mass that swirled about. His red eyes penetrated through Coda's thoughts. At first, Coda felt a tinge of anger toward Zoey. She was holding him back, weighing him down by clutching to him so tightly. He shook off the feeling and looked forward. Those weren't his thoughts. Those were Crepus' Dark Arts at work.

He trekked forward, but felt an energetic pull at his head.

263

He had the sudden urge to look back into Crepus's eyes. But why? He fought against the feeling, forcing himself to look forward, locking his neck muscles to stop from turning his head.

His head turned in spite of his best efforts to resist.

Around Crepus was an oval sphere of red light. The red light changed to black, then slowly crept through the fog toward them. Zoey shifted again, but held on tightly. The blackness wove its way through the Fog, inching eerily forward.

Coda couldn't turn his head back toward his goal—the other side of the Fog—no matter how hard he tried, and as the blackness neared, Coda knew it would hit them.

And it did.

The black mass surrounded them and silence filled the Fog. Then, terrifying screams darted at Coda like frigid icicles falling from the sky. He shuddered and fell to the ground, putting his paws over his ears. He couldn't take it. It was just too much. He wanted to close his eyes, but some mysterious force kept them open.

With all his might, he stood up.

"Go back to where you came from," commanded Crepus's voice. It was frightening and squeezed his heart. Fear began to devour him and he felt lost, as if he'd walked into a jungle of terror, not knowing where to go to next. His mind spun in circles and he became dizzy. He wanted to scream. Instead, he yelled, "Zoey! Go on without me!"

There was silence. Not because of the absence of Zoey's reply, but from the lack of any sound at all. The glaring screams, the rushing jet engine sounds of the fog, and Crepus's voice was gone. It was completely and absolutely soundless.

"Zoey?"

A white light pierced the darkness, instantly calming everything. Coda's clear mind was back and his heart felt light. *Who turned on the light?*

It was Zoey.

She hovered above him. Her feathers glowed white light, penetrating the darkness, erasing any negative feelings coming from the black mass. Around them, the swirl of the Fog slowed as Zoey flapped her wings, spreading the light even more.

Suddenly, someone pushed Coda from behind. Looking back, Coda saw Nova nudging him with her shoulder. He started to walk, heading toward what he hoped was the other side of the Fog. Up ahead, Zoey hovered at what seemed to be the edge of it, making sure the darkness didn't return.

Yes! There, just past Zoey, Coda could see it. The end of the Fog. His heart beat with delight and he gave an audible *yes!* He walked under Zoey's hovering body, breaking through the Fog.

"Well done," said Chev, who stood at what looked to be the beginning of a passage at the bottom of a narrow canyon. It was nearly dark, but the outline of high canyon walls were still visible. Coda guessed that the Circle of Elders was deep within this canyon, surrounded by these large walls. He knew he was correct when some of the elders started walking that way.

Coda turned around, seeing Zoey come through the Fog. There was a tinge of white light around her. Her eyes, though, looked tired. She glided to the ground, falling over in front of Coda and Chev. Coda ran to her side. "What's wrong?"

"She used too much of her own energy," responded Nova, as she padded next to him. "She'll have to learn how to control that."

Nova approached Zoey's exhausted little body, placing her paws on her wing. Nova took in a deep breath, and pumped Prana into Zoey. Coda could see Zoey's eyes come to life with each passing second. Then she shook her head, plumped her feathers, and jumped up. "Much better!" She looked at Nova, mouthing *thank you*. Then she hopped onto Coda's back, ready to move on.

"How did you do that?"

"Do what?" replied Zoey.

"How did you glow like that?"

"I don't know. I went into my heart. I just couldn't take it anymore." There was still some tiredness remaining in her eyes, but Coda knew she'd be fine. His sister was changing with each day. She amazed him more than he ever imagined possible.

∞

As they pressed on to their destination, Coda caught up with Nova at the front of the pack. He still had a question burning in his mind.

"Um, Nova? What was that inside the Large Boulder?"

Keeping a steady gaze on her surroundings, Nova replied, "The Large Boulder is also known as the Boulder of Records. As you saw, it has thousands of tablets lined with our prophecies, as well as the history of each tribe in Ohm Totem. It used to be the home of the PureLight Order, as well, until it disappeared." She deftly stepped over a large rock. "Tomorrow I'll go through the Large Boulder with you and Zoey."

Coda was excited at the prospect of doing that, and also asked, "What about the Zolts below? How did they get there?"

"I'm not sure. It's something I mean to discover. They were there when we arrived in Ohm Totem. We call the tunnels 'The Gateway'. It's our fastest route to other territories and tribes. We don't use it anymore though. The tunnels aren't safe for most PureLights."

Coda could feel Zoey tightly clutching his fur. Her weight on his back was getting heavier; he could tell that she was tiring the longer they walked. Coda felt sorry for her, wondering why she had to go through this ordeal, just to go to the Circle of Elders.

"Why did we have to come to the Circle of Elders with you all?" Coda asked.

Nova stopped, and kindly gazed into his eyes. "I understand your frustration. It's part of our custom. We bring every new student here, because the Circle of Elders will advance you by planting seeds into your mind. These seeds will grow, expanding your horizons, your heart, and your mind, even if you don't immediately feel these effects." She shook her head. "We're not here in Ohm Totem to be safe and secure. That's impossible. We're here to learn and spread love, any way we can. This isn't a place for the weak of heart. This Fog, that fear, this struggle, will strengthen you and Zoey." She sniffed the air carefully, and added, "Be strong."

Nova resumed walking again and Coda followed. "If we're to be so strong, then why don't we attack the Dims, so you can get every tribe's land back?"

"Attack them? Only fools rush in. You must have faith in the flow of life—the way of The Great Spirit." Nova's frown almost consumed her nose. "What have I been teaching you, Coda? That goes against our ways, against the PureLight Order."

"I know, but why?" asked Coda.

"Because going against the flow by attacking someone is an extension of fear."

"I still don't understand. What do you mean?" Coda asked, looking up to her for answers. He saw that the stars were full, and the moon was bright, helping to light their way.

"Even the thought of attacking someone is against our custom. The thought is violent in and of itself, bringing the emotional body and mind out of balance. Sometimes it's hard for others, even VioletLights, not to succumb to those dark thoughts and feelings."

She took a deep breath and patiently explained, "It's important to realize, however, that those thoughts and feelings not only hurt others, they also hurt yourself. And those thoughts have the ability to create violent situations in real life. So, be careful what you focus on."

They both gracefully leaped over a rock, then Nova continued, "When attacking another living Being, you're doing so out of anger, malice, power, dominance; all of which arise out of fear. That fear reverberates to everything around you, sending ripple affects across the consciousness of every Being, creating more and more violence with each ripple. The opposite, that of the thoughts and actions of peace, send ripples of love, healing, and understanding to everyone. Choosing one over the other not only affects your life, but everyone else's around you."

"But attacking them and defeating them would finally stop them from taking over. You'll have peace again. You wouldn't have to worry about the Dims anymore," Coda said, quite sensibly.

"How could I rejoice in victory and delight in the slaughter of others? There's no victory in that. You talk of peace, but peace doesn't come through violence. It never has. It has always led to eventual bloodshed." She laughed. "VioletLights are a different breed than what you're used to. You'll never see a VioletLight attack another living being out of spite or anger. I, in truth, could kill twenty Dims with a single swipe of the tail, even if they're a hundred leopard lengths away. If I did, however, then it would be a massacre. It'd be out of power, ego, and fear. It'd be heartless and if that were to occur, then I wouldn't be able to counsel the Sihu Tribe wisely. That's why I prefer to stun my opponents, rather than to kill them. I do so in the hopes that one day that opponent would eventually see the light and change from a Dim to a PureLight."

She smiled after she saw the confused look in Coda's eyes. "We VioletLights are different than the rest of you PureLights. However, I do not judge those who must injure or kill another in defense of their own life.

"But, VioletLights have the ability to avoid harm, even though it may appear that we are hurt. You may see this as magical, but we have mastered our own auras to the point that when a body part is injured or dismembered, we rejuvenate it at any moment we choose. We know that the aura or energy around that injured or missing body part never disappears. Because of this, I'm able to rebuild that area in an instant. It may not make sense now, but it will later.

"This doesn't mean that I can't be killed. That's far from the truth. However, when a Being gets to a complete state of love, all things fall into place, and that Being becomes increasingly difficult to kill. That's the state that VioletLights are in. And, it's because of this state of love that spirit animals look up to VioletLights, heeding our advice, not because we govern them, but because they trust us. Not because we lead through violence, but because we lead through love. The eventual goal of this all is to help everyone, even you Coda, attain a VioletLight state of life where nothing can harm you, not even

Crepus. That's one reason Crepus is doing his best to find a way to change or to kill us all, including the VioletLights. He's convinced he's going to find a way to end us. And, if anyone could do it, it would be him."

Coda nodded. He still wasn't convinced, but knew he couldn't change her mind, and why should he? She was wise and knew what she was doing. Then Skint popped into his mind. There was something wrong about letting him into the PureLight's training. "What about Skint? He came over here and spied on us. Shouldn't we stop that?"

"There have been many of Crepus' operatives that have come to spy on us, but instead were turned into full fledged PureLights—living a life of love, rather than fear. Honani was one of them. He changed for the better and we're that much better off with him around."

"What!?" Coda stopped dead in his tracks. "Really?"

"Yes," replied Nova, not stopping, indicating that the conversation was over for now.

Coda's thoughts turned to Zoey again. He was worried about her. She hadn't said much of anything after coming through the Fog.

Nova halted just outside a large circular opening in the canyon. It was surrounded with high rock walls and trees growing on top and near the edges of the cliffs above. "Let Zoey off of your back, Coda. She needs more Prana."

He crouched down and Zoey hopped off. Her legs were weak, and as she landed, her small legs buckled beneath her and she fell on her side. Nova put her paws on her, peering into Coda's eyes as she did so. "Remember, The Great Spirit stands at peace, not taking a 'good side' or a 'bad side'. It gives blood, air, and water to both the light and the dark, the negative and the positive, the evil and the good. Just like the Great Spirit, I don't draw a line. I accept both sides in my enlightened wish that both can find balance within.

"Don't get me wrong, I defend this sacred ground as much as I defend the tribe's life. But we refuse to attack because it's against the PureLight Order to invade another being's space." She glanced to her left. "The tide is changing though. The light of Ohm Totem is becoming brighter as the darkness recedes. There are always ebbs and flows, but when the light takes one step back, it rebounds with two steps forward."

She took her paws from Zoey, who glowed with light again. Zoey thanked her, then eyed the circled canyon before her. "Is this where the Circle of Elders takes place?"

Nova bowed her head. "It is. Welcome."

Chapter 26

The waning moon was set at its highest arc, way above the growing fire illuminating the nine elders around the circle. The elders sat quietly, staring into the depths of the orange, yellow, and light bluish flames that rose from the large pit. Chev, Zoey, and Coda sat closely behind them.

"Let's close our eyes, clear our thoughts, and open our hearts," began Isi. She curled up, lying slightly on her right side, exposing the left side of her body to the warm fire.

Zoey didn't know if she should close her eyes like they did. She didn't want to disrespect their custom or worse, ruin their fire ritual. Or, maybe, she thought, she wasn't supposed to close her eyes at all. The journey to The Circle of Elders had been tough and draining, and she was tired. In fact, she really just wanted to curl up into a ball and fall fast asleep.

Coda sat on Zoey's right. She noticed that he was off in his own world, staring at the fire. She followed his gaze, then San came to mind. She felt a pang of sadness, then exhaled it out. She should probably be as positive as she can. She took a deep breath and looked at Chev on her left, who was breathing deeply. His eyes were wide open, and knowing the respect Chev held for others, and probably for The Circle of Elders, Zoey felt better that her eyes were open.

The elders remained silent, taking deep, rhythmic breaths that seemed to match each other's. As they did this, the fire seemed to breathe in and out in sync with the elders. This went on for a long time before Isi spoke.

"Please speak freely amongst The Circle of Elders and under the moon of The Great Spirit. Allow each individual to speak without interruption." As she spoke, she looked at each and every elder around the fire. Her voice was very sweet and soothing, making Zoey want to hear more. She finished with a bow of her head. "Proceed with your heart."

The zebra, Ke, stepped forward, bowing his head to each elder. His voice was determined, booming loudly around the circle.

"I want to revisit holding rooms for stunned Dims. I know the idea is foreign, and long lost in the memory banks of everyone, but it's essential, nonetheless."

He took a deep breath, standing even taller. "I've come to the conclusion that this is the best idea. Instead of continuing to allow the stunned Dims to simply go back home after each attack, we keep them, and put them in holding rooms, or prisons, then the Dims numbers are depleted. Their strength would stop growing."

He paused, waiting for a reply.

Nova stood up, also stepping forward. "Yes, you spoke of this at the last circle and my position remains the same. I see only one outcome. Government. Governing our tribe, or in this case, governing the Dims within our own tribe, is the beginning of the Sihu Tribe's ultimate end."

Ke shook his head at Nova's reply, and after a few moments of silence within the circle, he spoke, "I understand your good intentions. But the time of change is now. We lose more family and friends with each and every attack. We gain nothing in return. If we capture and confine the stunned Dims, their numbers start to fall, making each attack thereafter weaker."

Nova nodded, "And in the meantime, what shall we do with the prisoners?"

"Good question," said Ke. "I thought it would be wise to slowly teach them our ways."

Nova smiled, "And, our ways would be what? They wouldn't be the ways we share now. They'd learn the ways of a tribe that has introduced prisons into their culture."

"You see, Nova, nothing would change but prisons," insisted Ke.

Nova took her eyes from Ke, turning them toward the fire. She stared for a few moments into the hot flames. "I'd rather us change by expanding our hearts, instead of closing them. Remember, our way of life comes from the heart, and gives us freedom in all ways. The only government we have is the government of thine own self be true. I govern myself and you govern yourself. It's not up to us, no matter how cruel and destructive the Dims are, to capture and govern them. We don't force anything on anyone."

Ke shook his head vehemently as Nova continued.

"Where there's force, there's a counterforce, Ke. What we force upon others grows in all directions, and turns its ugly head toward us. I know you're well-intentioned, and care very much for everyone in the Sihu Tribe. However, introducing a prison will eventually imprison us all."

"Words. These are merely words," Ke disagreed. "Actions are what we need, not words. I'm tired of losing friends and family. If we create holding rooms or prisons, then the Dims will have something to think about, and perhaps stop attacking us. We can stop our loved ones from dying. I vote for prisons, and will do so at each and every circle. Some day you'll all come to your senses. We need some sort of law that says that each Dim we find on this land after each attack shall go to prison. Period."

Ke took a step back and sat down. His face was as stern as a stone. Nothing was going to change his mind.

Nova understood his argument, and took his counterpoints with compassion and calmness. "Thank you for allowing me my say, Ke."

He gave a nod, but continued to stare unflinchingly at the fire.

Zoey had watched this exchange with utmost interest. She'd never thought of prisons in this way before, nor had she ever had a need to do so. She lived in a cozy house where life was rather simple. You make a mess, you clean it up. You hug your mom, she'll hug you in return. You sneak a cookie without asking, you get in trouble because you didn't ask. Simple.

Isi stood up, taking a pace toward the fire. Her head was held high as she looked at each individual, even Coda and Zoey.

"I agree with Nova," she said. "It's true that force always has a counterforce. I see the wisdom in that. A holding room will only bring the energy of imprisonment to the Sihu Tribe and..."

Ke furrowed his brow, breaking The Circle of Elders sacred agreement by interrupting. "Are your eyes closed? Haven't you seen that the Dims already take some of us as prisoners each time they attack us? I'd say, beyond a shadow of a doubt, that the energy of imprisonment is already here!"

Isi, taking exception to the interruption, shot back with an irritated look. Zoey could tell this wasn't the first time Ke had gotten under her skin.

"Of course, I see this, Tasunke. I'm not blind to the fact that they capture tribe-mates and put them into slavery, imprison them, or brainwash them to attack us. Your ideas of a prison brings a bigger picture to my heart, though, and the picture I see is nothing but failure."

"Failure?" retorted Ke. "How can something we've never tried be a failure? We must try it first." He paced around the circle, between the elders and the fire. His hooves hit the dirt with each step, making soft clopping sounds. Finally, his pent up anger erupted. "We are cowards! We shrink back in fear when any new idea is presented to the circle!"

He stopped in stride when he came to Nova. "And you," he pointed, "you're the worst of them all! You call yourself a PureLight, or worse yet, you call yourself a VioletLight?"

Nova smiled. "Yes, that I am."

Zoey thought this was probably how Crepus had turned from a VioletLight to being a Dim. *Was he once voicing his opinions like Ke in the Circle of Elders by going against the PureLight Order?*

Ke rolled his eyes as he walked back to his spot in the circle directly across from Nova. He sat down with a curt snort.

Lootah, a black bear, stepped forward with his ears held high. "I'm not a historian of any means. But, what I've seen throughout the moons of visiting the archive tablets in the Large Boulder is a pattern that emerges among societies. Although we've never had a prison in Sihu Tribe, history shows us that if we set one up, then it's not only the Dims that become imprisoned, but it would eventually be us, too. I found this to be a literal lesson. It would be a form of prison for us to

274

have to guard prisoners, and eventually, we would throw our own Sihu brothers and sisters into the prisons, as well."

"I don't see that coming," countered Ke. "That's impossible. Our mere character as a tribe wouldn't allow it. No one would do such a thing."

Nova, nodding to Lootah, made sure that it was okay for her to speak. Lootah nodded back, giving her the floor.

"You said 'our mere character as a tribe wouldn't allow it', yet you would already do such a thing, Ke. You just said so yourself. You'd throw a Dim into a prison."

"Yes, I said a Dim, not anyone from Sihu. I'd never throw a tribes-mate in there."

"Throwing a Dim into a prison is no different than a Sihu tribes-mate. What you do to another, you do to yourself. In this case, what you do to another tribe, you do to your own tribe."

Nova's eyes narrowed. "This lesson has repeated in history over and over again. A prison would bring about a massive change in thinking. We would veer away from the PureLight Order."

"The Order, the Order, the Order," Ke intoned, flipping his head back and forth. "Where is this Order? I've never seen it! None of us but Nova claims to have seen it. It disappeared for a reason. It disappeared because The Great Spirit wanted it to."

"From what I remember," said the red-tailed hawk that had stepped forward, "Crepus stole the PureLight Order. From my knowledge, it wasn't The Great Spirit."

"Yes, Shikoba, Crepus may have stolen it," replied Nova. "Still, we have to look more clearly into the change that Ke wants to make. Because of this change, Ke," she looked deeply into his eyes across the fire, "our very way of thinking and doing things would change. Laws and government would be created for the sole purpose of this prison. An energy shift would stir and spin its way to everyone in the Sihu Tribe.

"Since prisons are also an internal border—someone goes in, but can't get out—the idea of internal borders in the Sihu Tribe enters our mindset. Some, if not all, would slowly but surely claim ownership to certain areas of this land. We'd be under the impression that we own something, and that this land we walk on is our land. We'd forget that this land was created by The Great Spirit, and is to be shared with everyone. Once ownership is established, laws are established. We'd need laws for the land we'd own, so others couldn't take it from us. One thing always leads to another."

Nova could see that none of this was sinking in. "We'd no longer allow everyone in Ohm Totem to govern themselves. We'd be doing the governing for them. Laws would be created, and because they'd be created, they'd be broken," she tried again. "We'd become a Dim. This is what Crepus wants. This is his grand plan to take everything and everyone over. He wants us to create laws. He wants us to destroy ourselves from the inside. He knows this is the only way to end our very existence. What he wants is everything set up for him, so he can govern us all. To govern the entire island of Ohm Totem."

Ke groaned, "A law is a law and merely a law. All the harm that a law would do is keep spirit animals in line."

Nova shook her head, getting the attention of the rest of the circle. For a reason Zoey couldn't explain, she felt that Nova now knew something about Ke that no one else knew. Nova tilted her head. "You've changed, Tasunke. You aren't seeing as clearly as you once did. From my point of view, I see that a law is a great idea in a world of terrible illness, an illness of the mind. We've never lived by a set of laws. We've lived by an Order. An Order that's been ingrained in every Being from the beginning. It's never steered us into a negative direction. It's only when we choose to ignore the Order that things start to get out of hand. We stop helping others. We start becoming greedy, and do things only for ourselves. We act like others are going to take everything from us, when in truth, we have nothing to begin with. In the true sense of life, we own nothing. We don't own anyone's soul, body, or mind. Imprisoning another just to help ourselves would create a completely new mindset in our tribe. The mindset would slowly take over each and every tribes-mate, eventually taking over our tribe.

276

"Those who choose to ignore the PureLight Order, choose to dim their light. Those who don't ignore it, brighten their light for all the world to see. Hear me well, Ke, it's not my plan to become a Dim. However, I must ask, is it your plan to become one? I know you're intelligent, so I see no other explanation of your need for laws, other than to secretly help Crepus."

Ke's face twisted in anger, but he held his tongue and glared at the trees in the distance. The other elders flinched, astonished that Nova would say such a thing.

Lootah nodded to Nova and spoke up. "I don't think that Ke wants to be a Dim. I disagree with you there. I agree, though, that when a prison is formed, then a government in some way must be created to police the prison system. When government is created, it meddles in the affairs of those that it governs. If we governed, we'd stop acting for the benefit of others. We'd have to place trust in the government, hence, we'd stop trusting each other. Once that happens, even trusting our own selves would be difficult. We'd be living a lie." He looked at everyone around the circle, even Zoey, Chev, and Coda.

"Ke, we have to trust that the Dims have to do what they do, and leave them alone. They have their own lessons to learn. The only way to deal with a giant boulder tumbling down a mountainside is to get out of its way. If you try to stop or change its direction, it will either kill or carry you down the hill with it. If you come to the understanding that you can't control the boulder, and never could, then you've understood the flow of life."

Lootah, having felt that what needed to be said was said, sat down. Nova did the same, but added one last comment.

"Drop all desire for the well being of others, and in so doing, well being will be as plentiful as the trees, Ke."

Ke turned his eyes to Nova. "Is that the message you want to send to them?" His eyes were like small creases holding a burning ember held behind them. "So, we don't do anything to help them? Is that your message, Nova? Let Crepus bring continued suffering to the spirit animals living in the Dim

Lands? Is that your message to our world?"

Nova remained calm. She bowed her head to Ke, saying quietly, "My life is my message. I live my life as an example to others. As you've seen for thousands of moons, when a Dim crosses over our land for help, we help. However, I don't push my way into their life and into their affairs. There will be a point, Ke, when our task as PureLights will be to cross through the Fog and protect those who suffer the torment of Crepus Dim. The best way to do so is through patience, compassion, and love. I don't rush into a violent crowd that's not ready to hear my voice. Prisons, in a sense, will lengthen the span in which the Dims maintain control of Ohm Totem."

Ke responded, "And, again, my position is..." his voice trailed off as a loud bang echoed in the sky just above them. A bright, white light flashed, lighting up all of Ohm Totem, and then, as quick as it came, vanished.

Zoey crouched low to the ground, half expecting the night sky to fall on her. She looked up a second too late, missing the bright light, but saw what looked to be a silver comet, followed by the large bang. It had a tail full of color the full spectrum of the rainbow. It shot in a slow moving arc across the sky, coming from the east, passing in front of the moon and disappearing in the west, showering sparkles of colors throughout the sky.

In unison, Coda and Zoey looked at Chev and whispered, "What was that?"

Nova, turning away from the comet, glanced at the elders, then peered at her feet. A rolled up scroll sat next to her paws. She gently nudged it open and stared into it.

She read and then narrowed her eyes at Zoey. "This can't be! Everyone surround Zoey and protect her—now!"

Chapter 27

Suddenly a rustling sound came from every direction. Coda looked up to the cliffs surrounding the circle. Hundreds of spirit animals stood all around the edges. The Dims!

The PureLights huddled around Zoey, and Coda took his place amongst them. He stood guard, determined that no feather on Zoey would be touched. Through the narrow canyon passage leading to the fire appeared a familiar figure. Crepus!

"I've come for my prize," he roared, his head held high and his tail lashing back and forth. Behind him were hundreds of Dims.

This is impossible. We have no chance, despaired Coda.

Echoing his thoughts, Chev shrieked, "This is nearly impossible! How can we get out of here?" Chev's eyes darted back and forth in wild-eyed panic. If Coda could, he'd send Chev home, but that wasn't an option. He worried that Chev could make things worse. He'd have to protect Chev, as well as Zoey.

Nova rested her tail on Coda's back, saying, "You're Zoey's Guardian. Get her out of these Dim Lands safely. I'll make a way for your exit. Just stay close behind." She voiced the obvious to the group. "We're greatly outnumbered here." Nova nodded to Shikoba, the red-tail hawk, instructing, "At my signal, fly as fast as you can back to Sihu Tribe. We'll need their help."

Shikoba dipped her head in acknowledgement.

Coda asked anxiously, "Can't you just lift up the Dims and move them away from us? The way you did with me?"

Nova shook her head. There was sympathy in her eyes. "I wish. It doesn't work that way. If we were all VioletLights, then we could all do just that. We'd have the ability to lift most of them. I'm not yet that evolved to lift an entire tribe." She bowed slightly, stepping out of the circle to slowly approach

Crepus. Crepus continued to come toward them, undaunted by Nova's presence. They stopped two body lengths away from each other, glaring into each other's eyes.

Coda didn't know if he was to follow her or stay right where he was. Was she making the way for him and Zoey right now? He looked at Chev. Chev shook his head, indicating for Coda to stay put.

Nova bowed. "Greetings, Crepus."

Coda narrowed his eyes. *Why doesn't she just tear him apart right here, right now?*

Crepus tipped his head in greeting. "Welcome to the Dim Lands, Nova. Every full moon you trespass on my lands for this silly Circle of Elders and I hope you're grateful that I have allowed it. But tonight, I just can't allow it anymore."

Nova looked up at the moon. "As you can see, Crepus, there isn't a full moon tonight. How did you know that I'd travel to The Circle five moons after the full moon?"

Crepus's tail swiped against the ground, flinging soft dirt to his left. Grinning wickedly, he chortled, "You don't know?" Crepus glanced over his shoulder. Skint walked forward. He, too, had a cunning grin.

Nova turned toward Ke, and saw by the look of shock on his face that he had no idea that Skint was a spy. Nova blinked with satisfaction. "Ke, please be more careful whom you share our news with...and I apologize for my mistake. I accused you of wanting to be a Dim. I'm grateful that I was wrong."

Ke blinked back, then turned his eyes on Skint. Skint glared back at Ke. A new rivalry seemed to form right then and there.

Nova turned her attention back to Crepus. "What do you want?" she inquired flatly.

Coda couldn't tell if she was angry or calm. Seeing the hundreds of Dims surrounding them, his body ached with fear. *They could attack us at any moment. We have no chance.*

"I want the skylark. You can have Orion."

Orion? Coda wanted to scream that he wasn't Orion. He wanted to tell Crepus that Zoey wasn't the skylark he was looking for. He shook his head. He knew it wouldn't matter to the dragon.

"Zoey? Would you like to go with Crepus Dim?"

Zoey lurched back. She composed herself, stating an emphatic "no." She almost felt sick that Nova would even ask that question. She didn't know what was going on and Coda sensed her bewilderment. Coda knew she just wanted to get out of here and go home. And now, here by The Circle of Elders in the Dim Lands, she was facing one of her worst fears—being put on the spot.

"She said 'no,' Crepus, and her will reflects mine."

Crepus snarled. "Then so be it." He spit on the ground in front of Nova. It singed the brown sandy dirt. A small cloud of smoke rose in front of her.

Nova's tail slowly raised, then flicked back and forth three times. A loud screech erupted behind Coda. Twisting around, he saw that it was Shikoba. She jumped high, spreading her wings out wide. Like a lightning bolt, she shot forward, flying at a high speed over the Dims, toward the Sihu Tribe.

"Attack!" came Crepus's voice, taking everyone's focus away from the hawk, and to the moment at hand. Instantly, hundreds of Dims gave a war cry and ran forward.

Nova ran quickly to the edge of the circle and stood in front of Coda. "I'll make a way for you to get Zoey across the Fog. If you lose me, defend her the best you can. She isn't as trained as you are. She'll rely on you for your skill." She glanced at Zoey. "Do you understand?"

Zoey, seeming determined and ready, nodded her head yes.

Just then, a large Dim looking like a rhinoceros, barreled into Nova. Nova fell back, then recovered with incredible skill. The rhinoceros came at her again, but was suddenly flipped on its back, with alarming speed. Nova jumped on its chest, pressed on its gray crystal and twisted her paw, stunning it unconscious.

Coda glanced behind him. There were his friends, even Ke, defending with all of their hearts. He saw the amazing speed and accuracy of their moves. They far outmatched the Dims, except for Chev. If it weren't for his brute strength and large bulk, Coda knew that he'd be the first PureLight down. Regardless, the Dims outnumbered them. He didn't know how long the PureLights could last.

Then Coda's stomach lurched. *Where's Zoey?*

Spinning in circles, he searched everywhere. *Where is she?* "Zoey!"

She was nowhere to be seen. *Did she enter the battle?* He panicked, yelling again, "Zoey!"

Realizing that no one could hear him over the sounds of the ensuing fight, he decided to run through the battle to search for her, but with his first few steps he was suddenly tripped and fell face-first into the sandy ground. He shook the dirt off and saw Sigun, the tiger who tried to stop him from following Skint the other night. Sigun bared his teeth, sending a clear message with his low growl. Two coyotes appeared beside him. The two from the other day!

Coda didn't have a moment to spare. He had to look for his sister, but was trapped. Two more Dims stood next to the coyotes, and then three more. He looked around. More and more Dims were racing in his direction.

He looked for Nova, and saw that she had created a split in the crowd. How she did it amazed Coda. With one flick of a tail here and another there, Dims tumbled backward or fell sideways, unhurt from her invisible magic. She was a master at this. And, at the same moment, she was using the Art of Defense. He saw her flip a large cat and stun it, then flick her tail, using her magic to throw another Dim that was about to attack her.

Coda felt the fur on the back of his neck stand on end. *Uh oh!*

Several Dims landed on him, pinning him to the ground. A coyote snarled, dripping sticky saliva on his forehead. Then three more animals held him down.

"End him!" growled Sigun.

Coda spun on the ground, dislodging the many paws and hooves that were on him. He stood up to face them, but was pummeled from behind. The thought that this fight was impossible entered his mind again, but quickly faded when he hit hard against the dirt. Stars filled his vision. Just as quickly, he shook his head clear, diving sideways, barely escaping a large hoof that landed on the spot he had just occupied a moment ago.

Jumping forward, Coda dodged another attack, landing expertly on all fours, crouching in a defensive stance. His training was becoming evident.

Two more Dims, a bear and a wolverine, sprang at him. He sidestepped the bear, then undercut the wolverine, sending it spinning into the air. The wolverine landed on its back and Coda quickly jumped on it, planting his paw on its gray crystal, stunning him.

Coda was amazed at his own agility. He was even faster in battle than in training. *How am I doing this so well?*

The momentary loss of focus betrayed him as the two coyotes swiped at him, striking a severe bite against his left flank. He buckled in sudden pain, falling to the dirt. The ground seeped red with his blood. His eyes widened when he saw the two coyotes rise on their hind legs. They were about to deliver him a deadly bite.

As they lunged, Coda flipped on his back and rolled backwards. They missed, getting tangled up with each other on the ground. Coda jumped forward, landing a paw against each one of their crystals. Out they went.

He glanced at his injury. It dripped with blood and though his adrenaline seemed to mask the pain, he knew that if he survived this he'd be in a lot pain afterwards.

Zoey! Where is she?

In between dodging the numerous swipes and blows coming from the onslaught of Dims, he desperately looked for her. *Where could she have gone?*

Pained by the thought that the Dims might have somehow taken her, he searched that much harder. Frantically, he moved through the canyon, scouring the cliffs, hoping she'd be flying high, but knew that was unlikely, since winged Dims darted everywhere above him. *Was she hiding in the brush*? He hoped so.

Regaining his wits, he found himself completely alone. He was in the corner of the circular, southern end of the canyon. Where's Sigun? He crouched low, waiting for him to pounce, but after a few moments nothing happened. He surveyed the battle and realized that the Dims weren't paying attention to him anymore. They were focused on the north, attacking furiously at something. *Was it Nova?*

He narrowed his eyes, searching the northern sky. What he saw nearly caused his heart to sing with joy. The reinforcements were here! PureLight Wings were diving into the crowd of Dims, scattering the Dims' focus in too many directions. Relief flooded through Coda.

A growl quickly turned his relief upside down. Only a few yards away stood Sigun. "I will always have you in my sights, Orion," spat Sigun. "I will kill you." A thick golden eagle, fallen from a wound, hit face-first on the ground next to Sigun, sliding into the tiger's hind legs. Sigun turned, pounced on the eagle, and pressed his large paw hard on its throat.

"No!" yelled Coda, as he ran at the tiger, ramming his shoulder into him, sending the angry traitor toppling on his side. Sigun slowly shook his head, then rose to his full height. Coda's eyes widened at the large, muscular tiger before him.

Uh oh! Coda quickly glanced at the eagle. He couldn't tell if it was alive or dead.

Coda ducked as he felt a large paw coming at him, swiping the air just above Coda's head. Coda rolled to his right, again avoiding another blow from Sigun. The tiger was as fast as lightning and landed the next couple of blows, tearing flesh from Coda's shoulder, splattering his blood to the earth.

Coda cringed, then assessed the situation. There was Sigun, bearing his teeth down upon him, ready to crush Coda's neck. This tiger was twice the size of Coda, but not as brilliant. Coda, for the first time in his life, knew his intelligence far outweighed many spirit animals when it came to the Art of Defense. He dodged to the side, easily avoiding Sigun. Then, to change the energy, Coda decided to close his eyes.

Sigun stopped, confused. "Open your eyes, you coward."

Coda shook his head" no".

Sigun flung dirt at Coda, hitting Coda in the face. "Open them!"

Coda shook his head yet again.

"I want you to watch your death through open eyes," growled Sigun.

"There is no death," responded Coda.

"There is today." Sigun jumped toward Coda, spinning in the air, bringing his hind claws to bear down on Coda. Coda, feeling the inevitable impact, turned, caught and trapped Sigun's nearest hind leg with both forepaws. Coda then hooked one forepaw over the trapped leg, moved both forepaws in a clockwise direction, turned and stepped toward Sigun. This reversed Sigun's force, flipping him, sending him straight on his back. A moment later Coda stunned him, then opened his eyes. He was astonished by what he had just done. This all happened in a matter of seconds—and with with his eyes closed! Maybe he was this Orion character after all?

Dismissing the thought, Coda returned to the fray around him. He could tell that the fight had turned for the better, and the canyon was filled with stunned Dims lying on their sides. Their eyes were closed, dazed to the world.

For a moment the air was silent and everything was still. Then Coda heard Chev yell his name. Turning around, he saw the gray elephant. Tears flowed down his gray cheeks. He had slash wounds similar to his own, but Chev's were by far deeper and more serious. But Coda knew that's not why he was crying.

Chev fell to his knees. "I couldn't save her. I couldn't do it. I tried, but I—"

"Who?" demanded Coda. "Zoey?" His mind went in circles and his belly cramped with bleak fear. *Is she dead?*

Nova materialized beside Coda. "Zoey was taken. Crepus has her," she reported, with a pained expression.

Coda's momentary elation of Zoey still being alive snapped to anger. He must get her, find her, and stop Crepus from all this bloodshed he brought to Ohm Totem.

"How was she taken?" Coda looked around, thinking he could spot Zoey somewhere.

"Isi saw a Dim swoop down and take her the moment Crepus called the attack."

"What?" Coda glared past the western cliffs, and into the night sky. "I'm going to find her!'"

"Stop!" yelled Nova. "You'll die before you reach the Southern Fog. You must mend your wounds. We'll take a scouting party to look for her, but until you're better, you stay with the Sihu Tribe."

"But they'll kill her," Coda protested.

"If they do, then Crepus will die as well. He needs her, so I don't see Crepus making that decision."

Coda suddenly became weak and his legs buckled. His vision blurred and he took a deep breath. He wanted to ask for help, but even the strength to speak had left him. He was losing a lot of blood.

"Numee!" called Nova.

"Right here," replied the raccoon, swiftly leaving Chev's side. She'd been mending his wounds, which looked as if they were already healing. Chev was peacefully snoring away.

"Please see to Coda while I get a scouting party together. And when Coda's strong, you, Coda, Chev, Shikoba, and I are crossing the northern Fog to rescue Zoey."

"You want Chev to go?" asked Numee dubiously. Then she nodded, knowing Nova had her reasons. She placed her paws on Coda's wounds. He felt the Prana enter his body, and instantly, his strength began to come back.

Coda stood. "Nova?"

"Get your rest, dear one. Tomorrow we'll go through the Fog. Your sister will be safe. I've sent a call out to a fellow VioletLight."

"Okay," he agreed quietly. "But, what did the scroll say?"

Nova hesitated. "It's not for you to concern yourself about. You must rest."

"But, you said, 'This can't be'." Nova wrinkled her nose. She didn't want to tell him, but why? He persisted. "Why did you say that, Nova?"

Nova sat in front of Coda, tenderly stroking his cheek with her tail. "It said, 'The sacred heart has sung her sacred song and the dragon listens intently. The dragon whispers for her and she shies away. Death arrives at her doorstep, malevolently.'"

Coda frantically tried to decode the meaning. *Is she going to die?* "I thought you said she'll be safe?" Coda tried to run toward the Fog as fast as he could, but after a few steps the pain still ached in his side and he fell back down.

"They mean nothing. Scrolls are mere prophecy, and not set in stone. They are warnings to be heeded."

Coda stared into her eyes. She sounded confident, making Coda feel the same way. Nova then bowed to him, and turned to go. Looking back, she said, "You're her Guardian, Coda. You'll find her. It's what you do."

"But, Crepus will kill her if we don't get to her fast."

Nova shook her head. "He'll do no such thing."

"Yes he will!" cried Coda.

Nova nodded. "I know you fear this, but know that if Crepus kills your sister, then he has no chance of survival."

Chapter 28

Coda shifted on his paws as he stood in front of the northern Fog. It spanned the entire distance of the island from east to west. There was no way around it, except through it. Last night, he had entered the southern Fog, which was no walk in the park. The northern Fog was probably no different. Glancing left and right, he inwardly cringed. He didn't want to go through the Fog again. Then he thought of Zoey. Crepus had kidnapped her! He swore to himself that Crepus was not going to get away with it. He bared his teeth in a growl. A stupid Fog wasn't going to stop him. Somehow, he'd find a way to rescue her.

Coda pondered his changing feelings for his sister. Wanting his sister to be safe was odd. He never knew he cared this much for her, but here in Ohm Totem things had changed quickly. Only a day ago he had thought she was annoying. Now he had do anything in his power to make sure she got back home, happily doing her irritating things again. His stomach twisted into a ball of fury. He wanted to take on the entire Dim army.

"That's exactly what Crepus Dim wants, Coda," Nova replied in response to his silent thoughts. "He wants rage. He wants you to display and feel all the emotions of fear. He feeds off of it, especially inside the Fog."

Coda nodded in understanding. "I know. I just want my sister back. She's...she's okay, right?"

"She's okay. I trust Crepus with her, but there's something else out there, beyond the Fog, that I don't trust. Last night's scroll warned us about it. I can't quite put my paw on what it is."

Coda glared at Nova, ignoring her last words, aghast at what she just said. "You trust Crepus?"

"For one simple reason. He knows that if Zoey dies, then he

surely dies. He'll do everything in his power to keep her alive."
Nova then bounded forward as fast as a bullet, parting the Fog
for a millisecond, giving Coda a glimpse of a large hill on the
other side. Just as quickly, the Fog closed again.

What? If Zoey dies, then he dies? Why would that happen?
Coda heard those same words last night, but didn't quite
understand them.

A hefty pat on his back prompted Coda to glance behind
him. It was Chev. "I guess I'll see you when you get back from
the Dim Lands."

"You're not going?"

Chev shook his head as he peered into the Fog, his face
twisted with reluctance. "Nah, I don't want to." Suddenly, he
jumped up in surprise. "Ow! Who bit me?"

"I bit you, you silly oaf," chided Numee. "You're going
whether you like it or not." She nipped at his back leg again.
Chev quickly moved out of range of any further nips. "Come
on, Chev. Get moving," ordered Numee.

Chev sighed. "What happened to free will?" He shrugged.
"Oh boy. Here we go again." He closed his eyes, took in a
rather large breath, then ran through the swirling mist. It
whirled around him like tongues slurping up a meal,
swallowing him whole.

Coda glanced behind him to see Shikoba, the red tailed
hawk, and Numee standing there. They nodded at him. He
guessed that meant for him to go. Gathering himself, he stared
at the Fog. He took in a deep breath, just like Chev, and
whispered, "I can do this. I can do this."

Here I go. He closed his eyes, and entered the Fog.

Silence seemed to swallow him. He opened his eyes,
glancing around suspiciously, waiting for Crepus to jump out
at him at any moment. He flinched, ducking down when a
sudden roar of screams flew past him, trailing off to his left.
Then he looked to his left and saw a dark, floating mass
forming like blood weeping from a wound. Above him soared
another scream. Taking his eyes away from the dark mass, he
crawled forward, but his mind told him to turn around and
remain in the Sihu Tribe. *Nova could deal with it. Nova could*

save Zoey. They don't need me on this trip. At least not on this day. Maybe tomorrow?

He shook his head, clawing the ground. *No*, he thought, *I must save my sister!* He looked left again, seeing the dark mass coming closer. It shuddered for a moment, then started spinning toward him.

He stood up, lurching forward, but moved no more than a step or two. His legs felt like they were stuck in thick mud. He looked down, but saw only hard soil. He took another step forward as a gust of heavy, stale air pushed against his movement. He flexed all of his muscles, marching forward with all of his might, but didn't get very far. Then, wondering if the dark mass was almost upon him, he peered to the left and jerked back in surprise. It was nearly touching him! Coda ducked, hoping it would fly over him. The opposite occurred, and the mass wrapped itself around him, strangling his body and legs.

Coda wrenched with fear. But, he knew it didn't come from him. It came from the Fog. The fear felt like stinging punches, with every hit.

"Help!" he cried out.

Nobody answered his call, so he grabbed hard, cold soil, pulling himself onward. Another mass, filled with hideous laughter, careened toward him, landing on top of him, knocking the wind out of him and forcing him to the ground.

He panted hard, trying to breathe, but the harder the masses pushed and strangled, the harder it was to take a breath. Lifting his head, he took as big a breath as he could, then stretched his front legs forward, grabbing the dirt in front him, pulling himself closer to the Dim Lands.

A scream in his right ear startled him, and he let go of the earth to cover his ears. But the screams only became louder.

"Help!" he cried.

"Shhh," said Numee's voice, and with her sweet tone the screams instantly stopped.

"The screaming," yelled Coda, "I can't stand it!"

Numee brushed against him. "Sink into your heart."

Another scream erupted above Coda. Startled, he went into

a fetal position. His blood rushed through his veins as his heart pounded.

Yes, my heart.

Coda sank into his heart, listening to it beat like a drum, ignoring the chaos around him. The more he listened, the more its rhythm slowed, calming him. He closed his eyes, bringing the fear down into his heart, and imagined smothering it with pink colors. When he was finally able to take a deep breath, he stood up, and felt much better.

He opened his eyes and saw Numee's soft face. He could see her smiling through the gray mist hovering around her. "Follow me, Coda."

The Fog was heavy, but seemed to step aside for Numee. How she did that, he didn't know. A moment later they were out of the Fog.

He dropped onto moss-covered ground. He was in the northern Dim Lands now. The home of Crepus. Things, he thought, aren't going to get any easier.

Nova leaned against Coda to comfort and send him healing energy. She whispered in his ear, "Thank you for being so brave."

The Adventure Continues...

Book II:

The PureLights

&

the PureLight Order

www.brandon-ellis.com